STUDIES IN CRITICAL IDIOM OF LITERATURE

STUDIES IN CRITICAL IDIOM OF LITERATURE

M.P. Kotter
Lawrance D'Souza

CYBER TECH PUBLICATIONS
4264/3, Ansari Road, Daryaganj, New Delhi-110002 (India)
Ph.: 011-23244078, 011-43559448 Fax: 011-23280028
E-Mail: cyberpublicationsdelhi@yahoo.com
Website: www.cybertechpublications.com

STUDIES IN CRITICAL IDIOM OF LITERATURE

M.P. Kotter, Lawrance D'Souza

First Edition 2011

Published by :

G.S. Rawat for **Cyber Tech Publications**
4264/3, Ansari Road, Daryaganj, New Delhi-110002 (India)
Ph.: 011-23244078, 011-43559448 Fax: 011-23280028
E-Mail: cyberpublicationsdelhi@yahoo.com
Website: www.cybertechpublications.com

CONTENTS

Preface

For nearly four hundred years, and throughout several revisions of its English form, the King James Bible has been deeply revered among the English-speaking peoples of the world. The precision of translation for which it is historically renowned, and its majesty of style, have enabled that monumental version of the Word of God to become the mainspring of the religion, language, and legal foundations of our civilization.

Along with this awakened concern for the classics came a flourishing companion in interest in the Scriptures, an interest that was enlivened by the conviction that the manuscripts were providentially handed down and were a trustworthy record of the inspired Word of God. The King James translators were committed to producing an English Bible that would be a precise translation, and by no means a paraphrase or a broadly approximate rendering. On the one hand, the scholars were almost as familiar with the original languages of the Bible as with their native English.

George Bernard Shaw became a literary legend in our century because of his severe and often humorous criticisms of our most cherished values. Surprisingly, however, Shaw pays the following tribute to the scholars commissioned by King James: "The translation was extraordinarily well done because to the translators what they were translating was not merely a curious collection of ancient books written by different authors in different stages of culture, but the Word of God divinely revealed through Therefore, while seeking to unveil the excellent form of the traditional English Bible, special care has also been taken in the present edition to preserve the work of precision which is the legacy of the 1611 translators.

— *Author*

1

Introduction

SOME (NON-) DEFINITIONS

As I face the part-daunting, part-comical prospect of writing a short book on the vast topic of 'Literature', I am reminded of my favourite film-title: Mel Brookes's *A History of the World, Part One.* So much literature has been produced world-wide over such a long period of time, and—all the more worrying— so much has been written about it, that knowing where to start, where to end, and what might go in between, could lead to the book never progressing beyond these preliminary mus-ings. A very short book, indeed, then!

But a clue is provided here: it *is* to be a *short* book, and so, in the nature of things, it can only do certain things and only be of a certain kind. For one thing, it cannot be a *big* book—with all the promise of authority and definitiveness that big books tend to convey. I would prefer to think of the present study as an essay: at once a composition of limited length and all of a piece, and—as the dictionary also glosses it—an 'attempt', a 'try', a 'tentative effort'—to define, not 'what literature *is*', but what it might mean, provisionally and tentatively, for us on the cusp of the millenium.

So, first of all and according to convention in Introductions, let me say what this essay is not. It does not attempt to survey or engage with the voluminous, aesthetics-driven 'What is Lit-erature?' debate. The very formulation of the question suggests a way of conceptualising literature which runs entirely counter to my project here. Neither can it be a history of literature (not even 'Part One') of the Homer to Heller variety, nor a literary-critical/theoretical history of its protean definitions over the centuries (Plato to Foucault)—although a succinct historical account of the changing *notion* of the term 'literature' will be offered as part of the overall argument. Rather, the essay is principally conceived as a reflection on the contemporary nature, place and function, within general cultural production, of what, for now, I will go on calling literature, but will prefer to designate the domain of 'the literary'.

By the late-twentieth century, 'literature', as a concept and as a term, has become so problematical—either through ideo-logical contamination as the high cultural 'Canon', or, con-versely, through demystification and deconstruction by radical critical theory—that it approaches the unuseable, at least with-out contorted apologetics. Perhaps the only way to represent it, as *passe* presence or determinate absence, is 'under erasure'.

For what has gone on, and continues to go on, in its sullied name, and under its tattered banner, appears to remain such a crucial component of human activity and experience that it suggests the need to be rescued from itself: to be *re-accredited*—rather than shamefacedly subsumed, as has recently been the case, within general concepts of 'writing', 'rhetoric', 'discourse' or 'cultural production'.

Hence, I agree with Terry Eagleton when he writes: 'Literature must indeed be re-situated within the field of general cultural production; but each mode of such production demands a semiology of its own, which is not conflatable with some universal "cultural" discourse' (Eagleton [1976] 1978:166).

Let me begin by looking in some detail, in the contemporary context, at the word 'literature' itself. If nothing else, this will offer us what I have awkwardly called 'Some (non-)definitions' with which to problematise the heavily naturalised term as it appears in current usage and common parlance. If I offer the reader the following sentence, devoid of any explanatory con-text, what might s/he understand by it: 'At the moment, I am reading some interesting literature on this very subject'?

- Would it be fair to assume that I am speaking as a student who is currently reading novels, poems and plays as part of my *literature* course: 'I'm doing literature at college'?

- Would I be reading some 'secondary' critical *literature* on those literary texts: 'I need to cover a bit of the literature on Dickens to write my essay'?
- As the author of this book, might I be speaking about the diverse and gripping theoretical *literature* on the question, precisely, of 'What is Literature'?
- Might I be a budding creative writer, who is attempting to enter the profession of *literature* by reading novels, for example, which focus on how a young person becomes a novelist ('portraits of the artist as young wo/men'): 'I'm determined to go in for literature when I grow up'.
- Might I be a commuter (employed in the tourist catering industry) talking about the sort of *literature* (novels, diaries, autobiographies, say) which they buy at the book-sellers on the station to wile away delays on the rail net-work and which, through preference, tends always to be about the Caribbean: 'I'll read any literature about the Caribbean you've got'?
- Might I be the same commuter who is perusing the promo-tional or technical *literature* on refrigeration: 'I must famil-iarise myself with the literature on commercial freezers before we get to Macclesfield' ?

Of course, out of context, I could be speaking about any of these things, so it becomes apparent that the word 'literature' in itself can be used in a number of ways. However, in normal usage, a distinction tends to be drawn and signalled by the fact that when we are speaking of critical, theoretical or promo-tional literature, for example, we tend to put the definite arti-cle in front of the word: 'I'm reading the literature on...'. Whereas, when we are referring to 'literary' writings, we leave it out, hence denoting that some (unexplained) generic distinc-tion has already been made: 'I love reading literature in my spare time'/'I'm studying Literature at the university'. But notice that I have made a further generic distinction in passing here: by using a lower-case 'l' in the first instance and an upper-case 'L' in the second. The significance of that tiny typo-graphical shift will constitute much of the content of this book, but I am willing to wager that it is the sense with the capital 'L' that is uppermost in the minds of the vast majority of you in understanding what is now normally implied by the word 'literature'. 'Literature' with an upper-case 'L' and inverted commas round it signifies here the conception of that global body of literary writing which has been accredited with being— pointedly to borrow Matthew Arnold's famous utterance—'the best that has been known and said in the world' (Arnold [1869] 1971:6). It has been ascribed the highest achievement of aesthetic and moral merit, and has acquired the status of a kind of universal resource of formal and ethical models for humankind: as Ben Jonson said of Shakespeare, it is 'not of an age, but for all time'; and as Ezra Pound defined it, it is 'news that STAYS news'.

In the case of national literatures, writers and works may be included that might not make it into the 'World' category, and there will be some marginal argument as to who or what *should* be included, but, by and large, the same received principles of evaluation will obtain.

We will also recognise collocations of such authors and texts as constituting 'The Classics', 'The (Great) Tradition, 'The Canon', and the standard 'Set Authors/ Books' on all secondary and tertiary education syllabuses. On the other hand, 'literature' with a small T and no inverted commas is used either when I am employing the word in a neutral discursive capacity, or to rep-resent the undifferentiated corpus of writing which is 'literary' in the sense—more fully explained later—that it identifies itself quite self-consciously as belonging to the artificial (i.e. pertain-ing to 'artifice') discursive realm of 'creative' or 'imaginative' writing as opposed to other, more quotidian forms of written communication.

If we turn now to the dictionary and other reference works, we will find that they confirm and expand the various definitions identified by my glossing of the made-up sentence given ear-lier. *The Oxford English Dictionary* offers a series of meanings for the word *literature,* and I will have occasion to return to them—and to their etymological implications—within their historical location. The first meaning given is:

1. Acquaintance with 'letters' or books; polite or humane learning; literary culture. Now *rare* and *obsolescent.*

Because of the rider, this is not a usage we have encountered above, but its longevity as the principal meaning of the word will be of great significance when we come to see how—and when—*our* principal understanding of it developed. (This should be held in conjunction with the *OED's* note on its 3a. definition as adduced below.) The second sense is:

2. Literary work or production; the activity or profession of a man of letters; the realm of letters.

We noted this meaning as still active in our everyday usages above, but it is perhaps worth clarifying that 'work' here means the business of producing a literary 'work' (not the 'work' itself, which belongs with a subsequent meaning: 'a work of literature'), and that this is again not the principal meaning I assume most of you will have in mind at the moment. The latter is, in fact, part 3a. of the third sense the *OED* presents, but I want to leave this until after I have noted parts 3b. and 3c, so that it will lead us more conveniently into a fuller exposition of the nature of the problem which lies at the heart of the matter in this book.

Sub-sections 3b. and 3c, then, are respectively as follows: 'The body of books and writ-ing that treat of a particular subject' (as in our critical, theoret-ical, technical usage above: '*the* literature on...'); and '*colloq.* Printed matter of any kind' (I did not give an instance of this earlier, but it is clearly a colloquial variant of 3b.—as in: 'a great pile of advertising literature fell though my letter-box this morning').

Although both of the above definitions, but particularly 3b., are in wide current usage, it is the *OED's* sense 3a.—*without* the direct article—which is arguably the primary and priori-tised sense in our culture:

3a. Literary productions as a whole; the body of writings produced in a particular country or period, or in the world in general. Now also in a more restricted sense, applied to writing which has claim to consideration on the ground of beauty of form or emotional effect....

...This sense is of very recent emergence both in Eng. and Fr.

Now, we may feel, we are getting to it, and indeed we are: 'English Literature', 'French Literature', 'eighteenth-century Literature', 'Contemporary Literature', 'World Literature'— our familiar bearings are established: 'Literature', the great generic category of written creativity which we can all recog-nise. Much fuller analysis of this meaning will follow later; but, for now, let us just register two points about the *OED's* definition. First, it becomes problematical as soon as it ceases to be merely descriptive and shifts to being evaluative, i.e. in its second sentence.

'In a more restricted sense' is ambiguous anyway, since it is intended to mean here that the scope of the word literature is restricted if it only applies to the kind described by the dictionary entry's following clauses, whereas we might think literature so described is the least 'restricted' sense of the word and the one with the greatest currency. But the problems really start to emerge in the designation of the qualities such literature may be supposed to have: what does 'on the ground of beauty of form or emotional effect' mean? What, for example, is 'beauty': how do we define it; how do we recognise it; is it the same to all people; is a sense of it innate or is it learnt? What, for that matter, is 'form'?

Given the range of possible meanings any dictionary will give for that word, it is difficult to be even remotely precise: but 'mode of being', 'mode of arrangement', 'structural unity in music, litera-ture, etc.', 'that in which the essence of a thing consists' may, *inter alia,* be apposite, while still leaving us with imponderable problems. Is form separable from content, then; if a piece of writing lacks 'unity' can it not be literature; if a work of litera-ture cannot exist *without* form, how do we discern some form as beautiful and some as not—a short-circuit back to the prob-lems we registered with the notion of 'beauty'? Is the creation of 'emotional effect' special only to the 'restricted sense' of lit-erature (consider 'tear-jerkers', 'thrillers' and pornography); or does the *OED* mean 'beauty of...emotional effect'? In which case, how do we discriminate between those effects that are and those that aren't? And so on.

What we see here are attributions to the notion of 'Literature' (with the capital letter) which are subliminally assump-tive, partial and imprecise, but so heavily naturalised that they are, indeed, an inescapable aspect of its definition—at least its relatively recent definition. For the second point to notice in the dictionary's entry is the subscript note appended: 'This sense is of very recent emergence...'. It will be the business of the following chapter to sketch in the moment of this emer-gence, and the implications of it, but we may note in passing here that it belongs roughly to the nineteenth and twentieth centuries.

It is, therefore, a historically constructed—rather than an 'essential' or 'natural'—category, so, while a notion of 'the literary' (i.e. writings which in some way distinguish them-selves from common communicative discourses) has been around since ancient times, the concept of 'Literature' in that 'restricted sense' has not. In other words, while the *thing* is recognisable in all cultural periods, the concept and term has not been: Shakespeare, perhaps, had a sense of what I mean by 'the literary' (although, like other contemporaries, he might have thought of it as 'Poesie/Poetrie'—see Chapter 2, pp. 26-7, 33-4), but not of 'Literature'.

Richard Terry, in arguing that it is a mistake to conflate 'the history of the word [with] a his-tory of the concept that has come to be associated with that word' (Terry 1997:84), goes on to propose that not only was there a recognisable notion of literature in existence by the end of the sixteenth century in England, but also a clear process of constructing an English 'canon' of literary works—albeit one which could not then have been graced by our term 'Litera-ture' {*ibid,* 94-8).

To reinforce our sense of the dizzying problematics at the heart of this naturalised word, we can turn briefly to other standard modern reference works. The entry in *The New Ency-clopaedia Britannica: Micropaedia,* for example, reads: 'a body of written works. The name is often applied to those imagina-tive works of poetry and prose distinguished by the intentions of their authors and the excellence of their execution'. This seems to imply that drama is not literature (*pace* Shakespeare); introduces the notion of 'imagination' as the defining character-istic of *literary* writing (see pp. 17-18); and discriminates in favour of those writings 'distinguished by the intentions of their authors'.

Leaving aside its apparent dismissal of the unre-solved 'Intentional Fallacy' debate which has been going on for the last 50 years, it is unclear here how an author's intention 'distinguishes' a work as literature (does having a clearly per-ceptible one automatically qualify a work as literature—or is it the *quality* of the intention which makes the work 'distin-guished' and hence literature?). Finally, it falls back on 'excel-lence of their [the works themselves or the authors' 'intentions'?] execution', an evaluative judgement which has all the definitional problems of the *OED's* 'beauty of form' writ large. What we may register for later discussion, however, is the way (usually vague and unexamined) criteria of judge-ment and evaluation are structurally built in to the very defini-tion of literature.

As its title suggests, the essay on 'The Art of Literature', in *The New Encyclopaedia Britannica: Macropaedia,* is an even more partial and partisan affair. While fumbling for defini-tions of 'Literature' which it can never deliver, the essay notes that individual examples of 'certain forms of writing [unspeci-fied] are said to succeed if they possess *something called artis-tic merit* and to fail if they do not. The nature of artistic merit is less easy to define *than to recognise'* (my emphases). The self-fulfilling question-begging here is astonishing: 'artistic merit' is passed off as 'something' which unequivocally exists and happens to be 'called artistic merit', and which the essay-writer cannot 'define' but—by implication, along with other *cognoscenti*—can 'recognise' intuitively. Such a deeply exclu-sive, and hence elitist, literary-critical stance lies at the heart of the assumptive evaluative judgements which, as I noted above, are structured into the conventional definition of 'Literature', so that truly 'literary' works are then perceived to contain their own innate 'artistic merit' which they secrete or emit and which the person of taste 'recognises'.

The circularity of the argument—around a definitional vacuum—is that 'artistic merit' is self-evident to those who attribute its self-evidence in the first place. As Terry Eagleton has observed: 'Valuable text and valuable reader are reversible.... The valuable reader is constituted as valuable by the texts which he constitues as such; ideological value is projected into the Tradition to re-enter the present as meta-physical confirmation or critique. The name of this tautology is Literature...' (Eagleton [1976] 1978:164). Ironically, the only assistance for my project that I can take from the whole *Macropaedia* essay is the author's touching admission that 'it becomes more and more difficult to categorise literature, for in modern civilisation words are everywhere' (like other pests), and that 'a further complica-tion' in classifying the wretched stuff is that 'literature as a whole and in its parts means varying things to various writers, critics, and historians' (87, 86). And there we have the nub of the problem.

No one by now—not even the most dyed-in-the-wool tradi-tional literary critic—can easily accept either a notion of a unitary 'Literature' or that there can be a meaningful essentialist definition of the concept: that there is an innate, self-identifying 'essence' of literature. The above author's oddly insecure phrase 'literature as a whole and in its parts' points to the heterodox nature of literature and to the fact that there are indeed many *literatures* rather than one 'Literature'. However, the admission that literature means different things to different people signals the contemporary recognition that the theoreti-cal position— and we must also now accept that there always is one, however tacit, subliminal or unacknowledged— informing the stances 'various writers, critics, and historians' take to literature in effect both defines and constitutes the 'lit-erariness' of the literature they then 'objectively study.

I might also add that modern critical theories, as we shall see in Chapter 3, propose that literary texts are, in a sense, 're-written' in every act of reading by every reader—not just by the processes of professional analysis: that literature is reconsti-tuted in the endlessly unstable dialectics of the author/ text/ reader nexus in history. Just as the author's control and author-ity over their text is relinquished as the text is written and published, so the reading-positions from which readers read it are different both throughout history and through their cul-tural location at any given moment—and 'the text' becomes the *product* of those differences. How these positions have been arrived at—especially over the past 30 years or so— together with a fuller account of the theoretical and critical positions implied in what I have just written, will be the subject of Chapter 3. For now, I merely state the case, and point to the fact that the untenable word 'Literature' must now indeed be placed under erasure.

One final foray here into the reference books will throw up other crucial terms in the (non-)definition of 'Literature'— albeit potentially helpful ones in progressing my argument. The entry in the (generally excellent) *The Oxford Companion to the English Language* identifies the two main current mean-ings of the word that we have already encountered:

'(1) Artistic creation through language and its products: *French Literature, literature in English....*

(2) The texts of a group or sub-ject: *scientific and technical literature, the latest literature on computers'*—noting, as we have, that while the latter 'is cur-rently the minor sense, it is the historically prior meaning of the term'.

In the definition of the first sense, 'artistic' may seem to beg the question, although I will later return to it as a term of some force; equally so with 'creation'—which here has the active sense of 'creating', rather than being the substantive noun—hence the subsequent phrase 'and its products' (i.e. the 'creations'). But the fulcrum phrase—'through language'—is an important addition to the definitions we have seen so far, and will become a focal matter as my exploration continues. Under the heading '"Literary" literature', the *Companion* interestingly confirms my assertions in the preceding paragraph: 'It is impossible to define the now primary sense of literature precisely or to set rigid limits on its use.' However, it immediately slips into just such a problematical—if potentially fruitful—definition:

> Literary treatment of a subject requires creative use of the imagination: something is constructed which is related to 'real' experience, but is not of the same order. What has been created in language is known only through language, and the text does not give access to a reality other than itself.

Here again we have 'creative' and 'the imagination' appearing, but now also the notion of a problematical relation to 'reality' occasioned by literatures construction in language. Literature somehow alludes to the 'real' while being of a different order of reality precisely because it is constituted by language. I want to put these notions on hold for the time being, since they will need to be addressed when I come to present my own working definition of 'the literary'.

But one final comment in the *Oxford Companion* entry points us to a key term in the constitution of 'Literature':

> *The word* literature *tends to be used with approval of works perceived as having artistic merit, the evaluation of which may depend on social and linguistic as well as aes-thetic factors. If the criteria of quality become*

> *exacting, a* canon *may emerge, limited in its inclusions and exclu-sions, and the members of a society or group may be required (with varying degrees of pressure and success) to accept that canon and no other.* (ibid.)

You might register the reappearance of 'artistic merit'; note the imprecision of 'social and linguistic as well as aesthetic factors'; and puzzle over the proposition: 'If the criteria of qual-ity become exacting...' But ultimately we arrive at the crucial notion of an exclusive *'canon'*. Just as we have noticed along the way that 'Literature' incorporates the evaluative judge-ments made about it (from now on represented by the short-hand phrase 'literary value') into the very definition itself, so it takes in, too, the concept of 'the canon'. Indeed, it is difficult to see how it could do without it. 'Literature' requires the iden-tification of 'great works', which, *ipso facto,* become the benchmarks for judging all other literary production. In order to designate these as such, they must be elevated above other works, which are then, as a necessary reflex of this process, excluded from the canon.

Fair enough, one might think: what is wrong with wanting to say that some works may be better than others, and with demarcating such by extrapolating them from the ruck? The problem is, however, that the above canonising process is cog-nate with the discourse of evaluation I have considered earlier: the criteria are imprecise, unexplained, tacitly assumed, and thoroughly naturalised. The reasons given for the received canon rely, in other words, on notions of 'beauty of form', 'emotional effect', 'artistic merit', and on the judgement of those who can 'recognise' these qualities when they see them. Once again, the bottom line is that the canon is self-selecting, *given,* crystallising out of the history of literature as a whole— whereas, it is historically constructed on behalf of some very powerful and insistent ideolog-ical imperatives and vested interests.

If we start asking the questions: *who* constructed the canon, *when* and for *whom,* on *what* criteria and to *what* ends—as the critics and theorists have done from the late-1960s onwards —then the notions of 'Literature', 'canon' and 'literary value' are simultaneously demythologised and destabilised. If mean-ing is to be returned to them in some way and for some rea-son, they have to be re-thought and reconstituted to an extent that makes them unrecognisable in their previous guise. Some will immediately say: 'Well, in that case, why bother? Why not invent something quite new and radical to fill the space they have left?'. The answer this book attempts to give— and while much of the book is necessarily concerned with the processes which have gone to constructing and now decon-structing the dominant sense of 'Literature', it is the *answer* which is its real purpose and drive—is that literature ('the literary') remains too pervasive, too consuming and consumed, too open a space in our culture not to be reclaimed and recuper-ated from the ruins of its past incarnation.

In particular, I will offer there a range of examples to illustrate the uses of literature; to indicate what literature from the past may continue to give us as a form of 'special knowl-edge'; and especially to suggest what 'news' about our own culture is broadcast by contemporary literature—news which would otherwise be imperceptible until released by the specific textuality of its literary formulation.

A final word first, however, about some of the fundamental and undoubtedly contentious premises on which my argument here is based. I have, so far, drawn out from the materials of definition three central and interrelated—indeed, necessarily self-sustaining—concepts/terms: 'Literature', 'literary value' and 'canon'.

Literature, in this book, will refer to *written* works: by which I mean works whose originating form and final point of refer-ence is their existence as written textuality—however much individual texts may be performed, produced or reproduced in non-written form (hence plays but not film-scripts, perfor-mance poetry and poetry set to music but not song lyrics). I make the assumption that there is an area of human activity and production in which people choose *deliberately* to use writ-ten language in ways distinguishable from other forms of writ-ten communication: most obviously the genres of poetry, prose-fiction and drama. Their readers, therefore, are sensible of being in the presence of something which is self-consciously 'literary'—be it eighteenth-century elegy or performance poetry, Victorian novel or contemporary romance, Renais-sance tragedy or street theatre. I am not concerned, therefore, with pamphlets, histories, journalism, diaries, car manuals, menus, promotional literature on fridge-freezers, biographies or beer-mats, while recognising that some or all of these may display 'literary' characteristics (for example, in style or in their use of rhetorical devices), and that they may be indistin-guishable from literary texts in terms of their linguistic compo-sition. In this regard, I accept and retain the last two centuries' 'aestheticisation' of the concept, regarding literature as operat-ing within the domain of *artifice* (and hence 'artificial'): i.e. as 'fictive' in the broadest sense.

I am aware of the difficulties which various inflexions of linguistic theory and criticism (succinctly outlined by Roger Fowler in his helpful introductory essay, 'Literature', in the Roudedge *Encyclopaedia of Literature and Criticism)* pose for the definition of a discrete 'fictive' literary realm: of distinguish-ing between 'fictional' and 'non-fictional', 'literary' and 'non-literary', texts. Linguistically, they all share similar textual characteristics and deploy similar stylistic tropes, so that a 'fac-tual' text, in terms of its 'textual semantics', is just as much a construction of discourse as is a 'literary' one (Fowler 1990:16).

Nevertheless, I would claim that my discrimination of the term and concept is *cultural* (or 'functional') rather than linguistic (or 'ontological'), and so, while accepting Fowler's admonition that it is 'futile' to seek a 'single linguistic crite-rion, or set of criteria' for distinguishing 'literary' from 'non-literary' genres and texts, I would argue that 'literature' as a concept retains a meaningful cultural sense, and that is the functional one I work with here. In this regard, then, while agreeing with Fowler that the pursuit of literary-theoretical and aesthetic definitions of '"Literature" into innumerable dead ends is a waste of intellectual energy', I would disagree with him when he says: 'progress in understanding these matters [i.e. establishing that 'texts not normally...included in "Literature"' have similar characteristics to those that are] would be facilitated if we removed the complication of "liter-ary" status'. Peter Murphy has written of poetry (but it holds good for my notion of 'the literary' in general) that if one of its distinguishing characteristics is that it is 'something that people... choose to write' (Murphy 1993:3) in contradistinction to other forms of writing, then 'we must find a way to talk about what makes poetry different from other forms of writing'. I do not wish to proceed too readily, however, down the track of the kind of retooled humanistic formalism which Murphy seems to be proposing.

Equally, if what I appear to be saying smacks of the so-called 'new aesthetics' or 'new formalism' emerging principally in the United States, then I would immediately want to say that the present project does *not* favour a return to *belles-lettrism,* and that it is firmly cul-tural-materialist in grounding—insofar as it is abjures any notion of an 'essential' literariness, and is predicated on the assumption that literature, its uses and definitions, are invari-ably historically specific.

Indeed, even Tony Bennett, one of the most indomitable contemporary critics of the aesthetic con-ception of 'Literature' (be it idealist or Marxist), should be able to find it cognate with his own project to get 'Outside "Literature"'—a project which 'imbue[s literature] with a far more concrete existence' than can aesthetic theorisations, by 'more appropriately regard [ing it] as a historically specific, institutionally organised field of textual uses and effects' (Ben-nett 1990:10). Nevertheless, I can still follow Peter Murphy when he says 'there is a high critical value for us in encounter-ing the need for distinctions between writers', and calls for evaluative judgements to be made (Murphy 1993:2), because otherwise we lose all the advantages of deploying and perceiv-ing *difference,* and can function only with the ungainly mono-lith of an undifferentiated 'writing'. I will pick up Murphy's point again when I discuss 'literary value' on pp. 20-1.

I assume, too, then—and here I appropriate some of the terms I registered in passing from the entry in the *Oxford Companion* as potentially still necessary for defining 'literary' activity—that these productions are 'creative' and 'imaginative' in that they are 'made-up' (which the *OED* defines as 'to con-coct, invent, fabricate [in the sense of "put together by art and labour"]', 'to compose'—thus, 'an invention or fiction), and are therefore 'original' insofar as they are a unique invention. Their specificity, in other words, constitutes their originality.

Further, I assume them to be constructions of written language whose 'reality' is comprised by that linguistic construction (their reality, in other words, is that encoded in their 'fabrica-tion'—however much they may allude to a reality beyond their own). Similarly, they are 'imaginary' (products of the imagina-tion) whose relationship to experiential reality in the material world exists only by way of their formal contrivance. The orig-inal derivation of the words 'poet' and 'poetry'—the generic terms for literary writer and writing until relatively recently (see pp. 26-7)—from the Greek *poiein,* 'to make, create', is of central importance to my understanding of what 'the literary' might mean.

An age-old (but false) opposition—that between *poiesis* ('creative production', i.e. the artistic 'making' of 'con-trived' realities) and *mimesis* ('imitation', i.e. the artistic 'repre-sentation of 'real' realities), where the written art of *mimesis* must logically still be subsumed within *poiesis*—focuses the trajectory of my argument. It draws attention to the fact that all literature is always an original process of *making* 'realities', and that its formal articulation is precisely what enables read-ers to perceive those (newly fabricated) 'poietic realities' for the first time. I will employ the term '*poietic* whenever I wish to signal this throughout the book which follows.

One further restriction in range and focus must be announced here: although my subject is *literature*—which implies its global totality—my treatment of it will perforce be limited in both historical definition and textual example. For while I will attempt to make reference to a wide spectrum of periods of literary production, my knowledge of other litera-tures beyond the Western tradition and its colonial/postcolonial diaspora—in terms both of their definitional con-ception and of their textual representation—is minimal. Equally, while the word *literature* has 'cognates in other Euro-pean languages', as Roger Fowler points out, 'for France, or Germany, or Russia, the history and the possible theoretical positions would be different..."Literature" exists universally but is regarded, or realized, differently in different cultures' (Fowler 1990:10).

Again, my detailed knowledge of these dif-ferent cultural inflexions is too inadequate to make my range of reference comprehensive, and so I must acknowledge at once that the present study of this topic is primarily anglo-centric in focus. My attention will be mainly directed, there-fore, to what I will call 'literatures in English'—in order to indicate the diverse range of literature drawing on a basic common language—and as a consequence, I shall only use the term 'English Literature' when I mean something specific by it (for example, the 'English Canon or 'The National Literature'). Nevertheless, it is perhaps not too presumptuous to acknowledge that 'Eng. Lit.'—in its indicatively familiar diminutive—has itself been, and remains, a global cultural presence (especially in Commonwealth and former Common-wealth countries, and in the United States); that 'great' English writers have figured prominently both in the conspectus of 'World Literature' and in the international 'exchange' of liter-ary influence, reaction and interaction; and that, as Marilyn Butler has suggested, 'the literature in the language the world uses ["thanks to the world dominance of America"] is...a world literature' (Butler [1989] 1990:10).

LITERARY VALUE

A wide-ranging, complex and unresolved debate surrounds the notion of 'literary value', and it will implicitly inform much of the rest of this book. I have used it hitherto to identify those discriminative judgements of evaluation made about literary works within conventional critical discourse—usually impre-cise and naturalised—in order to 'define' the 'artistic merit' of a work and so position it in relation to 'the Canon'. As a reflex of this, I have suggested, the notion of 'literary value' is ascribed to the work itself, so that it is perceived as containing and revealing 'literary value' rather than merely being *judged* as possessing it. The circular argument can then proceed with the critic/judge 'recognising' the 'literary value' inherent in the work, and having their judgement of its artistic merit con-firmed (for more on this 'tautology', see p. 10), whereas it is precisely the *ascription* of value which *constructs* the nature of criticism's object as the object it then perceives.

I shall use the term 'literary value' by and large to signal the process just described. But I should not be misunderstood to be recommending that we throw the baby out with the bathwa-ter. Certainly, I would wish to reject the notion of innate value which is 'recognised' by the 'disinterested' critic and used to construct a naturalised hierarchy of texts which are self-evidently 'Literature', while excluding others which are self-evidently not. But, equally, I would not want to relinquish the possibility of judgement and evaluation.

The point is that 'liter-ary value', and its product 'the Canon, *pre-empt* judgement by closing down evaluative analysis of works within the canon, and by closing out the vast body of 'literature' which falls out-side it. As Marilyn Butler tellingly observes, in her plea for a more

'Open Literary History' in the contemporary world-context, the canon reduces the number of texts available for reading and study—and the questions one can ask about those texts—to the point where 'evaluation itself is threatened: how can you operate the techniques for telling who a major writer is, if you don't know what a minor one looks like?' (Butler [1989] 1990:15).

If we do away with this pre-emptive and restrictive process, however, judgement can become variable and the range of material available for this variable judgement hugely increased. For stated and explicit reasons—and explicitness is crucial— we can say that text A is more interesting, more effective, 'bet-ter', than text B—but it will be *in relation to our purpose far evaluating it so.* And this purpose can be diverse and multiplex:

- the preferred text gives more pleasure as holiday reading;
- is a better exemplificaion of realism in fiction;
- is a canonic text and therefore has available for analysis a wider variety of critical readings about it;
- is so much a part of the national cultural heritage that we cannot understand the latter without it;
- is an inter-text necessary for an understanding of another text which alludes to it as a primary referent;
- repeats and reworks matters dealt with in an earlier poem by the same poet;
- gives us more insight into eighteenth-century attitudes to sexuality;
- is a formative instance of the development of Modernist drama;
- was a crucial component of the living literary culture on which the now dead but great writer originally drew; and so on.

We are freed, therefore, from the static position of simply say-ing that *Madame Bovary* is unarguably 'better' than a popular romance, and that we should only give serious attention to the former, to a position where we *can* say that—but also the *opposite*—in the context of the explicitly articulated purpose for which we are reading/studying either text. Nor does this lead to an undifferentiating relativism, since a purpose-driven criticism determines and controls the hierarchy of evaluation in particular circumstances: rather than substituting a 'do-as-you-like' free market of judgement for the fixed and absolute criterion of canonic status, the 'purpose' proposes a rationale for evaluation in any individual case.

Just as we acknowledge that there are now many literatures in place of 'Literature'— and that the critical attention paid to them self-determiningly constitutes their definition *as* literature—so here we encounter many extrinsic definitions of 'literary value' to replace the uni-tary and unverifiable notion of 'literary value' as intrinsic to any given text. Even so redoubtable a defender of 'Literature' as Frank Kermode, in his wryly rear-guard essay, 'Value in Lit-erature', in Blackwell's *A Dictionary of Cultural and Critical Theory,* seems grudgingly to accept that there is a kind of 'radi-cal freedom' in the recognition that 'value' is 'dynamic, transac-tional, contingent'—if only because such contingency allows him to reassert expert knowledge as the basis of true judge-ment (Kermode 1996:551, 552, 555).

THE CANON

Similarly, 'Firing the Canon', as the neat phrase has it, is not to destroy or do away with the Canon *tout court,* but rather to deconstruct it as a naturalised hierarchy. Nevertheless, in say-ing this, I would, of course, be cast as a member of what Harold Bloom, in his book *The Western Canon,* calls 'the School of Resentment': one of those who has rejected 'the autonomy of the aesthetic' (Bloom [1994] 1995:10), refuses to 'confront greatness' (524), and will not accept 'the [or rather Bloom's] Western Canon' on trust.

The main reason why I am perversely happy to be in the 'School of Resentment' is that the only way to accept Bloom's 'Canon is indeed 'on trust', since no arguments are made for it which address any of the ques-tions that have problematised it in the first place.

On the contrary, the main intellectual mode of his writing is a testy, tendentious and blustering assertion which smacks of little more than shouting to keep your courage up—a mode seen at its most naturalised and essentialist best when Bloom wonders about the fate of the other arts, now that literature seems to have fallen to the barbarians of the left:

> *When the School of Resentment becomes as dominant among art historians and critics as it is among literary aca-demics, will Matisse go unattended while we all flock to view the daubings of the Guerrilla Girls? The lunacy of these questions is plain enough when it comes to the emi-nence of Matisse, while Stravinsky is clearly in no danger of being replaced by politically correct music for the ballet companies of the world. (527)*

Note especially the give-away phrases in the final sentence: 'plain enough', 'eminence', 'clearly'—phrases which encode the same unthinking assumptions as those equally unexamined criteria of 'artistic merit' and critical 'recognition' which we saw earlier as sustaining conventional notions of 'literary value' and 'canonisation'. Does the Canon need enemies with friends like this in the 1990s?

As it happens, however, it is quite possible to accept the con-tinued presence of the Canon—so long as it is recognised to be an artificially manufactured product within cultural history. Indeed, I would argue strongly that because it is *there,* and has been/is such a central component of our cultural history, we can only understand the latter and what it signifies if we retain a concept of the Canon and what *it* comprises.

To put it another way, 'The Canon' needs to be studied as the cultural formation it inescapably is. (Incidentally, this also helps us to perceive how canons are formed more generally, for while *the* Canon is what I have particularly in view, as Frank Kermode points out, 'every reading list is a canon of sorts' (Kermode 1996:552), and the erstwhile radical displacement of the 'great works' by hitherto disregarded ones may well substitute one canon for another.) Furthermore, we can argue that the works which are in the Canon—rather than being there because they are, in some anterior sense, self-evidently 'great'—have their 'greatness' conferred on them, or at least continually recon-firmed, precisely by being in it: they *become* 'canonic texts', and therefore remain reference-points for other literary produc-tion.

However, they do so no longer as benchmarks of 'artistic merit', but as symptomatic instances at once of formal and ide-ological productions of past cultural conjunctures, and of the values descried in, and inscribed on, them in their reproduc-tion in subsequent cultural history.

In addition, perceived as 'canonic' in the denaturalised man-ner suggested above, such works can also be 're-read' in ways which release them from the limitations of their canonic status:

- Wordsworth's 'Ode: Intimations of Immortality', for exam-ple, can be defamiliarised as a poem encoding his complex political dilemma at the turn of the eighteenth century;
- *Adam Bede* (see pp. 141-8), for the way its narrative struc-ture reveals a fraught engagement with female sexuality and the 'Woman Question' in nineteenth-century England;
- *The Tempest, Mansfield Park* or *jane Eyre* for the way they sub-textually articulate a colonialist mentality;
- *Tess of the d'Urbervilles* as heteroglossic, stylistically riven, anti-realist textuality.

As an analogy, we may consider how little bits of 'great' liter-ary works become familiar quotations—so familiar, indeed, that we cease to think of what they might mean inside or out-side their original textual location, and that we see them as 'self-evidently' self-selecting and self-defining examples of (to borrow an apposite example) 'what oft was thought but n'er so well expressed'. But if we rediscover them in their context, and can set aside their status as 'quotations', it is possible to read them quite newly—either as saying something other than their common usage allows, or as sufficiently unremarkable to make one wonder why they were extrapolated as 'canonic' quotations in the first place.

So, too, with the works in the canon. But without the *existence* of the canon (to reinflect Mar-ilyn Butler's argument in relation to evaluation noted on p. 20) there would be no perceptible coordinates of literary culture, and it is salutary to remember how often contemporary writers—especially those from national, social and sexual groups whose forebears were, *de facto,* excluded from the canon—still 'write back' to canonic texts, both as a point of reference and to revise and 're-vision' those texts themselves.

In my abbreviated account of the holy trinity of terms above, one procedural strategy in their emancipatory decon-struction has been common to all. In the process of denaturalis-ing and defamiliarising such categories—so that they may, if required, be reconstituted and recuperated—it is the business of giving them back their history which is of primary and fun-damental importance. Dehistoricised, the marks and meanings of their manufacture are erased, so that they do indeed appear 'natural', 'given' and impervious to challenge; rehistoricised, their partiality—in both senses—is restored to view, and their invulnerability as mythic monoliths is countered. It is to the historical construction of the notion of 'Literature', therefore— and to a lesser extent of 'English' or 'Eng. Lit.' as the academic site on which that process was underpinned, in the first half of the twentieth century, for the English-speaking world at least— that I now turn as the subject of my next chapter.

2

What has Literature Been?

A HISTORY OF THE CONCEPT, PART ONE: ORIGINS TO ORTHODOXIES

In setting out to chart the history of the concept *literature,* I return to my proposition in Chapter 1 that while the phe-nomenon of literature has existed since deepest antiquity, the notion of 'Literature' has not. Hence, the term 'literature' will only be used in what is an anachronistic sense in the early parts of the present chapter. Better, perhaps, to think in terms of 'poetry' (see Chapter 1, p. 8), since, at least throughout the classical era and down to the Romantic period at the turn of the eighteenth century, this was the generic term for what we know as literature. Poets, in other words, were simply 'makers', and poetry (including poetic drama and prose romances, fables and sagas) was what they created by 'the arte of making' (1586). As Sir Philip Sidney commented in c.1581: 'wee Englishmen haue mette with the Greekes, in calling him [the poet] a maker', noting also that 'One may bee a Poet with-out versing' and 'there have been many most excellent Poets, that never versified'; whilst James Beattie in 1776 could still nominate Shakespeare's play, *The Merry Wives of Windsor,* and Fielding's novel, *Tom Jones,* 'the two finest Comic poems...in the world'.

Forms of poetry, together with other recognisably literary genres, in the oral traditions of—note the word—*preliterate* cultures disappear into the mists of time (some would argue they were the primal and primary form of languages them-selves). Magical fertility spells and incantations, hymns, rid-dles, proverbs, myths, ballads, folktales, lyrics, epics, satires, were as organic an aspect of life as food, clothing, shelter and religion. In 'literate' cultures—i.e. in those where such modes of expression were written down—the earliest examples would include Sumerian poetry from the third millenium BC (like the *Epic of Gilgamesh)* and Egyptian poems and myths going back to 2,000 BC, whilst Indian, Chinese and Greek written poetry can be dated back many centuries before Christ.

In the move from preliterate to literate cultures, we may also perceive the way in which a division occurs between folk and elite (or 'polite') literatures. The written forms start to take on an eval-uative precedence over the oral ones, and begin to establish the notion of a canon of 'classic' texts (the primary meaning of 'classic/ classical' is 'of the first class, of acknowledged excellence'—*OED).* In this context, and to signal the later symbiotic relationship between 'Literature' and criticism (see p. 37ff.), it is also worth registering that it is precisely ancient literary *scholarship*—the self-conscious preservation of 'classi-cal' works—which begins to sustain a recorded literature for future generations. One of the most significant early epochs of such is focussed on the library and university of Alexandria from its foundation in 324 BC to its destruction in AD 640, and so it is to the Hellenistic Greek scholars there that we owe the survival of most of the classical Greek texts.

In the Western tradition, Homer's epic poems are regarded as dating from before 700 BC, and literary writing is signifi-cantly present in sixth and fifth century BC Greece (Aesop's fables, for example, date from the sixth; Aeschylus's, Sophocles's and Euripides's plays from the fifth), and it is in 4th century BC Greece, too, that we find the first, and lastingly influential, philosophical disquisition on the nature of the poet, and thus of poetry, in the works of Plato. It is worth pausing here for a moment to register some of the earliest (often conflicting and seemingly contradictory) characteristics of poetry identified by Plato and his followers, since they have informed—even *constituted*—the way in which 'Literature' has been conceived of since.

Paradoxically, Plato did not regard poetry favourably, and banned most of its types from his ideal Republic. Two main reasons lie behind this. First, while poetry could educate people in individual and social morality, it could also, by its persuasive power, corrupt them by inducing meretricious illusions, since it is also a *mimetic* art which 'imitates' objects and actions in the created world. As the latter, for Plato, were themselves imitations of their 'Ideal' form, poetic imitation was an imitation of an imitation, and hence more false than the objects and actions themselves. So that whilst poetry might be an entertaining pastime, it led dangerously away from the truth.

On the other hand, Plato speaks of the 'divine madness' of the poet—i.e. his 'inspiration'—in which transcendent state of mind a divine power speaks through the poet and puts him in touch with the 'Ideas' (ultimate realities/archetypes) behind the material world. Similarly, and despite his deprecation of poetry as meretriciously mimetic, Plato elsewhere and impor-tantly sees all art as being poetry and all poetry as being *cre-ation* (in the sense of *poiesis* that we noted in Chapter 1, p. 18): 'All that causes the passage of something from non-being into being is a "poesy" or creation'. It is these latter thoughts which are crucial to the establishing of 'poetry' as a supreme human achievement in later periods: now enshrined in our con-cept 'Literature'. Plato's disciple, Aristotle, in his *Poetics,* fosters this process by accepting the notion of *mimesis* ('art imitates life'), but proposes that this is, in fact, its high moral dimension, because in its synthetic and generalising tendency it is truer to reality than are the particularities of history. Aristotle was also the first to be systematically interested in the formal construction of literary texts, and thus initiates the *aes-thetic* discourse in the definition of 'Literature'.

Conversely perhaps, the first-century AD Greek treatise, *On the Sublime,* attributed to the 'pseudo-Longinus', focusses prin-cipally on the *expressive* quality of literature. In seeking to establish what makes 'great literature' great, 'Longinus' relates poetic excellence to the author's emotional and intellectual pro-fundity and seriousness. 'Sublimity', in other words, is above all things an effect *of the spirit,* an emotional charge that bonds the soul of the writer to the soul of the reader: 'Sublimity is the echo of greatness of spirit'. Significantly, 'Longinus's' treatise made no great mark on literary thinking until the late-seventeenth century, when it became deeply influ-ential in identifying the loftiness of feelings which, by that point, were beginning to be seen as an essential attribute of 'Literature'. This resulted at once in the subjectivising and psy-chologising of literature and the reader's experiencing of it; in notions of the free spirit of 'original genius'; and hence, in the concurrent development of Romanticism and of aesthetics as a newly discrete branch of philosophy (see below, pp. 35-6).

Finally, in this brief survey of the originating classical dis-courses of 'Literature', the Neoplatonist tradition, beginning with Plotinus (third century AD), took the Aristotelean posi-tion on 'imitation' much further. For Plotinus, poets had a truly noble role—almost God-like in their ability to create— since their art touched the realm of Platonic 'Ideas' on which, as we have heard, the created world was modelled. Ironically, then, Plato's own ideas about the unsatisfactoriness of the poet and poetry in the pursuit of truth were turned back against him by the Neoplatonists: poetic imitation was regarded as the highest of all imitations because it offered access to the divine archetypes rather than merely copying existing materialities. In the context of accounting for the conventional post-Romantic, 'aestheticised' notion of 'Literature' which follows, it is worth bearing in mind that such Neoplatonic views were profoundly influential throughout the Renaissance and down to the Romantic period, where, once again, their consonance with the new aesthetics is clearly apparent.

In the centuries after Plato, examples of developed 'literary' art abound throughout the Greek and Roman periods, as they do also in the so-called 'Dark Ages'; and they include, of course, works in vernacular languages as well as in the classi-cal ones. My following synoptic selection of some of the received 'classics' of the Western literary tradition is simply and strategically to establish the fact that literature in a wide range of languages and genres predates even the first appear-ance of the word *literature* in European languages, let alone its discriminative modern usage as 'Literature'. Obvious instances would be:

- Virgil's *Eclogues* and his epic poem the *Aeniad* (first cen-tury BC);
- Ovid's *Ars Amatoria* and *Metamorphoses* (first century BC/ first century AD);
- the early prose fictions (the *novel* as a defined genre, we should remember, belongs to the post-Renaissance period) of the Roman writers, Petronius (the *Satyricon,* first cen-tury AD) and

Apuleius (*The Golden Ass,* second century AD);

- the prose epic sagas of Iceland and Norway (dating from a c.ninth-century oral tradition but written down in the twelfth and thirteenth centuries);
- the Anglo-Saxon epic poem, *Beowulf;*
- the Middle High German epic, the *Nibelungenlied* (proba-bly twelfth century);
- Guillaume de Lorris's *Romance of the Rose* and the French courtly-love poems of Chretian de Troyes (twelfth century);
- the Irish stories of Cu Chulainn (dating from c.eigth cen-tury, although not written down until the twelfth);
- the thirteenth/fourteenth-century Italian poems of Dante (the *Commedia* and *La Vita Nuova)* and the fourteenth-century stories of Boccaccio (the *Decameron);*
- the lyric poetry of Medieval Latin, Provencal and Middle French;
- the Middle English alliterative poem, *Sir Gawain and the Green Knight* (and the shorter poems in the same manuscript, *Pearl, Patience* and *Purity);*
- and the works of the fourteenth-century English poet, Geof-frey Chaucer—most famously, *Troilus and Criseyde (c.* 1382-85) and *The Canterbury Tales (c.* 1388-1400).

All this writing is, of course, recognisably 'literary', but the point is that it could not have conceived of itself as comprising 'Literature'. Perhaps it is appropriate, then, that the word 'literature' itself enters the English language at about that point in the late-fourteenth century (the *OED's* first example is from 1375) when Chaucer was composing what was to become the foundation-stone of the English 'National Literature'.

The English word *literature* derives, either directly or by way of the cognate French *litterature,* from the Latin *litteratura,* the root-word for which is *littera* meaning 'a letter' (of the alphabet). Hence the Latin word and its European derivatives (Spanish, Italian and German, for example, also have direct cog-nates) all carry a similar general sense: 'letters' means what we would now call 'book learning', acquaintance/familiarity with books. A 'man of letters' (or 'literature') was someone who was widely read; would have had, as in the *OED's* first definition (see p. 5), 'polite or humane learning'; would have been someone who possessed 'literary culture': that is, a culture acquired through reading books. An inverse example from Bradshaw in 1513 pin-points this, and also indicates, as Roger Fowler suggests (1990:8), the element of social judge-ment implicit in having (or not having) such learning—which itself points forward to the discriminations inscribed in the much later notion of 'Literature': 'The comyn people... Whiche without lytterature and good informacyon Ben lyke to Brute beestes'.

The necessarily elitist nature of possessing 'lyt-terature' (to be 'literate' in this sense was a rare accomplish-ment and access to printed books—themselves new, costly and uncommon—was limited) is also signalled in Skelton's com-ment of 1529: 'I know your vertu and your lytterature', as it is too in Burne's remark of 1581: 'hes nocht sufficient literatur to vndirstand the scripture'. And Francis Bacon's compliment to King James I in 1605—'There hath not beene...any King...so learned in all literature and erudition, diuine and humane'— establishes this meaning, whilst also implying a value judge-ment, not just on the fact of possessing 'literature', but about the books which provide it. This sense of the word continues down to the mid-to-late-eighteenth century. The *OED* notes that this is the 'only sense' given in Dr Johnson's *Dictionary* (1755); and in his *Life of Milton* (1780), Johnson uses it twice in that way: 'He had probably more than common literature, as his son addresses him in one of his most elaborate Latin poems' (quoted in Williams 1976:151); 'His literature was unquestionably great. He read all the languages which are con-sidered either as learned or polite'.

At this point, then, as Raymond Williams suggests, 'litera-ture' corresponds to the modern 'literacy' (1976:151), albeit with an evaluative dimension well beyond our descriptive sense of simply being able to read and write. By the later eigh-teenth century, however, the word was acquiring the second of the *OED's* meanings: the profession or realm of letters. In Johnson's *Life of Cowley* (1779), Cowley's previous biogra-pher, Bishop Sprat, is described as: 'An author whose preg-nancy of imagination and elegance of language have deservedly set him high in the ranks of literature'. Here, John-son is referring not to the place of Sprat's work in a hierarchy of literary texts but to his status in the newly-emerging *profes-sion* of writing (nevertheless, Johnson's complimentary judge-ments on the quality of Sprat's writing point to the discrimina-tion of such typically 'literary' virtues later found to be the hallmarks of 'Literature').

Around the turn of the eighteenth century, then, Isaac D'lsraeli is quoted by the *OED* as saving: 'Literature, with us, exists independent of patronage or associa-tion, where 'literature' again implies the business of producing any kind of writing.

By 1830, Sir Walter Scott notes: 'I deter-mined that literature should be my staff, but not my crutch, and that the profits of my literary labour...should not... become necessary to my ordinary expenses'. This self-conscious pride in the paid professional status of the individual 'author' or 'writer'—words which themselves become more frequent in the later part of the eighteenth century—reveals the shift from aristocratic patronage as the matrix for the produc-tion of literary writing to a *commercial* environment in which individual authors sell different kinds of written wares in dif-ferent kinds of market. What we can perceive in this process is the emergence of the socio-cultural conditions in which the discrimination of a selective category of 'high' literature—as opposed to the 'hack' writing of 'Grub Street'—will conse-quently take place.

Symptomatically, too, although 'poet' and 'poetry' remain preferred terms for the whole spectrum of literary writing amongst the Romantic poets, those words, since the middle of the seventeenth century, had been gradually specialising out to mean, not creative writing ('making') in general, but *metrical composition* or *verse*—a process highlighted by Wordsworth's well-known grouse in the 'Preface' to the 1802 edition of *Lyrical Ballads:* 'I here use the word "Poetry" (though against my own judgement) as opposed to the word "Prose", and synonymous with metrical composition'.

As Raymond Williams suggests: 'It is probable that this specialisation of *poetry* to verse, together with the increasing importance of prose forms such as the *novel,* made literature the most available general word' (1976:153).

By the beginning of the nineteenth century, then, and impor-tantly fuelled by the status within Romanticism assigned to the role of the poet, the previous sense of 'literature' also gave way to the *OED's* third definition of the word, some of the prob-lems with which were considered on p. 7:

> Literary productions as a whole; the body of writings pro-duced in a particular country or period, or in the world in general. Now also in a more restricted sense, applied to writing which has claim to consideration on the ground of beauty of form or emotional effect....
>
> ...This sense is of very recent emergence both in Eng. and Fr.

What we can now further deduce from this 'very recent' usage is that the concept-word 'Literature' is fundamentally inscribed with notions of *period,* and, more importantly, of *nation* (the conception of it as a *world* species will resurface later in the status that Matthew Arnold and his disciples award it). It is, of course, important to avoid a slippage between a merely lexical and a conceptual history: George Puttenham, for example, in 1589, was already thinking in terms of a 'national' literature when he proposed that 'there may be an art of our English *Poesie,* as well as there is of the Latine and Greeke'. Nevertheless, my italicising of 'Poesie' there allows us to note that the *OED's* first example of the word *literature,* in its 'more restricted sense' (i.e. as 'Literature'), implicitly identifies it as having a national character: '*Their* literature, *their* works of art offer models that have never been excelled' (Davy 1812; my emphases).

But it is Buckle, in 1857, who makes this fully explicit: 'Literature, when it is in a healthy and unforced state, is simply the form in which the knowledge of a country is regis-tered'; and Green, by 1874, is using the word in the recognisably modern sense: 'The full glory of the new literature broke on England with Edmund Spenser'. However, Rene Wellek has offered quotations which show the usage to be appearing in Italian, French, German, and then English, from the mid-eighteenth century: George Colman in 1761 seeks to rescue Shakespeare and Milton from 'the general wreck of old English Literature'; Dr Johnson in 1774 speaks of the possibil-ity of reviving 'our antiquated literature'; and James Beattie in 1783 wants to explore 'the history and politics, the manners and the literature of these latter ages' (Wellek 1970:5-8).

Such critics are now talking of a kind of literary writing which is distinguished from other kinds of writing (e.g. history, philoso-phy, politics, theology) that had hitherto been subsumed under the category 'literature', and which is precisely so distinguished by its *aesthetic* character (as suggested in the second sentence of the *OED's* definition above). Wellek, indeed, claims that 'the word' underwent both a 'process of "nationalization" and..."aestheticization"' from the 1760s onwards *(ibid.)*.

But whatever the precise moment at which this process begins to develop, it remains a crucial one in the cultural his-tory of our term, since 'aestheticization' defines a particular kind of writing ('creative', 'imaginative'), but also, in effect, begins to ascribe a new and higher value to this discriminated sub-set. As Terry Eagleton makes clear:

> *It is no accident that the period we are discussing [the second half of the eighteenth century, leading into the Roman-tic period] sees the rise of modern 'aesthetics'.... It is mainly from this era, in the work of Kant, Hegel, Schiller, Coleridge and others, that we inherit our contemporary ideas of...'aesthetic experience', of 'aesthetic harmony' and the unique nature of the artefact. Previously men and women had written poems, staged plays or painted pic-tures for a variety of purposes, while others had read, watched or viewed them in a variety of ways. Now these concrete, historically variable practices were being sub-sumed into some special, mysterious faculty known as the 'aesthetic'.... The assumption that there was an unchang-ing object known as 'art', or an isolatable experience called 'beauty' or the 'aesthetic', was largely a product of the...alienation of art from social life.... The whole point of 'creative' writing was that it was gloriously useless, an 'end in itself loftily removed from any sordid social purpose.... Art was extricated from the material practices, social rela-tions and ideological meanings in which it is always caught up, and raised to the status of a solitary fetish. (Eagleton [1983] 1996:18-19)*

Paradoxically, however, this 'fetishisation' of the aesthetic offers itself, in the course of the nineteenth century, as a substi-tute for the rapidly waning spiritual force of religion, as we shall see later in respect of Matthew Arnold, and as a forma-tive element in the urgently needed construction of a cohesive national consciousness and identity in the context of the emer-gence of a new and heterogeneous industrial, urban, class society. So that Rene Wellek's other term, 'nationalisation, sig-nals the nation's appropriation of a valued selection of tran-scendent 'creative' texts in the national language as somehow articulating its 'best self (Arnold's phrase for an essential humane culture: Arnold [1869] 1971:108), which it then canonises as 'The National Literature'. As the process settles and matures, this construction will come to seem 'natural', but a national Canon is nevertheless deeply ideologically inscribed.

For the valued literature will be seen to represent, not merely 'aesthetic value', but rather, in Buckle's sharply perceptive phrase given earlier, 'the form in which the knowledge of a country is registered'. That is: the expression of what it per-ceives, or desires to be perceived, as its most admired spiritual and humane values, and thus of its 'true character'. Signifi-cantly, at around the same time, Charles Kingsley, one of the founding-fathers of 'English' as an academic subject, described literature as 'the autobiography of a nation'; while in 1835, in the context of establishing the civilising need to teach the peo-ple of India English, Lord Macaulay had based his case on the premise that 'the literature of England is now more valuable than that of classical antiquity' (Macaulay [1835] 1995:429).

This reciprocity between the aesthetic and the national, despite notions of a 'world literature' which transcends national boundaries, is what makes it so difficult to discuss 'Literature' abstracted from its determining national conditions of being, and drives the focus of my argument here constantly back to the particular case of 'English Literature'.

By the second half of the nineteenth century, then, a fully aestheticised notion of 'Literature' was becoming current. But a further factor in its constitution is its symbiotic relationship with *criticism*. Indeed, we may say that while literature exists independently of criticism, 'Literature' is only created *by* criti-cism: it is criticism which selects, evaluates and elevates those texts which are designated as such, and which identifies—more or less explicitly—those features of them that comprise their high 'literary value'. 'Literature', in other words, is made in the image of the criticism that regards it. Certainly, as Chris Baldick neatly points out, 'the real content of the school and college subject which goes under the name "English Literature" is not literature in the primary sense, but *criticism*' (Baldick 1983:4). In the English-speaking tradition at least, it is the Victorian poet and critic, Matthew Arnold, who is most influential in this respect, and who fundamentally establishes the dominant conception of an aestheticised 'Literature' of high cultural value for the modern period. Throughout his writ-ings, his use of such phrases as 'current English literature', 'good literature', 'the literature of France and Germany', 'great works of literature', 'the creation of a masterwork of literature', show that the *OED's* third sense has definitely arrived. So, too, does the status he ascribes to 'great literature', and thence to the literary critic.

However, although Arnold uses the word with its main mod-ern meaning, he also, on the one hand, retains 'poetry' both in the older generic sense and as indicating the highest realms of literary art, and, on the other, transposes 'literature' into the broader term 'culture'. Both of these usages, in different ways, have had an equally profound impact on later conceptions of the value and function of 'Literature'. In his essay, 'The Study of Poetry' *(Essays in Criticism: Second Series,* 1888), he makes an immense claim on behalf of 'poetry':

> *More and more mankind will discover that we have to turn to poetry to interpret life for us, to console us, to sustain us. Without poetry, our science will appear incomplete; and most of what now passes with us for religion and phi-losophy will be replaced by poetry. (Arnold 1970:340)*

We can see here how Eagleton's 'special, mysterious faculty [of] the aesthetic' ('poetry') is being substituted as the realm of the spiritual in modern 'scientific' society. And in 'The Func-tion of Criticism at the Present Time' *(Essays in Criticism,* 1865), Arnold famously defines what the object of attention for the person of culture (or 'critic') should be: 'the best that is known and thought in the world' (Arnold 1970:141); in *Cul-ture and Anarchy,* this becomes 'the best that has been thought and *said* in the world' (Arnold [1869] 1971:6; my emphasis).

It is here, for modern Anglo-American literary culture, that the notions of 'the tradition' and 'the canon' are established, although Arnold is not responsible for the concept-words themselves, nor, indeed, for the parochially 'nationalising' ten-dency that, as we have seen, goes hand-in-hand with the aestheticisation of 'Literature'. His own 'Hellenistic' view of the canon was, in fact, uncompromisingly cosmopolitan, and his life-work aimed at countering the 'philistine' provincialism of nineteenth-century English social culture. It is somewhat ironic, then, that he should have become the *eminence grise* behind the twentieth-century institutionalisation of 'The National Literature' as the 'form' of our national identity, and of 'English' as the academic processing-plant in which it is celebrated, nurtured and recycled on behalf of the nation's spiritual health.

> *But it is also in Arnold's views on the 'function of criticism' that further determinants of the modern conception of 'Litera-ture' may be jound. Indeed, his most important collections of essays, aside from* Culture and Anarchy, *are the two series enti-tled* Essays in Criticism. *Criticism, he says, must seek 'to know the best that is known and thought in the world' with* disinter-estedness—*'the free play of the mind on all subjects' (Arnold 1970:141-2)—and to make 'the best ideas prevail' (134). In this way, 'a current of true and fresh ideas' (141) is created, and out of 'this stir and growth come the creative epochs of literature' (134). It is important to note that, for Arnold, it is 'criticism first'—'when criticism has done its work' (142)— which creates the conditions for true creativity. And criticism, as the later 'The Study of Poetry' makes clear, involves 'a high standard and...a strict judgement' (Arnold 1970:341): for 'the best poetry is what we want' (342)—'poetry of a high order of excellence' (341)—since in poetry 'our race, as time goes on, will find an ever surer and surer stay' (340). In order to obtain this great cultural good, we must be able to 'appreciate the wide difference between it and all work which has not the same high character' (344); and to do this, we should have in mind the works of 'the great masters, and to apply them as a touchstone to other poetry' (347). This should not be an* abstract *process of ascertaining greatness, Arnold adds, but should be achieved by taking 'concrete examples...specimens of poetry of the high, the very highest quality, and [saying]: The characters of a high quality of poetry are what is expressed* there' *(349). In other words, what Arnold is propos-ing is the evaluative selection, by practical (not* theoretical) *discrimination and judgement, of the best 'Literature' as* the *spiritual/cultural prop in an era...in which we are to see multitudes of a common sort of readers, and masses of a common sort of literature ...readers [who] do not want and could not relish anything better than such literature...[the provision of which] is becoming a vast and profitable industry. (366)*

Represented as an elevated aesthetic domain to be defended for the race's benefit against the assault of commercialised mediocrity, it would be difficult to announce more clearly the ideological investment carried by the high-cultural concept 'Literature'. Equally, in *Culture and Anarchy*, whilst Arnold appropriates the wider term 'culture' to designate 'sweetness and light' (Arnold [1869] 1971:69), the 'pursuit of perfection', 'a man's total spiritual growth' (30), our 'best self (108), and the need to ensure that such ideas *'prevail'* (69), it is clearly *literary* culture ('the best which has been thought and *said* in the world' [6]) that he has in mind as the bulwark against the contemporary cultural 'anarchy' incident on the rise of a mod-ern, mass, class society.

Furthermore, his 'aliens'—individuals who are 'led, not by their class spirit, but by a general *humane* spirit, by the love of human perfection' (109)—sound remark-ably like those (literary) critics who can distinguish the 'best poetry' from the 'masses of a common sort of literature', and who therefore become the guardians of the cultural health of the modern world.

To register the strength of Arnold's influence in the construc-tion of the concept of 'Literature'—especially in respect of such equally influential Anglo-American twentieth-century crit-ics as T.S.Eliot and F.R.Leavis—and in the institutionalisation of 'Literature' in the education syllabus, let me sum up the key ideas in his work:

- there is the elevation of 'Literature' ('poetry', 'culture') as a crucial humanising force;
- the importance of recognising a tradition of great works from the past;
- the central place of a discriminating criticism in selecting 'the best' from the rest, in order to create a healthy culture in which creativity can thrive. This is a criticism based not on 'abstract' theory, but on an empirical intuition which can discern innate quality in 'concrete' examples of the poetry itself;
- the notion of an intellectual elite ('critics'/'aliens') who are the agents of this process, and who will help to make high (literary/ minority) culture 'prevail' in the face of a moder-nity characterised by loss of faith and values, by fragmenta-tion and alienation, and by an urban mass civilization.

However, before we see Arnold's ideas alchemised into the fully-blown Modernist institutionalisation of 'Literature', we should notice a parallel and contiguous process in the second half of the nineteenth century: the construction of 'Literature' as an academic subject.

It will be difficult in what follows to avoid slipping between offering a potted history of the rise of 'English' as an academic subject and keeping in focus our concern with the construction of the modern concept of 'Literature'. But in either case, it should be clearly recognised that I am constrained to a limited *national* perspective (albeit with some attempt to include an American dimension). What I will do, then, is pinpoint what seem to be significant features in the long and complex process by which 'Literature', in the context of this national cultural history, became more or less synonymous with 'English'.

In England, the earliest instruction in the English language and literature was offered by University College, London in the 1820s (the first Professor being appointed in 1828), with some emphasis on the moral and 'liberalising' study of litera-ture. This was followed by other London and provincial uni-versity colleges in the following decades (not, however, by the 'old' Oxbridge universities until much later in the century).

Even so, the syllabus was very variable, and the 'English sub-jects' could include language and philology, history, geography and economics, as well as literature. Much of the curriculum was comprised of a 'mapping' of the historical components of the national language and literature (the first book with the title *A History of English Language and Literature,* by Robert Chambers, was published in 1836), this process being at once symptomatised and underpinned by such later large-scale Vic-torian and Edwardian scholarly projects as the compilation of the *Oxford English Dictionary* (initiated 1878) and of the *Cambridge History of English Literature* (15 vols., 1907-27).

But it was in the Mechanics Institutes, working-men's colleges and the university extension lecture circuits, rather than in the universities proper, that 'English' was developed most dynamically by such Victorian evangelists as F.D.Maurice and Charles Kingsley. This was explicitly to foster a sense of national belonging and 'larger sympathies' amongst working men, and to create 'fellow-feeling' between them and other classes. While many working men did indeed feel enfranchised by the acquisition of 'Literature', it nevertheless remained an ideologically-driven initiative to 'humanise' and 'civilise' poten-tially disruptive social elements in a developing class-stratified society by providing them with a 'liberal' or 'humane' educa-tion. In this context, 'English Literature' became at once a vehicle of moral education and a cheap and accessible 'poor man's Classics', although how successful such a social mission was, and how far it remained 'the distinctive hallmark of liter-ary studies', are matters open to debate.

Equally formative in the development of 'English' was its early association with women. Around the middle of the cen-tury, the recognition of a 'surplus' of unmarried women, together with a perceived need to educate the nation's chil-dren, led to the training of women as school-teachers, a train-ing in which the 'personal' and 'intuitive' properties of 'English', and especially literature, played a crucial and suit-able role. Charles Kingsley, in his introductory lecture on becoming Professor of English at Queen's College for Women, London around the mid-century, stated that the reading of English Literature, so suited as it was to 'women's inborn *per-sonal interest'*, would contribute an understanding of the 'English spirit' amongst women, essential in a group who were, in effect, to become the 'teacher-mothers' of the nation's young.

The huge demand for school-teachers following the 1870 Education Act, especially for those with higher education, led to the entry into the universities of increasing numbers of women studying 'English'. It is significant in this context that, whilst Oxford had fought off a proposal, supported by a Royal Commission, to include in its syllabus the study of English in the 1850s, by 1873 the subject was included in the examinations for a Pass degree, and by 1893 the university had established an Honours School of English Language and Literature.

Up until the First World War, then, 'English' at Oxford was largely a 'women's subject', a 'soft' option unsuited to the intellectual powers of men, who took mathematics or 'Greats' (Classics), but one which was regarded, in its designation as 'pink sunsets' and 'mere chatter about Shelley', as admirably tailored to the 'feminine mind'. Not sur-prisingly perhaps, the first Professor of English Literature at Oxford (1904) was

Sir Walter Raleigh, while the first at Cam-bridge (1912) was Sir Arthur Quiller Couch, both 'men of letters' who saw their 'feminine' subject as essentially one of *belles-lettrist* 'appreciation'. Nevertheless, despite these unpro-pitious beginnings, but in the context of a co-existent decline in the popularity of a general classical education, 'English Lan-guage and Literature' began to supercede it as the new 'humane studies'.

In America, English departments in colleges and universities began to be founded in the last quarter of the nineteenth cen-tury, although they, too, were departments of 'Language and Literature'. The drive towards the professionalisation of 'English', indeed, came from the philologists, who were the first to develop home-grown graduate schools in the new discipline and who tended to use examples from literary texts for their linguistic explications.

But with a growing recognition that studying the examples might have a greater popularity than the grammatical theory, and with a concurrent scholarly and systematic processing of literary texts (editing new edi-tions, for example), a kind of literary-critical study began to emerge. This coincided with a concern among the wider non-academic community to see the development of a more humanistic and cultural general education as in the national interest. As Gerald Graff and Michael Warner put it in the introduction to *The Origins of Literary Studies in America:*

> *After the Civil War, educators and custodians of culture began to feel that the study of English literature had much to offer to a society whose sense of national unity seemed increasingly threatened by such divisive forces as indus-trial capitalism, European immigration, labor agitation and other forms of class conflict, and the increasing concentra-tion of Americans in cities at the same time as they became dispersed across the continent. The teaching of English literature in schools and colleges promised to serve as a binding principle for Americans who had less in common than they had had in the small-town America before the Civil War. (Graff and Warner 1989:5)*

As in the English context, then, a mixture of motives fuelled the development of the study of literature as a significant ele-ment in the education process: from perceptions that it might assist in political and social control, to more liberal views of its democratising, civilising and humanising potential.

Alongside the professionalisation fostered by the philolo-gists, however, and often in open warfare with them, were *belles-lettrist* critics who looked to Matthew Arnold and John Ruskin for guidance, and who saw literature as the repository of moral and spiritual values which could be mobilised on behalf of an all-round 'humane' education and of the enhance-ment of the national culture. As Graff makes clear, in the essay quoted above and in his *Professing Literature: An Institutional History*, the tensions and contradictions between the various constituent elements of 'Literary Studies' in America show 'a tale not of triumphant humanism, nationalism, or any single professional model, but a series of conflicts' which mark all of its future history (Graff: 1987, 14).

So that 'teaching the con-flicts', Graff (1992) claims, should now be the principal project for a 'literary studies' which can only be explained and made sense of by understanding its own determinate history, as indeed is also the case for the literature that is its object of attention. I will return to this issue in Chapter 3 (pp. 79-80). Nevertheless, the origins of 'Literary Studies' in the US suggest an ideological matrix for the creation of the conception of 'Lit-erature' which is cognate with that we have observed develop-ing in England: a growing regard for 'Literature's' value in engendering a humane national culture, and an increasing pro-fessionalisation in the critical study of the literary texts them-selves. We will see the acme of these tendencies when we consider American 'New Criticism' on pp. 56-9.

In England, following the Education Act of 1902, and the foundation of the English Association in 1907 with its Arnoldian principles and its brief to promote English literary culture in education, 'English' began more broadly to take its place at the heart of the school curriculum as the one subject essential for every child's education in a fully 'national' education system.

As a further refinement of this process, in the course of the later nineteenth and early twentieth centuries, there had been a tendency to separate out the study of the English Language and Literature, with the latter taking on a methodological character of its own and becoming regarded as central to the full personal development of the properly balanced citizen. This kind of mass social engineering may not have been quite what Matthew Arnold had in mind when he urged making the pursuit of culture 'prevail', but its ideologi-cal premises were not dissimilar.

Pre-First World War imperialism was a further factor in engendering the need to celebrate the national heritage of 'English Literature' in order to forge a sense of national identity (see Baldick 1983: chapter 3), but it was the War itself which at once intensified patriotic fervour for an 'Englishness' enshrined in its literature, and ensured the victory at Oxford and Cambridge of 'English' over its erstwhile enemy: the 'Teu-tonic' or 'Germanic' philology *(ibid:* 89). In this context, we need only think of the thousands of 'heroic' and/or Georgian early war poems, and of the huge popularity of Rupert Brooke's sonnet 'The Soldier' in particular. Conversely, the enormous cultural disruption of the war and its aftermath—all faiths and values undermined, class and gender patterns in turmoil, the post-war world unrecognisable to many—created a further need to reinforce the national consciousness, the sense of belonging to a shared national organism.

Once again, 'Literature' was seen to provide, in Arnold's phrase, 'an ever surer and surer stay'. The 1921 Board of Education 'Newbolt Report' on *The Teaching of English in England* is the most explicit expression of this. Time and again, its Arnoldian premises weave into the 'anarchy' of the post-war social fabric: a liberal education based on 'English' 'would form a new ele-ment of national unity, linking together the mental life of all classes.... Even more certainly should pride and joy in the national literature serve as such a bond'.

Literature was a 'spiritual influence' which might ameliorate the 'morbid condition of the body politic'; so that to avoid 'lamentable consequences', education should promote 'fellowship' by way of literature as 'an embodiment of the best thoughts of the best minds, the most direct and lasting communication of experience by man to men'. But, whilst it directs people to 'higher' things than 'the social problem', and the teaching of it 'involv [es] grave national issues', literature in itself is presented as entirely apolitical, merely being a civilising influence which teaches 'young men and women the use of leisure' and prepares them for 'life'.

Newbolt, of course, was primarily concerned with fostering the educational centrality of the 'National Literature'. In this, Shakespeare, 'our greatest English writer', is 'an inevitable and necessary part of school activity', and the creative 'fellowship' of a stable, homogenous and organic Elizabethan culture is its (pointedly) exemplary moment: 'It was no inglorious time of our history that Englishmen delighted altogether in dance and song and drama, nor were these pleasures the privilege of a few or a class'. But the Report also indicates more generally some of the by now conventionally received characteristics of the notion of 'Literature':

All great literature has in it two elements, the contempo-rary and the eternal.... To concentrate the study of litera-ture mainly on the first aspect...is to ignore its nobler, more... universal element. There is a sense—the most important of all—in which Homer and Dante and Milton, Aeschylus and Shakespeare, are all of the same age or of none. Great literature is only partly the reflection of a par-ticular year or generation: it is also a timeless thing, which can never become old fashioned or out of date....

With the nation once again in desperate need of a new genera-tion of English teachers, and with the Newbolt Report lurking behind their training, it is not hard to see how the dominant mid-twentieth-century definition of 'Literature' became widely broadcast and received.

Straddling the publication of the Newbolt Report was a fur-ther development in the evolution of 'Literature' as a modern cultural discourse, which, while much more intellectually sophisticated and influential, has some features in common with the Report's position. Cambridge University's 'Literature, Life and Thought' tripos was introduced in 1917, although it was not until 1926 that a degree in English alone could be taken. It included papers on Tragedy, Literary Criticism, Special Subjects, the English Moralists and—most importantly in our context here—'Practical Criticism'. With this last critical initiative, energised by the Cambridge academics most signifi-cantly associated with its practice (see Richards, Empson and Leavis, pp. 51-6), we might say that the recognisably modern conception of 'Literature', and of its professional critical study, had come into being. It is to the distinctive contribution of its immediate and influential precursor, T.S.Eliot, and then to the impact of this new 'Modernist' criticism in England and Amer-ica, that I now turn.

To state it succinctly, if over-simply: what is central and com-mon to the diverse inflections of the twentieth-century Anglo-American critical traditon is a profound, indeed reverential, regard for literary works themselves. This is manifest, first, in an obsessive concern with 'the text itself, nothing more nor less; second, in the deployment of literary texts as icons of human value against twentieth-century cultural barbarism; and third, in a 'scientific', 'objective', 'disinterested' (Arnold's word) critical close-reading of 'the words on the page'.

All together, these tendencies represent the ultimate humanist aestheticisation of 'Literature', and, as the components of a naturalised critical orthodoxy, they were to dominate literary culture throughout the middle decades of the century. Such an orthodoxy came to require—and received from the late 1960s onwards—urgent demystification and dismantling, if literature and criticism were to be re-enfranchised for the contemporary world.

The principal mediator of Matthew Arnold's thinking into the new critical movements, and himself the most influential common figure behind them, was the American (and then natu-ralised English) poet, dramatist and critic, T.S.Eliot. In his early essay, 'Tradition and the Individual Talent' (1919)— perhaps the single most formative work in twentieth-century Anglo-American criticism—Eliot emphasises that writers must have 'the historical sense': a sense, that is, of the *tradition* of literature in which they must situate themselves, and which will help them to achieve the essential quality of 'impersonal-ity' in their art (Eliot, T.S. [1919] 1969a: 16-17).

Eliot's notion of 'the Tradition, while being highly selective, idiosyncratic, and arguably designed to sustain and legitimate his own kind of 'difficult', 'witty' modern poetry, nevertheless harks back to Arnold's dictum of 'the best that has been thought and said in the world'. It is central in constructing the received mid-twentieth-century conception of 'Literature': a canon of great works which most successfully hold an essence of human experience in their poetic 'medium'. For the true poet (and we may note Eliot's privileging of poetry as the supreme genre, since this was to become the primary focus of much 'Practical' and 'New' criticism) is a kind of 'impersonal' vehicle, not of personal experience, but for the residual essence which constitutes the 'medium': the poem itself.

This last should then be the reader/critic's sole object of interest. In a famous phrase from another essay ('Hamlet'), Eliot describes the work of art as an 'objective correlative' (an idea closely related to the notion of 'the image' in Modernist poetics) for the 'real' experience which may have engendered it, and from which the poem, as 'impersonal' recreation, now stands autonomous (Eliot, T.S. [1919] 1969b: 145). The emphasis in Eliot's theory on the autonomous art-object is fundamental both to what we have seen to be the fetishisation of 'the text itself in Modernist criticism's conception of 'Literature' (see p. 49), and to the new/ practical criticism's 'scientific' and 'objective' focus on a 'close reading' of 'the words on the page'.

But Eliot's most potent contribution is his implicitly Arnoldian promotion of 'Literature' and 'the Tradition' (Arnold's 'Culture') as a spiritual-aesthetic 'stay' against the destructive mass civilisation of the post-war 'wasteland'.

In his cultural despair, he sees 'Literature'—itself vulnerable and threatened—as enshrining humane values in a world inimical to them. In this respect, the ending of his own poem *The Waste Land* may be regarded as articulating both a post-First-World-War confirmation of Arnold's worst cultural premoni-tions and the ideological core of Modernist criticism.

When Eliot writes: 'These fragments I have shored against my ruins', and lists brief quotations from the literary works of earlier dynamically creative cultures (Eliot, T.S. [1922] 1958:77), we can read 'Culture'/'Literature' for 'fragments', and 'Anarchy' for 'ruins'.

In the same period that Eliot was developing these ideas, 'English', as we have noticed, was being established as the cen-tral subject in the education curriculum, and was seeking, in the Cambridge tripos most particularly, to shed the older *belleslettrist* character which had dominated it hitherto. Under Eliot's influence, a new generation of professional critics emerged who had a thoroughly symbiotic relationship with contemporary Modernism, finding their own premises borne out both in its theory and in its literary practice. Key figures in generating the new kinds of 'practical-critical' analysis in the 1920s and 1930s were the Cambridge academics, I.A.Richards, William Empson and F.R.Leavis.

Richards produced his widely-influential and innovative books, *The Principles of Literary Criticism* (1924) and *Science and Poetry* (1926), in which he attempted to lay down an explicit theoretical base for literary study. Arguing that criti-cism should emulate the precision of science in its pursuit of a newly professional methodological identity, he sought to articulate the special character of literary language, differentiating the 'emotive' language of poetry from the 'referential' language of non-literary discourse. But for all his science and psychol-ogy, Richards retains a fundamentally aestheticist—indeed recognisably Arnoldian—conception of the role of poetry in the fraught 'anarchy of the post-war environment.

Since religion can no longer supply the spiritual dimension which people need in their lives, and science is emotionally neutral, it is poetry, Richards says, which 'is capable of saving us' (Richards 1926:82-3), poetry which offers order in its own harmonious 'reconciliation' of the disorganised impulses of lived experience. Even more influential—certainly in terms of the praxis its title enunciates—was *Practical Criticism* (1929), in which Richards provided examples of his students' woefully inadequate attempts at the critical analysis of short unidenti-fied poems, and sought, therefore, to establish basic tenets for the 'close reading' of poetry.

'Practical Criticism', which was itself a feature of the new Cambridge tripos, became, in both England and America, the central compulsory critical and ped-agogic tool of tertiary (and then secondary) 'English', and was rapidly naturalised there as *the* fundamental and objectively 'scientific' critical practice. Its virtues were that it encouraged attentive close reading of texts and, in its intellectual and his-torical abstraction, a kind of democratisation of literary study in the classroom, in which everyone was placed on an equal footing in the face of an 'unseen' text. This point will be re-emphasised in the context of American New Criticism later on pp. 56-7.

But 'Practical Criticism's effect was also to fetishise and reify the literary text ('poem') as a valued/valuable aesthetic object in itself, and to dehistoricise and abstract the study of litera-ture by focussing obsessively on 'the text itself in isolation from its informing contexts. It would be inaccurate to charac-terise William Empson, Richards's pupil, as being simply a 'Practical' or 'New' critic, but in our context here, his first, famously precocious book (written while still a student), *Seven Types of Ambiguity* (1930), may be seen as an exemplification of the principles of 'Practical Criticism' in action.

Its virtuoso feats of creative close-reading, its emphasis on 'ambiguity' as the defining characteristic of poetic language, and its detaching of literary texts from their social, historical and intellectual contexts in the process of mining their ambiguities, were all deeply influential in establishing both 'Practical' and 'New' criticism in this country and abroad throughout the 1930s, 1940s and 1950s.

Of all the new Cambridge critics, however, it is F.R.Leavis who most potently determines the notion of 'Literature' for the middle decades of this century. Even as late as 1983, Terry Eagleton was writing:

> *Whatever the 'failure' or 'success' of* Scrutiny *[the immensely influential journal launched by Leavis in 1932 and edited by him until 1953]...the fact remains that English students in England today are 'Leavisites' whether they know it or not, irremediably altered by that historic intervention. (Eagleton [1983] 1996:27)*

Profoundly influenced by Arnold and T.S.Eliot, Leavis's whole project was to establish 'English' (for which understand 'Litera-ture') at the very centre of the education syllabus.

His *Educa-tion and the University* (1943) was in part made up of such earlier essays as the widely-influential 'A Sketch for an "English School"' and the significantly-titled 'Mass Civilisa-tion and Minority Culture', and it bears witness to the fact that Leavis was as much an educator as he was a critic.

In addition to producing many volumes of literary and cultural criticism, he edited *Scrutiny*, which was widely read by thousands of members of the 'English' profession inside and outside the universities throughout its 20-year existence. He taught genera-tions of students, who themselves became 'Leavisites' out in the field of secondary and tertiary education and who still command a fair degree of influence even today; and he was the informing presence behind hundreds of critical works pro-duced by others—not least, for example, the hugely successful, markedly 'Leavisite' but ostensibly neutral, *The Pelican Guide to English Literature,* edited by Boris Ford in seven volumes (1954-61).

In many respects, Leavis has much in common with 'Practi-cal Criticism', not least in his equal concern with the formal specificity of 'the text itself, with 'the words on the page'. In 'Henry James and the Function of Criticism', in his book *The Common Pursuit,* where the references to Arnold and T.S. Eliot in the two titles are pointedly emphatic, he wrote: '[the critic] is concerned with the work in front of him as something that should contain within itself the reason why it is so and not otherwise' (Leavis: [1952] 1978:224).

And in a famous exchange with the American critic, Rene Wellek, he both con-firms this and reveals the strategically untheorised, 'practical' nature of his work: the business of the critic, he says, is to 'attain a peculiar completeness of response...[in order] to enter into possession of the given poem...in its concrete fulness' ('Literary Criticism and Philosophy, *ibid.:* 213).

Indeed, Leavis is the most resolutely anti-theoretical of all influential critics, and it is Arnold once more whom we hear behind the refusal of 'abstract' theorising and the direct response to 'concrete' examples of poetic art.

But simply to regard Leavis as an ahistorical and formalistic 'Practical Critic' would be a mistake, for his close attention to the text is only ever to establish the vitality of its 'felt life', its authenticity of 'experience', to prove its moral force, to demon-strate its excellence, and hence to be able to 'discriminate' its value in relation to lesser works.

The full quotation about 'the critic's task' from Eliot's essay, 'The Function of Criticism', which gave Leavis his title for *The Common Pursuit* is: 'the common pursuit of true judgement' (Eliot, T.S. [1923] 1969:25); and 'judgement' and 'discrimination', by way of close *'scrutiny'*, are at the very heart of the Leavisian project. Hence, the other indicatively-titled books: *Revaluation,* which comprises a T.S.Eliot-like extrapolation of the 'true' tradition of English poetry, and *The Great Tradition,* which opens with the characteristically tendentious 'judgement': 'The great English novelists are Jane Austen, George Eliot, Henry James and Joseph Conrad' (Leavis [1948] 1962:9).

Central to Leavis's work, then, is the need to identify the 'true' great works of 'Literature', to sift them out from the dross (espe-cially, for example, 'popular fiction' produced for the mass market), and to further establish the Arnoldian and Eliotian 'Tradition'. Such works, in their concrete experiential speci-ficity, will embody 'Life', that crucial, but always undefined, Leavisian term: in *The Great Tradition,* for example, he writes that 'the great English novelists...are all distinguished by a vital capacity for experience, a kind of reverent openness before life, and a marked moral intensity' *(ibid.:* 17).

As Terry Eagleton says of the invincible circularity of Leavis's position: 'either you felt Life or you did not. Great literature was a litera-ture reverently open to Life, and what Life was could be demonstrated by great literature' (Eagleton: [1983] 1996:36).

'True' literary works will mobilise their dynamic life-values against the forces of urban-industrial materialism and cultural barbarism produced by a 'Technologico-Benthamite' age (Leavis 1969: the phrase is part of his title for Chapter 4 there).

In effect, they represent a 'minority culture` embattled with a 'mass civilisation', and their identification and protec-tion as the (Great) Tradition is essential because these are the works which constitute the syllabus in a university 'English' course, where the crucial work of refining and revitalising the nation's cultural life goes on. And for Leavis, the focus is very much 'The National Literature', which enshrines the qualities of an essential 'Englishness'.

Just as Leavis's *moral* mission distinguishes him from an abstract and aesthetic critical formalism, so too does his socio-logical and historical sense. 'Literature', for him, is a weapon in the cultural politics of battling with the modern world; and the 'great' literature of the past (his chosen period is the seven-teenth century—i.e. before Eliot's 'dissociation of sensibility' [Eliot [1921] 1969:288] had taken place) bears witness to the organic strength and stability of pre-industrial cultures. In this, as for

Arnold, Eliot, and indeed the Newbolt Report as we have seen earlier, the past and past literature act as a yardstick for measuring the sterility of the present 'wasteland'. However, the work of 'great' moderns such as Eliot and D.H.Lawrence, for example, in its 'necessary' difficulty, complexity and com-mitment to cultural values, is also mobilised by Leavis on behalf of 'Life' in the barren destructiveness of a twentieth-century 'mass civilisation'.

It is not without point that in *New Bearings in English Poetry* (1932) Leavis effectively first taught people how to 'read' *The Waste Land* as a modern 'master-work', nor that the title of his later book, *D.H.Lawrence: Novelist* (1955), presents the author as the essence and acme of his genre. It is 'Literature', then—and especially 'English Literature'—in which humane values sur-vive, and it is 'Literature' which holds at bay the worst evils of contemporary life.

So attuned to the mindset of its period was this paradoxical mixture of radical affirmation and elitist pes-simism that it constituted the ideological heart of culturalist thinking throughout the middle of the century. It became effectively synonymous with 'Literary Studies' in England, and placed the Leavisian conception of 'Literature' centre-stage in the wider national and social arena.

In America, in the same period, the analagous movement in criticism and education was the 'New Criticism' which emerged during the late-1920s and 1930s, and which was espe-cially dominant in the 1940s and 1950s. Its origins were in the work of members of a group of traditionalist academics from the American South hostile to what they saw as the hard-nosed industrialism and materialism of a United States dominated by the North.

In this, a consanguinity with the conservative humanism of Arnold, Eliot and Leavis is to be descried. Its high point of influence during the Second World War, and the 'Cold War' succeeding it, may be explained by the way New Criticism seemed to offer a quietistic haven for whole genera-tions of academics and students overwrought by war and political strife.

Its privileging of literary texts whose 'order' and 'harmony' cause them to transcend history and ideology, and its own 'impersonal' analysis of what makes them great works of art, were well-suited to the *mentalite* of what E.P.Thompson called 'Natopolis' (Thompson 1960:144). In addition, with the huge expansion of the student population in the States in this period catering for second-generation prod-ucts of the American 'melting pot', New Criticism, with its 'practical' basis, was at once pedagogically orientated and eco-nomical (copies of short 'unseen' texts—primarily poems— could be distributed to everyone on an equal basis).

It was also a way of accommodating the disparate cultural needs of masses of individuals who had no history in common. In other words, the ahistorical, 'objective' nature of this critical practice, the study only of 'the words on the page', was an appar-ently equalising, democratic activity appropriate to twentieth-century American experience.

The movement acquired its name from the the title of John Crowe Ransoms book on, *inter alia,* Eliot and Richards, *The New Criticism* (1941); and his earlier essay, 'Criticism, Inc.' ([1937] 1972), laid down some of the ground-rules for it.

Criticism should be the 'business' of professionals (i.e. university professors); it should become 'more scientific...precise and systematic'; students should 'study literature, and not merely about literature'; criticism was not ethical, linguistic or historical studies, but should be able to exhibit, not the 'prose core' to which a poem may be reduced, but 'the differentia, residue, or tissue, which keeps the object poetical or entire' (Ransom [1937] 1972:229, 230, 232, 238).

Cleanth Brooks and Robert Penn Warren's textbooks *Understanding Poetry* (1938) and *Understanding Fiction* (1943) are widely regarded as having spread New Critical doctrine throughout generations of American literature students, and books of essays like W.K. Wimsatt's symptomatically-titled, *The Verbal Icon: Studies in the Meaning of Poetry* ([1954] 1970) and Cleanth Brooks's own volume of close readings, *The Well-Wrought Urn: Studies in the Structure of Poetry* ([1947] 1968), gave practical application to Ransom's precepts.

In his essay, 'Keats's Sylvan Historian: History Without Footnotes', for example, Brooks explicitly rejects the relevance of biography.

He focusses throughout on the 'Ode on a Grecian Urn's' exemplification of 'irony', 'paradox', 'dramatic propriety' and 'wholeness', and he admires the poem's own 'history' for its resolution of the 'clash between the ideas of war and peace...[in a] sense of sta-ble repose' (Brooks [1947] 1968:132).

He praises its 'insight into essential truth' (134)—in contradistinction, it is implied throughout, to our 'meaningless' 'accumulations of facts' and the 'scientific and philosophical generalisations which domi-nate our world' (134, 135): 'like eternity, its history is beyond time, outside time' (133)—and, in this, he locates its value for the present (1942—at the height of wartime 'history'). For Brooks, the 'Ode's' essential value seems to lie in the 'ironic fact' (his phrase) that, like Keats's urn itself, which is 'All breathing human passion far above', the poem 'stress[es] that all human passion *does* leave one cloyed; hence *the superiority of art*' (130; second emphasis mine). The New Critical 'aes-theticisation' of the art object is epitomised here.

Equally characteristic of this tendency are W.K.Wimsatt and Monroe C.Beardsley's two influential essays, 'The Intentional Fallacy' and 'The Affective Fallacy'. These set the 'classical objectivity' of New Criticism in opposition to both the bio-graphical-critical pursuit of the author's 'intention' in writing a poem, since the latter 'goes about the world beyond his power to intend about or control it' (Wimsatt and Beardsley [1946] 1972:335), and 'romantic reader psychology', which sets up a confusion between the poem and its 'psychological effects' where 'the poem, as an object of specifically critical judge-ment, tends to disappear' (Wimsatt and Beardsley [1949] 1972:354, 345).

For the New Critic, they contend, the impor-tance of the poem itself is that, by 'fixing emotions and mak-ing them more permanently perceptible', by the 'survival' of 'its clear and nicely interrelated meanings, its completeness, balance, and tension', it represents a transhistorically valuable artefact which offers a life-line to the denizens of twentieth-century chaos: 'In short, though cultures have changed, poems remain and explain' ([1949] 1972:356, 357).

Whatever the socio-cultural explanations for its provenance, and despite its differing inflections, New Criticism was clearly characterised in basic premise and practice. It celebrated the uniqueness of the literary art object in and for itself; it was not concerned with 'context', be it historical, biographical or philo-sophical; it privileged poetry but did not seek out a poem's meaning, being concerned rather with how it 'speaks itself (Archibald MacLeish's poem 'Ars Poetica', itself a synoptic New Critical manifesto, ends: 'A poem should not mean/But be'.)

Nor was New Criticism interested in the 'fallacies' of 'intention' or 'affect'. It was concerned solely with the poem as 'text': with its language and organisation—how the parts relate, how it achieves its 'order' and 'harmony', how it con-tains and resolves 'irony', 'paradox', 'tension', 'ambivalence' and 'ambiguity'—and with articulating the very 'poem-ness', the formal quintessence, of the poem itself.

But New Critical formalism was overdetermined ultimately by the *value* it ascribed to the poetic artefact: its very superiority to the chaos and strife of 'life', history, politics; its aesthetic resolution of contradiction and tension; its supreme achievement, precisely, of *not being* 'life'.

By the middle of the twentieth century, in the Anglo-American tradition, the concept 'Literature' was centrally established in the terms outlined above: a select(ive) and valuable aesthetic and moral resource to replenish those living in the spiritual desert of a mass civilisation.

My account will seem to have been focussed on the institutionalisation of 'Literature' in the academy, but after all, as Roland Barthes so neatly defined it: 'Literature is what gets taught'. Even so, the ideological force of its cultural assumptions and meanings permeates well beyond the realm of professional criticism.

To take just one example: however much 'non-academic' readers may find their material in the wide realms of the much-despised 'popular literature', it is precisely the marker 'Literature' which demands that qualification 'popular', and most people would recognise it as such without any first-hand knowledge of its contents. Boris Ford's 'General Introduction' to a volume in the first edi-tion of *The Pelican Guide to English Literature* is illuminating in this respect:

> *...it is well to remember that this is the age of the Digest and the Headline, of the Comic and the Tabloid, of the Bestseller and the Month's*

> *Masterpiece: an age when a 'deep-seated spiritual vulgarity...lies at the heart of our civilization'.... Perhaps in response to this, the twentieth century has also been a period of unusually lively criticism, a time when a small number of writers and critics have made a determined effort to elicit from literature what is of living value to us today; to reestablish...a sense of literary tradition and to define the high standards that this tradition implies. At the same time it is also important that this feel-ing for a* living *literature and for the values it embodies should be given as wide a currency as possible, and that literature—both today's literature and yesterday's—should have a real and not merely a nominal existence among a comparatively large number of general readers. (Ford 1954-61, vol. 6 [1958] 1963:7)*

I would suggest that this (now evidently) 'Leavisite' manifesto, with its scorn for mass culture, its unproblematical assumption as to what literature is, its emphasis on a minority clerisy's feel-ing for *'living'* value(s), and its messianic zeal to make this (high) culture 'prevail', would have been accepted as natural and unarguable amongst the vast majority of 'general readers' in the 1950s. It would have been, too, in the early 1960s when I went to Nottingham University to take an 'English' degree exported from Cambridge, whose 'Literature, Life and Thought' syllabus unsurprisingly had at its heart our old friend 'Practical Criticism'. Readers may have been differentiated as 'high-', 'middle-' and 'low-brow', and many different kinds and schools of criticism there certainly were, but no one at that point seriously challenged the notion of 'Literature' itself as represented in the later parts of the present chapter.

I might even propose that, despite the revolutionary assault on 'Literature' in theory and practice from the late-1960s onwards, the concept has retained its discriminatory force throughout the last three decades.

It is not without point that *The New Pelican Guide to English Literature,* first published in 1983, contained a 'General Introduction' which opened almost identically to the one cited above (including the same quotation from L.H.Myers about the 'spiritual vulgarity...[of] our civilization); nor that in 1980, the publisher Routledge & Kegan Paul, whose list already included examples of radical critical theory, also published a book entitled *The Anatomy of Literary Studies* by Marjorie Boulton which does credit to Arnold and the Newbolt Report.

There, Boulton presents liter-ature as having 'civilizing powers' which will 'broaden our sympathies, widen our tolerance' (Boulton 1980:12), while conceding, with pained incredulity, that despite taking a First in English at London University—and 'knowing some of the things he must have known to achieve this'—'Lord Haw Haw' (William Joyce) somehow still became a Nazi traitor (7)). Even in 1997, a *Guardian* reviewer could castigate a new novel by Ian McEwan in such untroubled cliches from the naturalised culture of 'Literature' as: 'McEwan is a good and not a great writer' whose 'novels are efficient fictional engines, but not true novels'; 'the book has a thinness of literary texture' which helps to 'demote its status as a literary artefact'; and so it fails to become 'a true literary achievement' (Wood 1997:9-10).

> *It is the case, too, that 'English Literature' still remains a key subject in secondary and higher education throughout large chunks of the world. The editors of* The Post-Colonial Studies Reader, *for example, note* in 1995 *that, despite challenges to the cultural dominance of 'English' in (ex-)colonial tertiary education institutions during the 1970s, since then little has really changed. Few 'English Departments' of Commonwealth and former Commonwealth countries have abolished the title, and most (including universities in the United States) still retain English literature as the core cur-riculum. And in spite of fundamental changes in literary theory most still remain Anglo-oriented if not Anglo-dominated. (Ashcroft* etal. *[eds] 1995:426)*

Equally indicative is the fact that many major publishers have popular series of literary 'Classics' (some now staggeringly cheap), together with extensive catalogues of criticism en titled 'Literature'; and that bookshops and libraries sectionalise their wares in a markedly hierarchical fashion ('Classics', 'Poetry', 'Romance', 'Popular Fiction', etc.). Further, if I ask 'non-academic' friends what they understand by the term 'Literature', they will name as many 'canonic' writers as they can remember, and define it in a recognisable version of the dominant sense we have encountered above, while often simultaneously—and unnecessarily shamefacedly—admitting that they themselves 'can't get on with' George Eliot or Jane Austen, despite having enjoyed the TV serialisations. Apropos, and in a paradoxical way, the persistent appearance of 'Classic' serials and film versions of canonic works also confirms the continuing widespread popular penetration of 'Literature'.

Nevertheless, something *did* happen from the late-1960s onwards. So that where, in 1961, F.R.Leavis could be found defending the 'life-values' of *Lady Chatterley's Lover* in the famous Penguin Books obscenity trial at the Old Bailey, by 1968 Kate Millett was making ferocious fun of that novel's phallocratic sexism (Millett [1969] 1971: chapter 5). So, too, that when I left university and England in 1968 to teach 'English Literature' in northern Sweden, not a cloud had crossed my received notion of 'Literature'; but by 1971, in the 'Humanities' department of a new London polytechnic, its fea-tures had become barely visible—so thoroughly was it at the eye of the prevailing intellectual storm.

3

What has Happened to Literature

A HISTORY OF THE CONCEPT, PART TWO: AFTER THE 1960S

A crude but effective way of signalling an answer to the ques-tion this chapter's title poses is to cite the acronym 'DWEMs'— or 'Dead White European Males' (with a silent 'H', perhaps, between the 'E' and the 'M' standing for 'Heterosexual').

Sometime during the so-called 'Culture Wars' which have been raging in the United States for the past two decades (see pp. 77-80), those five letters became the public announcement that 'Literature' as we have seen it develop in the previous chapter was deeply beleaguered. Whether they spell the end of 'Literature' remains a moot point, but it is incontrovertibly clear that the received orthodox notion of it is now intellectu-ally and culturally derelict.

It was from within feminism that the letters first emerged, and feminism has indeed been at the forefront of the deconstruction of 'Literature' (although, as we shall see, many other socio-cultural, political and theoretical movements and impulses have also contributed to this process). So that while it would be wrong finally to privilege the 'M' in 'DWEMs', it was nevertheless the *male* hegemony inscribed in 'Literature' and 'Literary Studies' which was originally pinpointed for attack. What 'DWEMs' *does* spell is 'Canon', a male construct comprised of male authors (and a very few honorary female ones) handed down by male critics and lecturers—in British higher education at least—to a largely female constituency of students.

What the new feminists of the late-1960s and beyond perceived and challenged was that the Canon of 'Literature', handed down as *'their'* cultural heritage, was made up of works by 'dead' (past, old, 'classic') male writers, who were also almost exclusively European in origin. The Canon, in other words, was unproblematically Eurocentric, despite the existence of other literary cultures predating or contemporary with it.

Furthermore, these male writers were 'white' (an exclusive Canon, therefore, in the context of contemporary multicul-tural societies); were chiefly written, we may add, by hetero-sexual males about heterosexual experience from a male perspective; and when they *were* by homosexual males, it was certainly not for any suggestion of sexual deviancy that they were read, admired and canonised. While there is nothing intrinsically wrong with being dead, white, European or male, the fact that the received Canon was so emphatically imbued with these characteristics revealed that it was neither 'natural' nor 'given, but rather was constructed, ideological and partial.

In the light of this recognition, the immediate project for feminist critics in the 1960s and 1970s was to recover, on behalf of women, female writers and a female literary tradition from their historical occlusion. Similar innovative work was going on simultaneously in other areas, and the title of the his-torian, Sheila Rowbotham's book, *Hidden from History* (1973), together with the brilliant feminist perception that history hitherto has indeed been 'his-story' not 'her-story', is the most concise and telling synopsis of the rationale for this project.

The titles of influential books such as Ellen Moers's *Literary Women* (1976), Elaine Showalter's *A Literature of Their Own* (1977), and Mary Jacobus's *Women Writing and Writing About Women* (1979), are also symptomatic short-hand signs from that period. In the same vein is the coterminous development of 'Gynocriticism' which sought to set up a female framework for the analysis of literature written by women, to focus on women's experience as expressed there, and to establish a female literary and cultural tradition (see Showalter 1977).

A related development was the reconstitution of the Canon to include many more female writers, signifi-cantly facilitated by the collateral initiative of setting up 'Women's Presses'. These published both well- and little-known women writers from the past whose works had long been out of print—'hidden from literature'—and whose evident previous 'minority' could now be called in question by the texts' availability for sympathetic re-reading and re-evaluation.

A new emphasis, too, on *contemporary* women's writing—'serious' and 'popular'—both hugely expanded the range of literature available for study, thereby controverting the historically determined disparity occasioned by women's previously limited access to literacy, and enfranchised hitherto excluded groups such as black and working-class women writers.

In addition, a radical new focus on female sexuality in its different forms at once challenged and problematised male sex-ual predominance, gave a voice to the sexually silenced, such as lesbians, and opened up sexual discourses in past literature to re-reading 'against the grain'. In all these respects, the femi-nist project, whether or not it had the deconstruction of 'Litera-ture' and the Canon primarily and strategically in view, was fundamentally instrumental in achieving precisely that.

But in foregrounding the founding contribution of feminism, we should not lose sight of another centrally important ele-ment encoded in 'DWEMs'. The implications of 'white' have been signalled above in respect of black women writers; and in the context of post-war American society, the dynamic emergence of black, Asian and Latino/a writers in particular, whether male or female, has been highly significant in de/reconstructing literary culture. Race, in other words, has an equally significant place in this process as gender, and it is as well to remember that even white feminist critical theory and practice have been shown to be oblivious to race (and thus tacitly racist) in their otherwise radical opposition to a patriarchal 'Literature'.

In her salutary essay, 'Three Women's Texts and a Critique of Imperialism', Gayatri Spivak shows how Anglo-American feminist critics, in elevating Charlotte Bronte's novel *Jane Eyre* to being 'a cult text of feminism' (Spivak 1985:263), fail to perceive how its meritocratic individualism is deeply inscribed with conventional nineteenth-century discourses of imperialism. Having a 'basically isolationist admiration for the literature of the female subject in Europe and Anglo-America' {*ibid.*, 262)—and so that 'Jane Eyre can become the feminist individualist heroine of British fiction' {*ibid.*, 270)—such Western criticism 'reproduces the axioms of imperialism' by ignoring the fact that Bertha Mason's firing of Thornfield Hall at the end of the novel can be read 'as an allegory of the general epistemic violence of imperialism, the construction of a self-immolating colonial subject for the glorification of the social mission of the colonizer' {*ibid.,* 262., 270). Western feminists may radically re-read 'the great tradition' and reappropriate it for women, but it will still be oppressive if the critical gaze remains partially sighted.

It is only in recognising the exclusions implied by 'European' in the acronym—especially when combined with 'white'—that the other crucial dimension in the assault on 'Literature' as an ideological formation comes fully into view. A Eurocentric conception of 'Literature' excludes the 'New World', the (white and black) 'Commonwealth', the 'Third World', and all the indigenous literatures that any of the cultures in the exclu-sion zone may ever have produced.

If we leave aside the United States—or at least those components of the American literary and critical traditions which may be contained within the broad European sense of 'Literature'—and focus on what were the old 'colonies' of European states, we find that it is in the challenges and subversions of postcolonial literary and critical thinking that the other major deconstructive drive against 'Literature' appears. An obvious instance of this, in the case of ex-British colonies, has been the attempt in the academy to achieve, in Ngugi wa Thiong'o's words, 'The Abolition of the English Department' (at the University of Nairobi in this instance); to 'reject the primacy of English literature and culture'; and to set up 'a Department of African Literature and Languages...in its place'.

So that, 'with Africa at the centre of things, not existing as an appendix or satellite of other coun-tries and literatures, things must be seen from the African perspective' (Thiongo'o [1972], in Ashcroft *et al.,* [eds] 1995:441). Equally, in white 'settler colonies' such as Canada and Australia, there has been a fierce rejection of the neocolo-nialism, or continuing cultural imperialism, implicit in the centrality of 'English Literature' in the university curriculum, where their own literatures are still only available as 'options'. Such 'cultural cringe', which represents a tacit admission of the superiority of the metropolitan centre, is rooted out by post-colonialist reversals of what Franz Fanon called the 'hierarchy of cultures' (quoted in Docker [1978], in Ashcroft *et al.,* [eds] 1995:443).

More broadly, the postcolonial project has been to challenge both the 'Western Canon' and 'colonialist' literature in seeking to recover from oblivion a 'literature of their own': to 'write' a history/articulate the experience of the unvoiced colonised, and to explore in positive terms the subsequent 'hybridity' of post-colonial subjects. Once again, the title of a pioneering critical book in this area highlights the projects trajectory: *The Empire Writes Back* (Ashcroft *et al*, [eds] 1989), with its telling allu-sion to the 'popular' 'Star Wars' movie, *The Empire Fights Back*.

Central to this notion of 'writing back', here, has been the way postcolonial writers and critics have 're-written' and 'reread' canonic texts both to expose their complicity in racial domination and to denaturalise their assumed 'value' as recep-tacles of universal wisdom in *'our'* cultural heritage: that is, one so designated on behalf of the colonised, too.

J.M.Coetzee's 'revision' of Daniel Defoe's *Robinson Crusoe* in his novel, *Foe* ([1986] 1987) (see Chapter 5, pp. 168-72), is an excellent example of this, as is Chinua Achebe's devastating critical essay on Joseph Conrad's *Heart of Darkness,* in which he proposes that Conrad was 'a thoroughgoing racist', who, by using Africa in his story only 'as setting and backdrop... eliminates the African as human factor...thus reducing Africa to the role of props for the break-up of one petty European mind' (Achebe [1988], in Brooker and Widdowson, [eds] 1996:267). The 'real question' this raises for Achebe is: 'whether a novel which celebrates this dehumanization, which depersonalizes a portion of the human race, can be called a great work of art' *(ibid.).* His own strategically controversial negative answer is difficult to counter from within a Western aesthetic conception of the canon of 'Literature'.

Significantly, some of the most destabilising recent postcolo-nial writing, literary and critical, has come from women writ-ers who have had to negotiate both the racial and the gender components of a DWEM 'Literature'; and here again we may note that the resulting necessary focus on *contemporary* writ-ing has radically loosened the hold of the Canon on how we think about literature.

For instance, the question of 'literary value' in relation to new works, unencumbered by the weight of historical ascription of 'classic' status, immediately brings into view the contingent, subjective and often arbitrary nature of evaluation, and thereby problematises the notion of innate 'literary value'.

We can observe, as they occur, the material market forces and cultural predilections of publishers, review-ers and critics which are visibly at work ascribing to a text those literary features and qualities which will then be 'found in' it to value or deprecate. In the light of this, the making of value-judgements, should now properly be seen to be only provisional, strategic and function-specific.

As crucial agents in the process, then, feminism and post-colonialism simultaneously deconstruct 'Literature' and the 'Western Canon' by exposing their partial and ideological nature; allow for a creative re-reading of past 'classic' works; and bring into view other literatures (especially, but not exclusively, contemporary ones) which articulate hitherto occluded areas of experience from those which are constrained within the conventional conspectus of 'Literature'. Thus we can see in these new literatures precisely that the 'making' of 'new realities' by way of their specific literary formulation which I will go on to claim (especially in Chapters 4 and 5) is the reason for not throwing out the literary baby with the bathwater of 'Literature'.

But feminism and postcolonialism were not the only factors to bring about the demise of the received notion of 'Literature'. By the libertarian, if politically unfocussed, mid-1960s, a more general disenchantment and rebelliousness were beginning to set in. Even in Cambridge, which for 30 years had been the source in higher education at least of 'English's' mission on behalf of 'Literature', the citadel was under threat. Having gone to that university in 1966 solely in order to be taught by the 'Marxist' Raymond Williams, David Hare describes his 'aversion to the drawing up of lists' of 'moral' writers who were given 'dignified approval' and of those who were not. The conventional teaching of 'English' seemed to be entirely comprised of such:

> *I had no desire to train to be a non-commissioned officer in the arts police, patrolling literature for capital offences such as 'failure of seriousness'.... The attitude of [the dons] implied such a contempt for the ordinary feelings of people that the inevitable result of all this list-making would surely be more to remove me from life than to plunge me into it.* (Hare 1989:2)

This kind of response was as yet a largely personal rebellion, but it found focus in the politicising process engendered by the 'events' of May 1968 throughout Europe and the United States, in which the whole traditional curriculum and the authoritarian relationship between lecturer and student were called in question. Changes to the 'English' or 'Literature' syl-labus were everywhere demanded in the midst of all this tur-moil, but it was in the newer institutions in Britain—the 'New Universities', the Open University, and, even more radically, in the recently created Polytechnics—that the changes were most rapid and apparent. Tnterdisciplinarity' was the buzz-word here, signalling that the old subject boundaries should be bro-ken down to create new combinations of studies, most charac-teristically called 'Humanities'.

In degree courses with this name, 'English' might well be a large participant, but it would be there not in its own right (as the Leavisian 'core') but in equal relation to other subjects, most usually history, sociol-ogy, politics and philosophy. In this context, the assumed and naturalised status of the canonical text was subjected to the ferocious glare of other subjects' interrogations. Historians would ask: why is *King Lear* essential reading for a study of early-seventeenth-century England; why is it more important than a contemporary sermon; what makes it a 'major' work compared to some other anonymous 'minor' play; who says so, when, and on what grounds?—just as the sociologists would wonder why the 'popular literature' of a period, that which ordinary people actually read, was of less significance than the canonic texts.

A Leavisian response, or one based on an aestheticist formalism, cut no ice; and as soon as such ques-tions demanded answers which went beyond the received literary-critical thinking, the inner process of dismantling 'Lit-erature' began. How *do we* know that George Eliot's *Adam Bede* (1859) is more important than Mrs Oliphant's contempo-raneous novel, *Salem Chapel* (1863); what are the intrinsic features that make it so; how do we identify them, and by what criteria; by what processes has this hierarchical evalua-tion come about; might it not be reversed in a specific context (e.g. *Salem Chapel* gives us a better insight into mid-nineteenth-century English religious life than does *Adam Bede)}* A self-parodying question from that period still indicates the force and logic of this mode of enquiry about cultural texts: 'Why *is Middlemarch* more important than a beer-mat?'

Of course, 'English Literature' had long been a misnomer for what was strictly 'Literary Studies'. Are Dunbar and Henryson, Balzac and Tolstoy (even in translation), Robert Burns, Dylan Thomas and Brendan Behan, James Joyce, Ezra Pound and William Faulkner, for example, usefully described by 'English'? But what became strikingly apparent in the 1970s and beyond—as Wole Soyinka, Margaret Atwood, the Chartist poets, Robert Tressell, Jackie Collins, Linton Kwesi Johnson, *Coronation Street,* Jacques Derrida and Julia Kristeva joined the syllabus—was that 'English' (or even 'Literature') now even less accurately described what went on in its name. In 1987, the cultural critic, Peter Brooker, was writing:

> *even while 'English' is employed as the public description of many University and Polytechnic departments, it stands above their doors, with all its ideological freight, as the false title to courses in literary and cultural theory, literature and society, American and European literature, popu-lar literature and women's writing.... We would do better to describe such courses as discourse analysis, or text analy-sis, or again, cultural studies. (Brooker 1987:27)*

The expansion of the syllabus included courses on hitherto despised sub-genres such as 'Gothic Literature', 'Romance', 'Fantasy', 'Working-class Writing', 'Women's Writing', 'Black Writing' and 'Popular Fiction'; on semiotics, linguistics, stylistics, film, comparative literature, rhetoric and creative writing. In place of the traditional 'Author' and 'Genre' courses also came 'Period Studies', in which the content was a vertical section of the written cultural production of a short period in the past (e.g. the 1790s, 1840s, 1900-14) undifferentiated by later canonic hierarchies. Pointedly, however, such courses often foundered on the absence in print of the disregarded 'minor works': with commercial publishing reinforcing canonic 'Litera-ture', the latter indeed remains, in Barthes's phrase, 'what gets taught'.

A growing focus on 'contemporary writing' also began to force the older periods and 'classic authors' off the syllabus. So that where in the early-1970s even the Council for National Academic Awards' (CNAA's) sole compulsory requirement for the 'English' courses it validated in the new polytechnics was that they should include the study of Shakespeare, as had been prescribed by the Newbolt Report (see p.

ƒ), by CNAA's demise in the early-1990s, it was perfectly possible to 'do English' without reading a line of his works. Above all, and I shall return to this later, 'Literary' or 'Critical Theory' courses were *de rigueur* in almost every degree pro-gramme in the UK, the main exception being Oxford s. It is worth noticing, too, that in the title of many of the kinds of courses identified above—which are now staple diet in English-degree provision—the word 'writing' has replaced 'literature'.

This, of course, was both to signal a distance from 'Literature' and to allow for the study of written discourse which falls out-side the conventional notion of 'the literary': autobiographies, memoirs, essays, songs, journalism, etc.—all in an egalitarian symbiosis with 'literary' writings.

Apropos—and to move the focus outside the academy—in 1970s Britain, there was a further democratisation of literature underway in the fostering of working-class writing and com-munity publishing by, *inter alia,* such groups as Centreprise Publishing Project (London), Commonword Writers' Work-shop (Manchester), East Bowling History Workshop (Bradford), Hackney Writers Workshop (London), QueenSpark Books (Brighton), Scotland Road Writers' Work-shop (Liverpool), Tollcross Writers' Workshop (Edinburgh) and Women and Words (Birmingham).

In 1976, these and oth-ers formed a loose amalgamation to become the Federation of Worker Writers and Community Publishers (FWWCP). The title of the collectively-compiled volume, *The Republic of Let-ters,* which describes its history and aims, pointedly combines 'letters'—from which the word 'literature', meaning 'the whole body of books and writing' (Williams 1976:151-2), originally developed—with the notion of an egalitarian and popular state. The rationale behind the FWWCP's foundation was to '"disestablish" literature, making writing a popular form of expression for all people rather than the preserve of a metropolitan or privileged elite' (Morley and Worpole [eds] 1982:1). It was particularly aimed at those hitherto most com-prehensively disenfranchised by all that 'Literature' repre-sented: the working class, women, racial minorities. In order to give them the possibility of finding a voice, it was necessary to create sympathetic communities outside the academy in which people could practice writing and exchange comment on the results, and to publish and distribute work indepen-dently, co-operatively and cheaply beyond the control of the mainstream commercial industry. This, as the authors say, put them 'on a collision course with literature as it is conceived and established' *(ibid.,* 43); since if the kind of literary production they were engaged in were to become the norm, it would put conventional publishing—'competitive, elitist, profit-controlled, labour-dividing, separating producer from consumer' *(ibid.)*—out of business.

It was against the *institutions* which determine what is 'literary' and what is not—with, as Ken Worpole has elsewhere put it, their 'narrowness of vision' and 'cultural paranoia' when it comes to defining 'English Literature' (Worpole 1984:4-5)—that the FWWCP launched its challenge, rather than against literature itself. But the new independent publishing initiatives also 'established new forms of writing, discovered new writers and new networks of read-ers' (5) which have contributed significantly to the general 'disestablishing' of 'Literature' and the consequent widening and invigorating of contemporary literary culture.

In the context of British higher education, a further factor in the dissolution of 'English'/'Literature' needs to be noted (one cognate with the extra-academic cultural politics of the com-munity writing and publishing groups glanced at above). The essay by Peter Brooker quoted on pp. 71-2 is sub-titled 'Is There English After Cultural Studies?', and it was with the development of 'Cultural Studies' out of and alongside 'English' and 'Literary Studies' that the emphatic notification was made that the focus of interest was shifting from 'Litera-ture' to all forms of cultural production and representation, and most centrally to 'popular culture'.

Its origins, signifi-cantly, lay in adult education: the widely influential Centre for Contemporary Cultural Studies (CCCS) at Birmingham University was founded in 1964 by Richard Hoggart, author of *The Uses of Literacy* (1957), and later developed by Raymond Williams, Stuart Hall and others. In its earlier phases, mass-circulation newspapers, the BBC, television, film, advertising, working-class 'culture' (in the greatly expanded sense of 'lived experience' or, in Williams's founding phrase, 'a whole way of life': [1958] 1961:18), sub-cultures (youth, sport), style (Mods and Rockers, punks, working-class teenage girls), literacy and mass education, became the objects of attention—all those dis-courses, in other words, that 'Literature' had more or less explicitly defined itself against, and in all of which the notion of 'the text' had to be fundamentally rethought.

More impor-tantly perhaps, Cultural Studies—intellectually 'impure', fiercely political, and an irritant on the margins of the academy —was never quite a new 'discipline', but rather, in Brooker's phrase, 'a radicalising mentality' (Brooker 1987:27), or what Richard Johnson, a former CCCS director, has called a mode of 'critique'; that is:

> *procedures by which other traditions are approached both for what they may yield and for what they inhibit. Critique involves stealing away the more useful elements and reject-ing the rest. ... From this point of view cultural studies is a process, a kind of alchemy for producing useful knowledge. (Johnson 1983, quoted in Brooker:* ibid.)

Cultural Studies, in other words, has been less a discrete 'sub-ject' and more a politicised way of thinking beyond the limita-tions of whatever field of enquiry it enters or recuperates.

Ironically in light of this, for a while in the 1970s and 1980s, it seemed that Cultural Studies might take the place of 'English' in British higher education institutions (the situation is somewhat different in the United States; see pp. 79-80), and that literature would be subsumed, as one element among many, within a broader conspectus of 'cultural history'. That this has not happened in the UK—that Cultural Studies as a named academic area in the mid-1990s seems to be on the wane, despite Antony Easthope's *Literary into Cultural Studies* (1991) with its proposals for a 'New Paradigm', while 'English' appears to thrive—can only be explained by reference to political, ideological, institutional and academic factors well beyond my scope here. But two points are worth making in the present context.

The first is that many of the constituent ele-ments and theoretical/ methodological praxes of Cultural Stud-ies (Johnson's 'procedures of critique') have implanted them-selves in other academic fields, such as Women's Studies, Third World Studies, Film, Media and Communication Studies. But they have also embedded themselves within 'English', which discipline, whilst retaining its 'false title' (see Brooker on p. 71), has been transformed in terms of content and intel-lectual orientation in the ways I have suggested earlier: 'canonic' texts resituated in their 'period'; different categories of 'writing' introduced alongside them without a hierarchy of 'value'; 'theory' and 'contemporary literatures' foregrounded.

Perhaps the most radical and pervasive dimension of all this, however, is in the following two ways:

(i) that the *subject itself* (as well as its content) has been *historicised,* where the histo-ries of 'Literature' and of 'English'/'Literary Studies' themselves are—or should be—primary components of all such degree courses; and

(ii) that it has been explicitly *politicised.* Any notions of 'disinterestedness', 'scientific' objectivity and 'ideological innocence' have been scuppered by the political analysis of Cultural Studies, as they have, too, by those of the latter's principal theoretical drives: Marxism, feminism and postcolonialism. In other words, the construct 'Literature', and the studying of what it comprised, have been denaturalised both as object and as practice.

The second point about the persistence of 'English'/'Literary Studies' (albeit radically reformulated in the mould of Cultural Studies) is partly explained by the rationale for the later parts of this book. For while 'Literature' may have been terminally wounded, literature in general has not been: rather, it is widely read and studied in late-twentieth-century 'mass communication' societies, and retains a discrete and distinct presence amongst other contemporary media—including 'writing' as a generic whole.

A similar process of destabilisation and redefinition has been going on in the United States during the same period. Women's and ethnic presses, such as Feminist Press, Aunt Lutte, Spinster's, Arte Publico and Tikun, have fulfilled a simi-lar function to the alternative presses in Britain glanced at earlier. But more broadly, from the late-1960s, it is the 'Cul-ture Wars' which have represented the battle between the radical Left and the conservative Right over what the educa-tion curriculum should contain—and the study of literature has been at the centre of them.

As Regenia Gagnier puts it, with the increasing democratisation of higher education follow-ing the 1960s, 'the problems of society have become the problems of higher education, including ethnic and racial conflict, gender conflict, political and economic inequality, intolerance and lack of consensus' (Gagnier 1997:4).

Crucially, in a multi-cultural society where African-American 'assertiveness', feminism, and gay liberation movements are dynamically active, the question of *whose* culture should be taught as the curriculum has been posed and vigorously contested over the past three decades. In his influential contribution to the current debates, *Beyond the Culture Wars* (1992; see also pp. 79-80), Gerald Graff has written:

> *Today's academic disputes over which texts should be taught in the humanities, over the competing claims of Western and non-Western culture, and over the pros and cons of affirmative action and codes regulating hate speech mirror broader social conflicts over race, ethnicity, and privilege. Even the quarrels sparked by esoteric liter-ary theories about the pertinence of gender questions to the study of Shapespeare echo debates over sex roles in the larger society provoked by feminists, gay activists, and the entry of women into the professional work force. (Graff 1992:9)*

With the rise of Reaganite 'neo-liberalism' in the 1980s, however, a right-wing reaction got underway against a cultural pluralism which was seen as destroying higher education and the sense of belonging to a common national culture. Heads of the National Endowment for the Humanities like William Ben-nett and Lynne Cheney began to attack what they saw as the dominance of the Left in the universities, in particular its 'dismissal' of the canonic classics of 'Culture' from the syllabus, and their views were reinforced by such books as Allan Bloom's *The Closing of the American Mind,* E.D.Hirsch's *Cul-tural Literacy* (both 1987), and more recently by Harold Blooms *The Western Canon* (1994; see pp. 22-3).

As a consequence, in the late-1980s and early-1990s, the 'Culture Wars' hit the national news in an unprecedented fashion: *Newsweek, Time,* the *New Republic,* the *Village Voice, Harper's, Atlantic,* the *New York Times Magazine,* the *Wall Street Journal* and the *National Review,* amongst many others, ran regular instalments on the controversies around 'political correctness', often focusing on such prestigious universities as Stanford and Duke.

Most infamously, the *Atlantic* published a piece by Dinesh D'Souza in 1991, entitled 'Illiberal Education' (rapidly turned into the book, *Illiberal Education: The Politics of Race and Sex on Campus,* 1992), which asserted that classics by 'white males' were being 'expelled' from universities' required-reading lists, and quoted a remark by Christopher Clausen, head of the English Department at Pennsylvania State University, in 1988, to the effect that he was willing to 'bet that [Alice Walker's novel] *The Color Purple* is taught in more English courses today than all of Shakespeare's plays com-bined'.

A furore broke out, with President Bush denouncing the tyranny of 'political correctness' at the University of Michigan, and *Time* magazine bewailing the subjection of stu-dents to 'a literature class that equates Shakespeare and the novelist Alice Walker not as artists but as fragments of sociology'. It added, significantly, that 'obfuscatory course titles and eccentric reading lists frequently are wedded to a combative political agenda or outlandish views of the nation's culture and values' (Gubar and Kamholtz [eds] 1993:2). 'Literature', in this context, clearly reveals itself as continuing to enshrine the ideological values we saw inscribed in it during its construction in the nineteenth and earlier-twentieth centuries. Whether Henry Louis Gates is right, therefore, when he says that the 'vulgar cultural nationalists...are whistling in the wind' (Gates 1992: xvi) remains to be seen.

Nevertheless, in the American context as in the British, an unproblematic conception and study of 'Literature' can no longer be sustained. Evidence of this is apparent in the prolifer-ation of courses in African-American, Women's, and Gay/ Lesbian writing and theory—to name but three obvious examples—and in the Deconstructionist and New Historicist theoretical approaches which inform much contemporary criticism and pedagogy. Further, as Regenia Gagnier points out, in the United States there is a move in the humanities towards a gen-uinely interdisciplinary 'Cultural Studies'.

This is driven partly by institutional/economic determinants which are demanding proof of 'relevance', and partly by the perceived inadequacy by academics themselves of single-discipline approaches to study in a multi-ethnic and multicultural society. Faculty members from many different disciplines work together to identify and explore 'the ways that individuals and groups represent themselves to themselves and thereby construct their identities' (Gagnier 1997:7). In this, literature and the study of it, can clearly contribute a great deal.

But perhaps the most influential intervention in current debates in the United States about the role and function of 'Literary Studies'—and one accepted by Gagnier as inevitably implemented in the new Cultural Studies—is Gerald Graff's project for 'teaching the conflicts'. We saw in Chapter 2 how Graff identifies conflict as marking the development of 'English' in the US from the start, while being disguised, for much of its history, under a blanket of catholicity and compre-hensive 'coverage' of the whole field of literature; and how the only sustainable project for Literary Studies is to take as its syllabus the conflicts which actually determine its constitution.

In his more recent book, *After the Culture Wars: How Teach-ing the Conflicts Can Revitalize American Education,* Graff now argues that the 'Wars' themselves are merely the most extreme latterday manifestation of these endemic conflicts; so that 'the history of modern American education has pitted the liberal pluralist solution (everyone do his or her own thing) against the conservative solution (everyone do the conservatives' thing)' (Graff 1992:10). The present 'Culture Wars' represent these positions; but they are 'two sides of the same coin; neither is able to imagine any positive role for cultural conflict' *(ibid.).*

To transcend the impasse, he says, we must 'teach the conflicts themselves, making them part of our object of study and using them as a new kind of organizing principle to give the curriculum the clarity and focus that almost all sides now agree it lacks' (12). By bringing into the classroom at once 'the conflicts themselves', the misrepresentations of them by the media, and our own cognate research problems to do, say, with methodology, canonicity or cultural politics: that is, *our own theoretical insertion* within the field, we may com-municate the intellectual relevance and vitality of literature and the contemporary study of it.

My closing emphasis above signals what is clearly missing so far from this account of what happened to 'Literature' from the end of the 1960s onwards: the place of 'Theory' in all this. In a way, of course, that *is* where I began—by focussing on feminism and postcolonialism. But while acknowledging that Theory does indeed underpin all the developments adduced so far, it was never intended that this chapter should simply be a potted digest of contemporary critical theory, nor to make it appear that it was principally theory which caused all the upheaval.

Neither will (can) what follows here be such a digest: it merely sketches in the ways certain recent theoretical movements have undermined the concept of 'Literature' and the resulting effects for literature at the present time.

The so-called 'Moment of Theory' may be charted from the late-1960s, through its heyday in the 1970s and 1980s, to the current situation in which some would argue that its 'Moment' is over, and others that it is now so much in the intellectual bloodstream that 'continuum' is a more accurate word to describe it. What is beyond dispute, however, is that from the early-1970s onwards, wave after wave of new (and some older) theories destabilised 'Literature' and transformed liter-ary criticism.

THE 'BAKHTIN SCHOOL'

The work of one earlier theoretical movement, the 'Bakhtin School' (in Russia in the late-1920s, and of which Mikhail Bakhtin is the best-known member), may be adduced first, since it became widely influential in the post-1960s period through its emphasis on the *social* nature of language. In its critique of Ferdinand de Saussure's identification of the arbitrary relationship between 'signifier' and 'signified' in the 'sign' (word) in language, and its resituating of this in a social context, the Bakhtinians saw that relationship as invariably fraught with interference and conflict, inasmuch as every utterance launched into social space implies a dialogue or a con-tested interpretation and is therefore potentially a site of struggle.

Hence, language is always contaminated by the semantic accretions deposited there in the endless process of human struggle and interaction. By relating this dynamic view of language to the study of literary texts,

Bakhtin himself emphasised, not the way texts reflect society or class interests, but the way in which their language may disrupt authority and liberate alternative voices. His theory of the 'polyphonic' or 'dialogic' novel, for example, stresses the presence in such of various 'voices' (heteroglossia) which express different points-of-view and are not subordinated to the author's controlling purpose. The *text,* therefore, articulates liberating and often subversive discourses beyond the author's authority (see Bakhtin 1981).

Bakhtin's identification of 'Carnival', as an aspect of this dialogism, has been particularly influential in the subversion of 'Literature'. Seeing carnivals as traditionally collective and popular, in which hierarchies are turned on their heads, oppo-sites mingle, the authoritarian and the sacred are profaned, subverted and mocked by the release of folk 'laughter', he developed the term 'Carnivalisation' to describe similar effects within literature (see Bakhtin 1984).

Such effects are precisely where voices are set free to speak subversively and shockingly beyond the author's control. Indeed, they may well refuse, mock or subvert even the author's own 'dominant' voice and viewpoint.

Bakhtin's revelation of 'Carnival' has been instru-mental in breaking up the hold on literature of the organicist aesthetic formalism which dominated much mid-twentieth-century criticism. By promoting the idea that literary works are multi-layered and resistant to unification, he problematised the notion of 'character' as a stable and unitary individual identity and loosened the grip of the author on his or her text. While Bakhtin's own work, in fact, still retains a firm sense of the writer's controlling artistry, its politicised crit-ical reading nevertheless anticipates major tendencies in later Structuralist, Poststructuralist and Psychoanalytic theories:

- in its destabilising of the notion of the unified human subject;
- in celebrating liberty and pleasure over authority and decorum;
- in privileging the 'polyphonic', 'dialogic', 'heteroglossic' or 'plural' text;
- and in opening up the potential dialogism of *all* literary works.

STRUCTURALISM

Structuralism was also indebted to Saussure's concept of the signifier/signified duality. But, in contrast to the Bakhtin School's social orientation, it developed the theory that as a signifying system which is meaningful only in respect of the internal linguistic 'codes' of which it is comprised, literature does not allude to any reality outside itself, and therefore can-not be truthful: it is neither 'mimetic' nor 'expressive' (see p. 29).

Hence follows, in Roland Barthes's famous formulation, 'the death of the author' (Barthes 1977), since there can be no 'humanistic' communication between author and reader by way of the literary work; and the sole object of a structuralist criticism, therefore, can only be to analyse the internal rela-tions between the levels of meaning within the closed system of the text itself.

MARXIST THEORY, THE NEW HISTORICISTS AND CULTURAL MATERIALISTS

Since most contemporary schools of theory are not discrete, but partake of elements of each other, recent Marxist theory (a loose catch-all term for what is better referred to as 'Material-ist' theory), while still concerned with the social, economic and cultural 'modes of production' which determine the literary work in its own historical moment, has also taken up a 'struc-turalist' position which sees a text as encoding and revealing aspects of the ideology which shaped it beyond its own con-scious 'knowing'.

Its textual 'gaps', 'omissions', 'lapses' and 'silences'—its 'not-said'—thus take on greater import than its explicit significations. So that, for the New Historicists and Cultural Materialists, for example, the prizing open of what the text cannot itself know is a route to understanding the problematics of, and resistances to, the dominant ideology of the conjuncture in which it was formed. In this, of course, they are also beholden to Michel Foucault's theory of 'discursive formations'—those discourses of power which determine and constrain the forms of knowledge and the types of 'normality' and 'subjectivity' that prevail in any given period, but which are also open to contestation. Texts of all kinds—literary ones amongst them—have a complex insertion into these processes, and can be made to reveal how this is inscribed in their own constituent discourses.

POSTSTRUCTURALISM AND DECONSTRUCTION

Poststructuralism (again a catch-all term for a multitude of different theories) takes the Structuralist position to the point of *sz\{-deconstruction;* for where Structuralism was based on the informing notion of a structure of language, Poststructural-ism denies the existence of such a structure—or, indeed, of any kind of fundamental structure. Emphasising the essentially unstable nature of signification, Poststructuralism undertakes a 'playful' (but deadly serious) exposure of the contradictory meanings any text may be shown to articulate, insofai as it consists of words inextricably inscribed in the multiple dis-courses that inform it.

Contra the aesthetic formalism of, say, New Criticism (see pp. 56-9), it is the *disunity* and *excess* of the literary work's heteroglossic textuality which is the source of our *'jouissance'* (extreme pleasure) in reading it. In the most influential of Poststructuralist theorisations, the Deconstruction of Jacques Derrida, any reading which 'makes sense' of a literary text can immediately be destabilised by way of the same text's signifying system.

Thus all writing deconstructs itself ('Texts deconstruct *themselves* by themselves' [Derrida 1986:123]). Such a position thus holds that, in another of Der-rida's famous statements, 'there is nothing outside the text' (Derrida [1967] 1976:158), no controlling of it by the author's 'intention', and no unitary or 'essential' truth to be gained from it. Inasmuch as we only know the world through language, and because 'reality' is inseparable from the discourses in which it is known, there can be no absolute certainty about anything, since everything exists only in the unstable play of textuality and discourse.

The most sophisticated literary-critical appropriation of Derridean Poststructuralism is American Deconstruction, sometimes also called 'Rhetorical Reading' or 'Cultural Poetics', which incorporates and supercedes the insights of Structuralism by showing the pressures and ironies which traverse the structural dualisms of Western discourse. In such work, the minute close reading of, or 'response to', the language of literary texts proves their infinitely complex, contradictory instability and 'iterability' (their susceptibility to being continually 're-written in the process of being read and 'interpreted' by different readers).

A Deconstructive reading, then, is governed by *aporia* (moments of absolute uncertainty), and the recognition and acceptance that all texts are ultimately *unreadable,* insofar as 'readability' implies that a text is reducible to a single 'definitive' interpretation.

Again, therefore, the author does not control the literary text, it does not contain '*a* meaning', and it cannot be seen to hold a 'final' truth which can be extrapolated from it. Nevertheless, American Deconstruction, with its detailed attention to the linguistic textuality of literature, makes it possible to recoup a notion of 'the literary' in terms of its specific formal composition.

READER-RESPONSE CRITICISM

Albeit based on different premises, Reader-Response Criticism has also been influential in emphasising the *reader's* participa-tion in the construction of meaning which a text promotes. Here, the reader does not mine the text for its 'innate' mean-ing, but acts upon it to produce meaning in the dialectical relationship between the textuality of the text and her or his experiencing of it as an individual reading-subject.

Thus for the German theorist, Wolfgang Iser, the text is a *potential* structure which is 'concretised' by an 'actual reader' filling in the *indeterminancies* or 'blanks' that any text must contain in relation to her or his life-experience, an experience which will itself be modified in the act of reading. Once more, the literary object is seen not as an anterior and determinate receptacle of meaning and value, but as a potential spectrum of possible readings, since its meaning is constructed in the adjustments and revisions which are brought about in the reader's mind during a specific act of reading.

Equally, the critic's task is not to explain the text, but to analyse the relationship between the 'implied reader' which the text creates for itself ('a network of response-inviting structures' which predispose us to read it in certain ways) and the 'actual reader' as defined above (Iser 1974, 1978).

POSTMODERNISM

Postmodernist theories extend the implications of Poststructuralism in positing the discursive nature of all experience, and the impossibility, therefore, of arriving at any certainty or truth. The 'grand narratives' (see Lyotard [1979] 1984) of social and intellectual progress initiated by the Enlightenment are discredited. Any grounding of such ideas in notions of 'his-tory' or 'reality' is no longer possible in the comprehensively 'textualised' world of images and simulations which characterise this age of mass consumption and advanced technologies.

But Postmodernism also celebrates the endless 'play', and re-playing, of meaning in any discursive 'simulacrum' (i.e. a deceptively 'real' representation of an always already unreal 'reality'): where there can be no absolute truths, there is a kind of anarchic freedom in the 'depthless' provisionality of the (re) cycling of signifiers. In all these respects, Postmodernist theo-ries, whilst having a more general social import in the defini-tion of 'modernity' and 'modernisation, have also radically challenged the hegemony of 'high culture'. So that 'Literature' becomes merely one set of discursive texts in the 'technologi-cal' continuum of popular-cultural production and reproduc-tion of all forms of art.

PSYCHOANALYTIC THEORY AND NEO-FREUDIANISM

Psychoanalytic theories, remodelled in the context of Poststruc-turalism by the Neo-Freudianism of Jacques Lacan, Julia Kristeva and others, also focus on the functioning of language, but particularly its part in the construction of subject identity. Lacan stresses that the ego is itself a construct, and that this 'ego-artefact', while seeming unified, consistent and determinately centred, is, in fact, a discursive fiction made up of disparate fragments yoked forcibly together and always on the verge of dissolution (Lacan [1973] 1979, 1977). Language is especially important in respect of the formation of sexual iden-tity, because males are held to enter the 'figurative' or 'symbolic order'—where words are substituted for objects themselves—more readily than women.

Since our lives are lived out within the 'symbolic order' (there is nothing beyond 'text' or 'discourse'), this relationship between language and gender is fundamental in sustaining the sexual inequality of a patriar-chal society. Such a theory's impact on literature and criticism has been at once to reconfirm the sense that language is neither referential nor expressive, but constitutive; that human subjec-tivity (the notion of individual, unitary and essential 'character') is in fact constructed, heterogenetic and unstable; that literary texts may be read psychoanalytically like dreams; and that they will encode complex and contradictory messages in the 'not-said' of their textuality.

FEMINISM

Such Neo-Freudian theory has had much to say to Feminism both in the way language constructs subjectivity, so that, for example, deconstructing it can assist in the deconstruction of imprisoning subject-positions; and in the quest for a kind of 'feminine language' which would articulate preoedipal, pre-verbal, pre-symbolic discourses, thus restoring connection with that lost order which is now only glimpsed in eruptions from the Unconscious. For Kristeva, poetic language introduces the subversive openness of what she calls the 'semiotic' across society's closed symbolic order (see Kristeva 1986). More broadly, as we have seen, Feminism has politicised 'Literature' and the study of it as a form of sexual politics in which a male Canon is denaturalised, a female tradition established, and a discourse unearthed which voices women's experience and sexuality in order to release their *difference*—a difference hitherto subsumed in the submission of feminine to masculine identity. The principal variations on this last initiative appear either in Anglo-American 'gynocriticism' (see p. 65), or in 'French' feminism's conception of *'ecriture feminine'*, which may be defined as a kind of writing which seeks to access the pre-figurative 'semiotic'/'poetic' experience of the female subject (see Eagleton, Mary [ed.] 1991).

GAY, LESBIAN AND QUEER THEORY

Developing out of Feminism (and out of Deconstruction) have been more recent, and arguably now more radical, Gay, Les-bian and Queer theories which at once explore the complex sexual discourses inscribed in past literature and seek to 'transgress', in literature and elsewhere, the constructed and constraining conventional binaries of sexual identity in order to reveal their more unsettled and dynamic relations. One sub-versively Postmodern instance of this transgressive sexual/ cultural politics is Donna Harraway's notion of the 'Cyborg'—a 'creature of a post-gender world' which is radically free of the dualities and polarities which underpin conventional West-ern organising structures of subjectivity.

The Cyborg's openness to technology opposes 'it' to all myths of origin, fulfilment and organic wholeness (including those implicit in Anglo-American and French feminist theories); and *writing*, significantly, is 'preeminently the technology of the cyborgs'. In the political struggle for meanings in language—'the Struggle against perfect communication, against the *one code* that translates all meaning perfectly, the central dogma of phallogo-centrism'—writing which works outside the constraints of an originary common language celebrates its own 'illegitimacy' as it works to subvert the central myths of Western culture (Harraway [1985] 1990, *passim)*.

POSTCOLONIALISM

Such thinking as the above clearly relates to Postcolonialism, where most of the theoretical positions sketched in earlier find a combined focus:

- in its exposing and challenging of Western hegemony and the construction of the colonial subject;
- in deconstructing the dominant logocentrism of Western culture;
- in seeking a 'decentred consciousness';
- and in creating a discourse which returns a voice to the unvoiced.

In respect of this last, it literally 'writes' a history for those denied a history, and restores the (unwritten) experience of being the colonial 'Other'. Postcolonialism thus posits *hybridity* (the condition of being the 'subject' of cultural cross-breeding) and *marginality* (the condition of being situated at the edges of metropolitan society) as challenging unity and cen-trality in the postcolonial world. Perhaps the most telling contemporary convergence of many of these theoretical positions is in the work of 'women-of-colour' and postcolonial feminists (for example, that of Gayatri Spivak in 'Can the Sub-altern Speak?' [1988], Trinh T.Minh-ha in *Woman, Native, Other* [1989], and Chandra Talpade Mohanty in 'Under Western Eyes' [1991]) who emphasise the 'double colonisation of women in the Third World or metropolitan racial minorities. Such women are the site of shifting and multiple identities; they are, in Gloria Anzaldua's words, 'border women, 'living on the borders and in the margins' of several sexual and racial formations (Anzaldua 1987). In promoting a more flexible, plural, unbounded and transcultural figuring of femininity, and in celebrating this 'cultured culturelessness' of the 'Border-lands', such postcolonial feminisms have a clear linkage with notions of 'Cyborg' identity, with transgressive sexual politics, with all the creative postmodern movements whose rationale is the continual breakingdown of unitary and universalising paradigms—and of which 'Literature' has surely been amongst the most powerful.

Diverse as these theories may be in their specific agendas and formulations, they have all had the effect of demolishing 'Liter-ature' and the hagiographic study of it:

- by historicising and politicising it;
- by challenging notions of the authority of the author, 'the text itself, inherent 'meaning', and essentialist 'interpretation';
- by revealing its 'not-said' and the contradictory discourses within it which it could not know itself;
- and by opening it up to infinite variations of re-reading in history.

Nevertheless, as is immediately apparent if one walks into any bookshop, literature as a whole has not gone away. On the contrary, and regardless of the multifarious forms of alterna-tive cultural production available in contemporary societies, reading seems to be widespread and popular as never before.

On the day I write, an article in *The Guardian* on the new 'lifestyle' bookstores, 'Books: Change in Store' (1997), notes that 'the largest bookshop to open in Britain for 50 years is unveiled today in Glasgow, boasting a stock of 350,000 vol-umes; that the collapse of the British Net Book Agreement has led to retail groups like the Asda supermarket chain joining the book-selling industry; and that, as a result, book sales overall have risen in volume 'probably by 11 per cent over the past year'. students on 'Literary Studies' courses, having supped full of Theory, are demanding to see how the theories work in practice in assisting their reading of what they had principally come to study in the first place: the 'primary material', as it is still ironically called in academic discourse; while much 'post-modern' literary writing now contains its own 'theory' as part and parcel of its self-reflexive textuality.

A movement also seems to be emerging, principally in the United States and per-haps as a reflex of the 'Culture Wars', to develop a 'new aes-thetics' or 'new formalism' in theory and criticism which can mount, as the titles of two recent books announce, 'A Defence of Poetry' in sophisticated post-Deconstructionist terms. One of these 'defends' poetry, significantly, as a 'need, not a commodity' in people's 'perennial and pancultural' demand for it (Fry 1995:2); the other, as 'any cultural creation that fruitfully exceeds destructive norms and passes beyond theory's reduc-tive explanatory powers' (Edmundson 1995:28).

So, while 'Literature' may now indeed be a straw *man,* literature in gen-eral seems to have come through the 'Theory Wars', and all the associated hostilities, renewed and refurbished. If this is indeed the case, then we certainly do need to establish what 'the literary' might mean to us, and what literature—in the light of such a definition—does, and can do, for us as we approach the postmodern millenium.

4

What is the Literary

If 'Literature' as a conceptual term is as discredited as we have seen it to be in the preceding chapter; but if, as I propose, we also wish to retain a discrete notion of the domain literature occupies within cultural production, then 'the literary' may be the best way to describe it. The following pages will therefore attempt to define what I think we should understand by that term.

Once again, this will not be done by outlining the multi-farious aesthetic and theoretical definitions which have accrued around the notion—if not the term itself—throughout history, although it will be readily apparent that my concep-tion of it is often beholden to an eclectic range of previous insights by others. Rather, my intention is to establish a coher-ent working term for the kind of written discourse I believe has some irreplaceable uses in our society, and without which our cultural lives would be impoverished and diminished. It is also to allow for the possibility of a metadiscourse to talk about 'the literary' as a specific category of the generic 'writing'.

It will be noticed immediately that I have adapted the usual part of speech, the adjective 'literary', into a substantive noun: 'the literary'—which is not by any means an original coinage, although the *OED* does not list this usage at all. This is partly to signal that what I am calling the 'domain of the literary' is a generic category of discursive practice which may be cognate with 'Literature', but is distinguished from it, and from its adjectival forms: as, for example, in such phrases as 'literary artefact' or 'literary achievement'. It is also to avoid using the noun 'literariness', both in its conventional sense: 'the quality of *being literary*', often now suggesting in a mannered or pre-cious way, and to distance my position from the more purely *formalistic* associations of the word as used by the Russian Formalists earlier this century.

It is only fair to admit here, however, that the Russian Formalist sense of 'literariness' as 'that which makes a given work a work of literature', and their emphasis on the need to study the specificity and distinctive-ness of literature not merely as a formalistic analysis of the art-object but as an instance of 'the autonomy of the aesthetic function', will find echoes in some of what I have to say later.

My notion of 'the literary', then, is intended to identify a category of writing which is distinguished, first, from 'writing' in general—both in its own self-consciousness of being 'literary' and in its reader's apprehension of that property; and second, from other conventionally related art-forms such as music, painting and film. These distinctions will be based principally on an assessment of the social and cultural *effects* of 'the literary' rather than on any attempt to locate intrinsic aesthetic or linguistic characteristics of 'literariness'.

As Derek Attridge has pointed out in the introduction to his book, *Peculiar Language: Literature as Difference from the Renaissance to James Joyce,* there is a fundamental contradic-tion, throughout the Western tradition of thought about litera-ture, between 'two mutually inconsistent demands—that the language of literature be recognizably different from the language we encounter in other contexts, and that it be recognizably the same' (Attridge 1988:3).

There has been no convincing proof that there is a language 'peculiar' to literature; but if it is indeed 'recognizably the same' as 'ordinary' language, then 'the existence of literature itself as a distinct entity' is endangered. The notion of literature as 'difference', there-fore, has to shift its ground from attempting to identify a spe-cial 'literary language' (as we will see the Russian Formalists try to do) to recognising that literature exists within, and is determined by, 'a shifting web of socially produced relations, judgements, and distinctions' and is consequently open to 'change and cultural variation. Thus Attridge aims to show why the domain of literature and of literary theory cannot provide its own self-sufficient and lasting answers to the question of the distinctiveness of literary language.... [T]he judgements that control its status and function as art must be related to the wider context in which they are formed, sustained, and modified.

Like his, my attempt to define the 'difference' of 'the literary' will also be culturalist and functionalist in orientation.

The reader will also notice in what follows that I make no distinctions in including within 'the literary' all types of writ-ing which meet the definitions I propose. So while I continue to respect the usefulness of basic generic differentiation, no categories are to be found here of the 'serious'/ 'popular', 'major'/ 'minor' variety. Thus there should be no possibility of thinking that 'the literary' is, in fact, comprised of some writing which is more 'literary' than other 'literary' writing, or that pre-emptive evaluations are being made: *all* writing which fits the bill comprises my conception of 'the literary'. In this way, it seeks to promote a 'commonwealth' or 'republic of letters' which enfranchises the diverse plenitude of literature, and in which, as a necessary reflex of this, evaluation is always provi-sional, variable and justified by function.

First of all, I would argue that 'the literary' is distinguished by its own sense of being *'of* the literary'. This apparently circular definition means that writing which presents itself as being 'creative', 'imaginative' and 'artificial' (i.e. composed of and by artifice) simultaneously conceives of itself as being different to other kinds of writing which do not so conceive of themselves. I do not have in mind here Aestheticism or the kind of strategic self-reflexivity associated currently with postmodernist texts —where there is an explicit internal commentary, for example, on the discursive practices of creating a fiction—but the sense in which *any* literary text emits a consciousness of understanding itself to be 'literary'.

The literary text is the product, first, of a writer who *elects* to write a poem, a drama or a prose fic-tion, itself a choice knowingly made within a cultural context which is also known to ascribe meaning to these genres. Sec-ond, it is the product of a reader who *recognises,* by way of their own 'literary competence' (see pp. 98-100), that what they are reading is indeed a literary text. In this respect, the text is so indelibly inscribed by these ascriptive consciousnesses that we may say that one of its determinate characteristics is its sense of being 'literary'.

To put it more simply, a poem identifies itself as belonging to the 'literary' genre of poetry, and its 'poem-ness' helps to determine how it is read. In exactly the same way, a novel's self-presentation as being of the 'literary' genre of prose fiction is a constituent feature of its *difference* from a piece of writing which does not have that self-consciousness. Both examples, I am suggesting, are in fact fundamentally constituted by announcing their location within 'the domain of the literary'.

It could, of course, be retorted, certainly in respect of peri-ods before the modern generic classifications became conven-tionally established, that a writer of drama would not be conscious of writing a 'play' or that an early novelist did not think of him or herself as writing a 'novel'; nor that the audience/reader in either case were aware of themselves as being in the presence of such. But as noted on pp. 8 and 34 lexical histories do not always match conceptual ones, so it does not necessarily follow that the anonymous authors and audiences of medieval miracle plays were unaware that they were creat-ing or watching something different from the Bible or liturgical services in church.

Nor would it be the case that Daniel Defoe and Henry Fielding were not conscious of composing what turned out to be 'novels' rather than kinds of writing which were 'factual accounts' or 'histories'—if for no other reason than that of their self-conscious preoccupation with their own fictional contrivance or with affirming that their stories were indeed 'true'. It is clearly apparent, too, that the rapidly established popular readership for this 'novel' kind of writing understood and appreciated its novelty or *difference* very well.

Leaving aside generic 'naming', then, my argument is that the matrix of conscious production and reception in which 'the literary' is formed metaphorically invests the self-consciousness of 'being literary' in the written work itself. So that while we accept that there is no such thing as a specifically 'literary', or 'peculiar', language, we nevertheless regard the language of a text as 'literary', rather than as an ordinary act of communication, because we read it *as* a 'literary' work. In Umberto Eco's words, 'a well-organised text' (for which read, a self-consciously 'literary' one) 'presupposes a model of competence coming, so to speak, from outside the text, but on the other hand works to build up, by merely textual means, such a competence' (Eco [1979] 1981:8). The 'external' competence of the reader will indeed make the text readable, but it is the text's own 'internal' textual strategies which summon and confirm that competence.

This is not the place to discuss in detail the concept of 'literary competence', but as I am using a broad notion of it here, some definition is called for. Drawing on Noam Chomsky's concept of 'linguistic competence' (those language rules internalised by native speakers that enable them to generate and understand grammatically correct sentences), 'literary competence' posits the existence of implicit knowledge or internalised rules—'conventions of reading', as Jonathan Culler calls them —which enable readers to discriminate, read and make sense of literary works (Culler 1975:114).

This indicates a distinction, therefore, between simple literacy and what we might call 'literaracy'. Put simply, 'competent' readers, when faced with a text, seem to have internalised norms and procedures which enable them to know how to understand it, and to decide what is, or is not, an appropriate 'interpretation'. While this literary competence may seem to shift the recognition and ascription of being 'literary' from text to reader, it is also the case that literary writers write on the assumption of it, since they write *as* literature what can be read as *literature.*

We acquire literary competence through our general acculturation, but most obviously in education. As one commenta-tor has put it:

We tend to forget the fact that reading is an unnatural act— left alone, no child would do it. Reading must be taught.... The child is taught not only to sound out the words, but to interpret their meaning— which is to say that literary criti-cism is there from the moment the child's parents begin to read to him or her or explain the meanings of signs on the street.

In other words, unlike 'natural' linguistic competence (we are not formally taught how to speak and understand grammatically correct sentences), 'literary competence' is learnt through *nurture* and, therefore, will be acquired differentially. Because we cannot then assume that the entire adult population will have such competence, it could be argued that, whereas the writer may have made a specific choice to produce a literary text, a reader without 'literary competence' will not be able to recognise the kind of literary 'self-consciousness' proposed earlier.

On my own terms, therefore, this cannot then be a defining characteristic of my notion of 'the literary'—which would certainly seem to make it meaningless. However, this requires the hypothesis of a reader who can indeed read, but who lacks the 'literary competence' to discriminate the poem they are faced with from other kinds of written text: the hypothetical reader, in other words, would have become literate while escaping any of the accompanying processes of acculturation. Paradoxically, therefore, this may be seen to prove my point instead: for the reader who is outside 'literary competence' means that they cannot recognise 'the literary' or ascribe the poem accordingly, so that the poem is not then 'of the literary'. This surely implies that ascription of 'the literary' is indeed a constituent of the poem as literary object.

My usage of the notion assumes, however, that the vast majority of people in late-twentieth-century societies where literacy is ubiquitous will, in fact, have internalised the 'con-ventions' which enable them at least to perceive the difference between different kinds of writing, and will have a greater or lesser 'competence' in reading literary ones. Such factors as schooling from an early age, in which the reading and writing of poems and stories is a common activity; the huge children's books industry, 'constantly swelled by 7,000 new titles a year' ('Dive into a book' 1997:3); the ubiquitous presence of book-shops and libraries, publishers' catalogues, literary festivals and prizes, reviewing in mass-media outlets, readings and adaptations on radio, TV and film, all constantly reinforce the acquisition of 'literary competence' and keep the specificity of 'the literary' in the general public eye. So that most readers may be presumed to function within the context of a culturally determined and received notion of 'literature'. Faced with a poem, in other words, they would be able to name it as such, even if they could not formulate what makes it 'a poem' rather than the football results—thus recognising its self-inscription as being 'of the literary'

My second defining characteristic of 'the literary' returns us to the concept of *poiesis* or 'making'. I noted on p. 26 that for a very long period of time the word 'poetry' stood for what later became known as 'literature', and that a synonym for this in English, especially during the Renaissance, was the 'arte of making'. This more literal notion of the business of composing literary texts was, of course, later overdetermined by the Romantics' emphasis on creativity, 'the imagination', and the role of 'the poet' as individual and original 'genius': the 'unconscious legislator of the world'; 'The Hero as Man of Letters'—'in a world of which he is the spiritual light'. But what I want to focus on here is the fact that literature, even when it purports to be a form of realistic *mimesis,* in 'copying nature' or 'representing reality', is actually 'making' what I have called *'poietic* realities'.

If we think of the modern adjective 'creative', which now has the looser meaning either of 'imaginative originality' in characterising someone's artistic talentedness, of 'imaginative writing' genetically, or of the practice of it ('creative writing'), and restore to it its primary sense, we are returned, in the *OED's* words, to 'that which creates'/ 'makes out of nothing'. In deploying the notion of a *writing which creates,* it is that basic meaning of the verb 'to create' which is what I wish to emphasise: 'to bring into being; *esp.* form out of nothing... Make, form, or constitute for the first time or afresh' *(OED).*

The force of that 'bring into being/form *out of nothing!* constitute *for the first time'* is what lies at the nub of my argu-ment; for whilst recognising that literary texts are, of course, created out of *something* (i.e. language), it is precisely the orig-inal 'form' in which language is organised which makes the new object indeed 'formed out of nothing'. This is reinforced by the *OED's* subsequent definition of the noun 'creation': 'The action of making, forming, producing, or constituting *for the first time... An original (esp. imaginative)* production of human intelligence' (my emphases). It is the apparent contradiction implicit in being brought into *being* (i.e. material existence) by way of the *imagination* (i.e. by an act of mental contrivance) that signals the crux of my definition of 'the liter-ary'.

It is no coincidence that James Joyce, in *A Portrait of the Artist as a Young Man,* causes Stephen Dedalus, descendant of the 'fabulous artificer' of Greek legend, to think of the mature artist as 'like the God of creation' (Joyce [1916] 1964:215), nor to believe himself, at the end of the novel—and subject to Joyce's irony—to be about 'to encounter...the reality of experi-ence and to *forge* in the smithy of my soul the *uncreated* con-science of my race' (253; my emphases). 'Forge', of course, means at once to 'make' and to 'fabricate', in the senses both of 'constructing' and 'inventing falsely'; but it is 'uncreated' which implies that in the process of this 'forging' something new will be made. My definition of 'the literary', then, rests on this basic sense of 'creative' as *making for the first time.*

We may also notice that other words than 'poet'/'maker' used in relation to literature carry similar connotations. For example, the word 'playwright' is indeed not *'playwrite(r)'* but cognate with, say, 'wheelwright' or 'shipwright'—where 'wright' is glossed by the dictionary simply as 'a maker'. A playwright 'makes plays'—or *'creates'* them, as defined above. Equally pointed in this context is the word 'fiction'. Derived from the Latin *fingere/fictum*—to 'fashion' or 'form'—by way of the substantive *fictio/fictionis*—'a shaping'—the modern word carries the sense both of imaginative prose narratives (novels) and of pure invention, often in respect of the deliberately deceptive.

Thus we use it to denote a feigned or false 'fabrication': as in, 'his story to the court was pure fiction' or 'little Johnny is not beyond telling a few fictions about his friends'. *The Oxford Companion to the English Language* (McArthur 1992:401-2) further reminds us of the usage involv-ing 'social or cultural constructs' ('a special kind of fact'), such as 'temporal fictions' (the days of the week) and 'geographical fictions' (the Equator). These, the *Companion* notes, are at once 'part of life' and the 'products of imaginative storytelling', so that 'fictively, Sherlock Holmes and the Equa-tor are on a par'. It adds that 'at a certain level of discussion the [English] language is itself fictive: something created by the human mind within a cultural system so as to serve certain social ends'. Two points emerge from all this in my context here.

First, whilst conscious that some of the concepts which follow have been prejudicially gendered within male critical discourse, I nevertheless want to highlight that sense in the etymology of 'fiction' which means that it is a kind of aesthetic 'forming', 'fashioning' or 'shaping'. Like other kinds of literary writing, fiction is a fashioning of language; but because the genre is characterised by a more overtly referential modality in purporting to relate to 'real life', it also seems to form or shape the raw material of lived experience into the 'world of the book'.

Coleridge's notion of the 'esemplastic' power of the 'secondary imagination' which 'dissolves, diffuses, dissipates, in order to recreate' represents a founding aesthetic formula-tion of this process. But Henry James, in his preface to *The Spoils of Poynton,* neatly points up its significance in my context here when he asserts that 'life persistently blunders and deviates, loses herself in the sand. The reason is, of course, that life has no direct sense whatever for the subject and is capable (luckily for us) of nothing but splendid waste. Hence the opportunity for the sublime economy of art...' (James [1907] 1962:120).

Art, in other words, precisely does 'have a sense of subject', which it 'rescues' from the 'splendid waste' of life, 'fashioning' a perceptible reality for us in its textual 'shaping' of the inchoate into comprehensible designs or patterns. In this respect, fiction is just as constitutively *poietic* as poetry itself. I will return to the notion of 'pattern' in a moment.

The second point is that the correlation between 'fiction' and 'fabrication'—and the ambiguous relations between the 'real' and the 'fictive'—reminds us that our comprehension of the world is constructed within discourse; that we are all formed by, and complicit in, 'telling stories'; that our systems of knowing, meaning and making sense are all textualised narratives. Exactly because of this, the evident textualising of 'the real' in 'the literary' is one of the pressing reasons why literature remains a salutary resource for us.

My proposition that '*poietic* making' has a fundamental defining role is not to argue, however, that 'the literary' does not allude to a 'real' material reality outside itself, but to estab-lish that *even at* its most realistic the literary discourse never-theless constructs the reality it purports to represent. Neither is it to argue that other kinds of writing are not 'creative' in the sense used earlier: a political pamphlet, for example, will 'make' an argument in language on behalf of a particular cause, which can then be 'unmade' by an opposing argument put forward in response; popular journalism daily creates its news in writing its news-stones (the word is indicative).

But in both these cases, there is, on the one hand, an assumed external context of 'real' reference which justifies or substantiates the pamphlet's and news-story's own engagement with it; and, on the other, a self-presumption on the part of such writings that they belong to the real world as 'truthful', 'factual' discourses (i.e. precisely *not* fictive), and that they will be taken on trust to be so by their readership. This assumption of not being 'of the literary', in other words, distinguishes them from even the most 'real-world' allusive of novels once the novel has 'self-consciously' disclosed itself to be such—which, as I have argued earlier, is central to its generic self-definition as being 'of the literary'.

But the most important feature of literary 'making', I am proposing, is that it creates '*poietic* realities' which would not otherwise exist. Without wishing to collude in a Romantic dis-course which sees 'originality' as the central attribute of 'genius', I would nevertheless claim that it is the unique speci-ficity of all literary works *by definition*—since only a word-for-word copy would exactly replicate the original—which allows them to bring into view newly perceptible 'subjects' from the 'splendid waste' of life. Here, we are at what Seamus Heaney has called 'the frontier of writing': 'the line that divides the actual conditions of our daily lives from the imaginative repre-sentation of those conditions in literature' (Heaney 1995: xvi). This kind of 'originality', however, is only an enabling characteristic of 'the literary', not a value-bestowing property: rather it is interpretation and evaluation—whilst always provisional and function-directed—which will make of the 'making' what they perceive and value there.

A reworking of one of Raymond Williams's earliest and vaguest, but most fertile, formulations will help to clarify what I mean here. In *The Long Revolution,* he famously defined 'cultural history' as 'the study of relationships between elements in a whole way of life', and added, importantly for my present purpose, that 'a key-word, in such analysis, is *pattern* (Williams [1961] 1971:63; my emphasis). By 'pattern', I under-stand him to mean what we have seen Henry James claim is art's ability to extrapolate a 'sense of subject' from the undifferentiated 'inclusion and confusion' of life. By way of this perception of 'pattern', Williams says, we can tap into the 'structure of feeling' of a period, and experience 'the particular living result of all the elements in the general organisation' of a community: that is, its 'culture'.

In the process of showing how fiction is a vital form of access to this 'structure of feeling', he makes a passing remark which I wish to focus on and then extrapolate to 'the literary' as a whole. Having noted, pertinently in my context here, that 'art *creates,* by new perceptions and responses, elements which the society, as such, is not able to realise', he writes: 'We find also, *in certain characteris-tic forms and devices,* evidence of the deadlocks and unsolved problems of the society: *often admitted to consciousness far the first time in this way'* (86; my emphases). What Williams is suggesting here is not merely access through *content,* but much more importantly that this access is by way of fictional *fashion-ing* ('certain...forms and devices') which produces new knowl-edge by 'shaping' a 'pattern' which 'consciousness' perceives *'for the first time* in this way'.

Whether we read the ambiguous phrase 'in this way as 'by these means' or 'in this specific form', what Williams seems to confirm is my argument that 'the literary' 'forms out of nothing... makes for the first time' new perceptual realities in its *creative* textuality. We will find a consonance between these views and those of Louis Althusser quoted later (pp. 118-19).

Williams developed these ideas in his later concept of the 'knowable community' ([1970] 1974:66). His argument, by way of George Eliot in particular, is that she 'extends the community of the novel', not so much by increasing its 'real social range', but by articulating it so that 'the known commu-nity, *creatively known* (67-8; my emphasis: that is, known through its creation in Eliot's text) is perceived to be the 'divided' relationship between the 'real social' community and the 'knowing' of it by the novelist's 'signifying consciousness': a consciousness 'not of the known or the knowable but of the to-be-known (69, 74).

What Eliot has bequeathed us in palpable form is that it is the 'signifying consciousness' itself, of the now partially estranged observer/ novelist, which defines the 'to-be-known' community she writes about. In other words, it is her *vision,* articulated in and as the text, which defamiliarises habitualised *sight,* and so allows us to 'know' a community which is unable to know itself as it gets on busily with living the 'splendid waste' of its 'real social' life. I will return to notions of 'defamiliarising vision' later (pp. 112-16).

Eliot's importance for Williams, then, lies in her ability to depict 'a knowable community, but *knowable in a new sense*' (73; my emphasis). She gives form to a consciousness which is 'thinking beyond, feeling beyond, the restrictions and limitations... [of] the defining weight, of a limited and frustrating world' (77): a consciousness 'running beyond' *(ibid.)* the present to embrace the change which historical process will bring as the future. Such a proleptic realism, to put it another way, embodies the 'to-be-known' as 'knowable'. In effect, it *creates*—Williams's own phrase, significantly, is *'literally made' (ibid.;* my emphasis)—a new form of historical knowledge by way of its textuality, and whose vision arguably has greater potential to 'think beyond, feel beyond' the determi-nate 'real social' community than, say, academic history.

To quote Seamus Heaney again, 'the literary' is 'more dedicated to the world-renewing potential of the imagined response than to the adequacy of the social one' (Heaney 1995: xvii). How such literary works are thereafter valued and hierarchised as regards their 'originality' is not presently my concern. For now, all I want to establish as a matter of definition, is that all literary works are 'creative' in respect of their original 'making' in language, whilst also potentially holding for us, in this, what Thomas Hardy called 'moments of vision' (see p. 112-15).

By way of illustrating 'the arte of making', and to mitigate the paradox that a book about literature has so far unremittingly disregarded specific examples of it, let me quote, and then offer a close reading of, Ted Hughes's poem 'The Thought-Fox' (Hughes 1957). This is not to make great claims *for* this particular poem; it is simply that the poem rather obviously and self-consciously helps to establish my substantive point:

I imagine this midnight moment's forest:

Something else is alive

Beside the clock's loneliness

And this blank page where my fingers move.

Through the window I see no star: Something more near Though deeper within darkness Is entering the loneliness:

Cold, delicately as the dark snow, A fox's nose touches twig, leaf; Two eyes serve a movement, that now And again now, and now, and now

Sets neat prints into the snow Between trees, and warily a lame Shadow lags by stump and in hollow Of a body that is bold to come

Across clearings, an eye, A widening deepening greenness, Brilliantly, concentratedly, Coming about its own business

Till, with a sudden sharp hot stink of fox

It enters the dark hole of the head.

The window is starless still; the clock ticks,

The page is printed. Let me analyse in some detail how the poem works. First, there is its internal time-frame: in stanza one, it is posited that this is a 'midnight *moment*'—which 'this...forest' belongs to ('midnight moment's' is a possessive); there is a clock, and 'this blank page where my fingers move'. We should note that the tense of 'move' implies a continuity in the present (surely invoking the famous lines, 'The Moving Finger writes; and, having writ,/Moves on', from Edward Fitzgerald's poem, *The Rubdiydt of Omar Khayyam);* and that, as we shall see, this continuity frames the whole of the rest of poem.

Stanza two opens with T seeing 'no star' through the window. If we then jump to the final two lines of the last stanza, we find that 'The window is starless still'—where 'starless still' may mean both the temporal 'still starless' and the physical 'starless *and* still', i.e. unmoving—which implies that nothing has changed in time or space during 'this midnight moment'. Equally, 'the clock ticks'—not, we may note, the continuous temporal pro-gression of, say, 'the clock ticks *on*'—again implying that between stanza one and stanza six only one tick occurs (a 'moment'), while the final line reads: 'The page is printed'. Whether 'printed' suggests that the 'moving fingers' in line four are *typing* on 'this blank page', or whether it is a metaphor for the page now having marks ('prints') upon it, is uncertain, but we will notice in a moment that the fox 'prints' the ('blank' sheet of) snow in stanza four.

In other words, the internal 'time' of the poem is exactly equated with the time of the poem's composition; so that the poem is indeed, to borrow D.G.Rossetti's apposite phrase, 'a moment's monument'.

This suggests that the line 'Something else is alive/Beside the clock's loneliness' in stanza one refers not only to the poem's fox, but also to the process of composing the poem in the poet's 'imagination'. Indeed, it opens explicitly with 'I imagine'. The crux here is the word 'Beside'—which can easily be misread as 'besides', meaning 'in addition to/as well as'— but which should be read as 'in close proximity to'/ 'next to'. That is to say, the poet's 'imagination' is located 'beside' the clock and 'this blank page where my fingers move'.

This reading can be sustained throughout the last three lines of stanza two, where the 'Something more near' may also be the onset of poetic creation which 'imagines' the poem in the 'loneliness' of 'the clock's' suspension of time (the 'moment' between 'ticks'). However, this is so far unrealised, since the page is not yet 'printed', and is thus confined 'deeper within darkness': that is, within the as yet only emergent creative process. If we again skip forward to the second line of the last stanza, we find this correlation of fox and poem picked up once more by the poem's fox entering 'the *dark* hole of the *head'* in its realised entirety, where the 'deeper darkness' of the earlier stanza is now being occupied, or possessed, by its own creation. In respect of all this, we may well feel that the poem's 'subject' is its own composition.

However, stanzas three to five of the poem clearly imply that 'Something else' and 'Something more near' is indeed 'something else': the physical presence of the approaching fox. Like many of Ted Hughes's animal and bird poems, these stanzas offer an empathetic attempt to realise the specific otherness of a non-human creature. Here, it would seem, we have a vivid poetic invocation of a fox's very foxness. The fox's cold nose 'touches twig, leaf as delicately as the falling 'dark snow' does, and its 'Two eyes serve a movement that.../Sets neat prints into the snow'.

'Serve', here, in what I will call its 'realis-tic' function, presumably means 'assists' or 'services' the fox's 'wary' movement—i.e. the fox's acute eyesight patrols the safety of its progress. But we should notice, too, that here the fox is only made up of some of the constituent elements of its being—its 'nose' and 'eyes'; and that while these may indeed be the physical features that we 'see' first when making out the presence of a fox, they are also being used here as a synec-doche for the fox as a totality. In this respect, the word 'serve' takes on a further sense: I suggest there is an 'as' tacitly under-stood between 'serve' and 'a movement', so that the two eyes, together with the nose, effectively define or delineate the fox's movement—they *'serve as'* its movement in the poem. In other words, the fox exists *only as* a trope of the poem's rhetorical strategies.

Returning to the 'realistic' depiction of the fox, we see how the staccato repetition of 'that now/And again now, and now, and now' tracks the precise movements of the fox as it 'Sets neat prints into the snow/Between trees', and we follow the 'lame/Shadow' as it 'warily' 'lags' (comes slowly, hangs back) through the forest landscape. Again, however, we should note that the 'movement' traced by the 'two eyes' only 'Sets neat *prints* in the snow', and, by implication, on the white ('blank') sheet of 'the page', as the form of its definition.

The full corpo-real presence remains unseen behind them, what we 'see' being only a 'shadow'—an 'image' or visual simulacrum—not the thing itself. The final line of this stanza announces the advent of the full reality: 'Of a body that is bold to come'. Here, the sense in which 'bold' is being used has to wait for the first line of the following stanza in order to be completed: the fox is 'bold to come/Across clearings', i.e. fearlessly out of the protec-tive 'darkness' of the 'forest'. But if we consider the meaning of 'a body bold to come' in that suspended moment between stanzas, then its sense is less clear: it seems possible to read the phrase as meaning that the body will 'come out bold', i.e. realise itself in bold definition unlike the 'shadow' we have seen hitherto (it is even possible to read 'bold', in relation to 'prints', as invoking the sense of an emphatic *type-face).*

Equally, the word 'clearings' in the next line may also suggest, not just the open spaces in the forest, but a 'clearing' of the matricial 'darkness' which has up to now enveloped the creation of the fox. The following lines in this stanza continue to portray the physical reality of the fox, its 'eye' becoming descriptively realised as itself rather than merely serving as one of the markers of the fox's 'movement': 'Coming about its own business'—'Brilliantly, concentratedly'.

But again, in my simultaneous double-reading of the poem, we may consider those two adverbs as at once felicitous descriptive words for a fox's eye, *and* a self-congratulatory comment on the poem's own realisation of *its* fox as it emerges in the poem so far. So that 'Coming about its own business' may also be a self-reflection on the poem's *'own business'*: which is to articulate itself. But at this point, the 'real' fox arrives in the sensuous form of 'a sudden sharp hot stink of fox'; although, as we have already noticed, it arrives in the 'dark hole of the *head*' (the poet's and then the reader's) and is transliterated into a 'printed page'.

The substantive point I want to make by way of this reading of Hughes's poem is that the fox and the poem are one and the same thing: fox is poem and poem is fox, since both are cre-ated simultaneously and neither would exist without the other. In other words, the 'reality' of both only resides in the linguis-tic textuality of the poem. No matter how much the poem may appear to refer to an external recognisable 'reality' of foxes, *this* way of seeing *this* fox is uniquely that of the poem as encoded in its language, just as the poem would have no sub-stance without its fabrication of the fox.

We should not forget that the opening two words of the poem—'I imagine'— determine everything which follows, nor that its title, 'The Thought-Fox', clearly attempts to signal the fox's mode of exis-tence (although 'The Poem-Fox' might be more apt). What the poem does, then, is to create a *'poietic* reality', unseen before but now realised in its specific formulation. It is this function of *creation,* together with the way in which literary texts simultaneously enable us to 'see' the new 'reality' *being* created, which lies at the heart of my definition of 'the literary'.

While accepting that not all (or even most) poems are so self-consciously 'about' their own fictive composition, I will never-theless want to propose—that the constitutive textuality of 'the literary' as a whole enables us to see the way in which any text's 'reality' is indeed textualised. However, two other possible objections must be dealt with, so that they do not seem to slide into the definition itself. First, while everything I have written above must imply that an indi-vidual text is *determinate* insofar as it is this one thing and no other, I am not claiming that this 'text-in-itself is the ultimate arbiter of its unitary 'essential' meaning.

The 'words on the page' are neither restricted in signification by the author's 'intention' nor by their unique linguistic specificity: my own reading of the poem above, in its strategic partiality of interpretation, is certain proof of this.

Second, neither am I claiming that the poem's *value* lies, in this instance, in the way it sends us back to 'life' with a new perception of 'fox-ness' (although 'the literary' may do that, as I will suggest later); rather, that it allows us to observe the *process* by which any extrinsic effectiv-ity it may have is achieved. In other words, in seeking a func-tionalist definition of 'the literary', I am simply saying *this* is what literary texts seem to *do* by dint of their self-conscious creation of themselves as '*poietic* realities'. That uses and virtues may stem from this quality I happily accept—indeed I will hope to enunciate some of them in the following chapter— but these lie in particular and partisan ascribed functions *result-ing from* this quality, not as a primary constituent of its definition.

Let us consider this quality of 'being literary' in a different way. Earlier, I quoted the phrase Thomas Hardy used as the title for one of his volumes of poems, *Moments of Vision.* A close inspection of this seemingly simple, but resonantly com-plex phrase will act as a further gloss on much of what I have said so far. The ambiguity of the word 'vision' is readily appar-ent: at once the literal 'seeing/sight' (as in '20/20 vision'); the meta-physical notion of imaginative revelation ('she had a vision'); and the proleptic ability to see through or beyond the immediate ('he has vision', 'her vision of the future').

The ambiguity of the cluster of inflexions around 'moments', how-ever, is rather less obvious. Of course, 'moments' are brief fractions of time, usually implying stopped fragments in the temporal process (as in 'this midnight moment', 'wait a moment', 'magic moments' or 'moment of truth'), and this is certainly the upper meaning in Hardy's title: particular instances of 'vision'. But there are two other senses which haunt the fringes of the word: first, that of serious conse-quence ('momentous', 'matters of pith and moment'); second, and for my purposes here more fertile, that within physics which means the measure of a turning effect (as in 'the moment of a force'). So Hardy's phrase may imply that the instants of vision are important ('moments' of great 'moment'), but also that the vision is somehow itself in motion: turning, pivoting, swinging round a point.

If we think, then, of the effect of a turning vision, in the most literal sense, we must conceive of a 'seeing' which moves round its object (consider astronauts observing earth from their circulating spacecraft), and which can theoretically move round it through 360 degrees in any direction. Move round your chair, *looking* at it, and you will al various stages see it from all sides and angles. In other words, you will be able to apprehend it as a totality, a three-dimensional entity. But two things may strike you: one, if you stopped the moment when you were theoretically looking straight up at it from below (chair suspended absolutely vertically above you), the 'image' from that 'moment of vision' would look remarkably unlike one's standard received image of a chair. (Think of that kind of trick-photography which takes pictures of familiar objects from unfamiliar angles: where a bucket, for example, taken directly from above, becomes no more than a set of concentric circles.)

Two, how on earth (and I use this phrase here, as will become apparent, not merely as a manner of speaking) would you represent, *in visual terms,* your total apprehension of the complete three-dimensional chair: the chair in all its chair-ness? How, indeed, would you 'see' it all, all in one moment? Two senses of 'moment'—turning and stopped instant of time —clash here in fundamental contradiction: one is, precisely, *in motion,* in time; the other, equally precisely, is still, 'stopped', out of temporal process. Is there any way of resolving this physical impossibility? Well, yes, but only if we return to the other term in the phrase under consideration: 'vision'.

For vision, in what I have called its metaphysical senses, allows us (but especially the creative artist) to break out of the space/time trap of the third dimension, and enter that zone of relativity beyond the determinate factors of time and space. Put simply and crudely, 'vision' allows us to 'see' the future, or 'envision' another world; but it would also enable us to see, in one totalising 'moment' (in this case, *both* stopped instant *and* full circular movement) all of our chair at the same time. This fourth-dimensional liberation from space/time, this *envisioned* 'simultaneity' of experience, was the principle on which the modernist painters early this century based their dislocations of conventional realist/mimetic form. That is why one can see both profiles of a face simultaneously in Cubist portraits, or a violin dismantled with all its planes simultaneously displayed on the two-dimensional picture-surface of a modernist still-life.

'Vision', then, both as a momentary revelation of the very 'this-ness' of something (what James Joyce, in *Stephen Hero*, called an 'epiphany' [1944/56] 1969:216-18) and as a 'turning' or destabilising perception, is a way of breaking with the conventional, familiar, naturalised representations approved by 'commonsense'. Indeed, it ruptures a world constructed very largely by such a 'realist' cultural ideology: one which has a profound antipathy to the strange, the disturbing, the unset-tling, the improbable or implausible, all of which qualities are themselves frequently the result of, precisely, vision and 'the visionary'.

'Vision', in this binary sense ('double vision'?), is to 're-vision' the always already visioned—both in terms of 'revis-ing' and of 're-envisioning'. To put it another way, it is a way of 'defamiliarising', of 'making strange', the naturalised or habitualised world of conventional perceptual reality, of 'seeing things as they really are'. I have strategically chosen the Russian Formalists' terms for the notion of 'estrangement' here so that I can return to it a little more fully in a moment.

But Hardy himself, in the specific context of distancing him-self from 'realism' in (literary) art, pinpoints the effect of the process incident on such 'moments of vision' when he writes:

> *Art is a disproportioning—(i.e. distorting, throwing out of proportion)—of realities, to show more clearly the features that matter in those realities, which, if merely copied or reported inventorially, might possibly be observed, but would more probably be overlooked. Hence, 'realism' is not Art. (F.E.Hardy, [1928/30] 1975:228-9)*

I will argue that realism is very much a part of literary 'Art', and that it does, in fact, 'disproportion' reality—perhaps most revealingly when at its most realistic, but when read against the 'natural' grain (see pp. 141-8). Nevertheless, we can still see in Hardy's formulation strong affinities with Henry James's notion of art identifying a 'subject' in the 'splendid waste' of life, and with Raymond Williams's sense of newly perceptible forms of consciousness emerging from the 'know-able communities' realised in literary fictions. But in this attempt here to define the *effect* of 'the literary', let us pick up the consonance between Hardy's concept of 'disproportioning' and the Russian Formalist notion of 'defamiliarising', since my definition will, in part, be seen to be cognate with certain aspects of Formalist thinking.

The concept of 'defamiliarisation' derives from the Russian word *ostranenie,* meaning 'making strange' or 'estrangement'. The critic Victor Shklovsky argued that we can never retain the freshness of our perceptions of things because the processes of our cultural and social life cause them to become 'naturalised' or 'automatised'.

The special task of literature is to give us back our awareness of things which have become habitualised in our daily perception of them, as though we were seeing them for the very first time (Shklovsky [1917] 1965:13). The 'pure' formalism of the earlier Formalists' work, however, lies in the fact that they were not so much interested in the perceptions themselves as in the nature of the devices which produce the effect of 'defamiliarisation'; an image, therefore, was merely a 'device of poetic language'. As Shklovsky wrote:

> *The technique of art is to make objects 'unfamiliar, to make forms difficult, to increase the difficulty and length of perception, because the process of perception is an aes-thetic end in itself and must be prolonged. Art* is a way of experiencing the artfulness of an object; the object is not important. (ibid.: *12; Shklovsky's emphasis)*

If we think of the Ted Hughes poem in this spirit, we would say that the fox as 'object' is 'not important', but that our per-ceiving of it by way of the defamiliarising 'devices' of the poem is 'an aesthetic end in itself. Conversely, my own reading of the poem suggests that what *is* 'important' is our perceiving of the 'artfulness' of *the poem itself* as 'object'—not as 'an aesthetic end in itself, but in its displaying of how 'the aesthetic' functions.

The Formalists' technical focus also led them to treat 'liter-ary' language as of a special kind, which achieves its distinctiveness by deviating from and distorting 'practical' language. While the latter is used for acts of communication, literary lan-guage has no practical function of this kind at all except to make us 'see' differently. What distinguishes it from 'practical' language is its *constructed* quality, whose special property is its 'foregrounding' of the rhetorical devices themselves, and which, in so doing, draws attention to the fact that the utter-ance is uncommon ('peculiar language'). This changes our mode of perception from the 'automatised' to the 'artistic', and hence renovates the resources of a language worn smooth by conventional usage.

It is on the tropes and figures of this 'constructedness' that Formalism concentrates, proposing that the way in which a literary text 'lays bare' its own devices is its most essential literary quality. The Formalists took Laurence Sterne's *Tristram Sbandyas* a key text in exposing its own fic-tiveness as a novel (see Shklovsky [1921] 1965), and thus, by implication, the artificiality of the whole genre's supposed 'real-ism'. But Bertolt Brecht's 'alienation effect' in the theatre, where the audience is forced by a play's self-revealing devices to recognise that it is indeed watching a *play,* and the self-reflexivity of much postmodernist fiction, would be equally good examples of the processs of 'laying bare'—albeit with political or strategic functions which go well beyond the For-malists' notion of it as defining 'literariness'.

However, in their belief that language was a social phe-nomenon and could not be separated from ideology, the theo-rists/critics associated with the 'Bakhtin School' (see pp. 81-3) returned 'the literary' to its wider cultural, historical and social relations. 'The language of art', Medvedev, for example, observes, 'is only a dialect of a single social language'. Further, by shifting the emphasis of interest from 'the device' (static) to 'function' (dynamic), 'defamiliarisation' becomes not an essential(ist) *property* of the literary, but an historically determinate *effect* of its textuality in resisting the relentless processes of naturalisation, habitualisation or automatisation. It also follows from this 'functional' conception of defamiliari-sation that literature's variability of function, meaning and evaluation in different societies and periods is a reflex of change and historical process, thereby undermining any idea of a fixed canon of 'Literature' in which eternal verities are enshrined.

Clearly, my own notion of 'the literary' has much in com-mon with this latter position, since, on the one hand, I accept that there can be no such thing as a distinct 'literary language' in terms of its linguistic or rhetorical properties (see pp. 15-16, and Attridge 1988, pp. 94-5); and, on the other, I wish to situ-ate a definition of 'the literary' in its historical, cultural and social locations, functions and effects, rather than in terms of its aesthetic essence.

But I also wish, nevertheless, in what I suppose may be called a formalist-materialist critical method, to tread a narrow line between affirming the extrinsic cultural definition of 'the literary' and retaining a sense of its inherent *difference* from both other forms of written discourse and other modes of cultural production, since it will be in this, finally, that the claims I make for 'the literary' as a discrete cultural category must reside.

Formalism influenced both Structuralist and Marxist critical and cultural theory, and it is to the 'Structuralist-Marxist' philosopher, Louis Althusser (see also p. 84, n. 7), that I now turn in order to try and negotiate the difficult manoeuvre out-lined above. Althusser spends very little time on literature in his works, but some brief comments in his short essay, 'A Let-ter on Art', are of some help here. He claims that the effect of 'the specificity' or 'peculiarity of art' (in contradistinction to 'knowledge' or 'science') is: 'to "make us see"..."make us per-ceive", "make us feel" something which *alludes* to reality... [that is] the *ideology* from which it is born, in which it bathes, from which it detaches itself as art, and to which it *alludes'* (Althusser [1966] 1977:204; Althusser's emphases here and below).

In other words, art achieves 'a *retreat,* an *internaldis-tantiation' (ibid.),* precisely because of its formal composition as art, from its informing ideology. Because novels give 'form' to ideology as 'the "lived" experience of individuals', they 'make us see' 'the spontaneous "lived experience" of ideology in its peculiar relationship to the real' (204-5), and in so doing critically unmask the ideology in which the novels are neverthe-less still 'held'. Althusser concludes that: 'the real difference between art and science lies in the *specific farm* in which they give us the same object in quite different ways: art in the form of "seeing" and "perceiving" or "feeling", science in the form of *knowledge* (in the strict sense, by concepts)' (205). What he also recognises is that we need 'an adequate (scientific) *knowl-edge* of the processes which produce the "aesthetic effect" of a work of art' (206); that he does not offer one is, I suspect, because the analysis of 'the processes', rather than the 'effects' themselves, would again lead up the Formalist blind alley.

Nevertheless, in an earlier essay focussed partly on Brecht, Althusser suggests that, rather than in its ordered surface unity, it is in the 'silences' or ideological suppressions and in 'the dynamic' of its 'latent asymmetrical-critical structure', that literature promotes the 'internal dissociation' which works upon and exposes ideology (Althusser [1962] 1977:142). It is to these that the critic must attend, not in an explanative hermeneutic reading, but in a 'symptomatic' one which reads the tell-tale signs of an informing but unacknowledged condi-tion below the surface.

My reference to Althusser's ideas here is not to emphasise 'ideology' in relation to 'the literary' (whether that is all it enables us to 'see' will be further examined in Chapter 5). Rather, it is to foreground his sense both that the 'different''*specific form*' of a literary text is a crucial factor in its 'defamiliarising' of the naturalised and automatised within the social and cultural order (ideology), and that it has a *social and cultural effect* in thus exposing the way ideology relates us to 'the real'. This dual perception of 'form' and 'effect' neatly brings together the various strands of my argument so far. For the crucial point is that the 'special' *function* of 'the literary'— that which distinguishes it from other kinds of cultural production—does indeed seem to lie in its *formal* 'making' of newly perceptible '*poietic* realities', in its textualised defamiliarising 'moments of vision', and in the 'patterns' or 'sense of subject' 'knowably' inscribed in its linguistic texture.

Two disclaimers must be made, however, in relation to this assertion. First, to emphasise 'the literary' as a special cate-gory, is to acknowledge that it is recognisable as such in all historical periods and cultures, but simultaneously to accept that it will be differently inflected within them. In other words, I am not defining *the category in itself* as unchanging and tran-shistorical. Second, in foregrounding the literary text's 'mak-ing' of a specific '*poietic* reality', I am not implying that this once and for all determines and fixes its meaning throughout history: that it is a 'moment of vision for all time.

On the con-trary, while the text itself may remain by and large the same, its readability, its meanings and functions, will be the product, precisely, of *that text's* insertion in history. In other words, it may defamiliarise differently in different historical and cultural locales, while also being itself defamiliarised by its insertion in them. Shakespeare's *The Tempest,* for example, while remaining textually the same, functions differently in the context of postcolonialism than it did, say, when colonialism was at its most ideologically dynamic.

Where once it may have helped subliminally to 'fix' the colonial relationship (Prospero and Caliban) between Europe and its 'others' by establishing, in Helen Tiffin's words, 'patterns of reading alterity at the same time as it inscribed the "fixity" of that alterity, naturalising difference within its own cognitive codes' (Tiffin [1987] 1995:98), it can now be seen to defamiliarise the ideology in which it is complicit. The *poietic* reality 'made' in *the specific textuality* of that text, to put it emphatically, is witness to its ability to provide a permanent 'pattern' or 'shaping' of histori-cal reality which can then be decoded differentially in and on behalf of later histories.

Of course, much of what I have said above about 'the literary' could just as well be said, too, of other art forms such as music, painting or film (including TV). They are also 'creative' in the senses I have noted earlier; they also construct 'aesthetic realities' which have an oblique relationship to lived reality; they also produce 'moments of vision' which defamiliarise the 'automatised' world, and so on. By nevertheless still insisting on its *difference* from, the other arts, and on the need to retain a discrete space or domain for it, I have no intention of trying to privilege 'the literary' or suggest that it is *superior* to music or painting or film. I merely wish to insist that it is indeed dif-ferent from, and does different things to, those art forms.

Here, the crucial factor is my original definition, of what constitutes the subject-matter of the present book: that literature is in *written* form, and that its originating modality and final point of reference is its existence as written (now printed) text.

While I hope to have established 'the literary's' difference from other kinds of written discourse by way of my remarks on its 'self-consciousness' and on 'literary competence', what makes it different to music, for example, is that the latter is not primarily a form of *linguistic* notation. Even when it has 'words' associated with it, and that although it is, in a sense, 'written (as sheet music or score), it is is not 'read' in the same way as the linguistic textuality of literature is. We do not read music to comprehend a conceptual totality made up of words which have a social and cultural referentiality beyond their specific formulation as 'the text', but in order to 'hear' it as a musical structure.

Furthermore, written music assumes *perfor-mance* by instrument or voice, which may be said to become its full realisation. As with produced or performed drama, therefore, a mediating interpretation intervenes between 'text' and recipient prior to the subjective act of interpretation which occurs when one reads a literary text for the first time. An indi-vidual performance is thus transient (even if 'memorable'); but, unlike drama, there is no linguistic text to return to after the event, since even recordings are only ever of the particular *per-formance.* So that, for example, at the very end of Samuel Beckett's *Waiting for Godot,* following Estragon and Vladimir's decision: 'Well? shall we go? ...Yes, let's go', we can still register the full force of that resonating final stage-direction: '*They do not move*' (Beckett [1956] 1970:94).

A play, then, is arguably a readable totality without necessarily being performed, and is, crucially, accessible to any person who can read but is without the more specialist skill of reading music. Those who have this ability, of course, can return to the score after the evanescent performance, but the system of nota-tion, unlike that of the ('literary') play-text, will still not be the fundamentally acculturated linguistic notation possessed by any literate person. In addition, and as we will also see below in respect of painting and film, the logistics of attending per-formances constitute a further distinguishing feature between music and 'the literary' (all you can listen to in bed, for instance, would be a *recording* of a concert). Music, to put it simply, functions in different kinds of ways to literature, precisely in not having a commonly accessible linguistic referent for private reading.

Apropos of the visual arts, we may say that, unlike music, we have a permanent perceptible referent in its totality (the painting or sculpture as physical object); but the difference here to 'the literary' is again that a painting, for example, is not made up of words, but of visual images constructed in paint on a surface for apprehension primarily through sight. If it were to be argued that reading words is *also* first of all an act of sight, we can counter this, in terms of the specificity of 'the literary', by saying that a blind person who has never seen a painting could indeed have it described to them, but the act of describing it would, in effect, be a mediating act of interpretation.

Conversely, a person having a literary work read to them would receive—except, perhaps, in the vocal inflections of the reader—as unmediated a sense of the text as if they been able to read it themselves in the first place. And if the reading were on tape, they would have a permanent reference as 'text'. By contrast, a tape-recording of someone describing the paint-ing would only perpetuate the mediating interpretative description, as, in a sense, does a recording of performed music.

A further significant difference between the visual arts and 'the literary' is also perceptible here, one which is also a cen-tral defining characteristic of the latter as a pervasive cultural medium. I have argued that one of the defining terms of 'the literary' is the 'originality' implicit in any text's uniqueness, and this is a central claim made for the individual visual art-object too. But the fact that the determinate medium of literature sinçe the invention of printing has been that it appears *in print* means that the 'original' work is expected to be exten-sively *reproducible* without damaging or detracting from the experiencing of the work itself. Photographic reproduction of paintings, on the other hand, while now of very high quality, is never regarded as equivalent to seeing 'the real thing': paint-ings are not 'made' to be reproduced, whereas literary works in our culture are.

It follows from this that to experience the totality of a painting one must go and see the original wher-ever it is located, in a museum, art gallery or art dealer's show-room. But it may be either entirely inaccessible, if it is in a private collection, say, or logistically difficult to refer to on countless occasions: to see the 'Mona Lisa' means going to Paris; and in what sense, following the earthquakes in central Italy, can the Cimabue frescoes now be seen in a form other than that of inadequate reproduction? The very reproducibility of literature means that it is readily and cheaply accessible for perusal, both in its general availability (shops, libraries) and in its physical permanence: if my *copy* (note the word) of *Anna Karenina* gets burnt, I can buy another 'copy' immediately, but that 'copy' will be no different or inferior to the 'copy' that was burnt. A 'copy' of a painting, on the other hand, however good, and even if done by another talented artist, will not sub-stitute for 'the original'—as sale prices, if nothing else, make clear. Indeed, the conflation of financial and aesthetic evalua-tion in respect of the visual arts is itself pointedly distinctive.

Film and forms of radio and television production, of course, have all the wide access and reproducibility I have been suggesting are characteristic of 'the literary', and it is often now argued that these media are the forms in which fictional narrative and drama find their most innovative contemporary expression. Nevertheless, as I have pointed out on a number of occasions in the course of this book, they do not seem to have curtailed the reading of literature; and the answer to this may lie in the difference again between these media and 'the literary'. First, we may note once more the fact that they are not primarily *written* forms; for while there is always a *script* on which the finished product is based, the script is granted lit-tle status or autonomy as an object of reading in and for itself. While this means that, like music and drama—if not more so— what we see in the cinema or living-room is the always already mediated/interpreted production or performance of an originary text. But *unlike* both music (score) or drama (play), only rarely do TV or film viewers get to see a script at all, and when they *are* published in print form, they arguably enter the 'domain of the literary' themselves. For example, both Michael Ondaatje's novel *The English Patient* and Anthony Minghella's screen-play for the film of the 'same'—which is, in fact, rather different—are currently on sale as discrete works with identical main titles: so that a careless buyer may well pick up either as 'the novel'.

A number of further distinctions also accrue from the fact that the terms *cinema/cinematic* derive from the word 'kinematic', i.e. pertaining to *motion:* from the Greek *kinemat, kinema:* 'movement', from *kinein:* 'move' (which also gives us the word 'kinetic': 'in motion, 'moving'), and are thus, as the early names for film make clear, 'moving pictures', 'motion pictures', 'movies'. The first point is that the primary modality of these media is indeed *pictures,* where most of the screen 'business' we observe is communicated visually and dialogue is secondary.

So that the script-writing of an adaptation of a literary text will involve the transference of much written dialogue into visually enacted forms; and, *therefore,* the experiencing of the 'text' will be quite different from that of reading the written word. Secondly, these pictures are, as we have heard, '*motion* pictures', which means that if we watch a film in a cinema, or a one-off television broadcast, differential logistics of the kind we noted in relation to music and painting also obtain. For instance, one cannot currently watch a film, or indeed a video-recording, on the bus, tube or train, because they are not 'portable' in the way books are.

Nor can we easily return to 'the text' in the way that we can with a literary work: we cannot keep returning to the cinema, with its regu-larly changing repertoire, summon up at will the 'repeat' we missed on television, or turn back the film/TV programme which is presently running, in order to 'review' in whole or in part what we have seen flash in front of us for the first time.

Of course, the wide availablity of video-recordings does now mean that we can both repeatedly see films or TV programmes we like, and, by dint of the rewind button, turn back con-stantly to parts we wish to study in detail.

Even so, we only turn back to 'pictures in motion', to the 'kinetic' modality which defines film and distinguishes it from literature, and can only hold it still by using the 'pause' button—a device which *ipso facto* interrupts the essentially kinetic modality of the form. Although individual words in a written text are in sequence and we read them in a progressive manner, they do not themselves 'move' as a determinate feature of their meaningfulness.

A comic but telling exemplification of this difference in liter-ary and cinematic modes is the last chapter of David Lodge's novel, *Changing Places*. Entitled 'Ending', it is presented as a film-script in which one of the characters is made to ask— ostensibly about the events she is involved in: 'Where is this all going to *end?*' (Lodge 1975:227). In fact, the question signals the whole chapter's self-reflexive commentary on the nature of endings in life, film and written fiction, as the closing para-graphs (pointedly running across the novel's final two pages) make explicit:

PHILIP: You remember that passage in Northanger Abbey where Jane Austen says she's afraid that her readers will have guessed that a happy ending is coming up at any moment.

MORRIS: (nods) Quote, "Seeing in the tell-tale compression of the pages before them that we are all hastening together to perfect felicity." Unquote.

PHILIP: That's it. Well, that's something the novelist can't help giving away, isn't it, that his book is shortly coming to an end? It may not be a happy ending, nowadays, but he can't dis-guise the tell-tale compression of the pages....

I mean, mentally, you brace yourself for the ending of a novel. As you're reading, you're aware of the fact that there's only a page or two left in the book, and you get ready to close it. But with a film [page-break in Lodge's own text] there's no way of telling, especially nowadays, when films are much more loosely structured, much more ambivalent, than they used to be.

There's no way of telling which frame is going to be the last. The film is going along, just as life goes along, people are behaving, doing things, drinking, talking, and we're watching them, and at any point the director chooses, without warning, without any-thing being resolved, or explained, or wound up, it can just...end.

PHILIP: (shrugs) The camera stops, freezing him in mid-gesture. (233-4)

There follow the last words of the novel: 'THE END'.

Lodge is, of course, amusingly having it both ways in destabilising the distinction between film and novel endings; but even so, *physi-cally* we know that we are indeed on the penultimate page of his novel before we turn the page and see 'THE END' (and then turn back to re-read it). In this, it confirms my point about the permanently static *presence* of the literary text com-pared to the continuously kinetic *absence* of the filmic one. But I may also point to the way Lodge's ending indicates how 'the literary' extrapolates, and *fixes* for perusal, a complex 'subject' from what Thomas Carlyle called 'the Chaos of Being' of lived experience (Carlyle [1830] 1971:55): the physical realisation, in the novel's printed textuality, of the arbitrariness of 'endings'.

In claiming as I have that a fundamental defining principle of 'the literary' is that it is reproducible in print, I may seem to be contradicting myself, since I have stated in Chapter 2 that liter-ature (if not 'Literature') unquestionably predates the inven-tion of printing by thousands of years. But it was precisely the transcription of literary works into written texts by the earliest scholars (see p. 27) which also made them available for mechanical reproduction when printing was invented. The canonic classics of the Western tradition, it could thus be argued, have only become such because they were susceptible to reproducibilty in print. In the post-Gutenbergian order, however, what the impact on 'the literary' of computerised discourses such as hypertext will be, it is too soon to know.

A recent newspaper article on the 'hypertext novel' suggests (sig-nificantly, in the context of what I have had to say about 'the literary' differing from other art forms) that, in its attempts 'to break the bounds of the printed page and the models of linear narrative implied by the printed page', this will be 'an original art form—literature with cinematic or live performance quali-ties—not a replacement for a book' (Lillington 1997:2). How-ever, the inclusion of hypertext fiction in the present *Norton Anthology of Postmodern American Fiction,* and the fact that the newspaper tells us that 'a comfortable reading device [for hypertext] is probably not far off *(ibid.),* may suggest other-wise. But if 'the book' *does* survive, and widespread repro-ducibility is indeed one of its informing characteristics, then CD Rom and the Internet alone suggest that the day of 'the literary' may only just be dawning.

A centrally determining characteristic of 'the literary', then, along with the other attributes I have attempted to assign to it, is that it is realised in a tangible object which is readily present for close inspection or re-reading, and that it does not have to be performed (preemptively interpreted) in order to be read for the first time as unmediated text. Of course, publishing, reviewing and academic criticism—if not, by definition, 'liter-ary competence' itself—mean that no literary text can ever be entirely unmediated (for example, by being described as 'a clas-sic', 'Caribbean poetry', 'a romance', 'Restoration Comedy', etc.).

But I am working on the hypothesis that a reader coming to such a text for the first time will read it 'for themselves' as the primary act of comprehension. As a result of this common accessibility and unmediatedness, therefore, 'the literary' is amongst the most democratic of art forms: as witnessed both in its pervasive popularity, and in its fear-induced censorship by those who most wish to curtail freedoms. It is for these reasons that its *uses,* both as a practice of writing and as an object of reading, have been and remain so legion, multifari-ous, and valued. But if this substantive functionalist claim for the importance of 'the literary'—and for its retention as a cru-cial 'space' in contemporary and future culture—is to be justi-fied and sustained, my definition of it will need to be grounded in the identification of some of those uses. It is to a more extended and illustrated analysis of 'the uses of the literary', therefore, that the next chapter now turns.

5

The Uses of the Word 'Literary'

NEWSTORIES

In answer to her own question: 'Why Read?', Diane Elam replies: precisely because 'reading literature has the great poten-tial to be totally useless.... Reading literature is not a guaran-tee; it is a possibility' (Elam 1997:12; her emphasis). Her argument concerns the need to preserve a space, specifically within the contemporary 'corporate' university, for the kind of thinking that literature promotes. Literature, she notes, is bound by its own temporality, but 'something always remains, a literary leftover, waiting to be read': so that reading is, in fact,

> *a re-thinking, a* literary questioning *that continues to ques-tion the question, including the very question of literature itself. ... [T]he nothingness and potential uselessness of reading keeps thought open as a question, as questioning, so that even answers are part of questioning. (13; her emphasis)*

I absolutely take her point, but would suggest that paradoxi-cally it is in that very 'nothingness and potential uselessness' that the *uses* of 'the literary' do indeed lie. If, as Elam says, something always remains in literature—'a residual, a leftover from the past demanding to be thought as a question for the future' *(ibid.),* and if we subsume within her notion of 'the past' a present which is always already past—then the contemporary *usefulness* of that resource cries out to be explored.

What this final chapter will seek to offer, by way of readings of selected literary texts from the different genres, kinds, peri-ods and cultures, are some specific examples of the diverse uses which that 'residual' inscribed in literature, both past and present, may hold for us today. I employ the word 'uses', therefore, rather less in the sense of productive agency (i.e. to what use was the writer putting 'the literary' as s/he wrote her text?) than in the receptive sense of its 'functions' or 'effects' with regard to contemporary readers.

My suggestions are necessarily partial, tentative and provisional, since the whole trajectory of my argument here is based on the recognition of the differences of reading which the synchronic and diachronic positioning of readers makes inevitable. Indeed, that is a central reason why the permanently accessible 'leftover' of literature is so important to us: it is always there, in Elam's phrase, 'waiting to be read', prompting variable questions *about* the world in which it was produced and *for* the world in which it is being consumed.

Apropos, I have crudely distinguished in what fol-lows between 'past literature' and 'contemporary literature', because, while all literature is, in a sense and as I have sug-gested, 'contemporary', we will find differently inflected 'uses' in relation to literature which has come down to us from the historical past, not least in its cultural inscription by way of the old concept, 'Literature'. But before I turn to some examples of these two broad categories, I want to introduce one free-floating 'use of the literary' which may appear frivolous but which is, in fact, fundamental to its continuing popularity and cultural prevalency.

As with other art forms—albeit in the determinate form which distinguishes it from them (see pp. 120-7)—literature gives *pleasure:* people simply seem to *like* reading it. Any num-ber of reasons may be adduced for this: insomnia, curiosity, to pass the time, to obviate boredom, to stimulate thought, for excitement or escape, to find out what happens, to admire ver-bal dexterity, to enter realms of otherwise inaccessible experience, to contemplate characters like/unlike ourselves, and so on.

Or alternatively there may be no adducible reason at all: just *liking*. It behoves literary professionals to acknowledge that behind all the science, theory and practice of literary study lies the fundamental and irrational premise of a contingent 'liking'. No doubt there are social, psychological, and cultural explanations for every individual reader's predilections—*their* acquisition of *their* particular variant of 'literary competence' (see pp. 98-100)—but given a particular example al a particu-lar moment, the hardest question to answer is just why we like reading, and, even more disturbingly, why we like reading some literary texts better than others. As a professional critic and teacher, I can come up with explanations and rationalisa-tions for my own preferences; and within the seminar-room, of course, when confronted with the response: 'I didn't really like this book', I will harry the poor student to explain that remark. But if I am honest, I know that residually I just *like* some things and not others.

I am ashamed to say that I have only recently read for the first time Gabriel Garcia Marquez's *One Hundred Years of Solitude* and Isabel Allende's *The House of the Spirits.* Other people tell me that Marquez's novel is magnificent, but I read the two books in the 'wrong' order (Allende before Marquez), and am aware that Allende's novel is profoundly influenced by Marquez's, if not parasitic on it. I can identify the characteristic achievements and prob-lems in both books—but deep down I must acknowledge that I simply *like* the Allende far better than the Marquez. Family and friends 'know' the kinds of books I will/am likely to like and which not.

Whether it was reading Donne's poetry and T.S.Eliot's 'The Love Song of J.Alfred Prufrock' at an early and formative moment, I still read them now with enormous pleasure, whereas I never readily go to Milton or Ezra Pound; I cannot get on with Shelley, while enjoying Keats; I infinitely prefer *King Lear* to *Othello;* I wish I had written Christopher Isherwood's 'Berlin novels but not Giinter Grass's *The Tin Drum;* and so on. It is simply important to accept that liking is the fundamental premise on which other potential 'uses' rest; without liking (and I am not suggesting that liking cannot be learnt), the functions and effects I outline below will never have a chance to be realised. In a way, I suppose, my notion of 'liking' is analogous to Diane Elam's positing of the 'nothing-ness of reading': it establishes the space in which the uses can emerge.

THE LITERARY' AS HISTORY

The quantity, diversity and heterogeneity of literature defies any even remote possibility of a comprehensive survey of 'the uses of the literary' at the present time, just as it also precludes the selection of speciously 'representative' examples. What fol-lows, therefore, is an evidently partial choice of literary writ-ing: texts selected for their accessibility and/or familiarity, but which nevertheless involve many different kinds of production and which focus, as a unique form of historical knowledge, issues of politics, race and gender. While I can imagine the gri-maces of the politically incorrect as they hear me trotting out the predictable trinity of terms from what they see as the new orthodoxy, I will only retort that those three issues do, in fact, incorporate rather a lot of what is central to human experi-ence, and that it would be a peculiarly impoverished literature and a feeble literary criticism which passed them by for other less 'fashionable' topics, whatever they may be.

The kinds of writing which I propose to consider all relate 'the literary' to history in various different ways, and all are what I will call 'newstories'. This elided word is intended to exploit the unresolved ambiguity between 'new stories' and 'news-stories', a slippage amusingly focussed by Sally Shering-ham's children's tale *Clifford the Sheep,* in which Clifford delivers newspapers: 'He was also an excellent story-teller, so when he was a bit short of news, he made up some stories' (Sheringham 1986:10). Such 'newstories', I want to argue, and with the correlation between 'history' and 'story' firmly in mind, somehow offer us a kind of history for our own times: special forms of access to the past ('old stories' re-read in the present invariably become 'newstories' too), and to the experience of living in contemporary culture which we ignore at our peril or loss. In this, and in diversely addressing the 'trinity' of issues mentioned above, these examples of 'the literary' cru-cially exemplify what Michael Dash has called 'a counter-culture of the imagination (Dash [1974] 1995:200).

It is worth noting that the words 'history' and 'story' in English both derive from the Greek *historia:* 'learning by inquiry'—from *histor:* 'a person who knows or sees'—so that, in its origin, 'story' implies a *form of knowledge,* a *way of knowing.* Our words come down to us by way of the earlier English usage in which both 'story' and 'history' can be 'an account of either imaginary events or of events supposed to be true' (Williams 1976:119). But where the modern French word *histoire* retains both the senses 'story' and 'history', from the fifteenth century onwards the English word bifurcates, with 'history' coming to mean 'an account of past real events', while 'story' includes 'less formal accounts of past events and accounts of imagined events' *(ibid).*

We should remember, though, that in the early period of the English novel, Henry Fielding entitled his 'new' work of fiction *The History of Tom Jones.* Furthermore, in the process of setting up a cluster of words and meanings in which it is possible to trace the correla-tion: story>history>knowledge, we may also note that the word 'narrative' (which originates in the Latin *narrarel narratum.* 'to tell or relate') is derived ultimately from the archaic word *gnarus,* which significantly meant 'knowing'. *Gnarus* is also the source of our word 'cognition': 'the act or faculty of knowing—the product of this, a perception or insight'. 'Perception' *(seeing)* and 'insight' *(vision)* are precisely what I am claiming 'the literary' offers us. Both 'story' and 'his-tory', then, are narratively organised ways of knowing about the past; and 'the past', of course, can be as recent as a moment ago.

But history, it may be argued, presents itself as uneqivocally concerned with 'the real world', with *fact,* with giving a seri-ous and truthful account of 'past real events'. So why am I pairing it with 'story'? As Thomas Carlyle pointed out long before postmodernism was heard of, where in 'acted History' events are *'simultaneous',* or what he calls a 'Chaos of Being', in written History' the record of them is as a *'series':* 'Narra-tive is *linear,* Action is *solid'* (Carlyle [1830] 1971:55; his emphases). Two consequences follow from this: first, that his-tory can only offer an inadequate account of the simultaneity of 'solid Action, one which is, by definition, partial, but which purports to be the whole truth; and second, that History-writing is indeed 'Narrative', a 'story' which makes knowledge possible by 'forging' 'patterns' or a 'sense of subject' out of the 'Chaos of Being' which is the totality of past and present experience. If we hear echoes in this of my definition of 'the literary' in Chapter 4, it will not be fortuitous.

Furthermore, as modern historiography itself insinuates, the facticity of fact is variable: when does a fact become a fact; who says it is one, and why; can there be an uninterpreted fact? Do not historians 'reproduce' or 'write' the past in terms of their own present ideological positioning;

and is not written history, then, just as *fabricated* as any other discourse? But this raises a further peremptory question: *whose* past is being passed off as *the* Past?—one central to non-Eurocentric histo-ries, for example, or to the 'herstory' of an anti-patriarchal women's history.

Until recently, women and colonised peoples had been written out of the colonialist/patriarchal discourses of 'his-story', except in the terms in which that dominant narrative chose to introduce and display them. Telling another, differently inflected, narrative al once proclaims the endemic partiality of 'hisstory' (indeed, of *any* history), and opens the possibility for alternative liberating histories which have been silenced by the 'official' discourses of Authorised History. The form in which these histories may be written, and the nature of what they do, is the subject of this chapter; and in this context, it is worth noting a comment by Juliet Mitchell on early women novelists.

They were trying, she says, 'to *create* a his-tory from a state of flux... The novel is the prime example of the way women start to *create* themselves as social subjects under bourgeois capitalism—*create* themselves as a category: women' (Mitchell [1966] 1984:288-9). I have italicised 'cre-ate' in this quotation because it illustrates what I have suggested in Chapter 4 is a fundamental characteristic of 'the literary': i.e. that it 'brings into being/forms out of nothing/ constitutes for the first time'. What we perceive here is 'the literary' as a proactive writing of history in order to discover— or rather, 'form out of nothing'— an identity in a social forma-tion whose dominant discourses would consign a repressed group to silence: 'hidden from/by hisstory', women wrote themselves in *story*—'herstory' precisely. I will return to such 'creative' [hi]story-writing in the contemporary context later in the chapter. The key-word in defining my term 'newstories', however, is indeed 'novel'—although in no sense do I limit my coinage to prose fiction alone. Both modern English senses of 'novel' (the literary genre, and 'new in one's experience, innovating, inge-nious, having an element of the unexpected') derive originally from the Latin *novus:* 'new'. But the former sense comes into English in the sixteenth century from the Italian *novella (storia):* 'a little new (story)'; while the latter derives from the French *nouvelle,* which in its modern form still carries the senses, at once, of 'new, novel' and—importantly—*'news'.*

The English literary term 'the novel', it can be argued, retains traces of all these senses: 'a new story'; 'new, innovating, strange'—perhaps even 'making strange or 'defamiliarising'; and offering 'news'—information or 'insights'—about social life. 'Newstories', to repeat then, are at once 'new' and 'news' stories which offer us histories (and herstories) of the past and the present. The nature of what they may tell us, and how they do it, will comprise the rest of this chapter. I will look first at some of the ways by which literature from the past may pro-vide us with 'new' historical understanding.

PAST AS HISTORY

The crucial differences between 'past literature' and that which I am calling 'contemporary' (i.e. roughly post-Second World War) are: first, that such writings are the product of historical societies and cultures which seem more or less remote from our own, and consequently that we may wish to read them in terms of what they convey to us about their own past. Second, given this, we may also want to ascertain why we still read them today, and what relevance they have to our lives.

Third, in part answer to the last point, they will have undergone a long process of evaluation and reproduction, especially if they are texts which have been 'canonised', and will carry with them, therefore, the accretions of their own extended cultural history in a way that contemporary works, which are only in the process of acquiring theirs, do not. With the former, we are presented with a kind of *fait accompli;* with the latter, a chance to observe those accretive processes at work. My inten-tion here, then, is to offer a synoptic and simultaneous response to all three of these issues by focussing on the ways in which two past examples of 'the literary' may be seen to illustrate the defining characteristics of that term as adduced in Chapter 4.

It is important to understand, however, that in claiming these 'old stories' as 'newstories' I am not subscribing to Ezra Pound's definition of literature as 'news that STAYS news'. For where Pound implies 'literary value' in the transhistorical or universal inscription of meaningfulness, I am pointing precisely to the new and differential activation of meanings in different histori-cal readings—albeit as potentialities inscribed in the determi-nate textuality of the works.

Let me start with Shakespeare's play *The Tempest.* Taken to be the last of his 'last plays', extant in only one text (the Folio of 1623), and considered the 'cleanest' of all his texts, *The Tempest* has a central place in the Shakespeare canon and in 'World Literature'. It has been admired, performed and critically interpreted *ad infinitum,* it has inspired or been 'written back to' by scores of other writers and artists; it has supplied us with the now mythic figures of Prospero, Caliban, Ariel and Miranda, along with dozens of familiar quotations (not least 'brave new world'). It has such an inescapable presence in global cultural history that it does indeed always remain there 'waiting to be read'.

Written as the colonial imperative was emerging most dynamically in the early-seventeenth century, the play would seem to underwrite that imperative in the colonising and civilising of the island by the humane learning of Prospero and in the play's representation of the 'savage' Caliban. Certainly, throughout the colonial project, the binary of Prospero/Caliban figured the (European) Self/Other opposition, and helped to 'fix' alterity in its characteristic hierarchical forms. Nevertheless, it is possible to say that the play's textuality has *always* contained within it tensions and ironies which problematise such 'fixings':

- Prospero's colonising is the result of his being 'exported' by European evil (Alonso, Antonio and Sebastian);
- the 'superior' race contains within it both the clowns, Stephano and Trinculo, and the ingenuous idealism of civilised womanhood, Miranda;
- the executive arm of Prospero's power (Ariel) carries out his orders under duress, and chafes to be free of it;
- that power is itself sustained by and as 'magic', and Prospero well understands the limits of its sustainability. When he relinquishes his 'so potent art' (pointedly also referred to in the same line as 'this rough magic' [Shakespeare (1610-11) 1975: V. 1. 50]), he knows that,

...like the baseless fabric of this vision,

The cloud-capped towers, the gorgeous palaces,

The solemn temples, the great globe itself,

Yea, all which it inherit, shall dissolve,

And, like this insubstantial pageant faded,
Leave not a rack behind. (IV. 1. 151-6)

It is not too obvious to point out that these subversive ele-ments of the play's discourse are now brought into bold relief in the postcolonialist context, and that the play can, as it were, be seen simultaneously to promote and problematise the colonial paradigm. It is as though, in Althusser's sense, *The Tempest* achieves a distantiation on the ideology in which it is nevertheless bathed. Most particularly, we may see a close correlation here between 'magic' and ideology—the factitious '"representation" of the imaginary relationship of individuals to their real conditions of existence' (Althusser [1970] 1977:152)—where Prospero's magic performs exactly that function in respect of the individuals shipwrecked on 'his' (or is it Calibans?) island. And, like magic, the 'baseless fabric' of (colonial) ideology only has to be exposed and 'dissolved' to lose its power to mystify and control.

But wherein does the power of Prospero's magic lie? The play is insistent that it is in the 'secret studies' of his beloved *books:* 'Knowing I loved my books', Gonzalo had furnished him 'with volumes that/I prize above my dukedom' (I. 2. 77, 166-8); with more 'business' to be done, Prospero says 'I'll to my book' (III. 1. 94-6); and at the end of the speech in which he 'abjures' his 'rough magic', he promises to 'drown my book' (V. 1. 57). However, if we register that the 'three hours' of the play's own duration is self-consciously reiterated throughout, we can see the whole play itself as comprised of 'magic', including the transfiguration of the 'bare island' of the stage ('Epilogue', line 8), the shipwreck, the action of the characters at all points, and the 'baseless fabric' of the pageant. It follows, then, that the constitutive discourse of Prospero's own magic is the very language of the 'book'/play itself, which Prospero/ Shakespeare's 'Epilogue' implies, when, in stepping outside of the play's charmed ambience, it admits it now 'want [s]/ Spirits to enforce, art to enchant' (13-14). But it is also in the 'magi-cal' power of language that the colonising of the island and its inhabitants lies.

The crucial scene here is Act I Scene 2, in which Caliban describes his trajectory from being 'mine own king' to being 'all the subjects that you have'. In so doing, he voices vividly the process of dispossession which follows the initial wooing of the indigenous inhabitant: 'This island's mine...which thou tak'st from me'—leaving him in 'this hard rock' (his 'native reservation'), 'whiles you do keep from me/The rest o' th'island'.

A central factor in this gradual dispossession is teaching Caliban the colonisers' language: they 'teach me how/ To *name* the bigger light, and how the less,/That burn by day and night. And then I loved thee...' (331-41, *passim;* my emphasis). Made complicit in his own enslavement by linguistic acculturation, Caliban is turned into a slave. It is the civilising European female idealist, Miranda, who is centrally instrumental in this, since it was she who

Took pains to make thee speak, taught thee each hour

One thing or other. When thou didst not, savage,

Know thine own meaning, but wouldst gabble like

A thing most brutish, I endowed thy purposes

With words that made them known. (354-8)

This is a crucial passage, for the way cultural imperialism works is indeed to devoice the colonised of their own lan-guage, on the supposition that the subject 'savage' does not know his 'own meaning' until it has been transliterated, and hence appropriated, into that of the coloniser and *her* meaning. Note how Miranda '*endowed* thy purposes/ With *words that made them known'.* Language, in other words, is the textualising process by which magic/ideology subjects the subject to complicity in their own subjection. Paradoxically, the acquisition of this 'sameness' also fixes their 'difference' and 'otherness'. But it is Caliban's famous riposte which focuses my point:

You taught me language, and my profit on't Is, I know how to curse.
The red plague rid you

For learning me your language! (363-5)

At one and the same moment, then, the play can be seen to articulate the cultural processes involved in colonisation and their self-subversion by way of the very factors which bring it about in the first place. A better example of the notion of post-colonial 'writing-back' it would be hard to find, and yet there it is in a play of 1613, a play which at another level may be seen to be instrumental in establishing the figuration of the colonial hierarchy.

My point is that it is in the extant textuality of *The Tempet's* own constitutive discourse that this formative moment of colonialism's power, and of the inherent contradictions which determine its dismantling, can be seen by future generations (i.e. by the contemporary reader/playgoer). But because we have already understood that both Prospero's and Shakespeare's 'magic' are themselves comprised of linguistic textuality, we are further enabled to see how magic/ideology functions by textualising subjects; and that, by observing such processes of textualisation, we can also register the subliminally imperceptible processes which textualise us all.

Equally, as Prospero's late speeches referred to above make clear, such textualisation ('potent art') is indeed deconstructible (it is, in the event, only 'rough magic'). The 'baseless fabric' of a 'vision' of Empire, of racial superiority, of (Western) civilisation, can be 'dissolved' by stepping outside the magic circle of discursive incorporation, as the (proto-Brechtian) 'alienation device' of Shakespeare's *envoi* seems to admit. By breaking the 'spell' in which the audience has been held, he (and we) are 'released' from his 'spirits to *enforce, art to enchant*' ('Epilogue', 14; my emphases). We are enabled to *be free* (as are Ariel and Caliban when Prospero's magic is lifted) by the very process of 'seeing' how language (including that of 'the literary') 'enchants' us. All this, I am arguing, the play enables us now to perceive in the context of our own historical conjuncture. In this respect, the text of *The Tempest* may be said to be 'waiting to be read' in this way.

My second example of what past literature may 'hold' for us is George Eliot's *Adam Bede*. Despite being a first novel by a largely unknown writer, it achieved immediate popularity and high regard, thereafter rapidly acquiring canonic status, in F.R. Leavis's phrase, as 'a classic in itself (Leavis 1961: vii). Leavis goes on to say that '[t]he historical value of *Adam Bede* lies in her novelist's *[sic]* creation of a past England—of a culture that has vanished with the triumph of industrialisation' (xii), and that: 'As sociologist and social historian [Eliot] is scrupu-lously precise' (xiv). The question I wish to pose is:

what kind of 'historical/ sociological value' may the novel now be seen to offer us?

Adam Bede resolutely assumes its own truthfulness in giving an account of the view of the world it espouses: a positivist humanism, or 'religion of humanity', in which the acquisition of 'sympathy', fellow-feeling and altruism will obviate the destructive egoism of human individuals in their natural, 'subjective' lowest form, and will gradually lead to the betterment of Society, which represents humankind in its 'objective' highest form. This essentially empiricist or 'realist' philosophy is in fact symbiotically related to George Eliot's 'truthful' fictional realism, since this is the vehicle for 'tell [ing] my simple story, without trying to make things seem better than they were; dreading nothing, indeed, but falsity' (Eliot, George [1859] 1961:176).

Such realism meant the detailed description of the particular histories of all sorts of common humanity as a way of revealing and understanding their otherness; and in this, it would help to obviate egoism and develop the altruistic sympa-thy necessary for social progress. In *Adam Bede*, what Eliot appears to give us in pursuit of this project is an entirely veracious account of a real world and material issues. Even though Chapter XVII, 'In Which the Story Pauses a Little', is a frame-break-like interruption in the seamless realism of the novel, and one in which Eliot effectively offers her *credo* as humanist-realist novelist, it serves merely to reinforce the 'reality' of the world she purports to describe. She does not hold it

> *the highest vocation of the novelist to represent things as they never have been and never will be. Then, of course, I might refashion life and character entirely after my own liking.... But it happens, on the contrary, that my strongest effort is to avoid any...arbitrary picture, and to give a faith-ful account of men and things as they have mirrored them-selves in my mind. The mirror is doubtless defective ...the reflection faint or confused; but I feel as much bound to tell you as precisely as I can what that reflection is, as if I were in the witness-box, narrating my experience on oath. (174)*

The entire discourse of 'accounting', 'picturing' and 'mirroring', rather than of 'refashioning', implies an anterior reality which is simply being reported or 'reflected', although as I have indicated on pp. 103 and 115, literary realism, by definition, makes/ creates *'poietic* realities' just as surely as any more overtly artificial literary discourse. But the effect of Eliot's intervention, especially her admission of the 'defectiveness' of her 'reflecting' consciousness, rather than causing us to perceive her partiality, seems to confirm her essential truthfulness. 'Telling things as they really are' here attains a totalising self-conviction which, in its turn, *convinces.*

Paradoxically, however, two contrary effects arise from the very solidity of the novel's realism. First, because the world of the book is so convincingly realised, it tends to invoke other extra-textual and material 'realities' which are implicit in it but not directly addressed there. A dialectic is established, in other words, between the text's realism, which results from its informing ideological view of reality, and the real social relations from the novel's historical contexts which that realism at once summons up and suppresses in its concrete specificity of depiction. I will give some examples of what I mean here in a moment. Second, as a reflex of the text's realist conviction and plausibility, wherever there appear 'gaps', aporias, irresolutions or silences in the text, we may assume that the limits of, and contradictions within, its ideological world-view—its determinate and defining *partiality*—are disturbing the other-wise coherent vision the realism articulates. In other words, realism *at its most solidly realised* provides Althusser's 'critical distance' on the ideology which sustains and legitimates it.

To give some brief examples of the two related points above: first, in respect of the absent 'contexts' I have suggested the novel's realism invokes. *Adam Bede* is set historically and geographically very precisely, in and around the village of 'Hayslope' in Warwickshire some sixty years prior to Eliot's publishing of the novel (1859), its first paragraph giving an exact date for the opening of the main action: '18, June 1799' (17; it ends in June 1807 [504]). In other words, the placing of the action in the past in a single small rural community is a crucial factor in establishing the (unacknowledged) limits within which the informing world-view will be realised as a material world.

It is as though a particular historical moment in a particular place has been sealed off as the world of the book; and it is noticeable, for example, that although there are scattered references throughout the novel to the French wars (revolutionary and then Napoleonic), these are never to do with the material bearing—in terms of prices, recruitment, shortage of labour, bereavement, etc.—that the wars would have had on the community, but only as individual characters' opinions. As John Goode pertinently observed, Eliot needs to 'choose an historical reality she can dehistoricise' (Goode 1970:21). We may then ask—since the novel's humanistic vision is, we are led to believe, universally valid for all times and places—why it was set sixty years in the past in an isolated rural village? Did George Eliot's own fractiously politicised society in the 1850s seem less susceptible to her 'religion of humanity' than the 'organic' Hayslope sixty years earlier (in the self-consciously 'truthful' Chapter XVII, she enigmatically reflects: 'Sixty years ago—it is a long time, so no wonder things have changed' [174])? Does the minimisation of the effects of the French wars, which kept prices high and exacer-bated the distress of the urban poor, represent a recognition that there is a public world impervious to the individualist focus of liberal humanism?

Further, Dinah Morris, one of the central characters in the novel, is that unusual figure in mid-nineteenth-century fiction, an itinerant *female* Methodist preacher. Within the book's moral schema, however, Dinah gradually loses her fiercely ide-alistic evangelistic edge, and finally becomes feminised and domesticated as Adam Bede's loving wife in the reformed humanistic idyll of Hayslope. Despite the importance given to Methodism in the novel, it is precisely its presence solely in the shape of the character of Dinah which *excludes* historical Methodism as a powerful (and disruptive) nineteenth-century religious and social movement—a movement of dissent, amongst others, which was energetically active and effective within acutely distressed urban industrial communities.

Why, we again might want to ask, is Methodism constrained, in the 'social history' the novel represents, to being exclusively located in Dinah Morris within a prosperous rural commu-nity? Was the exclusion of urban environments a recognition that such places might respond better to the proselytising and dissenting energy of Methodism than to the benevolence of bourgeois humanism? Is Dinah's brand of Méthodism a way of excluding other, more radical and working-class-directed, forms of dissent which were very much less susceptible to incorporation within the homogenised humanist community that Hayslope finally becomes?

But Dinah also opens up another 'context'. For much of the novel, she is represented as an independent and emancipated young woman (an itinerant preacher, after all, whose personal calling precludes marriage [45]). In the 1850s, as George Eliot prepared to write *Adam Bede,* the 'Woman Question was a passionately debated issue, as indeed were those around the increase in prostitution, the 'philosophy of free love', and the beginnings of a demand for female suffrage—all developments which destabilised the prevailing mid-Victorian patriarchal ideology of 'woman worship'.

The question then arises as to whether, in displaced ways, the novel invokes but suppresses those issues of its 'own' period. Is Dinah's Methodism, in other words, a figuration of the potential threats of female social mobility, sexuality and independence outside marriage, which Eliot's 'totalising' realist-humanism could not countenance or contain; and her final domestication an affirmation that the 'proper sphere' for women is indeed within the home and family? Significantly, in the 'Epilogue' we learn that the Methodist Conference 'has forbid the women preaching', and that Dinah has 'given it up'—a decision approved by the humanised Adam (by now the authoritative voice of the novel), who says: 'Most o' the women do more harm nor good with their preaching...and she's seen that, and she thought it right to set th' example o' submitting...'.

It could not be more plainly put. So does Dinah's curtailed independence as a woman give veiled utterance to the challenges posed by rival, nascent or emergent movements to the dominant sexual ideology in Eliot's own 1850s, only to erase them fictionally by removing the 'social history' of the novel to the 1790s when they could not be 'realistically' included in its fabric? What *Adam Bede* does, I am suggesting—and what its realism allows us to perceive it doing—is to construct an apparently real world made credible by its exclusions. But it is one so convinc-ing in its realistic fabrication that it simultaneously introduces into the text, from its material historical contexts, the determi-nate absences it has had to exclude in order to be able to realise itself in the first place.

Second, as an instance of the way a realist novel of this kind can reveal its suppressed contradictions and the limits of its own totalising project, let us focus on one moment when a destabilising uncertainty occurs—an example of fictive con-trivance enacted in the text's otherwise 'convincing' realist texture. But while it is precisely its *poietic* textuality which 'holds' this slippage as potentially visible to us, it requires some reading against the realistic grain to render it so. Hetty Sorrel, made pregnant outside wedlock by the young squire, Arthur Donnithorne, has been convicted of the murder of her new-born baby, and is in gaol awaiting execution.

Her reprieve comes in a chapter entitled, perhaps self-consciously, 'The Last Moment', one which is not only the shortest in the novel, but is only a single page long. The actual reprieve is con-tained in its final paragraph, which slips uneasily into the present tense and over-wrought prose: 'The horse is hot and distressed, but answers to the desperate spurring; the rider looks as if his eyes were glazed by madness... See, he has some-thing in his hand—he is holding it up as if it were a signal'—'a signal' indeed: but of what? No further mention of the event is made in the book, and no explanation is given of how Arthur obtained the '*hard won* release from death' {*ibid.;* my emphasis). Hetty is, in fact, transported and dies on her way home, as a single passing remark in the final chapter informs us. 'The Last Moment', in seeking to reduce a crucial event to nothing, stands out in stark and melodramatic relief from the rest of the book—'a signal', perhaps, of its own embarrassed recognition of the evident fabrication going on.

How do we explain this fissure in the firm terrain of the novel? Why could Hetty not have been hanged, as the logic might suggest; or, failing that, why not fuller treatment of how and why Arthur wins the reprieve? The short answer is that the moral conception of the book has no room for such material: Hetty, the epitome of myopic egoism and vanity, and, as such, a character entirely constructed within the novel's humanist-realist schema, has fulfilled her purpose within it and must be removed *hors de combat.*

Hanging her would intro-duce into its moral universe a note of barbarity (at the start of the chapter, Eliot has shuddered at 'the hideous symbol [the gallows—not named] of a deliberately inflicted death') out of tune with social and moral humanism. Perhaps more importantly, it would have invoked a recognition of public institutions and issues which could not be assimilated into the humanist pastoral of the novel. Similarly, any extended explanation of Arthur's use of privilege and class leverage in obtaining a reprieve would have introduced a political dimension which opposed the moral world-view George Eliot was propagating. Class politics, like Methodism and female independence, destabilise the homogenising project of liberal-humanist culture, as we also see in Matthew Arnold.

Furthermore, to allow Hetty to remain in, or return alive to, England would have been to raise questions about the social position of 'fallen women' and about prostitution. This was a burning contempo-rary issue which fuelled a 'literature of prostitution' (of which Eliot knew), and in which similar circumstances to those of Hetty and Arthur (young squire seducing dairymaid) were stereotypical. Hetty is a 'ruined maid', to borrow Thomas Hardy's later phrase for the ex-country-girl prostitute of his poem ('The Ruined Maid', in Hardy, T. 1901), and prostitution would very conceivably have been her destiny. That this is precluded is because it would radically disharmonise the domestic ideology which the end of the novel seems to endorse. The embarrassment of that short fictive moment, together with the summary dismissal of Hetty later, helps to expose—if we hypothesise the course the novel *might* have run —a sublimated recognition of the limits and exclusiveness of the novel's 'totalising' realism and its sustaining ideology.

My general point, then, in respect of Shakespeare's play and George Eliot's novel, and by extrapolation to other literary works from the past, is that within their own realisation of what they set out do, they also embody discourses which run counter to that original project but which are every bit as much a part of their totality. Hence, they offer future readers the opportunity to read the signs as they will, and so provide a different kind of 'social history' to the one they were inscribed by or believed they were providing. In literary texts, to restate my argument, the subtle and usually invisible processes which construct our lives within ideology are encoded in the complex and shifting '*poietic* realities' comprised by the works' determi-nate textuality. It is these processes which are then susceptible to retrieval and scrutiny. This is equally true of contemporary literature—to which we now turn—although there I shall shift the emphasis to more immediate and pressing 'uses of the literary'.

THE LITERARY' AS CONTEMPORARY HISTORY

The problematics of history have been compounded over the past 30 years or so by its place and function in the postmodern world. Indeed the deconstructive strategies central to 'herstory' and postcolonialism are arguably themselves instances of post-modernity. If, as Jean-Francois Lyotard has it, the 'postmodern condition' witnesses the discrediting of the 'grand *narratives*' (my emphasis) of post-Enlightenment civilisation and their replacement by the petits recits' (little stories) of localized import (Lyotard [1979] 1984), then an authoritative 'History' is surely one of the casualties.

Equally, when Jean Baudrillard ([1981] 1994) proposes that postmodernism means the 'loss of the real'—that 'history and reality' have become 'textualised' in our hyper-real world of images and simulations, and replaced by 'simulacra' (things, the dictionary tells us, 'made to resemble some other thing, an inferior or deceptive likeness') —then *knowing* anything in the sense that *historia* implies becomes deeply problematic. As Dick Hebdige has suggested, the conspicuous consumerism and advanced technologies of late-twentieth-century postmodern monopoly capitalism replace all meaning with parody and style:'we are left in a world of radically "empty" signifiers.

No meaning. No classes. No history. Just a ceaseless procession of simulacra' (Hebdige [1985] 1989:269). The fundamental political and cultural pes-simism this implies nonetheless signals a 'condition that does coincide with aspects of late-millenial life: Baudrillard may have been tastelessly *outre* in suggesting that the Gulf War was 'unreal', but his perception of it as a media event, a TV simulation, is not without point (Baudrillard 1991, 1995).

One of the primary problems of the postmodern world, then, is that of *how to know*. The information explosion is an irresistible and potentially beneficial feature of our society, but as anyone who watches much television (particularly 'News' programmes) or regularly visits websites on the Internet will appreciate, the more knowledge we apparently receive, the more an eerie sense of *unknowing* comes upon us. Henry James once remarked on 'the fatal futility of Fact' ([1907] 1962:122); and it is indeed the amount of information we have, *without* the attendant 'narratives' to explain, interpret and make sense of it, which is central to postmodern experi-ence. 'The literary', I am claiming—precisely by way of its 'forming' and 'fashioning' properties, its 'sense of subject', its identification of 'patterns' and 'knowable communities... creatively known...for the first time in this way'—gives us insight into the complex interactive relations which comprise our culture.

Cutting in vertical section, as it were, into the 'Chaos of Being' which is the experience of lived history as it is being lived, it helps solve Carlyle's problem with the 'linear narrative' of written history by providing a history which is otherwise inarticulate: it accesses the 'to-be-known in our own 'community' (see pp. 104-6), and in particular, how we are textualised by ideological narratives which traverse, construct and position us. If a central problem of postmodernity is the failure of the 'grand narratives' of contemporary history, poli-tics and culture in helping us to 'know' anything for certain, then some degree of empowerment in this 'condition' may be achieved if we understand *how* narrative works, *how* text con-structs, *how* histories (and herstories) get written.

The 'little [new] stories' of contemporary literature, I would argue, at once give form to flux, if only temporarily and provisionally, shape a (textual) 'community' which we can comprehend, and thus simultaneously proffer us a 'way of knowing' our own culture and how it determines us. 'The literary', in this respect, gives us the news that 'The News'—by which I mean all osten-sibly authoritative knowledge-sources—are also themselves narrative, text, and *thereby* the potent fictions ('telling stories') which script our lives.

Arguably, each and every piece of contemporary literary writing offers us some form of defamiliarising perspective on our own culture, and can therefore be regarded as helping to compose a 'history' of the post-war period. But while our main focus in the following sections will be on texts which have a *self-conscious* sense of writing a kind of history, not all contemporary 'newstories', of course, necessarily have any explicit historical inflection at all. Let me give some diverse examples, from a broad range of the latter variety, of the types of insights about the present which seem to me to be 'held' in their consti-tutive textuality. Harold Pinter's plays, so disturbing in their uncanny repro-duction of the rhythms and silences of everyday speech, reveal the libidinal menace (of power and sex) lurking within the ordinary, the familiar and the 'civilized'—what he himself once memorably called 'the weasel under the cocktail cabinet'. Ron Hutchinson's play, *Rat in the Skull,* gives stark expression to the corrosive violence fostered by the prejudice and ignorance which fuel the 'terrorist'/'security forces' relationship in North-ern Ireland. Brian Moore's 'thriller', *Lies of Silence,* offers an entree to the moral and psychological quandries incident on the 'circle of violence' prevalent in Ireland.

The novel does so in part by its own involuntary textual confirmation of the detachment from, and despair at, any solution to 'the North-ern Ireland problem' felt by those not directly involved, which is itself a crucial component of that problem. Barrie Keefe's ferocious play, *Sus,* whose action is set as the results of the 1979 General Election are coming through, anatomises the bigotry and violence in race relations—most particularly in the language of the sadistic police officer, Karn—which was to be a subtext of the 'Thatcher Revolution'.

Joan Riley's *The Unbe-longing,* a novel by a British-based Caribbean woman, offers a telling account of the displacement and double exploitation of a black adolescent female immigrant to England—not least in the unremittingly alienated tone of her narrative; while Mau-reen Ismay, also Caribbean-British, in her poem 'Frailty Is Not My Name', articulates the simplifying ease with which a black woman can be bounced, ping-pong-like, from one stereotype to another.

In rejecting the white patriarchal labelling first enunciated by Hamlet—'Frailty thy name is woman'—she further rejects the new 'mythology' that she must therefore be 'a big strong, black woman/iron hard and carrying/all the sor-rows of the world on my back' (Ismay: 1987). Caribbean poets also explore their consciousness of the complex implications of being postcolonial/multicultural 'subjects' (in both senses) by expanding the possible poetic languages available. In the retrieval of the culturally 'non-accredited' patois and rhythms of West Indian speech and music, a 'counter-cultural' discourse is recuperated which is not already 'owned' by the dominant culture. So, for example, Linton Kwesi

Johnson is able to write of racial and social injustice in 'Inglan Is a Bitch' with a resonance 'standard English' would not catch:

well mi dhu day wok an' mi dhu nite wok

mi dhu clean wok an' mi dhu dutty wok

dem seh dat black man is very lazy

but if y'u si how mi wok y'u woulda seh mi crazy

Inglan is a bitch dere's no escapin' it Inglan is a bitch y'u bettah face up to it

(Johnson [1980] 1991)

And so, too, of a sexual relationship, is Lillian Allen in 'Belly Woman's Lament':

A likkle seed

Of her love fe a man

Germinates in her gut

She dah breed

Cool breeze

It did nice

Im nuh waan no wife

just life

Wey fe do!

(Allen [1982] 1986)

('Cool breeze' is proverbial for 'good while it lasted'.) John Le Carre's spy thrillers offer credible access to the other-wise secret world of espionage—which may just as well be as 'true to' or as 'real as' the world they purport to describe since we have no way of knowing otherwise. But they also reveal the ideological dilemma at the heart of Le Carre's own liberal-humanist attempt to establish a 'neutral' space into which 'free' human subjects who retain the capacity for love can struggle as individuals out of the wrecked world of double-bluff and betrayal fostered by the politics of international confrontation.

Rosie Thomas's bestseller, the aptly-titled *A Woman of our Times,* and Julie Burchill's 'bonkbuster', *Ambi-tion* (which can be read as either formulaic exploitation or deconstructive parody of the genre), in their different ways reflect the problems within the so-called 'yuppie feminism' and ruthless entrepreneurialism spawned by the Reaganite and Thatcherite 'new economies' of the 1980s. Similarly, Caryl Churchill's play, *Top Girls,* and her rumbustious verse-drama, *Serious Money,* explore the complex ethical and political issues thrown up by de-regulated sexual and financial 'freedom'.

A list of examples of the 'front-line' news that contemporary 'newstories' offer us could go on and on, so I now want to focus on a selection of texts which have a more than contingent relation to the writing of history. That these are themselves numerous and diverse tends to confirm that a self-conscious correlation between history and 'the literary' is indeed a dominant trope in contemporary literature. Whether this recycling of history through the merging of the factual and the fictive is helpfully defined as 'postmodernist' depends on whether you see postmodernism as wilfully playful and politi-cally irresponsible, or as a serious attempt to dismantle the dominant 'truths' of past cultural knowledge.

Once again, there are many ways in which 'the literary' uses history, and many ends to which it is put. So let us again briefly survey a broad, if partial, range of these, before focussing on a few chosen texts in more detail. Arthur Miller, for example, by basing his play, *The Crucible,* on the Salem witch trials of the early 1690s, circumvented censorship in 1950s America when Macarthyite 'witch-hunts' represented a real threat to freedom of expression, and anatomised the very mindset which engendered the censorship in the first place. While self-consciously admitting, in 'A Note on the Historical Accuracy of this Play', that it 'is not history in the sense in which the word is used by the academic historian' (Miller [1953] 1959: xvii), Miller, in his 'commentary' in Act One on the (historical) characters on which his own are based, makes a passing comment of central relevance to my argument here for 'the literary'.

He says: 'No one can really know what their lives were like. They had no novelists...' (2). The implication here is that 'novels' (or dramatic fictions) are the historical source for knowing what past lives were '*really*...like', rather, perhaps, than the history of 'the academic historian'.

Based only on hints from the scant historical records of the trials and their participants, Miller imaginatively recreates the characters and their motives in order to reveal to a modern audience (and the play remains deeply compelling, way beyond its Macarthyite context) the unstable mixture of religious, sexual and materialistic elements that cause an entire community to be racked by a contagious madness which effectively parades 'vengeance' (74) as true righteousness.

At the most immediate level, Miller's play shows how American society has, in its his-torical genes, the illiberal potential for 'outing' and destroying those who, on others' hearsay evidence, are not considered fit to 'live in a Christian country' (135).

More recently, Timberlake Wertenbaker sets her play, *Our Country's Good,* two hundred years ago in a convict colony in New South Wales in 1788, in order to depict, and hence remind a modern audience of, the brutality of which English law has been capable; the punishment regime the convicts had to undergo; and the original circumstances, therefore, out of which the new state of Australia emerged. However, prompted by the civilising mission of the colony's liberal Governor-in-Chief, who recognises that the convicts will in time 'help to create a new society in this colony' and should therefore be 'encourage [d]... to think in a free and responsible manner' (Wertenbaker [1988] 1995:21), and under the direction of an increasingly humanised Second Lieutenant, the convicts—some of whom are sentenced to hang—are led to rehearse a play: George Farquhar's early-eighteenth-century comedy, *The Recruiting Officer.*

In the course of this exposure to 'refined, literate language' *(ibid.),* to high comedy, and to the structural irony of performing that play in these circumstances, the con-victs do indeed find some 'redemption': they discover their 'humanity [which] lies hidden under the rags and filth of a mangled life' (58). So, *Our Country's Good* is also about the civilising and redemptive power of the theatre; and in the con-text of late-1980s cuts in arts funding in Britain, by which the theatre was seriously threatened, this too was a timely warn-ing. As the Governor-in-Chief puts it: 'The theatre is an expres-sion of civilisation', and watching a play 'require[s] attention, judgement, patience, all social virtues' (21-2). Barbarity, Wertenbaker's play reminds us, is not only represented by penal colonies, flogging and the gallows, but also by those who fear that 'the theatre leads to threatening theory' or who regard it only as 'fandangl[ing] about with a lewdy play' (25).

The white South African novelist, J.M.Coetzee, set his alle-goric novel, *Waiting for the Barbarians,* in an outpost of an unnamed 'Empire' in an historically unlocated time in order to avoid the censorship of the then apartheid regime in South Africa. In this way, Coetzee could analyse its strategies and techniques of oppression, expose the inherent weaknesses which would result in its eventual demise, and put 'in the his-tory books' a history which the custodians of 'the Empire' would erase ('"There will be no history, the affair is too trivial"' (Coetzee [1980] 1982:114). But he could further indi-cate at once a white liberal's ('the Magistrate', but also Coetzee's own) complicity in, and the limits of his opposition to, that regime, and his inability to 'speak for' the truly oppressed native inhabitants (the 'barbarians').

His sense of the inadequacy of 'white' words to articulate that oppression is represented both by the Magistrate's failure to read the 'script' of the painted wooden slips he finds in the buried ruins of a previous civilisation, and by Coetzee's own deployment of the inscribed body as a form of expression which enunciates the silence of those prohibited from speaking for themselves (we will see this again in his novel, *Foe,* on p. 171).

The most significant instance of this is the native girl whom the Magistrate exploits sexually, and whose body shows 'the marks her tortur-ers have left upon her'—marks which the Magistrate contradic-torily both wishes were 'erased', so that 'she is restored to herself, and finds 'do not go deep enough' because he cannot interpret their significance: 'is it she I want or the traces of a history her body bears?' The only answer to this question that he can come up with is: 'whatever can be articulated is falsely put', but even these 'words grow more and more opaque before me; soon they have lost all meaning' (64-5).

Neither the Magistrate nor the novel can 'articulate' in 'words'—or only 'falsely'—the 'history' the girl's body bears witness to. All they can do is give an account of the failure to be able to do so. Nevetheless, this in itself is a kind of truth-telling which we need to face up to: that in order to 'begin to tell the truth' (154) there is a kind of 'living through' (65) which lies beyond 'the locutions of a civil servant with literary aspirations' (like Coetzee himself; 154).

Again, we might observe how Seamus Heaney explores the implications, contradictions and complexities of the political situation in Northern Ireland by way of the preserved corpses of prehistoric people recovered from the bogs. In the poem 'Punishment', for instance, after the initial third-person description of a young woman's body, and exactly in the middle of the poem, the 'Little adulteress' is addressed directly ('before they punished *you'),* and she becomes *'My* poor scapegoat' (my emphases). The poem continues:

> *I almost love you but would have cast, I know, the stones of silence. I am the artful voyeur*
>
> *of your brain's exposed and darkened combs, your muscles' webbing and all your numbered bones:*
>
> *I who have stood dumb when your betraying sisters, cauled in tar, wept by the railings, who would connive in civilised outrage yet understand the exact and tribal, intimate revenge. (Heaney 1975)*

Once we realise that your betraying sisters,/cauled in tar,' are the victims of contemporary factional violence ('punished' for dating someone of the 'wrong' religion or a British soldier), the oscillation between the remote past and the immediate present washes back through the poem so that the whole earlier description, from the opening lines, 'I can feel the tug/of the halter at the nape/of her neck' to 'her shaved head', now res-onates with the historical (and eroticised) analogy. But it is the passive complicity in the event(s) of the poet—'the artful *voyeur'*—which becomes the poem's main theme: 'I...would have cast, I know,/the stones of silence'; would also, of course, 'have stood dumb' in the present troubles; or worse, would connive/in civilised outrage'.

The poet, in other words, would have participated both in the execution by not speaking out against it and in the furtive horror of the civilised at such barbarity, while in fact being implicated in the basic atavism of the act: 'intimate revenge' suggesting the fundamental sexual fear of a 'betrayal' across 'tribal' (male/female) lines. What we have here is at once the sense that the present is no less bar-barous than the past, that no one is innocent in a political situation like that of Northern Ireland, and that the 'little scapegoat' is a figure for the overdetermining complicity of the male poet as 'artful voyeur' in the (sexual/political) barbarity he observes.

Explicit and 'telling' instances of the literary as history, especially in their capacity to alert us to our construction within narrative, are Graham Swift's novels, *Waterland* and *Out of this World*. In respect of what Linda Hutcheon calls 'historio-graphic metafiction' (Hutcheon [1989] 1993:14; i.e. self-reflexive postmodernist fiction, like Swift's, which explores a history and a society represented principally by 'realist' narratives), she proposes that 'formalist self-reflexivity and parody' confront 'documentary historical actuality'.

So that: 'a study of representation becomes...an exploration of the way in which narratives and images structure how we see ourselves and how we construct our notions of self, in the present and in the past' (*ibid.*). To put it another way: if much of our history right up to the present has been based on an essentially realist paradigm ('telling things as they really are'), demystifying such realist forms and ideologies shows us at the very least how we have been constructed and thus how we might reconstruct our understanding of how we live.

The epigraph to *Waterland* is a dictionary definition of the word *historia* (see p. 133) and its main narrator is a history teacher who substitutes a history of his own family and of the Fens over a 200-year period for the school history syllabus. It continually foregrounds the consonance between the public and private worlds of historical account and 'telling stories'— with all the fabrication that goes into both—thus 'baring the device' of its own textual fabrication.

The novel's main thrust is how narratives/stories/histories are made, and how all our lives (or is it 'lies'?) are woven of and in them. In its defamiliarisation of its own processes, then, it admits complicity with the discourses it critiques, but simultaneously offers us a 'way of knowing' how those processes construct and contain us too.

But let me concentrate on the undeservedly less admired *Out of this World*, which is an equally 'telling' attempt to write a large-scale history in full view of the reader: this time of the contaminations implicit in twentieth-century warfare, as represented by the Beech family whose fortune was made in armaments. All the main characters have had their emotional lives atrophied by violence in one way or another, and the novel is an account by flashbacks of that process. The dominant motif of this twentieth-century alienation is the century's own main form of self-representation, of 'knowing itself: photography.

The novel is, indeed, a meditation on the truthfulness or not of representation, using various forms of photographic 'picturing' as its focus. These are presented as a form of mechanical dehumanisation, a form of truth-telling, a form of lying—and an analogy, in all these respects, for the novel's own attempts to 'capture' how it was, to 'record' twentieth-century reality, to offer a 'portrait' or 'snapshot' of a family, as though all its hidden past would be visible in the image presented to the world.

Harry Beech, the son, and one of the novel's two main narra-tors (the other is his daughter, Sophie), has been an RAF aerial photographer in World War II; he has 'covered' the Nurem-berg trials; and later he becomes a famous war-photographer: 'this new kind of hero...a hero without a gun...but flinching at nothing to bring back the truth' (Swift 1988:118). Later still, living in rural Wiltshire and working as a peacetime aerial photographer, his 'shots' of Bronze Age field-systems nevertheless still show up MOD installations. All this, of course, is, a 'true' representation of twentieth-century experience, which does indeed dehumanise and brutalise; and as Harry says: 'Someone has to be witness, someone has to see'—although he signifi-cantly poses his following remark as a question: 'And tell? And tell?' (163).

But the question the *novel* poses (of a realist pho-tography and of itself), as it tries to expose the secrets and lies of the family history, to 'tell' the truth behind the reified and blank postures of the main characters, is: just how 'true' is real-istic 'representation'? How neutral and objective is it ever?

From first believing that 'the camera doesn't manufacture' (13), Harry, just back from Vietnam and watching the first moon-landing in 1969, now reflects: 'the camera first, then the event. The whole world is waiting just to get turned into film' *(ibid.)*. Later, thinking about the claim of photography that it 'can show you how the world really is' ('telling things as they really are' is also the central claim of realist fiction), he realises that the 'witness standing there looking al it is changing the way the world is anyway. If you're going to *tell us how things are,* then maybe we should start with you' (119; my emphasis). What the novel itself is doing, by way of its own 'unreliable' first-person narrators, is showing us the parallax which the 'witness', the hand that holds the camera, introduces. But Harry adds a further (postmodern) perception:

> Have you noticed how the whole world has changed? It's become this vast display of evidence, this exhibition of recorded data, this continuously running movie.
>
> *The problem is what you don't see... The problem is selection...the frame, the separation of the image from the thing. The extraction of the world from the world.* (ibid.)

This, of course, is the experience of living in and through simulacra (such as realism). A key event at the moment the novel is set is the Falklands War. Pre-empting Jean Baudrillard on the Gulf War (Baudrillard 1991), Harry observes that the Falklands 'is going to be the TV event of the year' (185)—'As if without [the cameras there] it could not take place' (189) —'because nowadays TV can never have enough "real life" footage...it's no longer easy to distinguish the real from the fake, or the world on the screen from the world off it' (188):

> the camera no longer recorded but conferred reality.... As if the world wanted to be claimed and possessed by the camera. To translate itself, as if afraid it might otherwise vanish, into the new myth of its own authentic-synthetic memory.

A central feature of the postmodern condition, the novel proposes, is that rather than dispelling myths, which the recording camera might have seemed to have the potential to do, it 'confers' a specious 'reality' (or simulacrum), 'selected' and 'framed' by the angle of vision—since 'the world always wants another world, a shadow, an echo, a model of itself (187). But a photograph, which, as we have heard, is 'the separation of the image from the thing. The extraction of the world from the world', is an object formally detached from its experiential referent: 'it becomes an icon, a totem, a curio. A piece of reality?

A fragment of the truth?' (120). Earlier, and this will return us to stories and histories, Harry has reflected:

People want stories. They don't want facts.... Of the news photo [journalists] say: Every picture tells a story.... But supposing it doesn't tell a story? Supposing it shows only unaccommodatable fact? Supposing it shows the point at which the story breaks down. The point at which narrative goes dumb.

What Swift seems to be suggesting here, faced with James's 'fatal futility of Fact', is that 'stories' are the only things by which people make sense of their lives. As *Waterland* had already posited, such [hi] stories may be 'untrue' and incomplete, but they are our only way of knowing how we have come to be what we are.

Indeed, 'telling (stories)' is set in counterpoint to the domi-nant and factitious 'realism' of news photography. It is Sophie's psychiatrist significantly, to whom she is telling *her* story, who makes the comparison most sharply: 'An image, my dear Sophie, is something without knowledge or memory. Do we see the truth or tell it?' (76). But it is the novel itself, of course, which is the overall 'telling': the 'story' which gets behind the 'dumb narrative' of 'unaccommodatable fact' in order to write a 'history' of the postmodern world. Does this, then, make the novel 'true'—or even 'truer'—than news stories and news photography? One reviewer of the novel turned its central perception about photography onto itself, praising it for 'not only recording reality but conferring it'.

The irony is that what the novel 'confers' is not, of course, 'reality', but a way of perceiving how notions of 'reality' are foisted upon us. The notion of 'a true story' is a fiction, just as is 'the camera cannot lie', for there is always another image behind the photograph, another story behind the story, another history behind the history—it all depends on who the 'witness' is. The bottom line, here, is that there is no bottom line: we construct narratives as narratives construct us. But an historiographic metafiction like *Out of this World* helps us to see how this happens, not least in its self-consciousness of complicity in the fashioning of narratives.

For example: Sophie's husband Joe, a travel-agent in New York, specialises in 'sell [ing] dreams' in the form of tours to England: 'golden memories of the Old World. Thatched cot-tages and stately homes.... Sweet, green visions' (15-16). When Sophie is herself flying home, she tells her sons that they will 'see all the things [they had] only seen so far, in pictures... So it will seem that England is really only a toy country. But you mustn't believe that' (192). Sophie knows that Joe has 'the knack...of ignoring what he knows and endorsing only the image' (77).

The reader knows, however, that the 'image' of a 'toy' England belies the fact that it is on its way to the Falk-land Islands, that MOD installations lurk in the rural idyll of the countryside, that arms manufacturers own 'stately homes' and get assassinated by the IRA. But the England Harry now inhabits is indeed that of Joe's dream-world: 'I was', he says, 'facing up to life in a picture-book cottage' (59)—although he adds: 'Picture-books aren't real? The fairy-tales all got discredited long ago, didn't they?' (79).

It is within this pastoral retreat—'out of this world'—that he lives with Jenny, 40 years his junior and 'beautiful. She's incredible. She's out of this world' (36). Harry, on an aerial photography flying trip, think-ing of his cottage and the pregnant Jenny down below, muses that he 'could almost be guilty of believing...the rest of the world doesn't matter' (39). Is this an optimistic, if minimalist, affirmation of love in the grisly twentieth-century world of warfare and simulacra—a beneficent pastoral to defeat the 'real' narratives of history? Or does the novel both sustain and disavow the 'guilty' fantasy of escaping 'out of this world': a pastoral narrative, that is to say, just as specious as that 'true' one of photographic news?

The novel does not tell us, of course, because it is itself composed of the 'stories' it has con-structed and related. How, then, do we get behind those of Harry and Sophie? How, indeed, do we get behind the novel's own constitutive narrative? The short answer is: we don't. All we are left with is a sense of their potency and a suspicion of all narratives claiming to 'record' reality. But equally, without its 'made up' [hi] story—its self-deconstructing recognition of its own textualisation of 'reality'—we would be deprived of the insight it provides of how our own knowledge of the world is composed of narratives which purport to be 'true'. *Out of this World* is a 'newstory' which suggests that 'telling stories' may be just as (or as little) truthful as news-stories.

An important sub-set of contemporary 'historiographic' meta-literature is 're-visionary' writing, which focuses on those formative textualising narratives that have been central to the construction of 'our', that is to say, European-male, consciousness.

The term 'revision' deploys a strategic ambiguity between the word *revise:* 'to examine and correct; to make a new, improved version of; to study anew', and *re-vision:* to see in another light; to revision or perceive differently; and thus to recast and re-evaluate the 'original'. It was given currency by the American lesbian-feminist poet, Adrienne Rich, who uses it to signal a politicised feminist poetics which would help to counter the domination of patriarchal culture by way of refashioning its (canonic) texts.

In her essay, 'When the Dead Awaken: Writing as Re-vision', Rich defines the project thus:

> *Re-vision—the act of looking back, of seeing with fresh eyes, of entering an old text from a new critical direction.... Until [women] can understand the assumptions in which we are drenched we cannot know ourselves.... A radical critique of literature, feminist in its impulse, would take the work first of all as a clue to how we live, how we have been living, how we have been led to imagine ourselves, how our language has trapped as well as liberated us.... We need to know the writing of the past, and know it differ-ently than we have ever known it; not to pass on a tradition but to break its hold over us. (Rich [1971] 1992:369)*

Such a 're-visioning' can be a purely critical activity, of the feminist and postcolonial kinds we encountered in Chapter 3, but the act of 'seeing with fresh eyes' and of 'entering an old text from a different...direction', also relates to various elements of my definition of 'the literary' itself, and especially its 'defamiliarising' effects. So that as a *literary* practice, it means the 're-writing' of texts which have been constructed and owned by another (usually dominant) interest such as cultural, patriar-chal, or imperial/colonial power.

The principal characteristics of 're-visionary' works are:

1 that they tend to 're-write' canonic texts—those 'classics' which have a high profile of admiration and popularity in our literary heritage;

2 that they keep the original text in clear view, so that it is not just the 'source' of a new modern version but a con-stantly invoked *intertext* for it;

3 that, in this way, they denaturalise the original in exposing those discourses which we no longer see in it because we have learnt to read it in restricted and conventional ways;

4 that they not only re-write the original as a different, separate, new work, but re-cast, and thus repossess and liber-ate, the original as itself a 'new' text to be read newly— enabling us to 'see' a different one to that we thought we knew as, say, *JaneEyre, Robinson Crusoe, King Lear, The Tempest* or 'An Elegy Written in a Country Church Yard';

5 that they make us see parallels (or contrasts) between the period of the original text's production and that of the modern work;

6 that they invariably have a clear cultural-political thrust, especially on behalf of those exploited, marginalised and silenced by dominant ideologies, in demanding that the political inscription and cultural complicity in oppression of past texts be revised and re-visioned as part of the pro-cess of restoring a voice, a history or an identity to the erstwhile oppressed.

'Re-visionary' writing, then, is a crucial component of 'the lit-erary' as a contemporary 'counter-culture of the imagination', which in 'writing back' to historical texts, and to the historical conjunctures which shaped them, re-writes Authorised History by way of revising its 'master-narratives'.

Examples of such re-visionary works would include: Sue Roe's *Estella: Her Expectations* (1982), which rewrites Charles Dickens's *Great Expectations* as the story of Miss Hav-isham's vengeance child, hence giving a voice to the repressed and largely silent 'heroine' of Dickens's novel; Marina Warner's *Indigo* (1992), which explores the story of Sycorax, Caliban and Ariel in a modern re-vision of Shakespeare's play *The Tempest;* and Emma Tennant's *Two Women of London: The Strange Case of Ms Jekyll and Mrs Hyde* (1989). A wittily 'exact' re-writing of Robert Louis Stevenson's famous original tale, this novella reappropriates a by now pervasive myth and redeploys it on behalf of contemporary women.

For this is now an analysis of the effects on women of living through that perverse inflection of patriarchy known as Thatcherism, where Ms Jekyll and Mrs Hyde—respectively the 'rich poor' and the 'poor poor'—are the 'same' woman exploited by capitalism and patriarchy. The immediate cause of her transformation between 'yuppie' and 'slattern' is a reliance on drugs, which start out as 'little helpers' but become, combined with other substances unscrupulously prescribed by male doctors, a destructive chemistry which causes her to be both (inauthentic) women at once, and so unable, as one of the story's multiple narrators puts it, 'to find herself (Tennant 1989:119).

And the rapist, who for much of the story we think Mrs Hyde has mur-dered, is a blurred amalgam in Jekyll/Hyde's mind of all the men who control and destroy her. Tennant's later novel, *Tess,* recasts Thomas Hardy's 'masterpiece', *Tess of the d'Urbervilles,* to reveal that in presenting his heroine in the way he does, as a desirable sex-object to the male gaze, Hardy is directly implicated in the patriarchal exploitation Tess suf-fers, even when the novel purports to be on her side. Beginning in the 1950s, Tennant's revision also suggests that the exploitation of women by men, and the difficulties women face in fulfilling their own sexuality freely, have not signifi-cantly changed since Hardy's time.

Equally, Jane Smiley's novel, *A Thousand Acres* ([1991] 1992), relocates Shakespeare's *King Lear* in a modern American context, as a tale narrated by Goneril ('Ginny'). Unlike Edward Bond, in his play *Lear,* which merely represents a different (even more bleakly violent) version of the story rather than a 'writing-back' to the original, Smiley at once underlines the continuing destructive 'madness' of patriarchal and capitalist 'monopoly' in modern America, and, in the light of this, re-visions the 'good/evil' binary of Goneril-Reagan/ Cordelia affirmed so potently by Shakespeare's play. The 'unvoiced' story of Goneril and Regan's behaviour in *King Lear* is thus retrieved and 'explained' (were they indeed victims of abuse?), so that our experiencing of the canonic play itself is also subversively redirected.

Perhaps the best-known and prototypical re-visionary texts, however, are the novels *Wide Sargasso Sea* by Jean Rhys (1966) and *Foe* by J.M.Coetzee ([1986] 1987). The former re-tells Charlotte Bronte's novel *Jane Eyre* as the story of Bertha Mason, Mr.Rochester's first wife and the now famous 'mad-woman in the attic' of feminist criticism. Told in the first-person narratives of Antoinette/Bertha and her husband during their time in the West Indies before their return to England and Thornfield Hall', the novel forces us to understand why Bertha might have become a madwoman in the first place, and who indeed—from 'Rochester's' narrative—is really mad, hence forcing us to reconsider *Jane Eyre's* naturalised charac-terisation of Bertha.

In so doing, it further causes us to see how patriarchy worked in the early-nineteenth century, and what the position of women might have been within it, whilst also leading us to reassess the pointedly racial bias of Bronte's presentation of Bertha as a 'savage' who appears, in her physical representation, to be negroid but who, as a 'creole', is in fact a white West Indian. Jean Rhys's novel, in other words, redirects our attention to the latent racism of a text which has a central place both in 'The Canon' and in the contemporary feminist canon (see Spivak 1985, on p. *66*).

Likewise, Coetzee's *Foe* is an explicit 'writing-back' to Daniel Defoe's fundamentally formative novel, *Robinson Cru-soe.* Not only is the latter one of the first and most famous novels in English, arguably establishing the model for fictional realism—Defoe, as 'editor' of what purport to be Crusoe's authentic memoirs, writes in the preface that he 'believes the thing to be just a history of fact; neither is there any appearance of fiction in it'—but its story, at a number of levels, also rapidly acquired a pervasive mythic force. Crusoe himself, in Coleridge's phrase, became 'the universal representative, the person, for whom every reader could substitute *himself* (quoted in Watt [1957] 1970:81; my emphasis). But he also became a figuration both of (especially male) bourgeois individualism in all its manifestations: religious, social, political and economic, and of European colonialism. Coetzee's novel addresses all these elements of *Robinson Crusoe's* potently tex-tualising narrative.

Until the sixth and final section, the first-person 'voice' is that of Susan Barton, a woman who was also shipwrecked on Crusoe's island but who, it is implied, Defoe silenced by 'writing out' of his-story. Significantly, it is Susan (not Cruso— Coetzee's spelling) who writes the account of their sojourn on the island with Friday, who brings it home to London, who seeks out the professional writer, Mr Foe, and who offers him her story to be transformed by 'the magic of words' (Coetzee [1986] 1987:58) into a publishable text.

What is implied, of course, is that Foe's 'art', in the making of *his* novel, fiction-alises and distorts Susan's 'true' account in order to create a good story, not least by removing Susan herself from it. A con-tinuous refrain in Coetzee's novel, therefore, is the factitious-ness of realistic fiction (indeed of any written discourse which purports to be 'telling the truth'); so that where an early critic (1718) of Defoe himself wrote of 'the little art he is truly master of, of forging a story, and imposing it on the world for truth', the words 'art', 'master', 'forging' and 'truth' all now resonate in Coetzee's theme.

At one level, then, *Foe* restores a voice to Susan and her-story, although, even here, it questions the truthfulness of this narrator by the strategy—adapted from another of Defoe's novels, *Roxana,* whose eponymous heroine also turns out to be called Susan—of never resolving whether she is or is not the mother of the daughter who claims her to be so. Indeed, on the final page of the novel, it is implied that Susan had drowned in the slave ship before she ever got onto Cruso s island (see p. 171 below).

But the novel also has as a central figure the black slave, Friday, whom Susan brings back to London with her as a kind of possession (even a white European woman is complicit in colonisation). In Coetzee's version, however, Friday is not the 'noble savage' of Defoe's tale but a thoroughly alien 'Other', who, pointedly, has had his tongue cut out. Where Defoe's Fri-day learns his master's language and is thus 'voiced', albeit with his own 'tongue' silenced by the acquisition of the coloniser's language, Coetzee's becomes, most emphatically, a symbol of the European 'unvoicing' of the colonised.

However, two points should be noted here. First, it is never made clear who has brutalised Friday in this way: the slave-traders who leave him on the island, Cruso, or, indeed, Susan Barton herself, since all the written accounts (including, by implication, the novel itself) are suspect in their 'truthfulness' and are not by Friday himself. In this respect, *all* the Europeans are complicit in silencing Friday. The second point is that, para-doxically, removing Friday's tongue does not deprive him of his own *language* in the way that the imposition of the coloniser's 'tongue' erases a native language. It merely means that he cannot speak. And indeed, Friday has his own forms of self-expression, namely his singing and dancing, which the novel can only inadequately represent in its written discourse. Thus, he has not lost his own powers of articulating his consciousness; they are simply beyond the powers of 'magic' white words to represent and contain. Significantly, too, at the end of Susan's narrative, she (and Mr Foe) are beginning to teach Friday how to write, although all he can manage at that point is the letter 'o'. This is clearly the gaping hole of his mouth, 'nothing', and a space which waits to be filled.

The final section of the novel is an enigmatic chapter, again told as an 'I' narrative, but set in the present (the house 'I' visits has 'a plaque...bolted to the wall. *Daniel Defoe, Author,* are the words, white on blue'; 155). 'I' (the author?) envisions a scene back in the eighteenth century in which the corpses of Foe, Susan and Friday lie in the room they inhabited at the time the 'original' story/(ies) were written. But Friday is not quite dead, and 'the author', 'with an ear to his mouth', is lis-tening to 'the faintest faraway roar' emanating from it: 'From his mouth, without a breath, issue the sounds of the island': 'I enter the hole' (154)—which is both Friday's mouth and the silent, as yet unpenetrated, hull of the wrecked slave-ship on which Friday and thousands of other slaves were transported.

This is significantly, a '*black* space' (my emphasis) where 'the water is still and dead, the same water as yesterday, as last year, as three hundred years ago' (156-7). The author 'crawl [s] beneath the bodies of Susan Barton and her dead captain, fat as pigs', and comes upon Friday with 'the chain about his throat', a chain which is the mark of his enslavement. He asks him: 'Friday...what is this ship?' But the novels answer is, indeed *has to be* 'But this is not a place of words.... This is a place where bodies are their own signs. It is the home of Fri-day' (157); and it ends with Friday's mouth opening:

From inside him comes a slow stream, without breath, without interruption. It flows up through his body and out upon me; it passes through the cabin, through the wreck; washing the cliffs and shores of the island, it runs north-ward and southward to the ends of the earth....'

This reversed allusion to the last line of Joseph Conrad's novella, *Heart of Darkness* (1898), where, from the river of the imperial metropolis ('leading to the uttermost ends of the earth'), Marlow's 'inconclusive' Eurocentric [hi]story has sought to penetrate 'into the heart of an immense darkness', suggests that the silenced 'true' story of colonialism and slav-ery still waits to be written. It also implies that it has every chance of being so, but only when the language of the silenced can 'crawl from beneath' the corpus of Western texts which, in constructing their [hi] story, have been centrally complicit in rendering 'tongue'-less the subjects of colonial power. As in *Waiting for the Barbarians* (see p. 156), white 'words' are specious—'whatever can be articulated is falsely put'—and only pass off fictions as 'the truth': 'forging a story and impos-ing it on the world for truth', indeed. In the 'black space' and silence of the 'true' history of colonialism, as yet only 'bodies are their own signs'. But the positive message of Coetzee's novel is that it can in itself both reveal the fabrication which words/stories/histories promote in textualising our lives, espe-cially those of the oppressed, and affirm the possibility that when Friday finds his 'tongue' once more by substituting it for the gaping silent hole ('o') at the centre of colonial discourse, he will be able to articulate the signs of the bodies as his own history of the last 'three hundred years'.

Fundamentally, then, *Foe* is about language and how it works simultaneously to rep-resent and misrepresent ourselves to ourselves.

Derek Walcott's 'Castaway poems also write back' to Defoe's novel, and the power of language is again a central concern. In the title-poem itself, while, as it were, 'casting' himself as Crusoe surveying 'his' island (in the Caribbean), the 'I' of the poem (the Caribbean poet?) observes 'a wrecked ship./ Clenched sea-wood nailed and white as a man's hand', where the assumption that a man's hand is 'white' implies the cul-tural imperialism of Defoe's myth (all quotations here and below from Walcott [1965] 1992).

In 'Crusoe's Island', the poetic 'I', meditating on a modern island, sees 'Friday's progeny,/The brood of Crusoe's slave' as 'Black little girls in pink/Organdy, crinolines', this being the Europeanised result, again, of the culture which *Robinson Crusoe* so pervasively has helped to sustain. And in 'Crusoe's Journal', which is prefaced by a quotation from the novel, the poet reflects on the power of Defoe's writing in creating the consciousness at once of coloniser and of colonised:

...even the bare necessities
of style are turned to use,
like those plain iron tools he salvages
from shipwreck, hewing a prose
as odorous as raw wood to the adze;
out of such timbers
came our first book, our profane Genesis
whose Adam speaks that prose...

It is 'our first book' because it is a founding document of the 'three-hundred-year' history which is to follow. Defoe/Crusoe

...bears
in speech mnemonic as a missionary's
the Word to savages,
its shape an earthen, water-bearing vessel's
whose sprinkling alters us
into good Fridays who recite His praise,
parroting our master's
style and voice, we make his language ours,
converted cannibals
we learn with him to eat the flesh of Christ.
All shapes, all objects multiplied from his, our ocean's Proteus...

Here again, it is language which is the primary *creating* force, insofar as it is Defoe's prose which shapes the whole world-view of those (the 'good Fridays') it gives form to in the first place. Walcott is, in effect, defining 'the literary' in ways which are clearly cognate with my own:

...his journals
assume a household use;
we learn to shape from them, where nothing was *the language*
of a race... (my emphasis)

It would be quite wrong to represent Walcott's poems here as an unequivocal and negative rebuttal of the colonising dis-course of *Robinson Crusoe,* since, amongst other things, the latter represents 'those fantasies of innocence' which 'all of us/ yearn for'. Rather, Walcott is drawing attention to the power of language, 'hewn' into literary form, which is such a funda-mental constituent of our perception of the world. Nevertheless, his poetry, like Coetzee's *Foe,* also suggests how centrally power-relations in the colonial situation are determined by *whose* language constructs them ('to shape...the language of a race'), and how we live inside the [hi]stories so articulated, whether they are true or false.

Indeed, what such literature establishes is that it is difficult, if not impossible, to conceive of a state of being which is not determined by narratives composed of language.

My final example of re-visionary writing is another work which has the deteminate and exclusive powers of language as its central concern. Tony Harrison's long poem V. is, amongst other things, a re-vision of Thomas Gray's famous eighteenth-century poem 'An Elegy Written in a Country Church Yard'. *V.* uses the same stanza form and rhyme-scheme as Gray's 'Elegy' (quatrains rhyming ab ab), is set in a graveyard, is a meditation on death, and also ends with an epitaph to the poet himself. But Harrison's graveyard is on a hill overlooking Leeds rather than in the pastoral setting of the 'Elegy', and is composed during the Miners' Strike of 1984-5 (with the Gulf War and the National Front also in mind), rather than in the rural peace of mid-eighteenth-century England.

It has a jaunty emphatic rhythm which accentuates the 'snap' of the rhyme-scheme, unlike Gray's meditative and elegaic measure which mellifluously disguises it, and, crucially, it is full of the crudest four-letter words ('CUNT', 'FUCK', 'SHIT', 'PISS'), in con-tradistinction to Gray's orotund poetic diction. Where Gray's epitaph, for example, ends with the solemnly valedictory lines requesting the visitor to leave the poet to his quiet 'repose' in 'The bosom of his father and his God' (Gray [1750] 1973:179-82), Harrison's jokes:

Beneath your feet's a poet, then a pit. Poetry supporter, if you're here to find how poems can grow from (beat you to it!) SHIT *find the beef, the beer, the bread, then look behind.* (Harrison [1985] 1991: p. 33)

'Those words', of course, caused the furore which greeted the poem when it was televised in a film version, and the reaction of those on the right of the cultural establishment (as announced, for instance, by 'the riff-raff takes over') ironically confirmed what we shall see to be one of its principal themes: the exclusiveness of a literary culture based on deco-rous canonic poems like Gray's 'Elegy'.

To what end and to what effect, then, is V. a re-vision of the earlier poem? While it is considerably longer than the 'Elegy' and makes little explicit reference to it, once we perceive Gray's poem to be its intertext, a cross-historical irony is set up between then and now: the meditative peace of Gray's eigh-teenth-century pastoral is shattered by the graffitti which decorate late-twentieth-century gravestones.

But where one might expect uncompromising outrage on the part of the mod-ern poet, and a bemoaning of the loss of innocence and deco-rum which is held to characterise the eighteenth-century past, *V.* goes in another direction. Gray's 'Elegy' purports to speak for 'The rude forefathers of the hamlet' (does Harrison tacitly recast the word 'rude' into its modern sense with regard to his skinhead football fans?), for 'Some village-Hampden', 'Some Cromwell' or 'Some mute inglorious Milton'.

But, in effect, it patronises and silences them by way of the smooth poetic diction such countrymen would never have used (being 'mute' and 'inglorious'): so that, as no more than cyphers in the poem, 'Along the cool sequestered vale of life/They kept the noiseless tenor of their way'. All that these ordinary 'flowers' of the village have to remember them by is: 'Some frail memo-rial' made up of 'uncouth rhymes' (note once more the shift in sense from the eighteenth-century to the modern) where 'Their name, their years, spelt by the unlettered muse/The place of fame and elegy supply'. In fact, of course, they now have immortal 'fame' in the 'elegy' written by Thomas Gray: but as what? Not as the 'rude' men they were (and they do indeed seem to have all been men), but as the 'mute', 'noiseless' lin-guistic cyphers of Gray's meditation.

Conversely, Harrison's poem does give his 'skins' a voice—hence the strategically unpoetic 'CUNTS' and 'FUCKS' etc. However, the poem itself is conscious of the dangers of a patronising as bad as Gray's silencing, so that when it explicitly claims to speak for the yobs' in the poet's imaginary conversation with one of them, it immediately undercuts its own claim:

'...the reason why I want this in a book

's to give ungrateful cunts like you a hearing!'

A book, yer stupid cunt, 's not worth a fuck!

The only reason why I write this poem at all on yobs like you who do the dirt on death 's to give some higher meaning to your scrawl.' *Don't fucking bother, cunt! Don't waste your breath!*

The 'yob' also says *'Don't treat me like I'm dumb'* (or 'mute'? *ibid.).* Nevertheless, the poem *does* encode the skin's discourse, however 'uncouth' and senseless it may appear to be; and willynilly, in a poem, it becomes an element of poetic diction. I need hardly add that this is diction which, while extensively prevalent in spoken discourse, seldom if ever finds its place in poetry. But the four-letter words are, in a sense, only there as emblems of a discourse which lies behind them. What the poem also voices on behalf of the yob is the rage and frustra-tion at being out of work in an unjust capitalist society, part of 'the unending violence of US and THEM'(ll):

Ah'll tell yer then what really riles a bloke. It's reading on their graves the jobs they did ...Me, I'll croak doing t' same nowt ah do now as a kid.

...Death after life on t' dole won't seem as 'ardi

It is small wonder that the yob feels *'it's not poetry we need in this class war'* (22), since he is entirely excluded from a culture which has at its heart poems like Gray's 'Elegy'. What the poem is in part about, then, is the responsibility of a divisive and exclusive culture for the formulaic knee-jerk emptiness of 'CUNT', 'SHIT', 'PAKI GIT', 'NIGGER' etc.: 'It isn't all his fault though. Much is ours' (13). 'Ours', here, identifies the stakeholders (the poet amongst them) in a bourgeois capitalist society which makes its money out of arms and 'HARP' (lager) — another four-letter word on which the 'HARPoholic yob' (23) gets 'pissed'—and which admires poetry as part of 'the national culture'.

Equally, the poet recognises that it is only his ability to climb out of the *'class yer were born into'* (22) which differentiates him from the 'skin': under the skin, we might say, the poet remains his alter ego. As the yob prepares to sign the 'UNITED' he has sprayed on the graves of the poet's parents, 'He aerosolled his name. And it was mine' *(ibid).* Under-standing at once that, as poet, he can no longer 'represent' the class he was born into, that 'poet' is, for some, also *'a crude four-letter word'* (19), but that 'This pen's all I have of magic wand' (15—with its echoes of Prospero), all the poet can do is to compose a poem which attempts to 'UNITE' elements of himself in a hybrid mix of high cultural reference (Gray, Mar-vell, Rimbaud, *Hamlet)* and the language of the yob, but which is constantly and endemically pulled apart by 'all the versuses of life' (11).

It is here that we may bring in the poem's title, for *V.*, of course, means a number of things, as the poem implies: 'versus', as we have heard; 'V-sign, as in 'fuck off and/or 'Victory'; 'cunt', as in 'he added a middle slit to one daubed V.' (22); and the abbreviation for 'Verses' ('versus' and 'Verses' can also sound identical). For the poem is fundamentally con-cerned with language, its ambiguities and its protean nature depending on where it is located socially. 'SHIT' and 'poem' are both 'four-letter words', but they seem to belong to differ-ent cultural registers: to be another 'Versus'.

But in the 'Verses' of the poem *V.*, 'SHIT' takes its place in the poetic register as just as much a part of it as are the 'fame' and 'elegy' of Gray's poem, and the word has as much, if not more, poetic resonance in establishing the presence of the 'mute' and 'inglorious' as Gray's culturally acceptable verses do. In this respect if no other, Harrison's poem at once indicates the limits of the famous 'Elegy' and the possibilities of an expanded poetic discourse which accomodates the shifting and potent language of social reality. The yob, in other words, needs to be incorporated in a poetry which attempts to contain the fundamental contradictions of life, and which in so doing hopes to render them 'UNITED'.

In one respect, however, V. does not revise Gray's 'Elegy'. The only woman in the latter is 'the busy housewife' who will 'no more...ply her evening care' for the departed 'rude forefa-thers of the village' ('For them no more the blazing hearth shall burn'). While recognising that one of 'all the versuses of life' is 'man v.wife'(11), the only women in Harrison's poem are his dead mother and the one invoked by the lines:

'Home, home to my woman, where the fire's lit/these still chilly mid-May evenings, home to you' (29), and 'the bride/I feel united to, *my* bride is coming into the bedroom, naked, to my side' (31).

The 'busy housewife' and 'my woman' seem remarkably similar in their presence merely as comfort for the males voiced by the poems. But what Harrison's poem furthermore seems symptomatically to be unconscious of is the fact that his imported yob's language—and especially 'CUNT'—is pro-foundly sexist. This is *male* language from a predominantly male culture (football, lager, war, coal-mining), and in this case, it is *not* transmuted by becoming a component of the poetic discourse of Harrison's poem.

The poem, in other words, and however subversive of conventional attitudes it may otherwise be, remains locked within and by the sexist lan-guage it simultaneously deploys and fails to deconstruct. In this subliminal textualised alerting of us to the persistence of language as a ubiquitous form of male sexism, *V.*, I would sug-gest, reveals yet another—albeit only negative—aspect of the 're-visioning' which 'the literary' makes available to us.

Perhaps the most innovative 'use' by which contemporary liter-ature contributes to history, however, is by writing it as fic-tion. We saw earlier how an historical novel, *Adam Bede,* offers us a 'social history' at both the conscious and the uncon-scious levels. But in the contemporary period, 'the literary' has strategically attempted to penetrate into that empty 'space' or echoing 'silence' which is the history of a people who have been vanquished and/or colonised by victors of one son or another, not least by way of the victors' 'history' becoming the Authorised History of what occurred.

In many such cases, the history of the vanquished has no, or very little, written docu-mentation to sustain contemporary acts of restitution. There-fore, the only way in which a people's past can be retrieved and restored is by an imaginative reconstruction of the com-plex processes of survival and opposition which the dominant power would have written out of its own history of victory and control. A particularly telling instance of this is 'Holo-caust' writing, where fiction, amongst other forms, becomes precisely a defeating of the 'silence' the Nazis intended by the total extermination of the Jewish people.

The victims of the 'final solution' were told that none of them would be left to bear witness, and that there would be no certainty about what had happened because the evidence would be destroyed together with the victims. In 'testifying' to the things they had seen and experienced, Primo Levi and other writers attempted to reconstruct a 'real' history to counterbalance the fiction that nothing had happened, to controvert an 'official' silence which would have written the extermination of the Jews out of history. To *record* became the motivating impulse; for while the liquidation of the Jews could not be halted by writing, it could at least be chronicled and remembered. The fact that *fiction* is a primary form in which this 'real history' gets recorded—in the potential absence of it from 'official history'—lies at the heart of my argument here.

Raymond Williams's last major project, *People of the Block Mountains,* a trilogy of novels of which only two were completed before his death, focuses my point even more explicitly. In an interview in 1983, while reflecting on the writing of the 'real history' of a people, Williams suggests that 'the ruling class...in its own time above all controls] the tradition...[in which process] certain important things are read out, simply excluded...This is the process I call the selective tradition' (Williams [1983] 1989:168-9). In the first volume of his novel, apropos of the history which existed prior to the written record, the idea is taken up again:

> After ten thousand generations of conscious life and mem-ory, these written traces, by convention, would be called the beginning of history: *the true, because recorded,* story of the land.
>
> Actual *stories* are told by both winners and losers. Yet what becomes history is a selection by the winners.
>
> (Williams 1989:325; my emphases)

We may register in passing here—so that I can return to it—Williams's strategic slippage from 'history' to 'story'. In a sec-ond interview (1987), he presses the fact that the trilogy of novels presents a history written very much...from below' (Williams 1987:7; the phrase, pointedly, is E.P.Thompson's, in the preface to his radically innovative history, *The Making of the English Working Class,* 1963). The rulers, Williams says, dominate history (and hence most conventional 'historical nov-els'), whereas his novel attempts to reintroduce the lives of the 'anonymous' working people *(ibid.)* who had to relate to the different forms of power (he never disputes their reality) of that minority of rulers ('the winners') whose own 'selective tradition' nevertheless then writes' the 'true...[hi]story of the land'.

The history of the people, barely literate over thousands of years, has been 'read out, simply excluded', silenced by the official 'false history' (8) of the ruling classes.

Most historical novels, because of the abundance of such records, are also 'written from the level of the dominant class, and the *others* are...off stage' (7; Williams's emphasis), whereas his own 'true historical novel' (3) aims to reverse this emphasis. But the important thing, he says, is that he is '*not* writing a history: it is a novel, and I claim imaginative rights over it' (8), the reason being that 'there is a sense...in which history which is both recorded and unrecorded can only find its way through to personal substance if it then becomes a novel, becomes a *story*' (13; my emphasis).

The novel form, with its 'imaginative' (Williams uses the word repeatedly) freedom, can 'put back these actual lives [of the people] into what would otherwise be a generalised history' (10) by reconstituting their history from even the most vestigial 'traces'. Thus, as the novel itself has it, it can recover 'a living memory' to defeat 'a long forgetting' (1989:10) by reaching 'a wider common flow, where touch and breath replaced record and analysis: *not history as narrative but stories as lives*' (12; my emphasis). 'The literary as history', I would argue, functions precisely as a way at once of obviating 'a long forgetting' and of giving 'personal substance' to occluded historical knowledge.

But the nub of my argument is that Williams *has to write a novel* in order to retrieve the unwritten, unrecorded history of the Welsh people. In these circumstances, a history *has to be* invented, or imaginatively reconstructed ('there is nothing in [the novel] which goes *against* what is factually known' [Williams 1987:8]), since there is no other way of knowing, say, what a cave-dweller, hunting horses in 23,000 BC (when the novel opens), would have thought, said and done, nor how an eleventh-century smith in the Border Country navigated the continually shifting relations of authority and loyalty at that time and place.

And if the official 'winners' history' comprises an account of its successful dominance and control, which would, of course, 'read out' its actual repressiveness, then the novel can release and restore a sense of the challenges and resis-tances which that power would have met at all points. So that Williams can 'fabricate', as potent and 'enduring symbol[s] of resistance' (1990:4), Derco, the renegade British slave, and Owain Glyndwr, the Welsh hero. Of Derco, people say: 'it is not known ...whether Derco lives or indeed whether there ever was such a man.

When the men of Menhebog are asked they say only that he is not here but will come' (19); and of Glyndwr, that 'he will never make his submission' (302): he '"will get a new banner.... He will lead us to victory. He is a magician. He appears everywhere there is fighting". "Have you seen this magician?" ..."No. But I have seen his banner"' (1990:300). Their 'magical' protean absence also means that neither folk-hero has to submit—which a 'winners' history' would no doubt require them to do.

It may be stretching it to claim Williams for the fictional subgenre of 'magic realism', but it is fair to note that in his attempt to subvert orthodox history in novel-form, such a combination of elements is present. For in addition to writing a 'losers' history' which proclaims resistance and difference, *People of the Black Mountains* also subverts expectations and evaluations of what a novel—more particularly a 'realist' fic-tion—should be.

Conventional literary-critical criteria of value and decorum are placed beside the point here. For example, how do we discuss a coherent plot in a novel whose first vol-ume begins in 23,000 BC and reaches 51 AD in 358 pages; how do we evaluate the 'characterisation' of a stone-age shep-herd, or the representation of the penetration of modernity' (1990:63) into fifth-century Wales; how do we judge the tone and style of a novel which has, as it were, to invent a language in order to articulate an unvoiced people?

Even sympathetic reviewers of the novel when it was first published felt the need to criticise its 'infelicities' of style, tone and structure ('infelici-ties', and the ability to spot them instinctively and unerringly, surely take us back to the naturalised and received culture of 'Literature'), and of damning it with faint praise: 'we can't deny that in fiction...we want something more than even good and true ideas'. The presumptive 'we' here means that 'we' remain firmly imprisoned within a conventional paradigm of 'the good novel', upset by the 'tensions in the writing' and 'the crisis of idioms' the book reveals.

Hence, 'we' are unable to respond positively to Williams's heterodox fictional 'fabrica-tion' of the means and methods for an alternative political and social history of the relations between 'winners' and 'losers'. Indeed, throughout his work, creative and critical, Williams's definition of realism was complex. For it included the notion of a proleptic realism which could be deployed to project beyond the commonsense realisms of existing determinations and forms; so that realising the unwritten past, as does the imag[in]ing of the experiential history of the silenced Welsh people in *People of the Black Mountains,* is a form of such a realism.

To put it another way: Williams's cultural-materialist project rests, paradoxically, on *imagination,* on the ability, as we heard him say of George Eliot on p. 106, to 'think beyond, feel beyond' the limits and limitations of the dominant ortho-doxies and authorities, of cultural and political hegemony, of an Authorised ('winners') History.

And if nothing else, his novel poses the question: how do we write even a fictional redressing of the received account if we are held within the ideology of existing generic modes, and if the language and forms of such are effectively geared (in the name of 'taste' and 'plausibility') to excluding the experience of 'the *others*'' (see p. 181)? It is one of the principal uses of 'the literary' that its imaginative or 'magical' properties can transgress the quotid-ian and the naturalised.

In its concern to retrieve a 'disappeared' history by way of its unstable combination of grainy realism and the 'magical', Williams's late work does seem to have something in common with other, rather more radical, examples of 'magic realism', a mode of writing which is comprised of a matter-of-fact juxtaposing of a recognisable material reality with the fantastical and supernatural. Itself a product and figuration of the 'hybridity' of colonial and now postcolonial cultures, magic realism has been crucial in the process of moving, in Michael Dash's phrase, 'Towards a Redefinition of History' (Dash [1974] 1995:199).

Drawing on the work of the Haitian novelist, Jacques Stephen Alexis, and the Guyanese writer, Wilson Harris, Dash's notion of 'a counter-culture of the imagination', quoted earlier, allows for 'a more speculative vision of history in which the consciousness of the dominated culture would predominate' (200). This involves 'so reordering] their reality as to reach beyond the tangible and concrete to acquire a new re-creative sensibility', one which is articulated by 'the myths, legends and superstitions of the folk...traces of a complex cul-ture of survival which was the response of the dominated to their oppressors' *(ibid.)*.

As we shall see, this recuperation of 'non-rational' discourses to express what Alexis calls a people's 'whole consciousness of reality by the use of the Marvellous' (Alexis [1956] 1995:195) is very much what Toni Morrison also means when she talks of the restitution of African-Americans' 'discredited knowledge' (see pp. 200-01). The blending, in contemporary writing, of such 'figurative' systems with 'the tangible and concrete' signifies, says Dash, 'an adoption of the positive imaginative reconstruction of reality developed in the consciousness of the folk' (Dash [1974] 1995:200-1), hence 'engaging in a conception of the past which would shatter the myths of "historylessness" or "non-achievement"' (200).

Perhaps the best-known example of magic realism is the South American novelist, Gabriel Garcia Marquez's seminal work in the genre, *One Hundred Years of Solitude*, which, amongst many other things, represents an 'unofficial' history of Columbia. Here, the 'marvellous' or 'magical' is employed to capture states of mind in a remote country emerging into modernity; to realise the impact of the 'secondary' colonialism of American capitalism (the banana farming); and the conse-quential development of a repressive modern state, which, for example, erases the massacre of three thousand striking workers (its own citizens) from the historical record.

'The official version...was finally accepted: there were no dead, the satisfied workers had gone back to their families' (Marquez [1967] 1972:315); so that only 'a hallucinated version' remains (that of the novel itself) 'because it was radically opposed to the false one that historians had created and consecrated in the schoolbooks' (355). Echoes of Kafka and Orwell are evident here. It is by way of the magic realism (and other forms of 'fantasy' made available by 'the literary'), in other words, that the 'unreality' of the real can be brought into view. In so doing, such modes help to solve the problem, once identified by Christopher Isherwood, as to how the modern writer can address the 'fantastic realities' of 'the everyday world' (Isher-wood 1972:33).

Similarly, Isabel Allende, in *The House of the Spirits,* uses magic realism to compose her 'history' of modern Chile, emphasising especially the subversive 'counter-culture of the imagination of the 'extraordinary women of this story', to whom the novel is dedicated. The women exist in a repressively patriarchal culture where the quintessential patriarch, Clara's husband, Estaban Trueba, regards 'magic, like cooking and religion, [as] a particularly feminine affair' (Allende [1985] 1986:162).

Of Clara's fantastical notebooks 'that bore witness to life' (138 and *passim),* Alba, her granddaughter who 'writes' the novel, observes: 'She filled innumerable note-books with her private observations, recording the events of those years, thanks to which they were not erased by the mists of forgetfulness and I can now use them to reclaim her memory' (95). Equally, the letters between Clara and her daughter Blanca have 'salvaged events from the mists of *improbable facts'* (283; my emphasis). Since it is Alba/Allende who sorts through her inherited materials, in 'the silence of the dead and disappeared', in order to 'construct this story' (39), it is, of course, *the novel itself* which actually provides the notebooks and letters, and so 'reclaims' a 'herstory' for the benefit of con-temporary readers that would otherwise have been 'erased' by the 'improbable facts' of his-story.

Apropos, and following Marquez, Allende also deploys magic realism to devastating effect in 'realistically' writing a 'losers' history' of the fall of President Allende's (her uncle's) government and the nightmare of the subsequent military ter-ror in Chile. The ferocious, Orwellian regime of General Pinochet replaces reality with unreality in the name of reality: 'with a stroke of the pen the military changed world history, erasing every incident, ideology, and historical figure of which the regime disapproved'; introduced blanket censorship, 'swept... from the lexicon' words such as 'freedom' and 'jus-tice'; and closed the school of philosophy in the university, which 'like many others...open the gateway of the mind' (435-6).

Allende's imaginative reconstruction, on the other hand, accesses the 'unreal' reality behind the 'real' unreality. During the euphoric and doomed chaos of Allende's revolution, short-ages of goods meant that 'shoe polish, needles, and coffee became luxury items to be gift-wrapped and given as presents for birthdays and other special occasions', while 'people who had never smoked wound up paying an exorbitant sum for a pack of cigarettes, and those without children found them-selves fighting over cans of baby food' (396-7).

In Pinochet's Chile, squalor, poverty and violence are hidden away to 'create the illusion' of peace and prosperity, so that 'the [capital] city had never looked more beautiful' (434); but 'in the silence of the night...the city lost its stage-set normality and operetta peace' (442). It is, of course, 'the *silence* of the night' which Allende's novel seeks to break, in which a significant element of the unreality of the time is the way those who benefit from, and thus collaborate with, the military regime preferred 'not... to know what was going on' in order to preserve the 'precari-ous stability' of their world (458, 453). Sustained by the women in the concentration camp whose spirit the authorities 'have not been able to destroy' (487), and inspired by the ghostly presence of her grandmother, Clara, Alba begins to keep a notebook 'to escape from the doghouse and live' (470). Clara, in a key passage, suggests that she

> *write a testimony that might one day call attention to the terrible secret she was living through, so that the world would know about this horror that was taking place parallel to the peaceful existence of those who did not want to know, who could afford the illusion of a normal life...who could deny ...despite all evidence, that only blocks away from their happy world there were others, these others who live or the on the dark side.* (ibid.)

Like the Holocaust writers mentioned earlier, Alba's 'testi-mony' (and Allende's novel) are an attempt to speak for those others who are 'disappeared' out of history, and to controvert the blind and deaf 'forgetting' of those who live in a 'neigh-bourhood...like another country' (487). Clara's and Alba's 'notebooks', retrieved by the magic realism of the novel— which, of course, *creates* them 'out of nothing...for the first time'—defeats the fact 'that memory is fragile' and allows Alba/Allende to 'reclaim the past and overcome terrors of my own' (11).

In so doing, she offers those of us who are contem-porary readers, and who literally and metaphorically inhabit 'another country', a 'newstory' without which the reality/ unreality of history would remain opaque. Most significantly, however, for my attempt to exemplify the 'uses of the literary', Alba closes the novel by commenting on what it has done, not-ing the way she has had to organise the 'incomprehensible' 'jigsaw puzzle' of all its constituent elements, so that 'the sepa-rate parts would each have meaning and the whole be harmonious': 'The space of a single life is brief, passing so quickly that we never get a chance to see the relationship between events.... That's why my Grandmother Clara wrote in her notebooks, in order to see things in their true dimension and to defy her own poor memory' (490-1). And that too is the reason for the 'magic' of the novel: for it is this which shapes a 'sense of subject' ('seeing the relationship between events... seeing things in their true dimension') out of 'improbable facts', real 'unrealities' and the 'long forgetting' of the 'Chaos of Being'. *The House of the Spirits* is a [hi] story which his-story would not have written.

A prime example of this, too, is Salman Rushdie's *Midnight's Children,* in which, as the narrator, Saleem Sinai (whose *Tristram-Shandy-like* 'autobiography' the novel pur-ports to be), puts it: 'the great work of preserving Memory, as well as fruit, is being saved from the corruption of the clocks' ([1981] 1982:38). Hence, Saleem's present occupation of mak-ing pickles or, rather, of testing 'the feasibility of the chutnifica-tion of history; the grand hope of the pickling of time! I, however, have pickled chapters' (459). But in writing his life, Saleem has simultaneously to write an inclusive history of India since independence (and then of the foundation of Pak-istan and Bangladesh), for as he says: 'To understand just one life, you have to swallow the world' (109), and later:

> *I am the sum total of everything that went before me.... Nor am I particularly exceptional in this matter; each 'I', every one of the now-six-hundred-million-plus of us, con-tains a similar multitude. I repeat for the last time: to under-stand me, you'll have to swallow a world. (383)*

And to do this, the author must invent, amongst many other 'marvellous' characters and events, both his 'muse', Padma, 'with her [significantly, in the context of magic realism] down-to-earthery, and her paradoxical superstition, her contradic-tory love of the fabulous' (38), and the 'fabulous' figure of Tai the boatman as the representative of the age-old oral tradition of legends, myths and tall-tales in Indian culture, which press down onto the present and must be included if the whole pic-ture is to be given. His 'magical talk' (15), 'fantastic, grandilo-quent and ceaseless' (14), 'represents' the immense and ancient pre-history of modern India, in which Saleem's 'history' is 'no more than one fleeting instant'(194).

One of the novel's principal themes, which is summed up in the sentence: "'What's real and what's true aren't necessarily the same'" (79), is indeed the status of the 'fabulous' and the 'fantastic'. For Saleem/ Rushdie, the 'true' is as likely to be found in 'stories' *(ibid.)* and the (apparently) 'fantastic' as in 'real' history. Hence the invention of the 'MCC (Midnight Children's Conference—an acronym reclaimed from the home of imperial cricket): those 'fabulous beings' born on the stroke of midnight ('August 15th, 1947' [9]) after which India's independence from British colonial rule would begin. They represent the multiplex and contradictory elements bequeathed to the new India (Saleem himself, it transpires, has a British father)—'in truth, a mirror of the nation' (255): 'the children of midnight were also the children *of the time:* fathered...by history. It can happen. Especially in a country which is itself a sort of dream' (118; Rushdie's emphasis). Hence, too, the recurrent motif in the novel of the cinema/film as a metaphor for the truthfulness/ reality of composing (espe-cially contemporary) history:

> *Reality is a question of perspective; the further you get from the past, the more concrete and plausible it seems— but as you approach the present, it inevitably seems more and more incredible. Suppose yourself in a large cinema, sitting at first in the back row, and gradually moving up, row by row, until your nose is almost pressed against the screen. Gradually the stars' faces dissolve into dancing grain; tiny details assume grotesque proportions; the illu-sion dissolves—or rather, it becomes clear that the illusion itself* is *reality...we have come from 1915 to 1956, so we're a good deal closer to the screen... (166)*

And by 1976 (shortly before the novel ends), during Indira Ghandhi s repressive 'Emergency' when the Midnight's Chil-dren are 'disappeared-off-the-face-of-the-earth' (435): 'right now we're too close to the cinema-screen, the picture is break-ing up into dots, only subjective judgements are possible' *(ibid.)*. 'Illusion' has indeed become 'reality'.

The novel itself, however, is obsessively concerned with its own capacity for error, while at the same time in pursuit of telling 'the whole truth' of the history it is writing. Saleem dis-covers 'an error in chronology' (he has given the wrong date on which Mahatma Ghandi was assassinated, so that 'in my India, Ghandi will continue to the at the wrong time' [166]). That neither he (nor Rushdie) correct the errors, which they could easily have done, is at once an admission of any [hi] story's ability to falsify and of how historical errors in effect become 'true'. But still, Saleem asks:

> *Does one error invalidate the entire fabric? Am I so far gone, in my desperate need for meaning, that I am pre-pared to distort everything—to re-write the whole history of my times purely in order to place myself in a central role?* (ibid.)

The answer is surely 'No'; but it remains a salutary reminder that text and discourse, however truthful, construct reality—as Saleem also acknowledges when he says:

> *the feeling came upon me that I was somehow* creating a world...*I was somehow* making *[things]* happen...*which is to say, I had entered into* the illusion of the artist, *and thought of the* multifarious realities *of the land as* the raw unshaped material *of my gift (174; my emphases)*

The echoes here of Stephen Dedalus al the very end of James Joyce's *A Portrait of the Artist as a Young Man* cannot be for-tuitous (see above, p. 101). The phrases emphasised above coincide with what I am claiming is the distinguishing feature of 'the literary', and Saleem/ Rushdie do not renege on that. Rather the opposite: for while offering a warning ('in autobiog-raphy, as in all literature, what actually happened is less impor-tant than what the author can manage to persuade his audi-ence to believe...' [270-1]), they actually see the 'illusion of the artist' as more nearly approaching 'the whole truth' than the partiality (in both senses) of a 'real' record ever can.

For one thing, the magic realism of the text can incorporate those (apparently) 'irrational' or 'fabulous' areas of experience which a rational and 'realistic' discourse, by definition, cannot: 'Reality can have a metaphorical content; that does not make it less real' (200). For another, it represents 'the greatest talent of all—the ability to look into the hearts and minds of men' *(ibid.)*; and for another, in the (fictive) 'great work of preserv-ing Memory': 'Memory [i]s truth, because memory has its own special kind. It selects, eliminates, alters, exaggerates, min-imises, glorifies, and vilifies also; but in the end it *creates its own reality*, its heterogeneous but *usually correct* version of events' (211; my emphases).

In 'creating its own reality, its...usually correct version of events', the magic realism of *Midnight's Children*, like that of Marquez and Allende, is deployed to refute the 'true' history of 'real' events which warfaring and repressive regimes engen-der in becoming the proud owners of a 'winners' history'. Apropos of the consolidation of the 'President of Pakistan's' power, Saleem comments that the process proved to him:

> *that, in a country where the truth is what it is instructed to be, reality quite literally ceases to exist, so that everything becomes possible except what we are told is the case... I was adrift, disorientated, amid an...infinite number of false-nesses, unrealities and lies. (326)*

On the dates of a border skirmish between India and Pakistan in 1965, Saleem reflects:

> *That much is fact; but everything else lies concealed behind the doubly hazy air of* unreality and make-believe *which affected all goings-on in those days, and especially all events in the* phantasmagoric *Rann...so that the story I am going to tell...is as likely to be true as anything; as any-thing, that is to say, except what we were officially told. (335; my emphases)*

Of course, the fantastic 'unreality' of the story the novel tells is a countering of the 'real history' put out by government propa-ganda machines ('I saw many things which were not true, which were not possible...it was not true because it could not have been true' [375]). But this is most effectively seen in the novel's culminating event: Mrs Ghandhi's 'Emergency', which signals to Saleem the final elimination of the potentialities the Midnight's Children—who are rounded up and rendered impo-tent in the government's repression—had represented for the emergent modern India.

The novel, here, conveys the unreal 'reality' of the time and attempts to reveal from beneath it, in the real 'unreality' of its own textuality, a true history of those events: 'she had white hair on one side and black on the other; the Emergency, too, had a white part—public, visible, docu-mented, *a matter for historians*—and a black part which, being secret macabre *untold*, must be *a matter for us*' (421; my emphases). What I am claiming for 'the literary' as a 'counter-culture of the imagination' could scarcely be more exactly put: not that it necessarily tells 'the truth', but that it at once coun-ters the official 'truths' which envelop our lives, and shows us, in its own self-conscious textual 'making', how those [hi] sto-ries are fabricated too.

In this context, it is worth drawing attention to the novel's self-consciousness of *form* as the medium in which the 'chutnification of history' is preserved. Reflecting on what he sees as a 'national longing for form', Saleem thinks of it as 'perhaps simply an expression of our deep belief that *forms lie hidden within reality*, that *meaning reveals itself only in flashes*' (300; my emphases). It is indeed the ability to see pattern within the flux of life, and to reveal 'flashes of meaning' ('moments of vision', 'insight'), which I am arguing constitute literature's continuing claim for attention. Towards the end of the novel, Saleem observes: 'Form—once again, recurrence and shape!— no escape from it'; and as it closes, thinking about the 'immor-tality' pickling gives, he says: 'The art is to change the flavour [of the 'raw materials'] in degree, but not in kind; and above all (in my thirty jars and a jar) to give it shape and form—that is to say, meaning' (461). Such is the effect of the 'art' of 'the literary', too.

The 'thirty jars' mentioned above are the thirty chapters of the thirty-year-old (soon to be thirty-one) Saleem's 'autobiog-raphy' (and of the novel itself). The non-existent thirty-first jar —'and a jar'—is, however, crucial, since it represents the possibility of a future: the door to the future is kept 'ajar'. For despite 'the smashing, the pulverizing, the irreversible discombobulation of the children of midnight' (427), and the acceler-ating decomposition of the narrator himself as *Midnight's Children* reaches its conclusion, Saleem does have a son who can now speak, and whose first words are the magic ones which are the title of the novel's own final chapter: 'Abra-cadabra' (459).

When Saleem is trapped in the timeless dark-ness, 'the isolating, artificial night', of the postmodern 'Mid-nite-Confidential Club'—'that place outside time, that nega-tion of history'—the eyes of his son Aadam (a new first man to replace the first modern man, Saleem's grandfather, Aadam Aziz) shine with light, and he is presented as 'a member of a second generation of magical children who would grow up far tougher than the first, not looking for their fate in prophecy or the stars, but forging it in the implacable furnaces of their wills' (447). The unwritten thirty-first chapter, in other words, is available for Aadam's generation, because 'the future cannot be preserved in a jar; one jar must remain empty...' (462). Even Rushdie's magic realism cannot pickle the future, because it 'has not taken place' *(ibid.)*; but it does, nevertheless, leave it 'a/jar'—preserving it as a space as yet unspiced.

My final two examples of 'the uses of the literary'—in tribute to the re-energising of literature brought about by the enfran-chising of erstwhile marginalised voices—are both by black women writers, and both use it to reinstate a history 'hidden from history'. The first is the sequence of poems, *i is a long memoried woman* by the Caribbean poet, Grace Nichols (Nichols 1983). Charting the consciousness of an African woman transported by slavery to 'the new world', the poems register her resistance to, and gradual independence from, the 'double colonisation' of being a black woman.

The first poem, 'One Continent/ To Another', begins with the simultaneously unknowable and unforgettable experience of the 'Middle Pas-sage' (i.e. on the slave ships crossing from Africa to the Ameri-cas; see also Toni Morrison's *Beloved,* on pp. 199-200 below): 'Child of the middle passage womb/...bleeding memories in the darkness'. But the woman nevertheless believes that 'We must hold fast to dreams/...all revolutions are rooted in dreams' ('Days That Fell'). This she does by invoking her 'Mother' and other legendary 'goddesses', and by affirming the pride and strength of women who voices go unheard' ('We The Women'). She asserts their sexuality:

woman
clad
in her loveliest woman
skin gleaming faintly

with oils breasts nippling
the wind
('...Like Clamouring Ghosts')

And she never forgets either her African origins; her betrayal by men, even those 'the colour of my own skin': 'No it isn't easy to forget/ what we refuse to remember' (an ambiguous atti-tude to memory analagous to that in *Beloved,* too); or the appalling treatment handed out by the slave-owners to 'all us rebel/ women' ('Ala'). But it is in the section pointedly entitled 'The Sorcery' that black women's 'magic' announces their 'revolution:

I coming back "Massa" I coming back
mistress of the underworld
I coming back
colour and shape of all that is evil I coming back
('I Coming Back')

In this way, the poems' persona can envisage a 'Return' in which freedom from racial and sexual oppression is possible:

let them sleep
they happy white sleep
Yes, Wind a change keep yuh coming fire secret
('Wind A Change')

What she seeks, as 'a woman...with all my lives/ strung out like beads/ before me', is

the power to be what I am/ a woman charting my own futures/ a woman holding my beads in my hand
('Holding My Beads')

An essential part of the process of achieving this, as the 'Epi-logue' indicates, is to restore a voice and a history of their own to black women, which is, of course, what *i is a long memo-ried woman* itself is doing:

I have crossed an ocean I have lost my tongue from the root of the old
One a new one has sprung

The parallels with Coetzee's Friday, and his *excised 'tongue' from which 'a new one' waits to 'spring', are inescapable.*

My final example of the usefulness of 'the literary' in restor-ing a 'tongue' is Toni Morrison's novel, *Beloved.* If this may seem a predictable choice, because of the way the novel has so rapidly become both hugely popular and a 'new canon' text, this very phenomenon also underwrites my view that 'fiction as history' continues to fulfill a pressing need in late-twentieth-century societies. An attempt to map imaginatively the history of African-Americans (one continued in the two later novels in this loose trilogy, *Jazz* [1992] and *Paradise* [1998]), the pri-mary historical focus of *Beloved* is that of the immediate aftermath of slavery.

It charts the lives of a group of freed slaves in 1873 in post-bellum America, i.e. ten years after emancipation and eight years after the end of the Civil War, although it also articulates, by way of the 'rememorying' (Mor-rison's word) of Sethe and Paul D, the earlier experience of being a slave proper. And behind that history again, it attempts to give a voice, as we shall see, to the whole folk-memory of the 'Sixty Million and more' (to whom the novel is dedicated) who died throughout the appalling history of slav-ery, and especially during the so-called 'Middle Passage' (the sea-crossing from Africa to America).

Thus, it seeks to restore a voice to a past which has few written documents to sustain it. In this, it is another 'losers' history': one which seeks to get behind the double oppression of black women by 'speaking' 'the thoughts of the women of 124 [Bluestone Road], unspeak-able thoughts, unspoken' (Morrison [1987] 1988:199), where the double sense of 'unspeakable' is telling. In so doing, it focuses on the problematics of freedom: 'Freeing yourself was one thing; claiming ownership of that freed self was another' (95).

In addition, and as a crucial aspect of this, the novel offers an extended meditation on the interpenetration of the past in the present—of what Raymond Williams called 'the pressure of the past...a sense almost of the *presence* of the past' (Williams 1987:4; his emphasis); on the processes and effects of memory; and on the question of how determinate the past is, or, more importantly, *should be,* on the present. For Morrison (in an interview entitled 'Rootedness: The Ancestor as Foundation'), the novel-form is a crucial contemporary resource:

new information has got to get out, and there are several ways to do it. One is *in the novel.*

> ...*It should have something in it that* enlightens; some-thing in it that opens the door and points the way. *Some-thing in it that* suggests what the conflicts are, what the problems are. *But it need not solve those problems because it is not a case study, it is not a recipe. (Morrison [1983] 1985:340-1; my emphases)*

I have italicised the phrases above because they seem to me to be consonant with my definition of 'the literary', in the sense that they imply the transmission of 'news' by way of bringing into view, 'for the first time in this way, a 'sense of subject' ('conflicts' and 'problems') otherwise obscured in the undiffer-entiated flux of lived experience: they 'enlighten'.

There are a number of 'enlightening' narrative strategies employed in Morrison's own novel to get the several receding histories written, and to establish what it recognises itself is ultimately impossible: 'what really happened'. In one of its many disguised self-reflexivities, the novel notes: 'Denver spoke, Beloved listened, and the two did the best they could to *create what really happened,* how it really was, something only Sethe knew because she alone had the mind for it and the time afterward *to shape if* (78; my emphases). The paradoxical notion of *'creating* what really happened' is central to my notion of 'the literary'; but even more so is the recognition that only Sethe, in *'shaping* it', could get at 'how it really was': which, of course, is exactly what the novel is doing in order to get *its* [hi] story told.

The disturbed chronology, which cuts backwards and forwards between the past and the present, intermingling the two in the process of 'rememorying', itself *represents* the presence of the past in the present and its hold on it: Sethe's sense that 'nothing ever dies' (36). A particularly powerful instance of this narrative chronology is the extremely slow unfolding of 'what really happened' in Paul D's and Sethe's past, and most particularly Sethe's killing of Beloved. This is slipped in for the first time almost exactly halfway through the book (104), and is only actually described some 40 pages later.

The effect is to prepare us for the event: knowing so much about Sethe's atrocious treatment in the past has created sympathy for her, so that what otherwise would have seemed a monstrous act, while not being justified, is nevether-less *explained.*

A second feature of the narration is its disconcerting blend of harsh 'historical' realism and the supernatural, the most obvious instance being the character of Beloved herself, who is at once presented as humanly real and as a ghost. Her function as the latter, amongst other things, is to allow Morrison to rep-resent in her [hi] story the unretrievable experience of the slaves on the slave-ships as they undergo the 'Middle Passage'. Within the four sections towards the end of the novel where Sethe's, Denver's and Beloved's minds weave into a stream of consciousness that articulates 'the thoughts of the women of 124, unspeakable thoughts, unspoken' (the closing sentence of the preceding chapter), Beloved 'rememories' the conditions in the hold of a slave-ship:

> *I am always crouching the man on my face is dead his face is not mine his mouth smells sweet but his eyes are locked some who eat nasty themselves I do not eat the men without skin bring us their morning water to drink we have none at night I cannot see the dead man on my face (210)*

As for Williams in his 'pre-historic' re-enactments, only the imaginative projection of 'the literary' can retrieve a past so occluded that it may be said simply not to exist. Realising—in both senses—its existence is, of course, exactly what I am want-ing to claim literature uniquely does.

In the interview with Morrison quoted earlier, she makes a crucial statement about what 'the literary' can indeed do in its 'making' of '*poietic* realities'. Reflecting on her earlier novel, *Song of Solomon,* she notes how it

> *blend[s] the acceptance of the supernatural and a pro-found rootedness in the real world at the same time with neither taking precedence over the other. It is indicative of the cosmology, the way in which Black people looked at the world. We are very practical people, very down-to-earth.... But within that practicality we also accepted what I suppose could be called superstition and magic, which is another way of knowing things. But to blend those two worlds together at the same time was enhancing, not limit-ing. And some of those things were 'discredited knowl-edge' that*

> *Black people had; discredited only because Black people were discredited therefore what they* knew *was 'discredited'. And also because the press toward upward social mobility would mean to get as far away from that kind of knowledge as possible. That kind of knowl-edge has a very strong place in my work. (Morrison [1983] 1985:342)*

What Morrison is describing is, of course, a version of 'magic realism' (see pp. 184-5). But the important thing to recognise is that it is only by way of 'story' as 'history' that 'another way of knowing things' can be articulated: some things can only get said through an imaginative agency which ruptures common-sense, rational 'realism'. This is especially the case with 'dis-credited knowledge'—that of 'the losers', which, as Williams puts it, has been 'read out' of history. Morrison's novel, in other words, legitimates Black 'discredited knowledge' by giv-ing it a voice, by presenting it as part of the experiential reality of Black lives.

That it also enables her to get the 'unspeakable' spoken—what we might call the psycho-history of slavery—is a further 'enhancement' which would otherwise be left mute. But what is equally important for my argument here, too, is the fact that Morrison is acutely aware that she is writing 100 years after the end of slavery for people who may well be for-getting, or even *trying to* forget, that past and that kind of 'discredited knowledge': those for whom 'the press of upward social mobility', for example, means ridding themselves of any trace of 'discreditedness'. The novel, therefore, is a means of 'rememorying' a history which, in Williams's phrase again, is in process of 'a long forgetting'.

But even this is to simplify the kind of 'newstory for the con-temporary world that *Beloved* is. For it is a novel structured by profound ambivalences: ambivalences, for instance, about the nature of whitefolks' (it does not seem unequivocally to underwrite Baby Suggs's utterance that 'there's no bad luck in the world but whitefolks' [89]), and about the effects of slav-ery (slavery degrades and dehumanises not just its victims but also its perpetrators). Both of these challenges to received posi-tions have made it a contentiously political novel. Indeed, Morrison is on the record as believing that novel-writing 'must be political. ... That's a pejorative term in critical circles now: if a work of art has any political influence in it, somehow it's tainted. My feeling is just the opposite: if it has none, it is tainted' (Morrison [1983] 1985:344-5).

But the novel's most important structuring ambivalence is its stance to the past and to the 'rememorying' of it, and hence to Sethe (right or wrong?) and to Beloved (good or bad?). While its own primary theme and strategy is indeed to recreate the past in the present —albeit aware that 'Anything dead coming back to life hurts' (35), and that Sethe and Paul D are constantly battling at 'keep-ing the past at bay' (42), al 'the serious work of beating back the past' (73)—the question it nevertheless poses is: is 'remem-orying' good or bad, helpful or disabling, liberating or impris-oning? Rather than 'solving' such a question, however, (it is not 'a recipe') the novel merely suggests in complex fashion what the conflicts are, what the problems are', and so gives the answer: Both.

Sethe is so obsessed by the past, hence the presence of the murdered Beloved, that even Paul D sees her as dehumanised: '"You got two feet, Sethe, not four," he said' (165). She is about to commit another murder—of the 'good white' Mr Bodwin—but is stopped, significantly, by her daughter Denver, Ella and other *black women* who see her as 'crazy' (265). It is the down-to-earth Ella who, despite having herself suffered extreme humiliation at the hands of'the lowest yet"', articu-lates the opposition to Sethe's paranoia:

> *Whatever Sethe had done, Ella didn't like the idea of past errors taking possession of the present.... Daily life took as much as she had. The future was sunset; the past something to leave behind. And if it didn't stay behind, well, you might have to stomp it out. Slave life; freed life— every day was a test and a trial. (256)*

Denver is important in this context. Born 'free', she represents a new generation who can leave behind 124 Bluestone Road, who can begin to accept 'whitefolks' (they are offering her edu-cation), and who can claim a future: it is Denver who grasps Baby Suggs's injunction: '"Know it, and go on out of the yard. Go on."' (244). This is the politics of 'claiming ownership of the freed self (95), and the novel seems to propose a kind of humanistic affirmation, where true 'freedom' is associated with the ability to love, which the novel's symptomatically ambiguous title—at once 'Belovecf and the imperative 'Beloved'—

seems to confirm. Scarred by her appalling past, Sethe is terrified of feeling anything: 'Would it be all right? Would it be all right to go ahead and feel? Go ahead and *count on something*}' (38; Morrison's italics); and Paul D concurs: 'For a used-to-be-slave woman to love anything that much was dangerous, especially if it was her children she had settled on to love' (45; later, in a resonant phrase which Sethe does not understand, he describes it as 'her too-thick love' [164-5]).

However, despite Baby Suggs's ultimate denial of hope, her sermon on 'love' is a central statement in the novel; Paul D's 'red heart' is restored to him from within the rusted-up 'tobacco tin buried in his chest' (72-3)—paradoxically by Beloved's 'shining' for him; he brings Sethe painfully back to life when he kisses her mutilated back and they make love; and it is he too, on returning to offer Sethe his love at the end, who says:' "Sethe...me and you, we got more yesterday than anybody.

We need some kind of tomorrow"' (273). But most importantly, it is Paul D who associates love with 'freedom': 'He knew exactly what she meant: to get to a place where you could love anything you chose—not to need permission for desire—well now, *that* was freedom' (162). Such perceptions, I would suggest, accrue precisely from the imaginative freedom accorded by 'the literary': the affirmative potential it allows, in Williams's phrase, to 'think beyond, feel beyond' the material and the determinate.

What the novel seems to be saying, then—and, importantly, to *enact* in its own formal narrative strategies—is that 'free' and contemporary African-Americans, but also the 'whitefolks' who are complicit in it, must own their own history in order to be free to develop, to have a future; but also, *simultane-ously,* to be free *of it:* to 'know it, and go on out of the yard.

Go on'. This seems to be the point of the deeply ambivalent short last chapter, which at once recommends 'forgetting' the 'disremembered and unaccounted for' Beloved—because 'Remembering seemed unwise' (274)—and continues to affirm her presence: the need *not* to forget her because she is *their* past, *their* identity, that which has made them the descendants of their 'Sixty Million and more' 'Ancestors' (as the title of her interview calls them).

The 'upwardly socially mobile' Denver and *her* descendants may forget Beloved—'the water too and what is down there' (275; a reference to the 'Middle Passage'); but she (and the Middle Passage) remain 'real', if only as 'an unpleasant dream during a troubling sleep' *(ibid.)*, which those descendants forget at their peril. Hence the novel's repeated concluding ambivalence: 'This is not a story to pass on' *(ibid.)*, where the phrase simultaneously means 'not a story to pass *on*' (i.e. to keep repeating) and 'not a story to *pass* on' (i.e. to ignore). And the novel's equally ambivalent final word—at once memorial inscription and present injunction—is: 'Beloved'. On that note, I rest my case for 'the uses of the literary'.

6

Metaphoric Criticism of English Literature

We can begin to consider the study of metaphor by considering the nature of text, and of the word 'text' itself. If we were to be asked for a definition of 'text', our first recourse might be to a dictionary, and here we would find what at first glance appears to be precisely the definition we need:

The wording of anything written or printed; the structure formed by the words in their order; the very words, phrases, and sentences as written.

This may seem as though it is a clear, 'literal' meaning, and certainly it absolutely summarises some of the everyday uses of the word that we might make when contemplating the study of literature - although even here we may suspect that the dictionary meanings do not quite cover the expansion of the word 'text' into phrases like, for example, 'text-messaging'.

However, when we delve further into the dictionary definition, even this apparently solid ground starts to appear distinctly more unstable. Indeed, the further history of the word is supplied at the very head of the dictionary entry: it comes from the Latin verb 'texere', which means to weave. Thus, we might say, 'text' is something which is woven; but what exactly do we mean by this? Do we mean to refer to the original structure of paper, or papyrus, as something which was woven; or do we mean to refer to writing itself as something woven? Can we fully distinguish between the two? We may say that we have two images here, one of the paper, one of the words on the paper; but in the word 'text' these two images are brought together, and it would be difficult to say which of them has primacy.

Here, then, we are within a process of metaphor; a process, to use the most common definition of all, by means of which one thing is made to stand in for another thing. When we speak of 'twenty head of cattle' (which is a specific use of metaphor), we do not mean - and know that our hearers, or readers, will not expect us to mean - that twenty cows' heads are careering across the countryside, or indeed standing peaceably in a field; here the word 'head' does not have the customary meaning we might expect but rather stands in for another thing, for the cattle themselves.

Specifically, this is an example of metonymy, the reduction of (in this case) the animal to a single representative element. And words, of course, especially common words like 'head', can have a multitude of meanings, often dependent on how and where they are used: the head of a school or other organisation, by which we mean the person in charge; the head of a river; the head by which we signify one side of a coin; the head of a weapon (such as we might find Geoffrey Chaucer alluding to in The Tale of Sir Thopas (1387) when he speaks of a spear being 'of fyn ciprees . . . The heed ful sharpe y-grounde' [Chaucer 1912: 504]); the head of a stringed musical instrument; the head of a bed; the head as the 'rounded leafy top of a tree or shrub', as the OED reminds us, giving an example of Edmund Spenser describing 'most dainty trees; that . . . seeme to bow their bloosming heads full lowe' (Spenser 2001: 702) - and so the list could go on. All these, we may say, are metaphorical usages, in that they adapt the root term 'head' as descriptive of a specific part of the body (human or otherwise) to other spheres of life; but as we look more closely, we may suspect that in fact the operations of metaphor go further than this. For all these usages rely, in one way or another, on the notion that the head is not merely the physically highest part of the human body; it is also, we have come to assume, the 'superior' part of the body in a less literal sense. It is true that this slippage can be justified by saying that we would not survive very long, or indeed at all, without a head; but neither would we last very long without a liver, or with no kidneys, yet we do not accord these organs the same status as the head.

What I mean to imply from this example, and to continue to explore in the following chapters, is that the processes of metaphor are everywhere at work in language. 'At work': and in using that term too I am venturing, inevitably, into the realm of the metaphorical. Of course, these processes are not sitting there, with a hammer and anvil, working away; when we say 'at work' we mean to suggest that something is happening, and that we need a suitable image in which to convey what it is that is happening.

If all language is metaphorical, or at least invested with a certain metaphorical potential, then it could also follow that we might want to say that all language is continually involved in a series of acts of translation: translating things which are difficult to apprehend into things which we can apprehend, or conceptualise, or visualise, more easily. After all, all uses of language, from the very simplest to the most complex, are acts of communication, or at least they set out to be acts of communication whether they succeed or whether they fail, and therefore there is some implied motivation behind them, at some level, which seeks to engage the reader or listener. Metaphor seems to be integral to this need for engagement: even if we could conceive of a language without metaphor, which would be difficult to the point of impossibility, it would be a deeply drab and extremely restricted language. It could be, and has been, argued that such an imaginary language would approach the condition of mathematics, but even this seems doubtful; certainly the Roman numeral system is in a sense metaphorical, or at least 'figurative', in that the number of marks on the paper makes some attempt to represent figuratively the notions of oneness, two-ness and so on.

One of the most frequent usages of metaphor is as simile. It has sometimes been supposed that simile is a different figure of speech from metaphor; but in fact it is a sub-species of metaphor, which is distinct only in that it keeps the notion of comparison explicit. In Graham Greene's Brighton Rock (1938), the anti-hero Pinkie experiences a moment when he almost repents of his many past villainies:

> *He felt constriction and saw - hopelessly out of reach - a limitless freedom: no fear, no hatred, no envy. It was as if he were dead and were remembering the effect of a good confession, the words of absolution: but*

> *being dead it was a memory only - he couldn't experience contrition - the ribs of his body were like steel bands which held him down to eternal unrepentance. (Greene 1970: 179)*

The simile here is expressed in 'like steel bands' (simile is always worded in terms of 'as' or 'like'): here Greene is comparing the spiritual constriction which afflicts Pinkie to a more physical, more conventionally material image, which both effects a specific connection with the reader and also expresses Pinkie's own need to translate his experience into something concrete.

Simile may be in one sense cruder than other forms of metaphor, in that it does not seek to conceal its artificiality; but alternatively one might say that it is the original form of metaphor. When camels are spoken of as 'ships of the desert', the missing word 'like' is, as it were, present but 'under erasure'; it has been omitted but the notion of 'likeness' continues.

As a different example of metaphor we might think about the word 'fascist'. Nowadays that word seems to have a field of precise connotations, largely held in political movements ('movements' is clearly another metaphor!) of the mid-twentieth century; but the word itself derives from another Latin term, the fasces, which were:

> A bundle of rods bound up with an axe in the middle and its blade projecting. These rods were carried by lectors before the superior magistrates at Rome as an emblem of their power.

We could fairly conjecture that when the fascist movement appropriated this image, this was done with an awareness of its metaphorical power; that what was being said, or indicated, was, for example, something about power and authority, and about the threat of violence at the heart of apparent order.

We do not necessarily think about, or even know of, these things now when we use the word 'fascist'; it would therefore be possible to suggest, as some critics and linguists have, that what we have here is a 'dead metaphor', in the sense of one where the original meanings and implications have been so eroded that they have become irrelevant to our processes of communication. But the question of when, or whether, a metaphor can ever be truly dead is a vexed one. Consider, for example, the first stanza of an apparently simple poem written by Philip Larkin, called 'How to Sleep' (1950):

> *Child in the womb, Or saint on a tomb - Which way shall I lie To fall asleep? The keen moon stares From the back of the sky, The clouds are all home Like driven sheep. (Larkin 1988: 35)*

Nobody, I think, would claim that the metaphors of a child in the womb and of a tomb effigy to represent sleep are new; indeed, they are so old that we barely perceive them as metaphorical at all. Indeed, when in a different poem, 'An Arundel Tomb' (1956), Larkin speaks of two such effigies on a tomb and says, 'They would not think to lie so long' (Larkin 1988: 110), the comparison between the stillness of the effigies and sleep is so quiet as to be barely perceptible. Similarly, the metaphor by means of which clouds become sheep is in no way new; on the contrary, it can be found in visual terms in hundreds of children's books.

Yet, it would be possible to contend that these apparently 'dead' metaphors are in fact revivified by their location in this stanza. Perhaps this is done by juxtaposition, because the image of the 'keen moon' staring 'from the back of the sky' is by no means moribund; the moon in Western tradition has a host of attributes (inconstant, deathly, pallid, but also, and sometimes contradictorily, regular, amorous, female) but 'keen' is not among them. This metaphor derives its force from the sense that the moon is not 'literally' 'keen' in either the sense of 'sharp and cutting' or 'enthusiastic or eager'. Indeed, the metaphor moves through the stanza, exercising a menacing force that might make us look again at the implicit violence of the image of the 'driven sheep'. In fact, by one of those complex tricks that language is constantly playing, the way 'keen' and 'moon' might really interact is by inviting us to see a picture of the moon 'keening' (a quite different word, meaning 'weeping' or 'mourning') over the scene, which in turn will colour in a mood and will induce us to doubt the apparent tranquillity of the child or the saint. This kind of phenomenon is very close to the force of the homonym, a term which refers to words which sound alike but have quite different meanings.

Let us briefly consider another metaphor. It occurs originally in a novel by Ian Fleming, Dr No (1958), but it has become the staple of the long series of James Bond films. We may note in passing that 'bond' is also a metaphor for the stability of the financial 'bond', and especially through a standard phrase, 'his word is his bond', it signifies honourableness or reliability. However, the particular phrases to which I want to call attention are: 'A medium Vodka dry Martini - with a slice of lemon peel. Shaken and not stirred' (Fleming 1958: 208). Almost every word of this quotation has metaphoric resonance. The word 'medium' signifies Bond's poise, his ability to remain centred while there is chaos around him. 'Dry' signifies a certain kind of 'dry wit', a wry amusement before the scenes of carnage which continually threaten to envelop him. The making of the martini with vodka - rather than, as more usually, with gin - signifies Bond's individuality, and simultaneously his calm and powerful ability to make the world accede to his wishes. The unusual precision of 'a slice of lemon peel' signifies his exactitude, his unwillingness to tolerate the second rate or second best.

As for 'shaken and not stirred', a whole litany of metaphorical equivalents could be read from this phrase. The contents are principally sexual and emotional: Bond as a character is perfectly willing to engage in sex (to be 'shaken'), but none of this will imply that he is 'stirred' (in its common metaphorical sense of being, or becoming, emotionally involved). In a broader sense, it implies Bond's willingness to become involved in the events around him without having the essence of his character changed. What is shaken returns eventually to its previous state; what is stirred might lose its pristine shape and become some kind of composite or compromise, but Bond's monosyllabic naming metaphorically signifies his essential separation from the world around him. And this spreads out to involve the reader, or the viewer of the films: we are expected to be 'shaken' by events, because otherwise we would not continue to follow the narrative in search of resolution; but in the end we are not expected to be stirred by them, because if we were we would be losing some of Bond's supposedly admirable sang-froid (a French term which could be translated as 'cold blood'). And so, from this brief comment, we find ourselves having metaphorical recourse to a whole myth of Englishness: calm amid surrounding pressures; resistant to the allurements of the foreign; capable of equipoise even under the most difficult of circumstances. Indeed, we might say that what Bond precisely does is to take elements of the foreign, such as vodka and martini, and 'translate' them into the props of an English myth.

In 1978, a conference on metaphor was held at the University of Chicago. One of the papers was by Wayne C. Booth, and it began as follows:

> *There were no conferences on metaphor, ever, in any culture, until our own century was already middle-aged. As late as 1927, John Middleton Murry, complaining about the superficiality of most discussions of metaphor, could say, 'There are not many of them' . . . Explicit discussions of something called metaphor have multiplied astronomically in the past fifty years. This increase is not simply parallel to the vast increase in scholarly and critical writing. Shakespeareans have multiplied too, as have scholars of Homer, of Dickens, and of Charles the Second. But students of metaphor have positively pullulated . . . We shall soon no doubt have more metaphoricians than metaphysicians . . . I have in fact extrapolated with my pocket calculator to the year 2039; at that point there will be more students of metaphor than people. (Booth in Sacks 1979: 47)*

Wayne Booth jests; nevertheless, and somewhat frighteningly, as I write we are almost up to the halfway point between 1978 and 2039, and the study of, and interest in, metaphor shows no signs of abating.

However, it is true that the study of metaphor has changed enormously over the last thirty years, and in ways which it would have been difficult to predict in 1978. The advent of new kinds of literary theory, the specific contributions of thinkers like Jacques Lacan and Jacques Derrida to the study of the text, the attention paid in new historicist and cultural materialist criticism to the formative power of tropes and rhetorics, all of these have in different ways contributed to revolutionising our thinking about metaphor.

But before we 'embark' on this narrative, let us consider a final example of a metaphor which, while apparently simple, carries a remarkable freight of meanings and that also points to the crucial importance of metaphor in our daily lives. This concerns a firm of London builders from Indian backgrounds, who some years ago painted on the side of their van the slogan: 'You've tried the cowboys; now try the Indians'. In a way, metaphors of this kind, which are also jokes, or at the very least involved in a complex field of irony, are difficult to talk about, partly because talking about them threatens to unbalance the delicate poise that sustains the metaphor, especially as a kind of 'speech act'. However, we can at least do something to describe the metaphorical field at play here. We could begin with the usual meaning of the clichéd phrase 'cowboys and Indians' to describe a certain American cultural genre, chiefly represented in the movies but also present in the fictions of Zane Grey and others. And we could say that this is a metaphor in itself: it has come to stand in for a whole period of American history, with the concomitant idea that the white men who are signified by the 'cowboys' represent the 'side of good' against the primitive world of the North American Indian. This, however, is cross-cut with another myth, which is of the 'outlaw': the perpetuation of the myth, which is still very much with us today, if only in the 'survivalist' conditions of the extreme American rural right or in the Texan rhetoric of George W. Bush, clearly supports the metaphor of the cowboy as somebody who lives outside the law and yet has his own codes and practices of honour. As Bob Dylan encapsulated the myth, 'to live outside the law, you must be honest' (Dylan 1994: 349).

This is a metaphor which has now come to support a notion of US individualism. We are a long way from a 1787 usage of the term, 'A Flaxen headed cow boy, as simple as may be' (Bickerstaffe et al. 1792: II, 36), where the term is used in support of a non-violent pastoral myth. Instead, we have here the cultural transition to the common trope of the 'cowboy builder', which carries various metaphorical connotations: lawless, certainly, but in a distinctly unpleasant sense, as somebody who rides in by day and rides out again by night, leaving the job unfinished, the stairs waiting to fall down as soon as they are trodden on.

But our builders have picked up on another stream of metaphorical meanings, concerning, first, the stereotypical treatment of the 'Indians' in Western films; this stereotype is based on a cardinal misnomer, however, since the reason American Indians are called 'Indians' at all is a reflection of the colossal mistakes of Western explorers concerning what they thought they had found, and where they thought they were, when they lighted on the shores of America. Here there is a more or less forcible rejoining of this meaning of 'Indian' to the older idea of somebody who comes from the subcontinent of India. There is thus a certain deliberate 'inappropriateness' to this metaphor; it is not designed to suggest or produce an exact 'fit' between two different ideas or images; rather, it is supposed to challenge the reader to look at the fissures, the cracks in our cultural conception of the 'Indian'.

And this, I suggest, we shall find whenever we look closely at metaphor; although metaphor undoubtedly deals in likeness, similarity, it also deals in unlikeness and dissimilarity. Metaphor makes us look at the world afresh, but it often does so by challenging our notions of the similarity that exists between things; how alike they are; and in what ways, in fact, they are irreconcilably unalike. Thus, metaphor represents a basic operation of language: it seeks to 'fix' our understanding, but at the same time it reveals how any such fixity, any such desire for stability and certainty, is constructed on shifting sands.

'Shifting sands', to conclude, is obviously a metaphor; here, I hope, it is one that is being used accurately in order to provide an image of dangerous uncertainty, and indeed the threat of engulfment. If we think of another 'sand' metaphor, 'to draw a line in the sand', it is remarkable how this metaphor has come, certainly in recent years, and perhaps especially in the hands of politicians, to reverse its own signification. 'To draw a line in the sand' is clearly an impossible, or at best a somewhat temporary, task; but when politicians seek to convince a sceptical public that they are about to seal off some dreadful past event or strategic failure, this seems to be the metaphor towards which they reach, unaware (we hope) that the metaphor is itself constantly undermining their claims to be in control of circumstances.

THE CLASSICAL PROBLEM

Let us now turn to the history of metaphor. Since at least the time of Aristotle, it would appear that Western literary, linguistic and critical traditions have been interested in the possibility of differentiating between literal and figurative language. Within that general process, attention has focused on establishing a system both on which to base this differentiation and within which to distinguish further between different types of the figurative. Within these extensive and complex traditions, it is possible to establish a continuing dialogue between different valuations of the figurative, and consequently between, on the one hand, views of metaphor as adornment or elaboration, and, on the other, metaphor as the basic structure of language, according to which representations offer 'versions' of referents and thus inevitably imply an 'originary' process of metaphorisation.

There is no better place to begin than with Aristotle, who is generally regarded as the first thinker to elaborate a theory of metaphor. In his Poetics (350 BC), Aristotle first characterises it as a sign of absolute linguistic mastery and, therefore, of a certain type of genius. As he says, 'It is the one thing that cannot be learnt from others, and it is also a sign of genius, since a good metaphor implies an intuitive perception of the similarity in dissimilars' (Aristotle 1909: 71).

Far more important, though, is that Aristotle located the specific use of metaphor in poetry rather than in either of the other great divisions of discourse: rhetoric and logic. By doing so, he makes it clear that he does not regard metaphor as integral to language's functioning; rather, it is a kind of decoration or ornament. It has the power to please, which is an exciting and perhaps, under some circumstances, a dangerous power; but it is in some sense an addition to the 'normal', by which we might infer 'literal', workings of language.

Aristotle further defines metaphor as 'giving the thing a name that belongs to something else; the transference being either from genus to species, or from species to genus, or from species to species, or on grounds of analogy' (Aristotle 1909: 63). Behind this there lies the notion that every 'thing' in nature has its own 'proper name'; metaphor constitutes a kind of infringement of this rule, whereby 'names' are conveyed from one thing to another.

This may be done, as we have seen earlier, in the literal comparisons of simile; or there may be a certain 'hidden-ness' which is more typical of other processes of metaphor. At all events, the underlying intent, according to Aristotle, is to point out resemblances; these resemblances may move the reader or hearer beyond the 'usual' linguistic and rhetorical rules of clarity and decorum, but they are justified because the reader is, as it were, 'brought up short'; he or she is in the presence of something unusual, something outside language's normal ambit, and this can serve to deepen the reader's experience, to bring a suddenly enriched apprehension of the world.

The actress Vivien Leigh once said of the dramatist and political thinker George Bernard Shaw: 'Shaw is like a train. One just speaks the words and sits in one's place. But Shakespeare is like bathing in the sea - one swims where one wants' (quoted in Nicolson 1968: 297). Now this is what we might well recognise as the simplest form of metaphor - simile, where the comparison, the 'transference' (metapherein) between the two entities, is explicitly signalled by the word 'like' (or sometimes 'as'). Some would say that this is the basic form of all metaphor; what causes metaphors which are not cast in the linguistic form of the simile to have greater power is precisely the omission of the 'like', an omission which brings the two compared entities far closer to each other in a way that challenges the reader or hearer to make sense of the assumed or alleged comparison rather than having it spelt out. The point here, however, is that the reader is expected to gain some additional understanding from the analogies presented. George Bernard Shaw is not, in fact, very much like a train; he was smaller, for a start, and had no engine.

However, there is sufficient similarity for the reader to pause, to have the opportunity to recognise a new connection; to, as Aristotle put it, 'get hold of something fresh'. The parallels here are to do with running tracks, with a certain lack of freedom, with inducing a certain passivity in the watcher, here equated with a passenger. William Shakespeare is, perhaps, also not much like the sea, although the array of metaphors which have been deployed to explain his pre-eminent position in drama and in the English national culture suggest an unceasing quest to find metaphors apt to convey the complexity, the freedom, the spaciousness of Shakespeare's drama. Ben Jonson, for example, referred to him as 'Sweet swan of Avon' (Jonson 1975: 265); Samuel Johnson compared Corneille to Shakespeare 'as a clipped hedge is to a forest' (quoted in Piozzi 1925: 41); John Dryden referred to Shakespeare as the 'very Janus of poets; he wears almost everywhere two faces; and you have scarce begun to admire the one, ere you despise the other' (Dryden 1926: I, 172); Samuel Taylor Coleridge referred to him as 'myriad-minded' (Coleridge 1956: 175), and also said that 'the body and substance of his works came out of the unfathomable depths of his own oceanic mind' (Coleridge 1990: I, 468). What this might suggest is that metaphor - and I am going to continue to suggest that 'metaphorisation', although perhaps a little clumsy, would be a better word - is not so much an occasional intrusion into 'normal' patterns of speech; rather, it constitutes a continuing process of 'translation'. Where a concept, an idea, an emotion may be hard to grasp in language, then a metaphor, an offering of perceived resemblances, may enable us the better to 'come to grips with' the issue in hand. To follow Shakespeare obliquely through another twist, in 1941 we find George Orwell searching for adequate metaphors to describe the contemporary state of England:

> *England is not the jewelled isle of Shakespeare's much-quoted passage, nor is it the inferno described by Dr Goebbels. More than either it resembles a family, a rather stuffy Victorian family, with not many black sheep in it but with all its cupboards bursting with skeletons . . . A family with the wrong members in control. (Orwell 1941: 35)*

This passage can helpfully introduce us to two further features of metaphor. First, it is clear that here Orwell has a political intent: he means to divorce the imagery of England from, on the one hand, the smug over-optimism with which Shakespeare's original image, whatever its intent, could be interpreted for a modern world; and probably more importantly, he wishes to divorce it, in time of war, from the antagonistic characterisation mounted by Goebbels, the Nazi propagandist, which itself, in the mind of Orwell or Goebbels, probably takes us back to Dante's description of hell in his Inferno (early fourteenth century). Metaphor, in other words, is rarely if ever innocent; it has designs on us, as Aristotle and the other Greek philosophers of language indeed recognised. Second, Orwell's comment reveals the way in which the complexity of metaphor often entails metaphors nesting, as it were, inside one another; the black sheep and the skeletons in the cupboard are themselves metaphors which Orwell brings to bear to sustain his 'master-metaphor' of the Victorian family as an image of the condition of England.

Already we are up against questions about metaphor as mere 'ornamen-tation'; to sustain such an argument would imply that

Shakespeare's admirers and critics, or Orwell, could in some sense have 'made their point' in some other, more 'literal' way. But this is, to say the least, highly arguable. To move to a radically different field: when the Conservative Party came up in 1978 with the election slogan 'Labour isn't working', the intention was to juxtapose two different ideas. The first, reinforced by the accompanying picture of a queue outside an unemployment office, was that under a Labour government unemployment was rife; the second was to imply that the Labour government was 'not working' in the sense that it was being ineffectual. But it is not easy to see how this slogan could have been expressed in any other form; certainly had such an attempt been made it would have been inordinately long and, perhaps more to the point, inordinately boring. Also, by spelling out the connection between the hidden statements, there would have been the danger of a certain subterfuge being exposed, of voters wondering whether the system of cause and effect proposed in the slogan really withstood closer scrutiny.

There is here a whole set of questions about latent and manifest meaning. The metaphor can be considered in some sense and under some circumstances to be a kind of sleight of hand by means of which meanings can be surreptitiously smuggled into an apparently innocent discourse. In this context, classical definitions of metaphor have tended to try to separate the material of the metaphor into two levels: the 'tenor', or the material which is supposed to be conveyed by the metaphor; and the 'vehicle', which is the term for the image doing the conveying. But in this particular slogan it is difficult, if not impossible, to provide such a hierarchical arrangement; the intention is to convey both ideas simultaneously, and to solder them together in the mind of the recipient. The use of metaphor, we might say, in the hands of politicians is nothing less than an attempt to rewire the brain, if only on a temporary basis; that this is also true of advertisers is perhaps too obvious to mention, although it is worth saying that Judith Williamson's pioneering Decoding Advertisements (1978) remains a crucial book to read in this connection.

The view of metaphor not as ornamentation but as integral to language emerges at various points in Western literary history, but perhaps most decisively with the romantic poets of the late eighteenth and early nineteenth centuries. Coleridge, for example, refers to what he calls the 'two cardinal points of poetry' as the following: 'the power of exciting the sympathy of the reader by a faithful adherence to the truth of nature, and the power of giving the interest of novelty by the modifying colours of the imagination' (Coleridge 1956: 168). These two skills, or faculties, cannot be separated; they are integrally joined in a particular use of language. And for Coleridge, as well as for other romantics, this use of language was as essential to criticism as it was to poetry or any other type of writing. Consider, for example, his remarkable comment on the prose style of the great historian Edward Gibbon:

> *When I read a chapter in Gibbon I seem to be looking through a luminous haze or fog, figures come and go, I know not how or why, all larger than life or distorted or discoloured; nothing is real, vivid, true; all is scenical, and by candle light as it were. (Coleridge 1990: I, 418-19)*

This extraordinary description is clearly metaphorical. We do not suppose that when Coleridge read Gibbon he felt himself to be literally enveloped in a luminous haze, but we do suppose that in the very attempt to convey with the utmost clarity to his own readers his feelings when he read Gibbon he ineluctably found himself searching for a metaphor which would be not only the most apt but, precisely and using his own terms, the most vivid way of communicating his own experience. This is a paradoxical clarity since what Coleridge is attempting to convey here is a kind of essence of unclarity.

Elsewhere in Coleridge's writing this use of metaphor is evident. Let us consider the opening to one of his best-known poems, 'Kubla Khan' (1798): In Xanadu did Kubla Khan A stately pleasure dome decree: Where Alph, the sacred river, ran Through caverns measureless to man

Down to a sunless sea. So twice five miles of fertile ground With walls and towers were girdled round: And there were gardens bright with sinuous rills, Where blossomed many an incense-bearing tree; And here were forests ancient as the hills, Enfolding sunny spots of greenery. (Coleridge 1967: 297)

It appears obvious from the very first line of this poem that we are here in the presence of a metaphorical structure; we do not suppose that this 'pleasure dome' is, or was, in some sense literal, partly because, were it indeed to be merely so, it would be difficult to see how it could interest us one way or the other as to whether a long-dead Mongol emperor happened to indulge his passion and wealth in such an architectural construction. We might instead view the beginning of this poem as what we might call an 'invitation to metaphorisation'; in other words, we expect, as perhaps we do with most poems, and often with other works of literature as well, there to be a metaphorical dimension, in this case to discover that this 'pleasure-dome' stands in for something else.

Coleridge famously claimed to have been interrupted in the writing of 'Kubla Khan' by the arrival of the infamous 'person on business from Porlock' (Coleridge 1967: 296), and so it has always been difficult to know whether the poem is in any sense a 'whole'. And yet, as we contemplate it in the form available to us, we need also to acknowledge that that process of metaphorisation is not closed; we may feel ourselves here to be in the presence of metaphor, but precisely what that metaphor is may well remain opaque. A metaphor then, we might reasonably surmise, is not necessarily a matter of simple one-to-one equivalents ('this stands in for that'), but neither is it a process of ornamentation of something that could have been more clearly said in another, simpler way; rather, in this case at least, as in the very different case of the party political slogan quoted above, it is the very substance of the discourse. A common error about metaphor is to suppose that it can be in some sense 'unpacked'. When that unpacking takes place, what is left is rarely of value; it seems a paltry and colourless thing when compared with the metaphor itself.

In some ways this connects metaphor to the language of dream, and this is a connection we shall explore later; suffice here to say that it is obviously no accident that Coleridge subtitled 'Kubla Khan' 'A Vision in a Dream'. It also places under scrutiny, as many philosophers of language from Max Black onwards have done, the whole question of meaning in relation to metaphor. Does a metaphor mean something more than, or different from, or in some sense beneath, what it appears to say; or is the meaning of a metaphor precisely what it does say? Joseph Conrad has a pertinent comment related to this issue in Heart of Darkness (1902), at the moment when the narrator is trying to describe Marlow's manner of telling a story:

> *The yarns of seamen have a direct simplicity, the whole meaning of which lies within the shell of a cracked nut. But Marlow was not typical (if his propensity to spin yarns be excepted), and to him the meaning of an episode was not inside like a kernel but outside, enveloping the tale which brought it out only as a glow brings out a haze, in the likeness of one of these misty halos that sometimes are made visible by the spectral illumination of moonshine. (Conrad 1983: 30)*

This, I suggest, might itself be a useful metaphor for the concept of metaphor; that it may not be revealed by an 'opening' or unpacking, but rather that it gives off its own meaning in a way that is difficult of apprehension but integral to communication and understanding. It is perhaps also worth bearing in mind that, later, Marlow himself refers to the attempt to render events into language in Coleridgean, or even Freudian, terms as indistinguishable from dream. 'Do you see the story?' he asks. 'Do you see anything?'

> *It seems to me I am trying to tell you a dream - making a vain attempt, because no relation of a dream can convey the dream-sensation, that commingling of absurdity, surprise, and bewilderment in a tremor of struggling revolt, that notion of being captured by the incredible which is of the very essence of dreams. (Conrad 1983: 57)*

And then, a little later, he adds, in a famous line, 'We live, as we dream - alone'.

It may seem as though we have moved a little way from metaphor here, but the point I am making is that as the view of language as predominantly metaphorical has gained ground, then this may be seen as an accompaniment to a re-examination of the whole question of the possibility of discourse delivering verifiable truths. This has come continuingly under question recently, not only in literature but also in the physical sciences, and what Conrad is here presciently recognising is that if all language is fundamentally metaphorical, then the meanings it enshrines cannot be re-expressed in any other way; they cannot be made clearer by some attempt to expunge metaphor from the linguistic register.

We might also wish to say that the critical discussion of metaphor has, since the romantic literary revolution, necessarily to an extent proceeded in the light of changes in literary, and perhaps especially poetic, practice. When we read, for example, a passage from the Augustan poet Alexander Pope it is not difficult to apprehend the concept of metaphor as ornamentation. There is a famously vitriolic episode in the Epistle to Dr Arbuthnot (1734) where Pope attacks the character whom he chooses to name Sporus:

Let Sporus tremble - 'What? that thing of silk, Sporus, that mere white curd of Ass's milk? Satire or sense, alas! can Sporus feel? Who breaks a butterfly upon a wheel?'

Yet let me flap this bug with gilded wings,
This painted child of dirt, that stinks and stings;
Whose buzz the witty and the fair annoys,
Yet wit ne'er tastes, and beauty ne'er enjoys:
So well-bred spaniels civilly delight
In mumbling of the game they dare not bite.
Eternal smiles his emptiness betray,
As shallow streams run dimpling all the way.
Whether in florid impotence he speaks,
And, as the prompter breathes, the puppet squeaks;
Or at the ear of Eve, familiar Toad,
Half froth, half venom, spits himself abroad,
In puns, or politics, or tales, or lies,
Or spite, or smut, or rhymes, or blasphemies.
His wit all see-saw, between that and this,
Now high, now low, now Master up, now Miss,
And he himself one vile Antithesis. (Pope 1966: 336-7)

Here we have a poetic method which deliberately and indeed ostentatiously displays the poet's control of metaphor; indeed, we notice that the poet's self-differentiation from Sporus is partly based on this factor. The wit of Pope's metaphors is precisely an enactment of his assumed literary, moral and characterological superiority over the unfortunate Sporus. And we notice too that in order to achieve this effect Pope does not reside within a single structure of equivalence. He compares Sporus first to a 'thing of silk' (tremulous and inconstant, but also anticipating through the figure of the silk-worm the later insect analogies); then to the 'curd of Ass's milk', with its connotations of something that has curdled - the metaphor 'white' here has been wrenched from its more usual connotations of purity and made instead to represent something pallid and sickly; then to a 'butterfly', something which has no weight, no solidity, something which we might say is, indeed, paradoxically unworthy of the very weight of metaphor which Pope is bringing to bear upon his subject.

The butterfly - which, after all, has residual metaphorical connotations of beauty and a wondrous fragility - is then transmuted into a 'bug' that 'stinks and stings'; by now this insect, whatever it is, is being regarded as simply a nuisance, a frivolous but damaging excrescence on society. But then again Pope changes his ground, to the image of the spaniel, not here being considered for its connotations of faithfulness and love, but rather for its 'fawning' quality. Next we come to the 'dimpling' stream, with its connotations of inconstancy and, more particularly, of a fair appearance which barely masks a worthless shallowness. It is worth remarking here that Pope is quite consciously reversing the very different metaphorical force which a 'dimpling stream' might have in a different kind of poem, of beauty and naturalness. We then move, again continuing the stream of animal metaphors, to the 'Toad', who, through the association with Eve, here clearly stands in for the Devil, yet even here the image of the toad is still further undermined as we are supposed to hear that the tempting voice he uses is not even his own but rather that of a puppet being manipulated by some greater force. The image by now constructed is therefore of somebody who is in no sense 'master' of himself, but rather of somebody who fawns upon other masters. Indeed, this is taken still further in the last lines of the extract, where the so far partly hidden accusations of gender uncertainty become explicit ('now Master up, now Miss'), and Pope more or less directly accuses Sporus of a sexual ambivalence which, in terms of the metaphorical structure of the passage, underlines his moral worth-lessness.

Pope here is not ashamed of 'decoration'; on the contrary, he is contemptuously demonstrating that his gift for the ornament is far superior to that of Sporus. The animal metaphors serve, all too viciously, their purpose; but in asserting similarity Pope is not meaning us in any sense to mistake one thing for another. On the contrary, he is seeking to encourage the reader to share his denigration of Sporus, and to have that reinforced by the poet's own mastery, his own linguistic and metaphorical skill.

When we place a pre-romantic poem like Pope's against a very different poem from the twentieth century, immediately we see how impossible it would be to paraphrase or describe this poem in terms of metaphor as ornamentation. Following the theme of animal metaphors, we might look at George MacBeth's remarkable poem 'Owl' (1963), of which the first three stanzas or so run as follows:

> *Owl is my favourite. Who flies like a nothing through the night, who-whoing. Is a feather duster in leafy corners ring-a-rosying boles of mice. Twice you hear him call. Who is he looking for? You hear him hoovering over the floor of the wood. O would you be gold rings in the driving skull if you could? Hooded and vulnerable by the winter suns owl looks. Is the grain of bark in the dark. Round beaks are at work in the pellety nest, resting. (MacBeth 1964: 117)*

There are many things one could say about this poem; one could talk about its rhyme scheme, and especially the remarkable use of internal rhyme. One could talk about the syntactical distortions (later phrases include 'Is a goad', 'Am an owl'). But here our concern is metaphor, and it is particularly interesting to see how this poem demonstrates a significant possibility for metaphor, namely that, at least as taken in one direction, it tends towards a certain kind of what we might reasonably call 'incarnation'. In a note to the poem, MacBeth writes: 'Someone, perhaps a child, who is fascinated by owls creates a sort of spell to bring an owl into being. By the end of the poem he has become the owl' (MacBeth 1964: 121).

We do not have to accept this view of the poem; authors' remarks on their own works do not constitute explanations, although they may very well constitute, in cases such as this, valuable addenda to the works in question. The point at stake here, in the poem and in MacBeth's comment on it, is rather to do with the way in which the key metaphor of the poem 'brings something into being'. For Pope and his contemporaries, such a contention would have seemed nonsensical: poems do not bring things into being; rather, they are exercises of wit, demonstrations of linguistic skill. If you had been foolish enough to ask Pope, 'Well, is Sporus actually a butterfly?', he would no doubt, and with good reason, have thought you mad.

The case here is not so simple. If you removed the metaphors from the Pope passage, you could still construct a searing indictment of Sporus from the suggestions that the metaphors encourage. To remove the owl from the MacBeth poem would be impossible, unthinkable; the relation between the metaphor and any 'literal' truth which it may be assumed to mask or code is far more condensed, even fused. The owl does not, for example, act as a substitute for any specific human qualities, any more than the human can be seen to stand in for the owl; rather, two dissimilars are brought together and 'yoked' (to use Samuel Johnson's rather disparaging word in the rather different context of metaphysical poetry) together.

In the service of this major metaphor, or indeed 'conceit' as the metaphysical poets would have called it, many 'minor metaphors' are brought into play. There is the notion of the owl as a 'nothing', bringing out his silence and, certainly from the point of view of his prey, invisibility. There is the comparison to a 'feather duster', which works both through the impression of an indistinct bundle of feathers and also through the less obvious attribution to the owl of a certain harmlessness, which is presumably how his victims are meant to see him until it is too late. There is the image of the children's game of 'Ring-a-Ring-a-Roses'; as readers we may or may not know that the origins of this game lie in the years of the Great Plague, but even if we do not we will still find something sinister in this metaphorical juxtaposition of the apparent innocence of a children's game with the violence of the owl's dealings with the world.

And this is only in the first stanza. The correlation is not merely between the human and the owl; rather, the metaphorical structure is extended as the owl becomes increasingly assimilated to a kind of 'spirit of place'. 'Is the grain of bark/in the dark': the surface implication is again about the owl's invisibility and his capacity for camouflage, about his ability to be unseen by those whom he is about to seize; but the metaphor also gives us a sense of the owl being an inalienable part of the world he inhabits. The owl works, we might say, within rather than against the grain; the implication is that he is perfectly designed, perfectly suited, to the life he leads, in a way which human beings, who have choices of a kind which an owl cannot experience, will never be.

Within the metaphor, then, there is thus also a certain kind of envy, a sense given of a different kind of life which is both rougher and more simple. 'O would you be gold/rings in the driving skull/if you could?': the force of this metaphor of the 'gold rings' is, at one level, to remind us of the physical shape of the owl's face, his eyes, but also to invoke a metaphor of value, of force. At the same time it also reminds us that the owl, as he appears to his victims, may indeed appear only to be a pair of 'gold rings', only the feathers around the eyes visible in that final moment of panic and death.

'Owl', then, represents a kind of metaphor which cannot be properly separated into 'vehicle' and 'tenor'. Rather, it reveals something of the metaphorical ground on which, by means of notions of similarity and difference, we construct our notions of what it is to be human, and also, by implication, of what it is that we conceal, repress, but continue to feel attracted to in the 'not human', in the creature of drives which, we might think after Freud, continues to inhabit us all.

A structure of metaphor which is both similar and different can be found in the American writer Cormac McCarthy's novel The Crossing (1993). Here we are partly inside the mind of a hungry, cold, lost wolf:

> *She wandered the eastern slopes of the Sierra de la Madera for a week. Her ancestors had hunted camels and primitive toy horses on these grounds. She found little to eat. Most of the game was slaughtered out of the country. Most of the forest cut to feed the boilers of the stamp-mills at the mines. The wolves in that country had been killing cattle for a long time but the ignorance of the animals was a puzzle to them. The cows bellowing and bleeding and stumbling through the mountain meadows with their shovel feet and their confusion, bawling and floundering through the fences and dragging posts and wires behind. The ranchers said they brutalized the cattle in a way they did not the wild game. As if the cows*

evoked in them some anger. As if they were offended by some violation of an old order. Old ceremonies. Old protocols. (McCarthy 2002: 331)

The metaphorical structure of this passage, especially as considered in terms of relations between the categories of the human and the animal, works in a number of different ways. Most obviously, what we have here is a sustained metaphor, in the figures of the wolves and the ranchers, for the relation between the wild and the tame. But within this structure, many things shift place. For example, the wolves are here credited with something akin to human memory, some inner longevity which quite belies their being as beasts of immediate, spontaneous impulse; thus, it is the wolves which are made to carry the history, indeed the prehistory, of the 'country', whatever country this is, while the ranchers are regarded as parvenus who know or remember nothing of the 'old order'.

Between these two poles of the metaphor, the cattle stumble and flounder. The implication clearly is that the wolves remember some older, more primitive form of hunting, where the prey had their own methods of evasion, their own competencies, because, precisely, they had themselves not been tamed. But these cattle, these tame beasts, the wolves cannot understand at all; they no longer belong in the domain of the wild - they have been weirdly transferred to the other side of the metaphorical structure, to the territory of man; which means, in turn, that they have lost the status of the beast - they no longer know where they are or where they have been.

The notion of 'anger' in this passage could hardly function without some notion of metaphor, or indeed without some kind of anthropomorphism or a concept of the 'transferred epithet', which begins to reveal something of one of the psychological roots of metaphor, which we will develop later. For the notioń that 'some old anger' is evoked in the wolves by the site of domestication is quite obviously here a kind of metaphorical reversal of the ranchers' feelings about the wolves themselves, feelings which become clearer in other passages in the book. Indeed, the whole notion of attributing to animals such negative attributes as 'savagery', 'bestiality', the commonplace but ludicrous simile 'he behaved like an animal', as though it were possible for an animal to behave in a 'depraved' way, can be read as a projection not of animal behaviour but rather of human fears. These fears would not only be reflections of our primitive fear of animals, and especially of predatory animals, themselves; it would also be a fear, commonplace throughout human history but perhaps especially noticeable, in Britain at least, in the wake of Darwinian discoveries, of an eruption of the beast inside the human self, of being forced to own to, or perhaps quail before, something within the category of the human which is distinctly not human. We may be reminded of this by our own warlike excesses or by our condemnatory attitudes to ordinary animal behaviour. This passage points one stage beyond that: in the world which the wolf is encountering, no 'naturalness' of any kind remains; all has been changed by what we might loosely term a 'human imperialist exploitation'. What has transformed the cattle will, in the end, also transform the wolf; or, if it does not, then the wolf will disappear, in terms not only of evolution but of narrative, because it will no longer have any part to play in the anthropomorphic unfolding of human drama.

EASTERN AND WESTERN METAPHOR

Western notions of metaphor, therefore, depend on specific registers of similarity and dissimilarity, but metaphor has occupied a quite different place in the long evolution of Eastern critical theories, and this is in part a consequence of the different emphases and valuations placed upon writing and speech. Thus, in order to pursue a history of metaphor, it is necessary to turn aside and look at the role of metaphor in the estab-lishment of Chinese and Japanese poetics. Here the relation between text and physicality takes a different turn, as does the relation between con-sciousness and the unconscious, and consequently the role of metaphor as mediation between self and 'not-self'. Metaphor in the Chinese tradi-tion, for example, is bound to a theory of 'appropriate styles'; but what is also important is that it is responsive to a quite different religious and political tradition, and thus these differences can be used to demonstrate the necessary instability of general definitions of metaphor, as I shall go on to show.

I have already mentioned various terms which are loosely associated with metaphor, and now is a moment to try to be clear about these terms as they have traditionally been used within the Western tradition.

The term 'metaphor' itself is seen to identify a verbal process whereby two discrete objects or ideas become linked, but in a very particular way, such that, for the duration of the metaphor, one of the items actually becomes the other, and vice versa: if we say, 'James is a beast', we are not merely inviting our listener to adjudicate on exactly in what way James displays any one or more of a range of beast-like qualities; rather, we are inviting the listener to identify James with a beast.

A simile, as we have seen, proposes a looser form of association. If we say, 'James behaves like a spaniel', we are inviting the listener to consider the way or ways in which James resembles a spaniel and, perhaps, even to adjudicate for him- or herself as to whether the comparison is apt. But similes depend, like all forms of metaphor, on a certain degree of common ground. If we were instead to have said, 'James is like an armadillo', we could reasonably expect considerably more puzzlement on the part of listeners as they try to work out in what way or ways James resembles an armadillo, which might be somewhat more testing in terms of our knowledge of, or assumptions about, natural history. It is also conventional to isolate as a separate category what is often referred to as an 'extended metaphor'. Here a metaphor might extend itself beyond a single point of comparison and run through an entire passage of text, or an entire poem, as it did in the MacBeth poem quoted in Chapter 1. Perhaps the greatest master of the extended metaphor is Charles Dickens. The following example is a passage from The Mystery of Edwin Drood (1870), introducing a chapter called 'A Dean, and a Chapter Also':

Whosoever has observed that sedate and clerical bird, the rook, may perhaps have noticed that when he wings his way homeward towards nightfall, in a sedate and clerical company, two rooks will suddenly detach themselves from the rest, will retrace their flight for some distance, and will there poise and linger; conveying to mere men the fancy that it is of some occult importance to the body politic, that this artful couple should pretend to have renounced connection with it.

> *Similarly, service being over in the old Cathedral with the square tower, and the choir scuffling out again, and divers venerable persons of rook-like aspect dispersing, two of these latter retrace their steps, and walk together in the echoing Close. (Dickens 1974: 40)*

Dickens sets the scene by an extended comparison between clergymen and rooks, in the course of which the similarities are drawn out in order to engage the attention and imagination. Sometimes he even develops a method whereby the name of a character, such as Mrs Gamp, for example, or Biler, continues throughout the particular novel to carry these metaphorical significations. Indeed, in certain cases, such as that of Mr Micawber, these associations, this 'continuous' process of metaphorisation, have entered into the culture in such a way that the name itself cannot be mentioned without drawing in its wake a chain of metaphorical associations.

The end-point, one might say, of these extended metaphorical processes is allegory. Here we would be talking about a text which assumes a readerly understanding that whenever a character or event is mentioned, it stands in for another character or event. Sometimes allegory is regarded as a particularly crude form of metaphor, in the sense that it invites the reader to do little work. Instead, it invites them into a pre-established framework of correspondences; cardinal cases of this process might include novels of anti-totalitarian satire such as Aldous Huxley's Brave New World (1932) and George Orwell's 1984 (1948). In other cases, such as Spenser's The Faerie Queene (1590-96), the allegory can be extremely subtle and rely on readerly understandings of a very complex kind.

The most obvious example in the history of allegory, John Bunyan's The Pilgrim's Progress (1676), achieves its effect not by asking the reader to form new con-nections but by inviting them into an existing network of metaphors: the names of Bunyan's characters - such as Christian and Faithful - mean exactly what they say, and there is little room for character subtlety or manoeuvre in their interpretation. If, however, we take a case which is in some way dependent on Bunyan but written much later, Wilkie Collins's The Woman in White (1860), where the protagonist is known as 'Hartright', we are in a more complex field: the name 'Hartright' may well suggest, in a Bunyanesque way, a hero of perfect moral rectitude, but in The Woman in White Collins is inviting us to inspect whether this is indeed an accurate epithet for his protagonist, or whether, as seems more likely, he is in fact somewhat blinded by his own rectitude as to what is going on around him.

Synecdoche is another term for a figure of speech which some would take to be a variant of metaphor, whereby part of an object is taken to stand in for the whole, as in 'sail' for ships or, as we have seen, 'head' for cattle; and there have, over the years, been many other terms devised for specific and detailed figures of speech, or tropes, which can be seen to be sub-categories of metaphor. Many metaphors are anthropomorphic, which means that the type of comparison they seek makes something non-human into something human. This may be something inanimate, and the constant reference to ships as 'she' is a case in point. Or it may be a non-human animal, as in the ways in which pets of various descriptions are endowed, sometimes to a bizarre extent, with quasi-human attributes. Indeed, it may be said that the whole kind of relationship suggested by the notion of the pet, which is quite culturally and historically specific, and not to be found in many cultures, is intrinsically metaphorical in that it seeks to replace the animality of the animal with a substituted human sensibility and with apparently human behaviours.

The term 'extended metaphor' can itself be further extended. To take one example: as is well known, there emerged in the late eighteenth century in Britain and Europe, and subsequently in America, a subgenre of fiction called 'Gothic'. When we think of Gothic, one thing that certainly comes to mind is the specific and limited range of metaphors with which the early texts played. For example, the list of Gothic works containing the word 'castle' in their title, let alone using the castle as the major setting for the action, is enormous, from Horace Walpole's The Castle of Otranto (1765), supposedly the originator of the genre, through Ann Radcliffe's The Castles of Athlin and Dunbayne (1789) and beyond. Although the word 'castle' does not appear in the title, Mervyn Peake's Gormenghast trilogy (1946-59) may well be regarded as a late avatar of the genre.

That the castle is some kind of metaphor would seem clear: after all, the contemporary reader's interest in castles as such is presumably limited. But for what is it a metaphor? Critics have suggested many options. The castle can be seen as a place of absolute political power, of a kind which is both hated and envied in the more volatile situation of late eighteenth-and early nineteenth-century Europe. It can be seen in psychological terms as a place of enclosure, a womb-like edifice which is, again, both feared and longed for, as a place of confinement and/or as a place of safety. In terms of gender, since many of these castles are scenes for the incarceration and persecution of 'innocent maiden' heroines, it can be seen as a metaphor, perhaps in some cases at a less than conscious level, for the plight of women under a patriarchal regime; although at the same time it has to be said, and has been said by many critics, that despite the terrors of the castle, these heroines usually contrive to escape. This points to a huge ambiguity at the heart of the metaphor: does the castle represent a political or psychological system which is frighteningly oppressive, or does it rather represent a kind of 'test' which has to be addressed and passed on the road to maturity? And behind all this there lies the castle as a route back into a kind of late medievalism, of which Robert Browning's 'Childe Roland to the Dark Tower came' (1855) is perhaps the most notable example.

When we come across such powerful and multivalent metaphors as this, another way of referring to them is as 'symbols', but in fact the dividing line between the metaphorical and the symbolic is tentative and shifting. It could be seen as a matter of intensity or cultural spread. By dint of its frequent use in English cultural life, the lion may fairly be regarded as a symbol, but the jaguar, for example, as in Ted Hughes's poems of that name, has a less fixed set of references and is thus available for the writer to imbue with different senses and suggested meanings. This flexibility can be seen in Hughes's poem 'Second Glance at a Jaguar' (1967):

Skinful of bowls he bowls them,
The hip going in and out of joint, dropping the spine
With the urgency of his hurry
Like a cat going along under thrown stones, under cover,
Glancing sideways, running
Under his spine. A terrible, stump-legged waddle
Like a thick Aztec disemboweller,
Club-swinging, trying to grind some square
Socket between his hind legs round,

Carrying his head like a brazier of spilling embers,
And the black bit of his mouth, he takes it
Between his back teeth, he has to wear his skin out,
He swipes a lap at a water-trough as he turns,
Swivelling the ball of his heel on the polished spot,
Showing his belly like a butterfly. (Hughes 1982: 72)

Here the poem appears to be trying to depict something which is utterly non-human; the movement and the shape of the jaguar challenge all our preconceptions about mind and body. But in order to convey this image, Hughes moves among a range of metaphors. There are the 'bowls', the heavy black spheres which appear in one sense to define the jaguar's shape and movement. There is the obviously rather apposite image of the cat; in this sense the phrase 'under cover' springs out, suggesting both the jaguar's need for concealment and the idea of the jaguar as some kind of 'secret agent', as something which cannot be fully seen, or at least not until it is too late. There is the commanding metaphor of the 'Aztec disemboweller', which juxtaposes ideas of antiquity, of an apparently inhuman or inexplicable violence, and of a particular kind of art which relies on a different kind of shaping of the universe from that which is commonplace in the modern West.

'Thick', too, is perhaps a metaphorical term, conjuring not only a shape but also a certain kind of incomprehension, but we are presumably here not meant to see this as a condemnation of the jaguar's stupidity, but more as a comment on his imperviousness to the demands of human reason, his incomprehensibility to an observer who could only be there if this were a jaguar observed in a zoo, as is suggested in the mention of the 'water-trough'. It would also be possible to see 'thick' as, again, a kind of 'transferred epithet', a metaphorical device whereby characteristics are transferred from one participant in a scene to another: what if, one might ask, it is the observer who is 'thick' in the sense of being forever challenged by the impossibility of seeing the world through the jaguar's eyes? The 'brazier of spilling embers' takes us into a different metaphorical field, whereby the jaguar becomes associated with fire and its destructive force, and this is partly continued through the association of the jaguar as something 'driven', driven as by the 'bit' in his mouth, although yet again we might have a hint of a transferred epithet here. After all, the jaguar is, above all, not tamed by the bit in the way in which a horse might be, so all our efforts to understand - and thereby, in a sense, to tame - the jaguar are futile. And thus we move to the final metaphor in this half of the poem, the 'belly like a butterfly', showing the inevitable vulnerability even of the jaguar, but perhaps also, through transference, of his prey.

At every stride he has to turn a corner In himself and correct it. His head

Is like the worn down stump of another whole jaguar,

His body is just the engine shoving it forward,

Lifting the air up and shoving on under,

The weight of his fangs hanging the mouth open,

Bottom jaw combing the ground. A gorged look,

Gangster, club-tail lumped along behind gracelessly,

He's wearing himself to heavy ovals,

Muttering some mantrah, some drum-song of murder

To keep his rage brightening, making his skin

Intolerable, spurred by the rosettes, the Cain-brands,

Wearing the spots off from the inside,

Rounding some revenge. Going like a prayer-wheel,

The head dragging forward, the body keeping up,

The hind legs lagging. He coils, he flourishes

The blackjack tail as if looking for a target,

Hurrying through the underworld, soundless. (Hughes 1982: 72)

One of the controlling images here in this second part of the poem is that of the machine, the body like an 'engine', although the machine is a crude one, as demonstrated in the repetition of the deliberately inelegant word 'shoving'. In the attempt to make the reader understand that which is not human, some kind of translation has to happen which will enable us to achieve a parallel understanding through metaphor. The text makes another attempt at this in 'translating' the jaguar into a 'gangster', which we might see as a development from the 'Aztec disemboweller', but now perhaps brought, more frighteningly, 'closer to home'. These metaphors, then, come to seem to depend on a certain tension between the familiar and the unfamiliar, the homely and the exotic, and this exotic moment is taken further forward in the notion of the 'mantrah' and the 'drum-song', where allusions to so-called 'primitive' cultures of Asia and Africa, respectively, serve to re-conjure the jaguar's strangeness, the idea that if he speaks a language at all, it is a language incomprehensible to 'civilised' ears.

The metaphor of the 'mantrah', however, does double duty: it also reminds us of the possibility of something 'sacred' about the jaguar, something which tells us of wider and wilder stretches of creation than we might otherwise conventionally know. And this is taken forward and also returned to a more familiar Christian context in the allusion to the 'Cain-brands', the marks of killing which are here read by the poet into the markings on the jaguar's skin and fur. This, then, builds up - at the same time as returning us to the notion of the jaguar being 'under cover' - towards the final line, where the metaphor of the underworld serves at least three functions. It reminds us of the gangster, of the jaguar's hidden, 'illicit' activity, as seen through human eyes. It takes us, through Cain, into hell and thus to the hinted representation of the jaguar as an incarnation of the Devil. But, through the very hesitancy of the word 'underworld', it also reminds us of different, again more 'primitive', religions, perhaps religions based more clearly on fear of the terrors of the natural world, and of different kinds of 'underworld', of which the jaguar, at least in anthropomorphised form, may 'know' a great deal more than we do as observers.

What might also be interesting about this poem in terms of metaphor is the title, 'Second Glance at a Jaguar'. We might say literally that this is simply because Hughes had already written and published a poem called 'The Jaguar', but the word 'glance' remains arresting, signifying as it does a quick look rather than a careful inspection. The metaphor reminds us that, at least in the wild, there would be little chance of a close look at a jaguar, either because the animal would be largely invisible or because, if we were its prey, our first look might well be our last. But 'glance' also reminds us of the stock phrase, almost a cliché, a 'glancing blow', signifying a blow which does not fall directly on its target. This might refer to a jaguar's method of attack; but if so, it certainly also becomes a transferred epithet in the sense that it simulataneously refers to our attempt fully to see the jaguar, which must always fail and become only a 'sideways' attempt to apprehend something which can never be grasped in its totality.

Thus, the notion of the 'glance' becomes a kind of metaphor for writing itself, which can never succeed in its self-professed task of fully incarnating its object, but must always be a mere 'glancing', momentary perception. A 'second glance', of course, could also be a way of reinspecting what has been inspected before, with a view to approaching a clearer vision of it; but this also, we suspect, is doomed to failure since, however many 'glances' at the jaguar we are afforded, they will never add up to a satisfactory picture of the whole animal, any more than a single metaphor, or even a chain of interlinked metaphors of the kind we have here, can fully grasp what is being portrayed.

I want to move to contrast the writerly assumptions behind this approach to metaphor, which in the case of Hughes is a highly self-conscious one, with a different approach to metaphor which we can find in writers in Eastern traditions.

Indeed, metaphor in classical Chinese poetry can be seen to operate differently. One critic, for example, describes the role of metaphor in the poetics in ancient China thus: 'the poetics of the second century BC and its interest in metaphoricity originate in philosophising on the phenomenon of illusion, that is, the deceptive resemblance . . . between disparate objects, the discrepancy between appearance and actuality' (Ekstroem 2002: 1). This emphasis on illusion, while deeply rooted in Eastern philosophical and religious traditions, has something in common with the uncanny aspect of metaphor, to which I will turn in a later chapter:

> *Illusion, thus defined, may appear as confusing or uncanny in everyday experience (the Doppelgänger, the mirage, the philanderer posing as saint, or linguistic ambiguity); yet this clash between form and content is an essential aspect of Confucian ritualism . . . observable in rules of mourning, or in the use of metaphorical poetry as ritualised discourse. (Ekstroem 2002: 1)*

This uncanny aspect of metaphor, then, makes an early appearance in Chinese critical assumptions; what is also interesting is that the use of metaphor is here solidly grounded in a set of cultural practices, such as the 'rules of mourning' and 'ritualised discourse'. And this hints at the constitutive nature of metaphor in Chinese thought:

> *Those who compare Western and Chinese philosophy are generally struck by the differences: formal logic never developed in China; metaphor seems to be emphasized over more rigorous argument forms in China . . . [There is an] ironical situation that Plato and Aristotle regard metaphors as second-rate tools for expressing the truth, yet they frequently invent metaphors. In contrast, Chinese thinkers express no qualms about metaphors, but often use repeatedly the same metaphors. (Van Norden 2004: 1-3)*

This, the writer goes on to claim, is because of a fundamental distinction between Chinese and Western metaphors. In the West, metaphor has been typically used to demonstrate a correspondence between two ontologically distinct domains, but, to quote the same writer at some length, in China the situation is somewhat different:

> *[The philosopher] Gaozi says that human nature is like water. Just as water will equally flow east or west depending on its environment, so will humans become good or bad depending on their environment. Mengzi [in the course of a famous debate] acknowledges that water is indifferent between east and west, but observes that it does show a preference for low over high . . . This exchange has puzzled and disappointed many interpreters, who see in the clash of metaphors empty rhetoric. However, Chinese thinkers often assume what has been called a 'correlative cosmology', according to which superficially diverse phenomena manifest the same qualitative patterns. Thus, 'the Chinese metaphor does not try to establish a parallelism between two domains, but rather wants to show that there is a convergence between them: the nature of water behaves in exactly the same way as the nature of man'. (Van Norden 2004: 4)*

It is this concept of 'convergence' which is critical for an understanding of Chinese metaphor. Metaphor, according to this interpretation, is not a question of demonstrating human wit or ingenuity in yoking together disparate realms; rather, it is a way of revealing or explaining the convergence of things, the ways in which they tend towards a common objective, as it were, echoing each other according to a wider natural law.

To separate Eastern and Western conceptions so neatly is always to risk distortion, however. For example, it would be possible to argue that the Jesuit priest and poet Gerard Manley Hopkins's use of metaphor, devoted as it is to exposing divine intention within natural phenomena through the process Hopkins refers to as 'inscape', approximates very closely to the Chinese model:

Glory be to God for dappled things -

For skies of couple-colour as a brinded cow;

For rose-moles all in stipple upon trout that swim;

Fresh-firecoal chestnut-falls; finches' wings;

Landscape plotted and pieced - fold, fallow, and plough; And all trades, their gear and tackle and trim.

All things counter, original, spare, strange;

Whatever is fickle, freckled (who knows how?) With swift, slow; sweet, sour; adazzle, dim; He fathers-forth whose beauty is past change:

Praise him. ('Pied Beauty' in Hopkins 1990: 144)

Here, it is clearly possible to see the whole world as a vast series of metaphors for God's creation, and in this respect Hopkins is following through an aspect of biblical thinking. Everything manifests, in one form or another, some attribute of the divine; as with William Blake, the divine is at the heart of everything, and we can only grasp the 'thing-ness' of a thing by seizing upon its divine representation. Nevertheless, in Hopkins, we might say, there is a highly wrought quality to his use of metaphor; these divine attributes may be present in the phenomena of the world, perhaps God-given, according to the romantic and post-romantic tradition. But it remains the duty of the poet to find new ways to manifest in linguistic and literary form the relevance of these metaphors. We might contrast Hopkins's 'Pied Beauty' (1877) with a mid-eighth-century Chinese poem:

When a single petal falls away,

it is spring's diminishment, a breeze that tosses thousands of flecks

quite makes a man dejected.

I watch them the while, till almost gone,
blossoms passing my eyes, weary not, though the harm be great,
of ale that enters lips.
At river's side small manors
Are roosts for kingfishers, high tomb barrows by the park
give unicorns' repose.
Careful research on the pattern of things
sends men to seek delight - what use to let hopes of tenuous glory
fetter this body of mine? ('Bending River' in Owen 1996: 424)

The entire metaphorical structure of this poem, written by the great Chinese poet Du Fu during the T'ang Dynasty, is devoted to establishing correspondences. At stake, at least seen from one angle, is the relation between the singular and the multiple: the 'single petal' is not merely itself; it represents, as it 'falls away', a much wider pattern, in this case the pattern of the seasons that is an enduring theme of Chinese poetry. But the question would be: what might the relationship be between these natural forces and human life? Is there some simple equation here, or is there disparity? And, perhaps more to the point, in what way do they converge?

There is a further metaphorical tension in the poem, between that kind of reflection that grants, or at least might grant, 'repose', and that other kind of reflection which tends rather to lean towards involvement in the world ('sends men to seek delight'). Seen from this perspective, the poem becomes a meditation upon metaphor itself, which indeed we also frequently see in the Chinese code for naming places. What, the poem seems to ask, is it to be a person? Although it should also be noted that, despite the meditative tone of the poem, this is not, as it were, an eternal question, but rather one that Du Fu is posing to himself in his specific context, as a poet recently returned to the relative safety of court in the midst of imperial battles.

The convergence, then, occurs at the point where the poet tries to assess the force and relevance of the metaphors to the particular predicament in which he finds himself, and this derives partly from the very different attitude taken by classical Chinese poets towards the question of originality. The task is not to forge new metaphors; rather, it is to reinspect the continuing relevance of old metaphors to current cultural and personal circumstances. Perhaps a clearer, although less self-reflective, example can be found in a poem written by Zhou Bang-yan to a lover in the late eleventh/early twelfth century:

At Peach Creek I did not stay
enjoying myself at leisure; once lotus roots break in fall,
they never can be rejoined. I waited for her back then
on the bridge with red rails, and today I follow all alone
a path of yellowed leaves.
Lines of hilltops in the mist
green beyond counting, geese turn their backs to evening sun
toward dusk growing redder. The person, like clouds coming after the wind
and moving onto the river; the passion, like floss that sticks to the ground
in the aftermath of rain.
('Spring in the Mansion of Jade' [Yu-lou chun] in Owen 1996: 577)

Here, we begin from a kind of metaphor which could be easily paralleled in Western poetry: the image of the broken root which can never be joined together again as a sign for the separation of the lovers. Whether this is a matter of mutual regret or a construction by the author, we can, as is the case with every love poem, never really know. But the overall point is that Zhou is using this repertoire of older metaphors that include most noticeably a panoply of colour coding, again based loosely on the seasons, to find some kind of convergence between the natural scene and the plight, the emotion which he is trying to develop. It needs, though, to be noted that the 'natural scene' is also anything but a natural scene, since it is deeply imbued with traditional Chinese tropes. So everything builds up, albeit extremely quietly, to the final four lines. The 'person' here, whoever or whatever it signifies, has an almost ghostly status, and thus becomes in itself a kind of metaphor for the insubstantiality of desire, which in turn is used as a metaphor for the equal insubstantiality of poetry, the impossibility of poetry, or of any other kind of writing, ever to reconstruct the object which it mourns. Yet, the poem concludes, perhaps such a reconstruction is indeed possible, but only and precisely through metaphor; perhaps the image of the 'floss that sticks to the ground/in the aftermath of rain' is an appropriate metaphor not only for the abandoned lover's plight but also for the task of poetry itself, which is to search ceaselessly for these elusive convergences between, for example, nature and artifice.

In this kind of poetry, then, there is self-conscious exercise of skill, but it is not designed to provoke awareness of strange and apparently bizarre coincidences between things, as in the manner of the metaphysical poets of the early seventeenth-century English tradition, who expressed their queries about divine rule through their ironised difficulties with scientific discoveries based on instruments which were then the new technology. It is designed rather to disclose a new and contemporary, if necessarily transient, correlation between the poet's condition and the stock of metaphors which he has inherited. Thus, we may fairly say of traditional Chinese poetry, as I have mentioned before, that it is better considered as a series of parts of a continuous process of metaphorisation; but the crucial point is to make this stock of metaphors converge, to find and reveal in them an underlying ground, so that a general term like 'passion', for example, 'takes root' in a sphere which spans natural imagery and the interior world of the poet considered as a human subject, in all the complex senses of that term.

What, though, of illusion? Perhaps at the heart of traditional Chinese metaphor there is frequently the sense that its purpose is to underline, to call attention to, the illusions by which we live. Hence the emphasis on transience, the dwelling on the past and the irrecoverable, as typically in this poem by Wang Jian, 'Passing by Lace-Crest Palace' (early ninth century):

Its jade mansions lean at a tilt,

the plaster walls are bare, green hills in layer on layer

surround the palace of old. The Warrior Emperor went away,

the gossamer sleeves are gone, the wildflowers and butterflies

hold sway over winds of spring. (Owen 1996: 455)

This is clearly a lament for the passing of a type of power, and of a way of life. What is perhaps more interesting, though, is the doubleness of the metaphor of 'gossamer', which simultaneously signifies a certain 'fineness' of the imperial past while reinforcing its fragility. This ambiguity, this sense of the transience of all things, even the most powerful, is carried over into the final line, where it is uncertain in quite what way the wildflowers and butterflies 'hold sway'. Is it that they are the very emanations of spring, in which case there might be within the poem a certain possibility of return, to or by the past? Or is it rather that these wildflowers and butterflies, with their beautiful indifference to human life and power, represent a force which will forever prevent the return of that particular, other kind of spring which might mark the renewal of the pride of empire?

It is possible to argue that both meanings are present, and are held within the poem. However, the force of the metaphorical structure is not to astound the reader, but rather to provide confirmation of a sense of illusion which is already assumed to be known as common cultural ground. As one critic says, the poem conjures a 'site of absence' and thereby provides a sense that metaphor cannot, in the end, give the reader confirmation that it has a grip on its object. What it might have instead is a grip, of some kind, on a certain mood, a certain state of emotion, akin perhaps in some ways to the Western romantic moods conjured by William Wordsworth's famous phrase 'emotion recollected in tranquillity' (Wordsworth and Coleridge 1968: 266), yet without the kind of possible redemptive status which is implicit in Wordsworth's formulation.

We have moved a long way from traditional descriptions of metaphor in terms of 'tenor' and 'vehicle' and perhaps the general point to make at this stage is that 'metaphor' itself is not a static, ahistorical term; it is not as though there is a pervasive, universal concept of metaphor which can be applied, like a template, to all ages and cultures. Rather, we need to historicise the term, to look as closely as possible at what different things might be considered to constitute metaphor under different historical, cultural and geographical circumstances. And this is before we even begin to look at the fundamental difference between different language systems which will play their parts in different definitions and usages of metaphor: the 'hieroglyphic' materiality of the Chinese language, for example, where it is still possible to see, even in its modern, stripped-down written forms, traces of the objects originally represented. In this sense, the whole operation of representation in Chinese differs from that available in alphabetical languages, and therefore the notion of metaphor and of the extent to which and the ways in which similarities among and differences between words on the printed page can relate to perceived differences and similarities among things will necessarily diverge.

PUBLIC METAPHOR

It is important to grasp that metaphor, however we might define it, con-stantly exceeds the literary even as it forms its basis; metaphor is the common substratum of the representation of institutions, corporations, public bodies. The French Marxist thinker Louis Althusser described how we are 'interpellated' through language (Althusser 1977: 162-70); that is to say, how we are constituted as subjects. We are given to believing, he said, that we are in some sense free agents, coherent subjects in our own right, when in fact we are at the mercy of an ideological flood that threatens to engulf us. Although Althusser did not say as much, we might suggest that the principal way in which we are interpellated is through metaphor, and also that we are interpellated as metaphor.

For example, as I open my newspaper today I see an article under the headline, 'Tobacco giants deny fraud in $280bn trial'. Now, it is obvious that tobacco companies are not actually giants, although equally it may not be easy to say what actually is a giant. What is being said here is that tobacco companies are very large, but this does not stop the flow of metaphor. For where there are giants there are giant-killers; and, as a reader of a liberal newspaper, I am being interpellated, hailed as part of a specific cultural and historical community, through this hardly remembered but still potent fairy-tale connection. I am being addressed as somebody who is on the side of the giant-killers, somebody for whom the size of the tobacco companies is itself grotesque, although this grotesquerie is in fact a compound of their size with the lethal nature of their dealings with human beings.

The 'Jack, the giant-killer' motif is actually entirely inapplicable to the story itself, which concerns a legal suit being brought against the tobacco companies not by the 'little people' implied in the metaphor but in fact by the US government. But this in no way prevents the play of metaphor: later in the story we read of a memo sent among the 'tobacco giants' saying that it was essential to provide smokers with the 'psychological crutch and some rationale to continue smoking'. The word 'crutch' in this context is obviously interesting; from being an essential device to help those with a disability, it has become here, in the communication system of the tobacco corporations, an accusation of feebleness implying contempt for their own customers. The memo was, we are told, somewhat ambiguously, 'secret'; despite this, however, one of the lawyers for the companies remains confident that they will win their case because, he says, 'fraud is a very high bar'.

Literally, he presumably means to imply that a successful prosecution for fraud requires a high level of proof; but the image comes from the world of sport, and implicitly by association reduces the life-or-death consequences of smoking to a game. As a final point in this single article, randomly chosen, we learn near the end that 'the courtroom battle is seen by anti-smoking advocates as the pinnacle of tobacco legislation'. All of these metaphors are commonplaces of journalism, but when added up and placed alongside a further reference to the 'pool' of smokers which is being constantly replenished to compensate for those who are 'dying off', we can perhaps begin to see what every lawyer and advertising person knows: that a 'case', whether at law or in the public mind, is as strong as the metaphors deployed to sustain it.

Metaphors, then, are integral to public life, and this is so not only at the verbal level, but also at the visual. One might consider the red rose which is the symbol of New Labour. The motivation behind the creation and adoption of this symbol, we might fairly suppose, is not merely to juxtapose but to jam together two indicators: the rose, as the symbol of Britain, or perhaps more properly of England, and the colour red signifying the, at least residual, traces of socialism in New Labour. The intention is to suggest that the natural colour of the rose is red; but this depends again on a set of metaphorical associations. Consider Blake's poem 'The Sick Rose' (1794):

Oh Rose, thou art sick! The invisible worm That flies in the night, In the howling storm,

Has found out thy bed Of crimson joy: And his dark secret love Does thy life destroy. (Blake 1966: 213)

For such a short poem, this is a highly complex one. We might initially feel that the metaphorical force of the rose is traditional, signifying beauty, purity, freshness, but this is not the only interpretation possible. This rose, indeed, may well have become sick because of the ministrations of the lethal worm; but on the other hand, it is equally possible that the sickness of the rose is precisely its complicity with the worm. If the worm has had to 'find out' the 'bed of crimson joy', then this implies something about secretive-ness, and thus that the rose may have colluded in its own corruption.

Here, at least, we are challenged to continue to accept a common belief, which is that commonplace objects have a limited range of metaphorical meanings. Even the rose, with its traditional connotations of fragrance and purity, can appear in different situations, which underlines the very important point that metaphor is primarily contextual. Consider, for example, an advertisement in the same issue of the newspaper which gave us 'tobacco giants'. It was for home shredding machines, under the headline 'The World's Toughest Shredders. Fight Our Fastest Growing Crime: Identity Fraud'.

There are many points one could make about this. One concerns the word 'toughest'. The metaphor by means of which the quality of these shredding machines is assured is cast, presumably not accidentally, in the context of the wider political connotations of the advertisement, in terms of the New Labour mantra 'Tough on crime; tough on the causes of crime'. By means of the metaphor, a certain level and type of modernity is proffered, and we are interpellated as citizens who wish to quell crime and who will somehow be contributing to this effort by buying a particular brand of shredder. But there is more to it than this, because current political rhetoric inexorably connects crime with asylum-seekers, those whose identity, in more than one sense, is uncertain; therefore, by joining in with this 'fight against crime', we are implicitly helping to repel an invasion, securing precisely our own identity against those who may wish or seek to encroach upon it. Thus, buying these shredders becomes, by a series of metaphorical shifts, virtually a public or patriotic duty, while at the same time it defines us as part of a community under siege. The paradox here, which is perhaps not entirely different from that in 'The Sick Rose', is that, when you think about it, the only way apparently on offer to preserve the purity of the State is through secrecy: 'The best way to protect yourself is to shred all personal information before you throw it away', the advertisement continues. Here, it is clear that shredding has itself become a metaphor; what is signified is that the State may be protective but it is also potentially intrusive, and the only way to preserve individuality is, paradoxically, to shred all evidence of it.

We might also want to consider the metaphorical structures which surround political movements. An example would be the pressure group 'Fathers4Justice', which sought to bring to people's attention the plight of fathers who were separated from the mothers of their children and regarded themselves as having inadequate access rights to those children. One of the things the name of the group might subliminally remind us of is the vast chain of toy shops formerly called 'Toys'R'Us'. By playing on this rhetoric, the group sought to establish that they are nice, friendly people, who fully understand children's needs and wish to play their part in infant upbringing.

This is supported by the symbol '4', which matches with the symbol 'R', but also calls to mind a realm of text messaging which again reassures the recipient of the message that this is a phenomenon which is thoroughly in tune with the young. But one of the principal methods the group used to bring themselves and their complaint to public attention was by dressing up as superheroes, a metaphor which works in several ways. In the first place, it underlines the notion that fathers are fully in touch with the world of their children. But because one of the facts about superheroes is that they are, at least in part, out of date, this is also designed to show that fathers retain their own memories of childhood, a detail designed to make the recipient of the metaphor feel closer to them and to incite sympathy. Then again, the notion of the superhero works in a quite different way, to remind us of the 'heroism' of the male; this is designed less to incite sympathy than to command respect. And finally, although there are certainly further connotations, the notion of the superhero returns full circle, because by dressing up and performing such stunts as climbing tall buildings, a certain irony comes into the equation: fathers, we are being implicitly told, are not merely serious persons deserving of respect; they are simultaneously able to laugh at themselves and at their own pretensions. They are serious yet playful.

Another contemporary example would be the Countryside Alliance. The word 'countryside' carries its own ideological weight: it conjures up a slightly old-fashioned view of rural life, which implicitly bolsters the Alliance's claim to represent a traditional way of life which is under threat from the forces of modernisation. 'Alliance', similarly, carries ideological baggage. An 'alliance', according to one of its dictionary definitions, is 'people united by kinship or friendship'; thus, the Countryside Alliance hopes to mark itself off from the common run of political parties or movements and to establish itself in the public mind as a loose group of like-minded people who, in the context of this looseness and friendliness of affiliation, represent in themselves the way of life in the countryside and thus become precisely an emblem for the communal habits and characteristics they claim to seek to preserve.

All public life sustains itself through metaphors. The recently redeveloped centre of the city of Bristol, for example, is marked by two enormous sculptures, known as 'the Sails', which, through particular arrangements of metal and fabric, resemble the sails of a ship and thus serve to act as a metaphor for Bristol's maritime past. Such a public metaphor seeks to control and restrict a chain of associations: it does not seek to remind us of the less currently acceptable aspects of this past - the slave trade, for example, or the trade in tobacco - but rather to play upon folk memories of sailing ships, of early explorers, of the danger, risk, thrill and adventure of life at sea in a rather less than specific period of history. The French thinker and critic Roland Barthes, in his famous essay 'Myth Today' (1957), referred to the whole collection of Western representations of China as 'sinity' (Barthes 1973: 121); following this thread, we might refer to this chain of associations in Bristol under the heading 'maritimity'. The most prestigious and influential commercial society in Bristol lays further claim to this set of historical associations by continuing to call itself the 'Merchant Venturers', and we can see a related rhetoric on a national scale with the advent of companies of risk funders referring to themselves under the heading 'Venture Capital'. Here again, there are demarcations around the word 'venture', which has a curious range of apparent meanings, from the timidity underlined in the phrase 'I venture to suggest that . . .' to the boldness implicit in the idea of 'venturing' onto the open seas, or into a theatre of danger.

What does this reveal about the general position of metaphor? It shows that metaphor is never static, and rarely innocent. A particularly interesting example in current speech, although a complex one to discuss, is the presence of the word 'like' in contemporary youth jargon. An example would be, 'I was, like, what is going on here?', a kind of speech which is brilliantly parodied in the television series Little Britain. What is happening here is, in one sense, a kind of act of impersonation.

Rather than simply reporting on the past, the word 'like' introduces what appears to be an actual recounting of how the person felt, what he or she was thinking, at the time. The complexity derives from the fact that the word 'like' is traditionally supposed to introduce precisely, as we have seen, a type of metaphor, a simile, but the use here has been subtly changed and one could argue that this also touches on the eruption of notions of virtual reality into everyday life. We might paraphrase the structure as implying, 'I did not actually think that; but it was "as though" I had thought that'. In a metaphorical usage like this, while in one sense past habits of speech may appear to grow closer and more vivid, they also become curiously intangible, reflecting wider cultural and social difficulties with public and private memory in an age when access to information through the worldwide web is virtually instantaneous and there is consequently little need to rely on the vagaries of personal remembrance. It could also be that there is a reference to a certain fragmentation of the self, to which I shall return in a moment.

In this sense metaphor is a crucial aspect of power; the control of public metaphor is a way of gaining and securing power. One may reasonably think of the still frequent use of the term 'the Crown' to signify the control of British society by royalty. And perhaps the most revealing metaphor in British cultural life shows up under this heading, namely the apparent fact that in the United Kingdom, as opposed to, say, in the United States or France, we are all conventionally referred to as 'subjects' of the monarch. It is perhaps critical to pause on this for a moment. I have referred to the term 'subject' several times now, and for many years it has been a crucial term in theoretical discourse, as I have hinted in my remarks on Althusser above. One of the results of this theoretical attention has been to criticise, even deconstruct or dismember, the term and thereby to expose its inner contradictions.

Put very briefly, the notion of the subject appears at first glance to presuppose something unified, whether this be in terms of the 'subject of an utterance', which means the person doing the uttering, or the subject of, for example, a conversation, in which case it refers to the apparent topic of such a conversation. But when one looks more closely at the word, especially in the political context, one is also referred back to its Latin root, as something or someone which is 'thrown under', as in the modern usage of 'subjected to'. The word 'subject' therefore alludes at the same time to a kind of unificatory power and to powerlessness, subservience. A poem by Dannie Abse, 'A Suburban Episode' (1968), begins with the following two stanzas:

Since you telephoned to say - in a tiny voice -
(how servile you are) intruders intruders walk
in pairs across the back lawn (I'm sorry, you say)
I say heartily, too heartily perhaps,
do not lock yourself in oh dear no,
go out, shout, challenge them, ask them why.
Since you say that some - the most impertinent -
and therefore you think (wrongly) the most important,
for instance, those in plum-coloured blazers,
are cutting down your tulips, snip snip snip,
one by one with small scissors, small nail-scissors,
I say with formidable aggression
stride out, ask them for credentials, stop them;
but remember walk with very long steps. (Abse 1977: 104)

It would be fair to say that what we have here is a sustained series of metaphors of public power and the powerlessness of the subject, but most of the metaphors contain or enact a certain ambiguity. To take just one example: the phrase 'tiny voice' in the first line has multiple referents. It could be that the voice is fairly literally 'tiny' in the sense of being very quiet or soft, although even here there is a metaphor at work, since the most obviously literal referent of 'tiny' is to physical size, and that is not a property which a voice can have. It could also, however, be that the narrator of the poem, whom we assume to be a man, regards the voice as 'tiny' because it seems to him comparatively insignificant, compared, for example, with the exaggerated 'heartiness' of his own response. It could also simply be 'tiny' because it is coming through a telephone, which might be seen as reducing volume, although here the question of how small a voice one might hear on a telephone is again a matter of power, since it is within the power of the hearer to adjust the distance between telephone and ear. But when we consider metaphor, we have also to consider not only the word itself, but also the adjacent possibilities of the word: so that 'tiny' might quite easily become 'tinny', which again could be seen either as a telephonic effect or as an implicit criticism by the narrator of the caller's voice, and hence of her - if we assume it to be a woman - complaint. If her complaint is 'tinny', then by a metaphorical extension we may consider it to be without foundation, without substance, hollow and rattling; but as we consider this, whether consciously or unconsciously, we are also therefore forming a judgement of how the narrator is receiving this call and what judgements he himself is bringing to bear on the caller.

Thus, an entire satire on the way bureaucracy deals with complaints or, indeed, desperate appeals, is already being formed in this first crucial metaphor. In the second stanza we might similarly think about the 'plum-coloured blazers'. The blazers themselves might well be a metaphor for a certain type of old-fashioned power or authority, and here again we may wish to pause for a moment and consider whether dress, fashion, the way of bedecking the human body is itself a type of metaphor. It is noticeable, for example, in television news broadcasts that Western male politicians and diplomats dress very differently from their counterparts from different cultures. The typical Western male dress, including suit, tie and belt, serves metaphorically to create a sense of completeness and power; jackets are cut to fit an exaggerated version of the male physique (and the notion of 'power-dressing' for women, which usually involves padded shoulders and nipped-in waists, enacts the same scenario).

Within this regime, power surges upwards to create a looming body which asserts its power through the strength of its shoulders and marks its boundaries carefully with sharp and clearly defined shapes and edges. There are many other forms of dress with which one could contrast this. To take one example, the Arabic djellaba provides no interior padding or shaping of any kind; it simply falls from the shoulders to cover the entire body without emphasising any particular feature of it. One could take this further by looking at the content of fashion sales catalogues: whereas in the West the emphasis is on clarity of line and, quite often and especially for women, exposure or accentuation of key bodily features, in catalogues for Arabic wear the emphasis is on covering, on removing the shape of the body from the gaze. In fact, this goes one step further, because in orthodox Islamic clothing catalogues, because of the taboo on the portrayal of the human form or face, the models have no heads. This, then, is also a version of public metaphor, a way in which an apparently minor cultural code carries a weightier signification.

To return to Dannie Abse and the 'plum-coloured blazers': the blazers themselves metaphorically signify membership of a club, class or caste. It is obviously one from which the caller considers herself to be excluded, whether by reason of gender or otherwise. However, the plum colouring reminds us of other things again, such as the metaphor of a 'plummy' accent, which was probably originally derived from the sense of the speaker having a 'plum in his mouth' but is now more broadly applied in class contexts. It may or may not be relevant to this specific context, but it is worth remembering that P.G. Wodehouse, the arch-chronicler of the early twentieth-century upper classes, was known as 'Plum'; ostensibly because as a small child this was the closest he got to pronouncing his own first name, Pelham, but we may suspect that the ongoing metaphor runs deeper than that.

The final stanza of the poem extends the series of metaphors and disturbs them, as the narrator makes us aware of the menace even he feels at least partly as a result of his caller's experience:

Do not apologise. For believe me
I believe you. I know your nation (I mean your nature)
and how cunning things can be, damnably cunning.
Why, have I not heard, even I, first cousin
of the mayor, heard in the night a stone falling?
No ordinary stone either, scraping the sheer ledges,
and later many stones, boulders even, leaping down out of earshot, down
the sides of hell. (Abse 1977: 105)

The pun on 'nation' and 'nature' reveals to the reader, at the very least, an implicit racism in the narrator. More importantly, though, what the stanza shows is a version of the disintegration of the subject; we come to feel ourselves to be in the presence of a character who is not, as he has claimed, immune to fear, but rather concerned with covering up and dismissing his fears. Hell here clearly serves a metaphorical purpose, of revealing to us the notion of a feared void within the narrator, a point at which all his apparent bureaucratic and official certainties no longer convince.

Thus, we have a set of metaphors on the terrain of power and power-lessness and of the ability of the subject to remain, or ever to be, in control of his or her own life, and we may speculate that this too is of the very essence of metaphor. Metaphor, of course, consists of comparison, but perhaps these comparisons can never be quite equal; perhaps they always also serve some purpose of aggrandisement or belittlement. And the notion of 'belittlement' can take us further into the relationship between public metaphor, power and childhood. We might pursue the theme of the telephone as metaphor, for distance, for incomprehension, for a type of communication which is, in a crucial way, unnatural. Sylvia Plath's well-known poem 'Daddy' (1962) contains the lines:

So daddy, I'm finally through. The black telephone's off at the root,
The voices just can't worm through. (Plath 1981: 224)

Here, the metaphorical structure involves an implicit comparison between the telephone and the voice, or voices, of the dead. The narrator of 'Daddy' is haunted by her father in a way which, we might suggest, is perennially applicable if we accept that the 'voices' we hear in our childhood, the voices of authority and power, never leave us but continue to inform our day-to-day actions and decisions. The fact of the narrator's father's death in no way affects this power over the subject; at least, that is what we might think while reading the poem up to this moment, when the assertion is made that the narrator has actually succeeded in 'killing the dead'. When she says, 'I'm finally through', it would seem that the force of the metaphor is double, and indeed more than double, it is virtually paradoxical: on the one hand, it implies that communication has been established, in the sense of having been 'put through' by the telephone exchange to the potential hearer; but, on the other hand, it implies that she is 'finished' with her father. This is confirmed in the final stanza, which also picks up on much further metaphor in the poem about Nazis, vampires and other creatures of evil and the night:

There's a stake in your fat black heart And the villagers never liked you.
They are dancing and stamping on you. They always knew it was you.
Daddy, daddy, you bastard, I'm through. (Plath 1981: 224)

From one point of view, one could say that the accumulation of metaphors here and throughout the poem is designed to permit the formation of a whole subject. The father is presented as what we might call constant interference on the line, as a voice, whether imagined or remembered, which is constantly preventing the subject from reaching a condition of entirety. Thus, by associating the father metaphorically with Nazism and vampirism, the self of the poem, which is presented as a kind of child-self, is seeking to use metaphor as a mode of explanation and also as a way of developing from a subjected position. To be 'through' is not only to be connected; it is also, in a quite different way, to have survived that condition. Furthermore, it is to be on the point of death, and so we may suspect that the metaphors run two ways: towards the evolution of a real power in the subject, but simultaneously towards an acknowledgement that such power will be deathly because it is only by accepting or otherwise dealing with the notion that the self, the subject, has been formed by others that one can come to an understanding of the individual's inescapable dependency on his or her own past.

It would now be possible, following one line of thought, to begin to see metaphor as that which 'stands in' for the human absence which marks and defines the subject of capitalist world-formation. The notion of resistance through remetaphorisation, through what the French thinkers Gilles Deleuze and Félix Guattari called a 'reterritorialisation' of conquered realms (Deleuze and Guattari 1988: 111-48), becomes a substrate of literary resistance itself. We might see it, for example, in the major literary theorist Maurice Blanchot's insistence on the inextricability of literature and death, in Samuel Beckett's refusal of elaborated discourse, or in Salman Rushdie's insistence on excess of speech as recompense for the refusal of the 'native' language. Perhaps the case of Beckett is particularly worth mentioning, as an example of a writer who, in one sense, resists the elaborations of metaphor, at least in part because of their contamination by public discourse. We might hypothesise that this is precisely why many of his characters experience difficulties with reality as it is usually presented to them. For example, in the 'Magdalen Mental Mercyseat' chapter in the novel Murphy (1938), reality is an altogether difficult matter, not to be apprehended by the normal means of comparison and translation but far more elusive:

> *The nature of outer reality remained obscure. The men, women and children of science would seem to have as many ways of kneeling to their facts as any other body of illuminati. The definition of outer reality, or of reality short and simple, varied according to the sensibility of the definer. But all seemed agreed that contact with it, even the layman's muzzy contact, was a rare privilege. (Beckett 1973: 101)*

We are a long way here from that condition of metaphor in which the poet, the writer or the advertiser can point to two phenomena and advise us that they have similarities. We are instead in a world where the common ground of such comparisons, the conviction that all of us, or at least all of us in some specific 'interpretive community', to quote the literary theorist Stanley Fish's phrase (Fish 1980), share common assumptions is no longer obvious, if it ever has been. The 'Magdalen Mental Mercyseat' is itself a marvellously satirical composite of metaphors. 'Magdalen' comes from a whole Christian and, in the Irish context of Beckett and Murphy, Catholic tradition. The word 'Mental', in this context, signifies the power of a 'scientific' establishment to classify people as 'mentally ill', as 'patients'.

'Mercyseat' takes us back in a sense to the religious register of metaphor, but in another way reminds us of the function of metaphor as euphemism, with something in it about the evasion of the dreadful facts of mental ill-health, incarceration and, eventually, death. The passage itself continues this violent mixture of metaphors. There are the scientists; there are the 'illuminati', the mention of whom suggests to us that perhaps so-called scientific rigour is not quite what it seems; and there is the kneeling, which again takes us back to church. Beckett's purpose in using these metaphors is, to employ a term which was often utilised when describing his drama, 'absurd': it is not that he wants his reader to gain new direct knowledge through these experiences and comparisons; it is rather that he wants to emphasise the vast variety of holds on reality according to which people live their lives, the disparity between the public formations and metaphors of institutions such as the Church and the mental health profession, and the struggle of the individual as he or she strives to find metaphors which actually work as they try to grasp the world around them.

This might lead us to think about Beckett's famous play Waiting for Godot (1955), and especially because here is a play which 'plays' to the utmost on a resistance to metaphorisation. The characters Vladimir and Estragon are, at least patchily, engaged in a struggle to discover meaning in the situation in which they find themselves and in the events which occasionally befall them, as well as in their hazy recollections of the past; but this never proves possible. And neither does it prove any more possible for readers and critics than it does for the characters themselves. The stage set for Waiting for Godot contains a single central object, a withered tree. It would seem obvious that, given its extraordinary prominence, it serves some kind of metaphorical function; but what kind? Does it represent a certain kind of barrenness, the hopelessness about change which is the lot of the two characters? Does it represent, on the contrary, the hope, however vestigial, of new life? Does it represent the already metaphorised 'tree' which is a synonym for the cross of Jesus Christ's crucifixion? Does it, in some sense, represent for Vladimir and Estragon the entire world, since there are no other objects or directions from which they can get their bearings?

All of these things are possible; but the point should probably be that the tree, in its barrenness, its reluctance to yield any kind of secret meaning, instead represents the exhaustion of metaphor. We shall come on to psychological and psychoanalytic readings of metaphor later; but we might say that one thing Waiting for Godot suggests is that the very process of constructing and understanding metaphor requires a certain energy in the life around us, which is the deeper ground behind the complexities of perception and reflection. For Vladimir and Estragon this energy is only sporadically available, and our fear at the end of the play is that this is unlikely to change. There is a name for the condition where the whole world seems as bleak as a withered tree and where there seems no possibility of escape from the unending and repetitive present. In fact, there are several names for it. Coleridge knew it, emblematically, in 'Dejection: An Ode' (1802) as dejection,

A grief without a pang, void, dark, and drear, A stifled, drowsy, unimpassioned grief, Which finds no natural outlet, no relief, In word, or sigh, or tear - (Coleridge 1967: 364)

And what he finds is that this mood, or condition, stifles his ability to 'metaphorise' the world:

All this long eve, so balmy and serene, Have I been gazing on the western sky,

And its peculiar tint of yellow green: And still I gaze - but with how blank an eye! (Coleridge 1967: 364)

Coleridge's dejection is manifested to him as an inability to make connections, to see more deeply into the heart of difference and similarity. We might reasonably say that there is a paradox in the poem since, while he is bemoaning his lack of imagination, he is nevertheless writing a brilliantly metaphorical poem. Another variant of the state would be 'melancholy'. But, to take this back to Waiting for Godot, the word we now more often use for this mood is 'depression': a sense of being stuck, of being unable to move outside ourselves in order to participate in the outer world, or even to manipulate it to our view. The poet Les Murray, among others including Winston Churchill, refers to it as 'the black dog' (Murray 1997).

Depression perhaps gives us a window through which to look at what it might be like to live in a non-metaphorical world. There are indeed people who live in such a world all the time, people whose mental illness consigns them to chronically 'concrete thought', which I shall consider in more detail in a later chapter; but if we consider depression to be a kind of 'retreat', or defile, in the continuous activity of metaphorising that makes us human, then this will open up the notion of metaphor as an essential ground of human activity.

However, to come back to 'public metaphor', there is clearly a two-edged sword at play here. On the one hand, our freedom to metaphorise is an essential aspect of our more general human freedom. If we think, to paraphrase Hamlet for rather different purposes, that a cloud looks very like a camel, we are free in a democratic society to say so, and at least to offer this perception to others, even if they disagree. But if, on the other hand, we see a picture of a camel on a pack of cigarettes called, unsurprisingly, 'Camel', then we are not free: we are constrained in our perception. We may choose to accept the implicit metaphor being offered, even if it might be very difficult to see quite what it is, other than the notion of a cigarette being an 'oasis-like' form of relief, or of a cigarette somehow reminding us of exotic Eastern mysteries, or of a cigarette being somehow a way of getting us, like a 'ship of the desert', through difficult times. Or we may choose to ignore it. Whichever we do, it is not going to go away; it is part of the huge system of 'embedded metaphor' which surrounds us at every point of our social lives, and with which we are dealing in one way or another at every moment.

7

Metaphor, Difference and Untranslatability

Deconstruction is a set of ideas and motifs which can remind us again that the possibility of a full translation, by means of which similarity can be verified, is always under suspension; to say that something is like something else is no longer to establish a similarity but to project such a similarity into an undecidable field, where the acceptance or recognition of such traces is always at the mercy of a more, or increasingly less, communal readership. The recognition of metaphor thus becomes not only a sign of power but also a powerful marker of cultural instability; metaphors need to be considered not only in terms of their endurance but also in terms of their passing away, their failure to fix language in untenable postures, the ways they have of vacating meanings and leaving us adrift, surrounded only by cliché, metaphor's ideological residue. One relevant question would be: what is a dead metaphor, and how may it be used to commercial and cultural advantage?

In order to explore this further, I want to turn to what may seem a surprising example, one to which I shall return at intervals in this chapter, some stanzas from a lyric by Bob Dylan:

When you're lost in the rain in Juarez and it's Eastertime too And your gravity fails and negativity don't pull you through Don't put on any airs when you're down on Rue Morgue Avenue They got some hungry women there and they really make a mess outa you

Now if you see Saint Annie please tell her thanks a lot

I cannot move, my fingers are all in a knot

I don't have the strength to get up and take another shot

And my best friend, my doctor, won't even say what it is I've got

Sweet Melinda, the peasants call her the goddess of gloom She speaks good English and she invites you up into her room And you're so kind and careful not to go to her too soon And she takes your voice and leaves you howling at the moon

Up on Housing Project Hill it's either fortune or fame

You must pick one or the other though neither of them are to be what they claim If you're lookin' to get silly you better go back to from where you came Because the cops don't need you and man they expect the same

I started out on burgundy but soon hit the harder stuff Everybody said they'd stand behind me when the game got rough But the joke was on me, there was nobody even there to call my bluff I'm going back to New York City, I do believe I've had enough (Dylan 1994: 315-16)

In thinking through the metaphorical structure of this lyric, one obvious starting-place would be Juarez on the Mexican border, antagonistically coupled with New York City in the final stanza. This is in some sense a visit, familiar from American literature, to Mexico, and in that sense, again familiar, a visit to a place which is 'below': in a conventional topography according to which, metaphorically, the north is superior to the south in the same way as the head is superior to the body, but also racially, socially, culturally. This is, as Freud or Hillman would say, a visit to the underworld; and the metaphorical structure of the lyric bears this out. There is no space here to dwell on all the relevant features; but we can at least consider Rue Morgue Avenue. What might suitably come to mind is Poe's 'The Murders in the Rue Morgue' (1841), a tale of crime and the beast. This is not to say that Dylan had Poe's text in mind when he wrote the lyric; that is something we shall never know. But it is to point to the ways in which common stocks of metaphor become elaborated.

I use this example in order to introduce the question of how far 'metaphorical correspondence' can go. If we think of the potential metaphorical field of a word like 'lion', for example, then obviously it stretches in many directions. To cast the metaphors in the alternative form of similes, one might think of 'as brave as a lion', 'as strong as a lion'; a zookeeper, perhaps with a rather more intimate relationship with lions, might prefer 'as smelly as a lion'; and with a little stretch of the imagination a visitor from the Planet Zog might opt, albeit perhaps only briefly, for 'as furry as a lion'.

In fact, at the risk of losing sight of Dylan's lyric for a moment, it is worth remaining in the company of our visitor from Zog, because what such a perspective underlines is the way in which, and the extent to which, metaphors function, and can only function, in relation to what Stanley Fish refers to as an 'interpretive community'. In other words, to put it very simply, metaphors are not universals. They depend upon cultural and social perceptions, but we can also go one stage further than this and say that metaphors actually ground our perceptions. The lion in English mythology, or the eagle in the corresponding US version, are national symbols; they will always have around them, to readers reading within those traditions, a penumbra which will not be available to readers reading from different cultural positions.

In a very interesting autobiographical novel called Passage to Juneau (2000), the travel writer Jonathan Raban, in the course of a lone yacht journey up the northwest coast of North America from Seattle to Alaska, calls attention to the characteristic forms of art practised by the seagoing aboriginals who used to populate the area. He points out that their art can seem strange to later Western eyes, since it sometimes appears to be composed of bits and pieces; in a particular piece of work, for example a woven blanket, we might find as we look closely the representation of an eye here, an ear there, with no apparent connection between them. The reason for this, Raban plausibly suggests, is that since water was so crucial to a people who spent most of their lives on or very near to it, their perception of the world was refracted through water; therefore, their representations of the world around, and consequently their metaphors for that world, reflect the broken, choppy surface of things when seen reflected in the waves.

These people's natural metaphors for life, therefore, consist in images of life on the water. The cycle of life is processed and represented as a sea journey, to the final point of air burial, with the body of the deceased hung high in trees in a canoe. From this kind of example, one might derive the thought that life is itself intrinsically metaphorical; that we make sense of our lives through metaphors which seem appropriate to it. Behind these large cultural metaphors lie vast swaths of cultural assumption: the intensely English metaphor of 'hearts of oak', to take a further but equally maritime example, would not be a thinkable way of construing the world (after all, one might think it meant merely 'hard-hearted' rather than 'brave') unless one knew that oak was the favoured, strongest wood for shipbuilding, and thus available as a cultural metaphor for a concept of power and courage appropriate to a nation which perceived itself, during the eighteenth and nineteenth centuries, when the metaphor came to its fullest fruition, as essentially maritime, dependent on naval supremacy.

To return to Dylan and to problems of translatability: in construing the metaphors in the lyric, it is important, but it is also natural to our reading or listening, to draw limits around the metaphors on offer. For example, the notion of 'Eastertime' clearly sets up a religious thread that crops up more than once in the lyric, for example in the image of 'Saint Annie' in the second stanza. But at the same time, it would be an error of reading to suppose that this is a controlling metaphor that runs through the whole of the lyric. It may indeed inflect the reference to 'Housing Project Hill' in the fourth stanza in such a way as to remind us of the Hill of Calvary, where Jesus was crucified, and it may further underpin a note of suffering that runs through the lyric; but metaphors have limits, and one of the crucial ways in which literature works is by setting one metaphor, or one field of metaphor, against another.

So here, for example, the metaphorisation of Mexico and the metaphorisation of religion enter into a complex interplay. We do not suppose for a moment that sweet Melinda is actually a goddess; neither, probably, because of the undertones of prostitution as a symbol of exploitation in the third stanza, do we seriously suppose that she has many of the attributes of a goddess. Instead, the metaphor functions within a certain field of reference, here to an extent ironic: it is possible to imagine that the lyric's protagonist, searching for a metaphor in which to describe this encounter, comes up with the notion of the goddess, but only in ironised form; the metaphor is used, in fact, not to point to a similarity but to a difference.

And here is another point at which the whole notion of metaphor becomes complicated, and where the methods of deconstruction can be helpful, because, again put very simply, deconstruction claims that words do not have fixed meanings. Building on the insights of structuralism, deconstruction claims that words, and thus by implication metaphors, are radically unstable; their meanings are always fluid, changing according to historical and cultural context, with the meanings trapped inside them constantly overflowing, refusing to be pinned down. To take the phrase 'howling at the moon', which Dylan is here borrowing from a stock of Negro blues lyrics and which may relate also to the blues singer Howlin' Wolf: the metaphor of the wolf is obvious, but we shall not appreciate the complex force of the metaphor unless we see that alongside its strength of representation there is also a certain 'hollowing out', a way in which, because the metaphor has been used so often, it has lost a great deal of its apparent force. Therefore, a protagonist who claims to be 'howling at the moon' is no longer using the metaphor to indicate a genuine throe of passion, but rather to demonstrate an ironically self-pitying view of a personal plight. This metaphor simultaneously deepens and betrays a certain shallowness.

'Howling at the moon' might, however, remind us of a further dimension to the relations between, shall we say, metaphor and the human, for it is the case that many of the root metaphors which we come across appear to attempt to establish some parity or opposition between the human and the rest of the animal world. We can stay with the case of the wolf, and with a remark made by Dean Inge (1919: 42-3): 'It takes in reality only one to make a quarrel. It is useless for the sheep to pass resolutions in favour of vegetarianism, while the wolf remains of a different opinion.' Here, a constellation of metaphors involving the wolf is conjured, but principally the 'big bad wolf' of folk legend, which here stands in for all those irresistibly violent and unstable forces that will, perhaps inevitably, upset all plans for human betterment, make sure that our plans 'gang aft agley' (Burns 2001: 96). And this metaphor of wolf also goes back to the roots of Western civilisation, or at least to Romulus and Remus, mythical founders of Rome, who were suckled by a she-wolf. Presumably this signifies that at the origin of civilisation there is a tamed, or at least maternal and nurturing, version of nature which has to be in some sense implicated in the founding act of the civilised. The deployment of this metaphor shows a deep, if unconscious, understanding of the precarious nature of civilisation; it also inevitably demonstrates something quite different, about the relationship between the so-called civilising impulse and the principle of femininity, such that the violence of the male wolf can in some sense be coerced or co-opted by the city as a means of reminding wild nature of its nurturing responsibilities.

And this can readily move us back directly into the heartland of psychoanalytical metaphor, by means of Freud's text Civilisation and its Discontents (1930), where he deploys one of the cultural master-metaphors of recent centuries. He details some of the history of Rome down the centuries, and then says:

> *Now let us, by a flight of imagination, suppose that Rome is not a human habitation but a psychical entity with a similarly long and copious past - an entity, that is to say, in which nothing that has once come into existence will have passed away and all the earlier phases of develop-ment continue to exist alongside the latest ones. (Freud 1964: 70)*

He then goes on to detail what this Rome would be like, with buildings from all centuries and periods (like, we might fairly suppose, the different reference points of Dylan's lyric) superimposed one upon another: 'And the observer would perhaps only have to change the direction of his glance or his position in order to call up the one view or the other' (Freud 1964: 70). Freud means this as an image of the unconscious, from which, according to psychoanalysis, nothing ever goes away. But seen in another light, or deconstructed in another way, we could see it as a metaphor for metaphor itself, in the sense that metaphor constantly reminds us of the depth of words, of the ways in which they cannot be separated from their centuries, even millennia, of accreted connotations.

In order to exemplify this depth, I want to introduce some further relevant instances of texts that try to revitalise or rewrite a tradition; a particularly apt example is Jean Rhys's Wide Sargasso Sea (1966), and it is interesting to demonstrate the shift in metaphorical structure that marks its 'difference' from Charlotte Brontë's Jane Eyre (1847), the text on which it is modelled and whose alternative story it tells. In these two texts, one might suggest, for example, that blindness is a controlling metaphor, but it is deployed quite differently in each. In Jane Eyre Rochester goes literally blind as a result of the fire which is the climactic moment of the text. But this blindness also serves a complex metaphorical function. Through a curious reversal, it underlines two further features: first, the equalisation of status which finally allows Rochester and Jane to come together by depriving Rochester of one of the props and guarantees of his superiority. Very near the end, we may recall, Jane says: 'being so much lower of stature than he, I served both for his prop and guide' (Brontë 1966: 473). We are thus reminded by the text that being of 'lower stature', which here metaphorically implies lower social rank as well as being of smaller build, may not only be conceived as a mark of inferiority, but also, or instead, as providing a necessary 'grounding'. The second implication of blindness in Jane Eyre is to remind us that Rochester has been blind all along to Jane's virtues. While possessed of sight, he has been unable to avoid being influenced in his relation to her both by her lower social status and by what she herself at least refers to on many occasions as her 'plainness'. It is worth noting that the word 'plain' is, in these contexts, also metaphorical, in that it refers to an admirable plainness of speech as well as a lack, according to conventional ideas, of beauty. Now deprived of sight, these problems fall away, and although it would be going too far to suggest that this new blindness is in some sense a recompense for an older, culturally conditioned blindness, the intensity and structural completeness of the text still owe a great deal to the relations between the two blindnesses.

No text, it is probably safe to say, has a single controlling metaphor; nevertheless, it is striking how these metaphors recur in refigured shape in Wide Sargasso Sea, which is essentially a retelling of part of the story of Jane Eyre from a narrative perspective close to Rochester's first wife, the 'madwoman in the attic' of Jane Eyre. The male protagonist, who is not actually named in the text, newly arrived in the Caribbean, finds sight deeply problematic from the outset: 'Everything is too much, I felt as I rode wearily after her. Too much blue, too much purple, too much green. The flowers too red, the mountains too high, the hills too near' (Rhys 1997: 42). What might otherwise be seen as a set of metaphors for scenic beauty (red flowers, high mountains, green hills) here acquires a quite different set of connotations, as that which afflicts sight, that before which the eye flinches. And this inability to see continues through his dealings with his wife:

> *The cold light was on her and I looked at the sad droop of her lips, the frown between her thick eyebrows, deep as if it had been cut with a knife. As I looked she moved and flung her arm out. I thought coldly, yes, very beautiful, the thin wrist, the sweet swell of the forearm, the rounded elbow, the curve of her shoulder into her upper arm. All present, all correct. As I watched, hating, her face grew smooth and very young again, she even seemed to smile. A trick of the light perhaps. What else? (Rhys 1997: 88)*

Here, there is what one might refer to as a willed blindness, a refusal to see because to see would involve emotional involvement and attachment. The fact that such attachment would be perilous beyond belief is indicated in the second word, in the metaphor of 'cold'; as we look at that word, we can see the various levels of metaphor at stake. Light cannot be cold, any more than it can be hot, according to the laws of physics; if it is cold here, it is because of the way the watcher chooses to construe it, and it is at the same time a description of his own emotional state; or perhaps better of the emotional state into which he is willing himself as he detaches himself from the beauty of her body and resorts to a 'cold' removal from emotion. And so the 'trick of the light': the metaphors here conspire towards a rejection, a refusal to see what is in front of him. We might consider also 'deep as if it had been cut with a knife'. This represents not only, or indeed perhaps not at all, a physical feature; instead, the metaphor of cutting moves us towards an understanding of the protagonist's half-suppressed wish to wound the girl, to damage her beauty, while at the same time, because of the precise positioning of the wound, suggesting a damage to sight, perhaps to his sight of her, which wounds his self-esteem; or perhaps to her own sight, because to be looked at by her makes him feel belittled. 'None so blind as will not see': so goes the old cliché; and it has to be repeated (as I have tried to evidence in the Dylan lyric) that the study of metaphor necessarily involves engaging with clichés, because clichés are frequently themselves metaphors which have been overused. But blindness itself, as well as the act or process of blinding, has almost endless extensions through Western textuality. It is eventually founded on the all-encompassing metaphor of 'enlightenment', insofar as it stands in for understanding, a term which is itself a metaphor. In shorthand terms, enlightenment in Western cultural mythology stands for resisting the darkness which is itself a metaphor for incomprehension, or a failure to grasp. Whereas Jane Eyre offers daylight to Jane as a result of Rochester's blinding, the protagonist of Wide Sargasso Sea, the alternative Rochester, has in the end to flee the site of too much sight, a sight which if he were to apprehend it correctly would fatally compromise the stability of his world. And hence the metaphor offered in the title of the novel, the 'Sargasso Sea', which mythologically stands in for a place where things are lost, where there is nothing on which to ground one's perceptions.

A further example of this rewriting of tradition, of remaking a text in the context of what Derrida calls différance, may be found in Blake's famous rewriting of John Milton in The Marriage of Heaven and Hell (1793). Blake was involved over more or less the whole of his writing life, and indeed also as an engraver and painter, with Milton, a writer whom he simultaneously loved and feared. In Plates 5-6 of The Marriage of Heaven and Hell Blake says that the history of the relations between reason and desire is written in Milton's Paradise Lost (1667-74):

But in Milton, the Father is Destiny, the Son a Ratio of the five senses, & the Holy-ghost Vacuum!

Note: The reason Milton wrote in fetters when he wrote of Angels & God, and at liberty when of Devils & Hell, is because he was a true Poet and of the Devil's party without knowing it. (Blake 1966: 150)

In this brief comment, Blake seeks to undo the whole of Milton's metaphorical structure, thereby endeavouring to demonstrate that metaphors themselves are time-bound and ideologically motivated. But, says Blake, even though Milton tried his hardest to demonstrate the goodness of God and the evil of the Devil, he was undone by his own writing, by the way in which his own metaphors were far more vivid when treating of Satan and his rebel angels than when treating of God and Jesus.

One of the crucial phrases here is 'without knowing it'. We might say that Blake is formulating a very early version of structuralism, in the sense that he is saying we cannot bend language to our will; language itself will always be stronger and will speak through our words rather than being bound by them. The metaphor of 'fetters' is clearly crucial in this respect.

Blake's aim here, as in many other parts of his work, is to recast, reforge, metaphor. Obviously, it would not be appropriate here to go into detail as to how he does that, or to quote the many other examples of his rewritings of biblical and Miltonic texts; but it is worth pointing out that he mounts a direct challenge to any notion of the stable authority of meaning, and in doing so prefigures deconstructionist arguments about fixity and fluidity, about the inevitable 'dissemination' of words, and in this case, because of the theological argument which underpins this passage, of 'the Word'.

It is significant that one of those arguments would be the one advanced by Derrida in his essay 'Edmond Jabès and the Question of the Book' (1964), where he says:

> *Absence of the writer toc. For to write is to draw back. Not to retire into one's tent, in order to write, but to draw back from one's writing itself. To be grounded far from one's language, to emancipate it or lose one's hold on it, to let it make its way alone and unarmed. To leave speech. To be a poet is to know how to leave speech. To let it speak alone, which it can do only in its written form. To leave writing is to be there only in order to provide its passageway, to be the diaphanous element of its going forth: everything and nothing. For the work, the writer is at once everything and nothing. Like God. (Derrida 1978b: 70)*

This takes up in one sense Blake's highly idiosyncratic theology, and perhaps especially his constant insistence that his work was the responsibility of spirits who spoke through him as much as it was of his own craftsmanlike efforts to give their words mortal form. But it also goes further than this, in implicitly suggesting that the very process of metaphoricity has been wrongly conceived. For Derrida, it would follow that metaphor is not that which happens when the writer applies him- or herself to the craft; it is what happens when there is a drawing back, a willingness, conscious or unconscious, to let go of the writing, to abandon it to its fate. Metaphor, therefore, is not necessarily embedded in the text; it is rather a mark of what happens to the text when it achieves its freedom, which will only be in the company of other readers, other places, other times.

This is a difficult thought to grasp: much critical training lies in the idea that if we can descry and gather together the key metaphorical components of a work, then we can use this as a beginning of our interpretation. But what both Blake and Derrida suggest is rather that as we read and 'absorb' literature, the metaphorical structure of the work we are reading becomes, to use Blake's key-word, 'forged' anew.

The ambiguity of Blake's notion of forging should not be lost on us. On the one hand, it signifies forging in the sense of the blacksmith's forge, the sense of iron-making and, by metaphorical translation, imposing some formed solidity on the flux of life. But, on the other hand, it implies virtually its exact opposite, namely the act of forgery; not perhaps in the sense of conscious deception but rather as an acknowledgement that all our attempts at originality are in fact suspect, held, as Derrida would say, sous rature, 'under erasure' (Derrida 1976: 19), because they can figure only as part of a continuing palimpsest, beneath the later stages of which there are always other texts, other perceptions, other translations, shadows hovering on the edges of visibility.

We might consider a comment by the Nobel Prize-winning novelist Saul Bellow: 'A novel is balanced between a few true impressions and the multitude of false ones that make up most of what we call life. It tells us that for every human being there is a diversity of existences, that the single existence is itself an illusion' (Bellow in Allen 1993: 142). This points us towards the inevitability of forgery as part of the essence of fiction; and we can place alongside the critic David Lodge's famous comment on the American novelist Herman Melville, author of Moby-Dick (1851). Melville, he said, 'split the atom of the traditional novel in the effort to make whaling a universal metaphor' (Lodge 1975: 195). We might take from Lodge's comment that, in fact, no attempt to construct a truly universal metaphor can wholly succeed, for obvious reasons of cultural diversity and difference; but that, nevertheless, the effort to construct such metaphors, or to revitalise them, or to reforge them for particular times and places, is also integral to literature, even if here it is, in some sense, safeguarded by being itself couched in the Promethean metaphor of heroic struggle.

CONCLUSION

I hope to have described so far some of the many complexities of language which begin to open out when we think about metaphor and its continual operations on the communicative stage. In order to round off this dis-cussion, it might be appropriate to begin this conclusion with a brief set of comments on some of the metaphors writers have used to describe their own activity of writing. Here, for example, is William Congreve on the failure of inspiration or, in one of its metaphorical incarnations, 'writer's block':

Invention flags, his Brain goes muddy, And black Despair succeeds brown Study. (Congreve 1923: IV, 160)

What is interesting here is again the nesting of metaphors one within the other. Clearly the principal metaphor is of a kind of swamp, or swamping, used to denote a condition in which nothing is clear, and also in which one is dragged down. But within this there is the phrase 'brown Study'; suitably describing the initial phase of being dragged down into the swamp or marsh when one's footsteps, like invention, 'flag', but also resonating with the notion of the study where the writer plies his craft. Words and metaphors are here, as everywhere, treacherous: taken out of context 'flags' and 'succeeds' clearly have positive connotations as much as they have negative ones. There is a further sense here of the writer's condition vis-à-vis the outside world, for a 'brown study' is a state in which one has lost one's awareness of one's surroundings, and is therefore all the more likely to fall into the swamp. One might be in a 'serious reverie, thought-ful absent-mindedness', to mention two definitions of the phrase; one might be in the lonely condition of the writer, as in an example given in the dictionary: 'Lack of company will soon lead a man into a brown study' (Walker 1850: 31).

These metaphors cannot be taken singularly or on their own; they are not coined, minted afresh by any particular writer; rather, they have a history, what we might term the history of a metaphor. Similarly with the idea of writing as some kind of consumable or comestible; as

Shakespeare puts it in Love's Labour's Lost (1595), 'he hath never fed of the dainties that are bred in a book./He hath not eat paper, as it were, he hath not drunk ink' (Shakespeare 1990: 153). Perhaps what is most interesting about this set of metaphors is the inserted phrase, 'as it were'. 'As it were' signifies something close to the word 'like' or 'as' in a simile; all these apparently signify that we are not meant to take the text literally. But it is more complicated than this. Even if the words 'as it were' had not been there, we, the readers or watchers, would nevertheless not have taken things literally, for we know that nobody, one hopes, drinks ink; rather, the insertion of the qualifying phrase serves a communicative function; it serves to assure us that the writer is on the same side as we are, that he understands human limitations and follies with a clear eye, and is not to be taken in by the potentially overweening power of metaphor.

The image of consumption recurs in, for example, Elizabeth Gaskell's comments on all the books she has not yet read: 'I have not had time yet. But I look at them as a child looks at a cake, - with glittering eyes & watering mouth, imagining the pleasure that awaits him' (Gaskell 1966: 567). It would, then, be difficult to imagine the act of writing aside from the deployment of metaphor. To say, 'I pick up my pen and place it on the page', or to say, 'I press various keys on my keyboard', might be adequate to the physical description of writing (although even thus it would be far from complete); but the conveying of the significance of the act of constructing an imaginary world and of inviting readers into it has taxed writers down the ages. One might therefore say that at the origin of metaphor, or as one of the origins of metaphor, there lies the impossibility of conveying the act of writing itself. Writing a metaphor is thus simultaneously an act of metaphorisation of writing, without which no writer can describe his or her craft. It is the fortune and the doom of the writer to be dealing in the very materials which render the craft opaque. Seen from one angle, metaphors of writing are a series of attempts to transfer transparency onto this activity; while seen from another they merely serve to reinforce the necessary opacity of a process which is always, in some crucial sense, other than itself.

Robert Frost has more to say about this in his apposite 1931 essay 'Education by Poetry':

> *[Enthusiasm] is taken through the prism of the intellect and spread on the screen in a colour, all the way from hyperbole or overstatement at one end to understatement at the other end. It is a long strip of dark lines and many colours . . . I would be willing to throw away everything else but that: enthusiasm tuned by metaphors. (Frost 1966: 36)*

One of the interesting features of this comment is its dependence on synaesthesia, the replacement, translation, transference of terms from one sensory sphere to another. Here, Frost transmutes verbal activity first into the painterly ('prism', 'colour') and second into the musical ('tuned'). What, though, might it mean for 'enthusiasm' to be 'tuned' by metaphors? Here the metaphor is clearly seen not as an exercise of the wild imagination, or of Aristotelian genius, but rather the reverse, as a regulatory mechanism which provides a translation whereby the otherwise incomprehensible is rendered into some kind of harmony with what we might term the 'reading mind'.

The past two thousand years of Western tradition have seen a continuous oscillation around the notion of language and the figurative, which has paralleled a set of uncertainties over the notion of origins. This can be figured in terms of myth, as well as in ideas about writing and speech. In the current situation it is becoming increasingly clear that metaphor is a key to unlocking the structures of cultural relativity, and this has an obvious and immediate public impact in terms of, for example, the languages of prejudice and the representation of trauma. What, we might ask, will happen to metaphor next on its journey? But in asking that question, we are only repeating an adventurist, adventitious, but, alas, not very adventurous metaphor. What is important is that we insist upon an understanding that the overall notion of metaphor is no more a pre-given datum than are metaphors themselves, but is responsive to historical and linguistic development; we construct metaphors for our times, but we also construct a concept of the metaphorical for our times.

As an example of this historical process, let us consider some aspects of the evolution of the word 'shrew'. The dictionary points out to us that the shrew is a term for 'any of the small insectivorous mammals, belonging to the genus Sorex or the family Soricidae, much resembling mice but having a long sharp snout'. However, when

Shakespeare wrote The Taming of the Shrew (1594) it was not this type of shrew he had in mind. What might be more critical is a further note in the dictionary, to the effect that 'the shrew was popularly held to be venomous and otherwise injurious'. Being a dictionary, naturally it does not go on to explore reasons why this might have been the case, but we might feel that there is something, first, in the shape of the shrew, and, second, in its smallness and rapidity of movement which may have conduced to this otherwise curious fear.

At all events, as the dictionary moves on it becomes clear that the meaning of 'shrew' intended by Shakespeare - as an uppity, uncontrollable woman, ripe for taming by a suitable man, or perhaps indeed by the whole complex force of patriarchy - is figurative, or metaphorical. There were rumours in the sixteenth century, for example, that a shrew could damage or hurt a domestic animal, obviously a deeply troubling thought in an age highly dependent on such animals economically; thus, the shrew turns into a malign force, and indeed into a figure for the Devil himself. One might reasonably wonder whether the long tail is an additional metaphorised feature here; as Chaucer puts it, 'Though that the feend noght in our sighte him shewe,/I trowe he with us be, that ilke shrewe!' (Chaucer 1912: 661).

But it is only later that this general attribution of malignancy (or perhaps it would now be better to think of it in terms of unnaturalness) becomes specifically applied to women. A classic example from 1839 is: 'He brought home with him a wife, who seemed to be a shrew, and to have the upper hand of him' (Irving 1894: 5). In this quotation we see the metaphor consolidating what was perhaps its final transformation, and becoming specifically a term of abuse to be directed at women who do not assume their supposedly correct place in a patriarchal hierarchy. The long nose of inquisitiveness, the long tail of devilry, the surreptitious and unpredictable set of movements; all have been brought together, as they partially were in Shakespeare's time, into a figure for all those traits in women which, seen from a patriarchal position, serve to undermine men's authority and men's straightforward, honourable purposes.

If we look back at Shakespeare's The Taming of the Shrew, it has often been critically noted that it is far from easy to determine the level of irony in the play.

To put it very crudely, does the play support a view that women who get beyond their assigned station are to be tamed? Or does it say that women in such a position are in fact unhappy, and that therefore their taming is somehow conducive to their own well-being, as well as to the well-being of a properly ordered society?

Or is Shakespeare at least partly mocking the pretensions of those foolish men who believe that such taming can actually be effective or productive? The force of the metaphor is so strong that it makes these questions difficult to answer. Although metaphors may appear to offer a certain precision, in the sense we have already mentioned of a translation from that which is difficult to describe to something which is more 'familiar', in another sense metaphor is opaque; it conjoins dissimilars, not always for the purposes of enlightenment but sometimes in order to prevent or deflect criticism of unthought assumptions.

'To shrew', a verb now obsolete, was in the later Middle Ages and for some time afterwards a synonym for 'to curse', or to cast the evil eye; it is hard to evade the possibility that there are suggestions of witchcraft in this collocation.

Thus, a small animal and one which is harmless, except of course to insects, cuts, as it were, a figure in the world; it becomes taken up and put through a series of historical and textual transmutations which end with the image of the overweening, displaced woman. Or rather, we should add, did end there, since the term 'shrew' in any of these meanings is hardly any more in common use, partly because more violent protestations of frightened male dominance such as 'bitch' and 'cow' have become more prevalent.

Thus, again, we need to see metaphor not only as something which is made or constructed by, for example, particular literary writers, but also as something inherited, something unexamined, something belonging to the cultural unconscious. And all this without examining the complex connections between the shrew and that word which is still in common currency, 'shrewd', which, as we might by now expect, derives from the same source, and bore the metaphorical weight of malignancy and cunning long before it became rehabilitated, albeit in a somewhat ambiguous way, to refer to cleverness and insight.

However, in order to complete our summary of the complexities of metaphor, it is necessary to return to deconstruction, and especially to the specific succession within deconstruction between Martin Heidegger and Jacques Derrida. In his masterly book Derrida, Heidegger, Blanchot (1992) Timothy Clark quotes a significant passage from Derrida's essay 'The Retrait of Metaphor' (1978a) on what he refers to as the 'doubling of metaphor':

> *As this withdrawal of the metaphoric leaves no place free for a discourse of the proper or the literal it will have at the same time the sense of a refold (re-pli), of what retreats like a wave on the shoreline, and of a re-turn (re-tour), of the overcharging repetition of a supplementary trait, of yet another metaphor, of a double trait (re-trait) of metaphor, a discourse whose rhetorical border is no longer determinable according to a simple and indivisible line, according to a linear and indecomposable trait. (Clark 1992: 119)*

This may seem at first glance a characteristically difficult and complicated passage of Derrida's, but the thinking behind it is really quite simple. Essentially, if I may dare to use such a term, Derrida is saying that no attempt to isolate metaphor as part of a poetic practice or as part of a critical activity can be truly successful; the processes of metaphor are already deeply twined around the evolution of language and around the rhetorical skills, unconscious or otherwise, which we need to learn to acquire in order to be able to communicate with each other.

The image of the shoreline might remind us of a similar image, in Iain Banks's novel The Bridge, an image based on classical sources, of a man whose destiny appears to be to beat at the waves with a flail.

This, obviously, is not a particularly useful activity; it perhaps bears comparison with the sad hopes of the Walrus in Lewis Carroll's 'The Walrus and the Carpenter' (1872) concerning the possibility of counting the grains of sand on a beach. For all will be disturbed by, among other things, the thought of 'what retreats like a wave on the shoreline'. I read this metaphor of Derrida's in several different ways. First, the 'wave' itself disappears; it is no longer there. Similarly, the operation of metaphor, at least in one sense, leaves no visible trace; metaphor comes and goes, it moves towards the margin, the verge of intelligibility, and then again it retreats.

But second, despite this apparent evanescence, it is of the utmost power: not only the sand but also the rocks and cliffs that constitute the shoreline have, in the end, been mainly formed by the waves, which even now possess the power to crumble whole shorelines into dust and, as we are increasingly appreciating in the aftermath of modernity's worship of the god of development, similarly to obliterate whole island nations. So there is in metaphor an uncanny combination of evanescence and permanence, of power and vulnerability, of resistance to change and the spread of change.

But third, in the Derrida passage, one can point to what might be called the sinister power, the left-handed power, of metaphor, which 'leaves no place free for a discourse of the proper or the literal'. It is not that the world of language is neatly divided into two provinces of the literal and the metaphorical, any more than we can say that the Earth is divided into two provinces of the land and the sea.

Geologically these formations only arise or indeed submerge as a result of complex and unending interactions with one another. Who can say where the sea ends and the land begins, or vice versa? It is perhaps interesting that, at least in the British context, the shoreline is Crown property.

We may construe this in several ways: as a demonstration of monarchical power, as the necessity of maintaining central control over the marginal, but also, surely, as a way of maintaining some kind of national boundary precisely at that point where the very notion of a stable boundary is most under threat.

We might in this context consider, or perhaps reconsider, T.S. Eliot's well-known lines in 'East Coker':

> *each venture Is a new beginning, a raid on the inarticulate With shabby equipment always deteriorating In the general mess of imprecision of feeling (Eliot 1963: 203)*

'East Coker' was written, probably, in 1940, and thus it is unsurprising to find Eliot using military metaphors like the 'raid' and the 'shabby equipment'. It is, however, open to the reader to decide quite what weight to place on the 'general mess', a phrase which in time of war might have unconsciously extended the obvious meaning of 'general' to include the role of a military commander, and the meaning of 'mess' to include the common military description of the place where soldiers eat.

The point, though, would be to figure the process of organising language ('I gotta use words when I talk to you') as one where there is an inevitability about a sequence of successes and failures 'where ignorant armies clash by night' (Arnold 1950: 212), to quote Matthew Arnold. The successful, and by implication metaphorical, use of language then becomes a series of manoeuvres; and perhaps even more to the point, the humble practitioners of language, which includes all of us, are rarely in a position ourselves to declare whether these 'raids' have been successful or unsuccessful.

What remains certain, if anything does, is that the shoreline will remain the same, according to some kind of timescale, but it will also never be the same from day to day, from minute to minute, as suitable metaphors are cast and recast, forged and reforged, always under the pressure of what might seem intelligible from the shore, but always difficult to perceive at the time of, for example, what W.S. Graham refers to as the 'night bell' (Graham 2004: 105), which summons us to the shoreline but always under conditions of obscurity and uncertainty.

A little later in his book, Clark comments that: 'What is ineluctable is not primarily language commonly conceived as representation, mirroring a realm of objects, nor yet language as presentation, rather, as it were, a mirror that faces inward in the re-mark' (Clark 1992: 123). This kind of phrasing might fairly remind us of J.H. Prynne's wrestling with language, almost as though the 're-mark', the moment when, as I interpret it, language makes its own statement, comes into clear focus. This statement will have at most an oblique relation to the statement we might have thought we were making when we dreamt of the forever receding possibility of using it. It turns to face us with a declaration, one which is always uncanny, always half in twilight, that the perennial attempt to rid language of its ambiguities is doomed and perhaps weirdly counterproductive, an attempt again to draw that notorious metaphor, a 'line in the sand'.

If I may venture a final metaphorical interpretation: mirrors are made of sand. The apparently clear glass of language as classically conceived is composed out of the most opaque of media - precisely that sand which, according to E.T.A. Hoffmann (1979), Freud and the various folkloric originators of their respective narratives, when rubbed into the eyes robs the possessor of those eyes of sight, understanding and eventually, perhaps, of the eyes themselves.

We are therefore reminded of whatever those eyes might signify in psychoanalytical terms of the mastery of difficult and confusing materials. The cumulative metaphors of Western civilisation are certainly based on sight, as we have seen; but equally they are based on the terror of a blindness which would place us in a night, on a tremulous shoreline, where our other senses, vestiges and atrophies as they are, would be of little avail.

What, then, is metaphor? The suggestions I have tried to offer in this book, and the examples I have provided, point to the fact that there is no single, universal, ahistorical definition of 'metaphor'. Metaphor is what metaphor has been taken to be at various times and in various cultures. Nevertheless, we cannot leave the concept in this unsatisfactory condition. We can say that the term 'metaphor' has usually been used to denote a peculiarity, or perhaps better an innate property, of language. This property is one of constant excess or dissemination.

The simplest of words ('head', 'home', 'animal') have metaphorical ramifications which cannot be simply denied or evaded, although it is possible, to a limited extent, to select among them in a contextual way. Metaphor is perhaps the principal sign that words do not stand in isolation; so long as they have histories - and all words do, even ones that appear newly coined - then they will have a metaphorical field of their own. I return again to the newspaper, where I happen today to read (not, I suspect, for the first time): 'Belfast sighs as peace deal slips away again'. Of course, Belfast does not sigh; a city cannot sigh any more than it can sleep, or rejoice, or do any of the other anthropomorphic things that newspaper headlines would have it do. It is possible that the people within it may sigh, although it is unlikely that they would all do so at the same time; and that would be a prime example of metonymy, the process whereby an interchange occurs between the whole and the part, between Belfast and its human inhabitants.

But the 'sigh of Belfast' here is a metaphor; it is a metaphor for a state of mind, but even to say that is too simple, for whose state of mind is this? Belfast, it says; but might one not equally say that this 'sigh' is at least in part the presumed reaction of the reader of the newspaper, the observer of the scene of defeat of hope? The hope of a peace deal 'slips away'; again, not literally, but perhaps this image confronts us more starkly with the problem of metaphor, because the metaphor of something slipping away, something which might be a hope, a relationship, a life, is so closely embedded within the language that it is difficult, if not impossible, to perceive its metaphoric force.

Bibliography

Baker, Nancy L. & Nancy Huling: *A Research Guide for Undergraduate Students: English and American Literature*, New York: Modern Language Association of America, 2002.

Beene, Lynndianne: *Guide to British Prose Fiction Explication: Nineteenth and Twentieth Centuries*, New York : G.K. Hall ; London: Prentice Hall International, 1999.

Bracken, James K.: *Reference Works in British and American Literature*, Englewood, CO: Libraries Unlimited, 1992.

Eugene Benson and L.W. Conolly: *Encyclopedia of Post-Colonial Literatures in English*, London; New York: Routledge, 1996.

Ferber, Michael: *A Dictionary of Literary Symbols*, Cambridge; New York: Cambridge University Press, 1999.

Joyce Moss: *British and Irish Literature and Its Times: the Victoria Era to the Present (1837-)*, Detroit: Gale Group, 2001.

Marcuse, Michael J.: *A Reference Guide for English Studies*, Berkeley: U of California Press, 2004.

Mark Hawkins-Dady: *Reader's Guide to Literature in English*, London; Chicago: Fitzroy Dearborn Publishers, 1996.

Steven R. Serafin and Valerie Grosvenor Myer: *The Continuum Encyclopedia of British Literature*, New York: Continuum, 2003.

Index